CAUGHT...

It was without a doubt the most beautiful and charming bracelet Kylee had ever seen. Amazing because this wasn't something just made out of pressed metal in molds. No, someone had taken the time to make each small door individually and lovingly—from the back it looked almost as good as the front.

She lay the bracelet across her wrist.

Put it on. It was as if someone whispered just behind her. She jerked around, a cold chill up her back, but of course there was no one there. She draped the bracelet over her arm again. The silver looked wonderful against her golden tan. Perfect, almost. Like it belonged there. On a whim she fumbled the key through the lock so it formed a perfect circle around her wrist and shook her arm so that the bracelet could just settle into place. A shiver ran through her, almost of excitement.

It was surprisingly light and the small series of doors fit like a loose cuff down over her wrist bones, but almost seemed to meld to her arm as if it was made for her. Someone was sure to love this bracelet, because she did. If she had the money she'd buy it right now. Maybe she could make some sort of arrangement with Lila. If she did, she'd never take it off.

And there she went again, falling in love. She sighed.

Who was she kidding? She already owed Lila money just for the kindness she was showing her.

"Kylee? Could you come give us a hand out here?" As if her thoughts had materialized, Lila pushed her head into the kitchen.

Caught red handed, Kylee stood mortified.

BOOKS BY THE AUTHOR

Romance
Ashes and Light
Shades of Moonlight
Judas Kiss
Second Spring
A Different Nightmusic
Shadow Play
Unlocking Her Heart
Unlocking Her History

Fantasy
***The Cartographer Universe* series:**
The Warden of Power
The Cartographer's Daughter
Afterburn
Aftershock
Aftermath
Afterimage

Terra Incognita
Terra Infirma
Terra Nueva

Also by the Author
Mutable Things
Emberstone
Ice Dragon
Crystal Courtesan

UNLOCKING HER HEART

Karen L. Abrahamson

**Dedicated to Nanette and Matt.
Inspiration, support and friendship.
Who could ask for more?
Thank you.**

UNLOCKING HER HEART

CHAPTER 1

Kylee Jensen drove her car toward the edge of a cliff.

At least that was what it felt like. The descent went on forever, so steep that even though she took her foot off the gas, the old silver Honda Civic continued to pick up speed until she was practically standing on the brake *all the time* even though she knew the car's brakes probably couldn't take it. They'd been squealing even before she left Vancouver for the Okanagan via the Coquihalla Highway but now it was like the brake pads didn't want to be in a relationship at all, and she was terrifyingly free-wheeling it.

The steep hill had stripped her from the top of Pennask Summit, down from the treed tops of the mountains through noon-day sunshine, following the side of a long valley that led to some place invisible below and eastward. The valley's steep sides were green with pine, here and there stained lighter with what must be poplar or aspen, still carrying their spring shade this early in June. Scars cut into the treescape marked logging roads that ran even more steeply down the mountainsides. That was it. She was flipping driving herself off the side of a *mountain* and whose silly idea was it coming here anyway?

She tromped the brakes again and a horrible squeal filled the cab of the car. Figured. She was going to go careening over the side of the road, and the burned-out brakes and the stink of metal on metal would be a fitting metaphor for the way her whole darn life had gone full-on out of control. Actually, the whole damn mad slide was a symbol of her life—chasing after something she could never quite catch up to, until she was running wild toward disaster after disaster.

Yup. That was Kylee Jensen, all right. Relationship Typhoid Mary.

The road curved around a bend and sunlight through the trees banded the four lanes of pavement. A black shape burst up in front of her car and she had a momentary image of wings and huge black beak and eyes.

What the heck? She jerked the car sideways and slammed on the brakes again. The shriek shrilled through the car and she careened to a stop at the side of the highway and sat there shaking in sudden silence. Her chest tightened and she wanted to cry.

Darn it, she was better than this. Bigger than this. It was a crow. A single crow. Sure, it was the biggest darned crow she'd ever seen, but it was only a bird and this was just a road that cars and even logging trucks drove down every single day. It was *her* that was out of control. The trucks and cars had been passing her for the last five miles of the trip, so obviously she wasn't going to drive off the cliff, if she kept her head about her and babied her car. She had to baby the car. It was the last thing larger than a suitcase that she owned in the world. Heck, she could end up living in the darn thing if things didn't work out in Peachland.

So enough sitting here feeling sorry for herself. She dropped the car into gear and pulled out onto the road again. It really had been the *biggest* darn crow she'd ever seen.

Was it a bad omen of what awaited ahead?

It was a bird. Think of it as a phoenix symbolizing her finding a new life out of the ashes of what had come before. She snorted. Grasping at straws much?

The road curved again and ahead the steep-sided valley she'd been following opened up to reveal a distant dry mountainside. At least that looked familiar, like the hills on the far side of Okanagan Lake.

As if on cue, the road curved again and flattened out, and then the car climbed up to a long flat stretch that revealed the massive lake—almost 84 miles long she'd once been told—stretched north to south below her. Its blue water was the same shade as the sky, its waves glitter-topped with sunlight. Beautiful and cool and welcoming compared with the heat through her windshield. Just down one more hill and she'd be there.

To the right of the highway, the land dropped down to small pastures, orchards and vineyards. This was the heart of British Columbia's wine and orchard country, though the old family orchards were too quickly being turned into vineyards or housing developments. She took the sharp turnoff for Peachland and joined the highway that ducked down steep treed bluffs toward the water. In places the trees were replaced by a stunning growth in building. Broad swathes of houses filled the hillside. Other areas where orchards had been, now held fancy houses between the highway and the water. Not what she'd expected.

Peachland, just by its name was supposed to be a sleepy little village that curved in a long string of cottages and houses along the waterside of a large bay. It was supposed to be surrounded by rolling orchards full of huge ripening peaches. Why else would it have that name? But this—this was like it was a suburb or something and if she wanted a suburb she could have stayed in Vancouver. Or Seattle. She had her green card. Maybe she should just turn the old Civic around and head back home. Or where home once had been, once upon a time when Kevin was in her life. Get real, Kylee. That was just the most recent place you lived. None of them have ever truly been home.

Her throat tightened as she fought off the tears. Her fists clenched on the steering wheel. A small shopping center with a grocery store, gas station, liquor store and library sprang up on her right and a stoplight interrupted the highway traffic.

Okay, maybe this wasn't the big city, because where in the big city world did you ever see highway traffic stopped by a stoplight. Nope, that was definitely small town. She clicked on her turn signal and glanced down at the open address book on the seat next to her.

Fifteen-twenty Beach Avenue. It evoked images of sand and blue water and friends on beach towels. It evoked memories of her friend Lila so long ago when they'd been kids in high school and had taken a trip up here to visit Lila's grandparents. They'd been fifteen then and she was thirty now. Thirty going on a hundred and forty and her life felt like it was over. Again.

She turned left onto Beach Avenue and found herself on the lakeshore: a narrow strip of public beach, shady weeping willows, picnic tables and park benches separating her from the water. Here and there people had towels spread across the pea-gravel beach and were sunning themselves just like she remembered. She smiled and the tension from the drive evaporated just like the heat haze over the water.

She pulled a u-turn and parked the car in a shady spot across from the beach and climbed out. Peachland was no longer quite so small, but it was still strung along the lakefront. She'd been driving for three and a half hours and really could use the chance to stretch her legs. Besides, it would give her a chance to 'sess out the town and decide just how crazy she was to come here. Lila could have sold her grandparent's house and moved on. They hadn't been in touch in a long time except for a few postcards Kylee had sent from overseas. But no. Lila loved the old house by the lake. She was loyal.

The wind off the lake ruffled her pixy-cut short blonde hair and played at the hem of her floral travel dress. It was one of the few things she had left that didn't look totally worn and drab from travel. She'd bought it on the spur of the moment with the foolish belief that Kevin and she might get married somewhere on their trip. After all, they'd been engaged two years before they left on the trip of a lifetime. She'd thought that this time things really were right.

Well, that was *another* lifetime. Certainly not this one. She spun on her ballet-flat heel and started walking, her trusty daypack over her shoulder. The breeze wafted scents of suntan lotion and barbecue picnics. Out on the lake, a powerboat hauled two laughing kids on an inner tube and closer to shore two kayakers glided like ghosts over the water. Voices called to each other, laughed. An elderly couple smiled and said hello as they passed her, walking hand in hand along the promenade. She turned to watch them go, two grayed heads curved toward each other like magnets, their shoulders a little bent by the years, but happy. Their smiles had said so. The way they held hands said so.

She looked down at her empty hands, and tears welled up again.

No. It was over. Here she stood, right now, in this lovely town. She would find Lila and they would talk and she would find a job and make a new life and Kevin and his new girlfriend could just go fall off the earth for all she cared.

She could. She would. They should.

She strode down the promenade and imagined herself as someone who lived here, someone who belonged. She'd smile at everyone. She'd say hello and comment on what a beautiful day it was, for it really was, with the soft breeze off the water and the sunny skies. Even people who lived here noticed it, judging by the good-looking guy sitting in his car looking out the open window. She caught a whiff of what smelled like ripe, sun-warmed, sweet grapes and—coffee. Strong coffee. Good.

Following her nose, she found a quaint, brick-sided café with tables spilling out onto the sidewalk and the divine scent of fresh baking and espresso enough to drive a person hungry. Her stomach growled, but she really needed to watch her pennies.

Full of regret, she passed the establishment by. She also passed a cute little clothing boutique, a kitchen and garden knick-knack store, and a day spa before finding the address she'd been looking for. Not that she needed the address. She'd recognize the house anywhere, even after all the years that separated her from that long-ago summer.

Sure, the heritage-style two-story home might have been repainted a blazing white, but it still had its broad porch on three sides of the main floor and red trim around the windows. New plantings of brilliant red and white garden beds contained well established hedges and an emerald green expanse of lawn that hadn't been there before, but the same hanging copper planters around the porch held lush baskets of more red and white flowers. A new, neat red and white sandwich board sign set by the curb said: *This & That: Jewelry and Unsung Treasures* in a Celtic script. A discreet little sign in the window said "open."

It was the same house—at least she thought so. Except way back when there'd been no *This & That* sign and the place in her memory had been a little run down. Lila's grandparents had been old enough they'd had trouble keeping the place up. But that summer had been a wonderful time in her life and maybe, just maybe, she could reclaim it. Besides, she needed a safe place to pick up the pieces of herself and put herself back together into someone who didn't just go running after the first guy who said he liked her. Back then, Peachland and Lila had helped her when she'd been broken-hearted after her first boyfriend broke up with her.

Maybe Peachland and her old friend could help, now, too.

It was a sorry comment on her life that she was sort of counting on it.

CHAPTER 2

Brett Main spotted the woman while he was putting off dealing with the inevitable. He sat in his racing green Miata with the top up under a shade tree with the windows rolled down trying to get up the courage to face his sister. It was a long time coming, this meeting, and he wasn't looking forward to dealing with Chloe and her 'magic' stones and all her woo-woo, half-baked spiritual stuff, but he had to see her to deal with Mom and Dad's estate. He swallowed back the too-familiar lump of grief that choked his breath for a moment and looked out at the lake, clear as a good Riesling wine. The swimming beach would be packed with teenage girls showing off their shiny new bodies and moms would be riding herd on their youngsters like a vintner waiting for his wine's maturation. The lifeguards would have their hands full today.

It was better not to think of the loss of his folks and just focus on the business of the day—the science of living. Just like winemaking, each year's success was the result of last year's careful thought and planning of the use of his varietals and if this year didn't fully work, then next year's would take into account what had worked or not worked in the past. Treat this whole darn thing as one more logical step toward life and put his loss behind him. In this instance he needed Chloe's sign-off on the sale of their parents' house. His hypothesis was that the incentive of a little cash in her pocket might make that option attractive, regardless of the layers of memories stacked up in the old homestead along with too much furniture. Yes, that was the tack he was going to take.

He reached for his briefcase, but a shock of color went strolling by like a nicely chilled Chardonnay.

Well, perhaps not strolled—danced more like. She was small, petite, but the word "pixy" came to mind—from where, he wasn't sure given fairytale creatures weren't exactly his thing. Sunlight caught in her golden hair like a crown and she wore one of those loose, brightly colored sundresses that he usually abhorred for their shapelessness, but on this woman it didn't look shapeless at all. Nope. The breeze pressed it in softly in all the right places and the sunlight shone through just a little too brightly and showed the shadows of long slim legs through the fabric. Pretty. Very pretty from the back and practical, too, given the flat heels of her shoes and that the daypack she carried was pretty similar to the one he carried when he went out tramping the vineyard checking the vines. Definitely not anyone he knew from Peachland, so she had to be one of the summer people.

He watched her flutter down the street like a zing of pepper on the palate and wished she'd turn around. He'd step out of his car and maybe just happen to strike up a conversation, just like he'd done too many other times to count. A group of young women would stop by the vineyard's tasting room and be impressed that the assistant vintner took the time to explain the wines. Then he carefully selected the woman he liked best and asked her out for dinner. Just like that. He could do it with his eyes closed. But he'd sworn off summer people after Mom and Dad died. They'd longed to see him settle down. The trouble was, he never really was the settling down kind.

And the girl walking away down the promenade wasn't exactly his type, anyway. Too small, too blonde and likely too practical, too. Given the shoes. Yup, not his type at all. Definitely not the type who would swoon into his arms after one too many samples at the Elkhart Winery tasting room.

Focus, Main. Focus. You came here today with a specific purpose—now get it done and get back to your office. Besides, you swore off skirt-chasing, remember? Take a break after your parents' deaths?

He gave the woman in the bright floral dress one last look of regret. Climbing out of the car, he grabbed his briefcase that held all the research on area housing sales figures and realtor options. Faced with the information, there was only one logical course of action.

Of course when had his sister ever been logical?

§

Holding her breath, Kylee pushed open the door to *This & That* and a small bell chimed that reminded her of Asian temples. Coming up the stairs had been a challenge to her determination. Stepping inside? Well that was the test. It meant admitting defeat and asking for help. She hadn't done that since she was a kid, but everything else was gone now and she just needed a friend. That was all. Just Lila's friendship would give her the strength to start again.

The faint scent of incense and a sense of being watched met her like a cloud when she stepped inside. The former came from a burning incense stick uncoiling smoke from a spot near an ancient cash register. The latter came from a woman maybe a few years older than her who looking up expectantly from her spot behind the counter. Not Lila. Not Lila by a long shot, and Kylee almost turned on her heel and left.

But the shop was intriguing with its bevy of gleaming glass cases that filled its aubergine and gray-painted walls. It had old fashioned wire mannequins draped in Tibetan turquoise and coral necklaces she recognized from her time in India. Unique amber pieces as large as her thumb hung from copper hooks along one wall. Another wall was filled with a glass cupboard that seemed to hold a cornucopia of what looked like Mexican and Indian silver earrings as well as pieces from places she didn't know. The glass counters held what must be expensive, custom jewelry. In corners and in the window displays were peacock-shade scarves and what looked like finely crafted gloves and handbags. The richness of the decor shouldn't surprise her because Lila had always been a unique person of exquisite taste. It was a shop she'd love to spend time in, to explore and gather the many wonders from so many places in the world.

The woman behind the counter absently shifted her single long brown braid over her shoulder. She'd obviously been examining the books on the counter. She was of average height—still tall to Kylee, and wore a long flowy caftan thing and matching flowing trousers the color of clotted cream that only emphasized her slim figure. The three quarter sleeves exposed arms covered in silver and stone bracelets that matched the tangle of chains and stone pendants that hung around her neck. She had a pretty face and smooth skin and deep blue eyes that seemed to verge on lavender. Whatever she'd been waiting for, at the sight of Kylee, a look of surprise crossed her face. An inner tension seemed to drain away and the woman radiated a calm that Kylee could never imagine feeling.

Around the shop, pot lights spotlighted glass jewelry showcases to advantage and kept the store a comfortable cool despite the baking Okanagan day.

"May I help you?" The woman glided around the counter. She had bare feet with red toenails. She smiled and it was like being welcomed into a room with a fireplace and a cup of hot cocoa or something and that was strange. In all her travels, she'd never felt that welcome.

"Um. I'm just looking I guess." Escape out the door, or accept the welcome? Hadn't she been running long enough? She had to stop somewhere.

The woman cocked her head and her eyes narrowed a little. "Heart," she said.

Kylee froze. "Excuse me?"

The woman grinned and waved away Kylee's momentary tension. "Sorry. I do that. I meet someone and a word comes to mind. It usually is a true descriptor of the person. In your case I got two. Words that is. Heart and capable." She frowned and looked Kylee up and down. "That doesn't mean you have a capable heart because yours has some bruises on it."

Kylee would have laughed at that thought if the whole thing hadn't been so strange.

"Of course it might, given time. People often have to learn to assimilate their two halves into a whole." She flourished her arm around the shop. "I'm Chloe. Chloe Main. Welcome to *This & That*."

Chloe ran her hands down the long silver and stone necklaces she wore. Many of them were pale yellow.

She must have caught Kylee's glance because she held one of the stones up. "Chrysoberyl for calming. I'm expecting someone and not looking forward to it."

Which must be why she'd looked surprised when Kylee arrived, but the woman seemed okay, if a little strange. Like someone lost from the 1960s or '70s flower child age.

Kylee looked around, trying to end the conversation, or find the way to ask about Lila.

"Well, you feel free to browse. There's lots to see. Are you looking for anything in particular?" Chloe asked.

"Uh...." Come on Kylee spit it out would ya? "I—I was looking for Lila—Lila Weber—but I guess she doesn't live here anymore."

The woman—this Chloe—seemed to close right in on herself. She crossed her arms. Her chin came down, and even her beatific smile turned down slightly as if she suspected Kylee of some kind of crime.

"Fan of hers, are you?" Her voice was light, but it felt like a trap.

Kylee nodded. "We were friends in high school. I was hoping to reconnect."

"Really? What high school was that?" Chloe asked.

"Centennial Secondary. In Coquitlam and then Port Moody when they changed the school catchment boundaries." She glanced up at Chloe, but the woman's intense gaze made her uncomfortable. She looked away and noticed a display of unique sterling jewelry made of silver discs embellished with Sanskrit blessings and Buddhist symbols. She went over to it and hung over the glass display, her hands behind her back. "I haven't seen her in years, but one of my favorite memories is of coming up to Peachland one summer with her to stay with her grandparents. This was their house. I knew she'd moved here so I thought I'd pop in to see her." If Lila had sold the place and moved on, just what was she going to do? It hurt to think that she might have lost her friend for good.

She leaned more closely over the case. Such intricate work, it reminded her of snake scales or chain mail. It would feel cool and smooth against the skin. "These are really beautiful."

Chloe straightened and she instantly dropped her Earth-Mother persona to become a sales person. "You've got good taste. Those are custom-made pieces by Regulus, a local designer. They've been popular enough that they've even shown up on New York catwalks.

Interesting. To some people it might even be impressive. But when you're broke it really didn't mean anything at all.

"I love those earrings with the small disc and the temple bell." Her hand went to the simple gold hoops in her earlobes. "I'll bet they're expensive, though."

"Let's check, shall we?" Chloe grabbed her set of keys, the necklaces rattling around her neck as she unlocked the cabinet. She pulled out the earrings for Kylee to examine. She felt the woman's study like a hot brand on her skin—probably picking up on her dress's signs of wear and the old daypack on her shoulder—not exactly the kind of customer who could afford one-of-a-kind jewelry. But she had to hand it to Chloe. She was polite.

Kylee held the earrings up to her ear and peered into the hand mirror Chloe steadied for her. They'd show off her neck and jaw line. Kylee flipped over the discreet price tag, shook her head sadly, and handed the earrings back.

"Too rich for my blood, I'm afraid. I've just come back from six months of travelling." She stuck out her hand. "I'm Kylee Jensen."

Chloe didn't hesitate to accept her hand yet it seemed to make her thoughtful. Then she brightened. Her hand was warm. "Pleased to meet you. I really am. Like I said, I'm Chloe. Lila isn't here right now, but she'll be back later. I'm one of her partners."

It was like Kylee had passed a test or something, because suddenly Chloe's suspicion disappeared. The woman still studied her as if she could categorize her like she did her stones. Chrysoberyl for calming, indeed. Get real, please. But Chloe's gaze seemed like a sponge that took in everything from the slight fraying around the neck of Kylee's dress, to the state of her well-chewed fingernails.

The door bell chimed behind them and Chloe seemed to stiffen.

"Hey, Chloe."

The deep masculine voice turned Kylee around.

Unlike most men, this one didn't look foreign to a shop so purpose-built for women. He stepped farther into the room and a faint scent of sunshine and warm grapes heady as wine reached her. Him.

Tall, she thought. Good looking, just like she'd thought when she'd spotted him sitting in his car. Brown hair in a thick rumpled thatch that kept falling into his eyes like a kid. He shoved it impatiently back over his forehead as his gaze skittered from Chloe to Kylee and back, as if he couldn't decide who to focus on. That sent an instant flush up her shoulders.

He had high cheekbones and a narrow, refined nose that led down to a full mouth that was a lot like Chloe's. Same shade of hair, too. A brother? Related, certainly. But though Chloe's eyes were deep blue that seemed to change color almost to violet as she moved around the room, this man's eyes were a pale green like the first poplar leaves in spring. He wore tan khakis and a rich brown polo shirt that set off his eyes very nicely, thank you very much.

"Uh, hi," he said and nodded in Kylee's direction. His gaze lingered a moment too long so she had to look away. Then he stepped up to Chloe. "I need to talk to you." But his gaze snuck back to Kylee for a moment.

Chloe seemed to stiffen and all the warm shop-keeper persona disappeared into that suspicion Kylee had seen earlier. This time it was directed at the intruder. All the air seemed to have been sucked out of the room and Kylee's chest closed up. There was conflict here.

She didn't do conflict anymore—not if she could help it.

So hard to breathe. So hard to move. Just like all the times Kevin had yelled at her. Even if this guy wasn't yelling, even if he was Chloe's relative, he was no one the woman wanted to see at the moment, that was clear from the way Chloe folded her arms over her chest and retreated behind the counter. Kylee so didn't want to get caught in the middle of someone else's family drama. She'd had enough drama of her own for a lifetime. The shop that had seemed so friendly and intriguing with all its unique displays suddenly seemed too cluttered, crowded, dark. She really needed to get out of here—back to the sunshine and wait somewhere else until Lila returned.

Brett and Chloe's attention was on each other so she edged toward the door. Just a few more feet and she could be out of here.

"Kylee? Where are you going? You don't have to go. Brett here, is just leaving."

Two sets of too intense eyes turned toward her and her voice escaped her. But Brett didn't really look like he was going anywhere any time soon.

She shook her head mutely, pushed out the door and ran.

The wooden stairs thumped under the rush of her footsteps. At the sidewalk she looked left-right-left, uncertain where to turn. Her car was that way. Maybe just get in the car and drive again? To somewhere else? The trouble was, coming to see Lila had seemed like her last stand. She'd been running so long that she really had nowhere else to go.

Head down, she hurried toward her car, threading blindly past the summer-clad people blissfully walking their dogs or jogging together down the promenade. Everyone was with someone. The sunlight placed too-bright dancing motes on the rippled water. The willows swayed long limbs to catch her. No. That was being silly. She stopped and leaned her hands on her knees and just inhaled. Moisture and heat and coconut suntan lotion that just took her away to that happy summer so long ago. She'd loved Peachland then and she thought she could love it now, except for that Brett guy. He was too pushy, too forceful and focused on himself and she'd had enough of guys like that. She took a deep breath, straightened and marched down the sidewalk following the scent of the coffee shop, and stepped inside. No way was she going to let Brett whatever his name was, chase her away from Peachland.

When she left it would be her decision.

Maybe.

CHAPTER 3

"Nice one, brother. Real nice. Scare the poor thing, why don't you? Maybe you should just stand outside and let that sour face chase all my customers away. Stop them from taking the trouble to come inside and see what we have to offer. Lila will be so pleased."

Brett turned from watching the woman in the floral dress retreat down the porch and into the street. There was something about her. The gamine blond hair and large eyes almost reminded him of Audrey Hepburn. The way her lithe body moved it was like she couldn't do anything but glide—and dance. He had seen her dance and actually he liked her better like that. Happy. She didn't look happy now. She *did* almost seem afraid.

He looked at Chloe who faced him with her hands on her hips, her slim legs parted in what could have been a warrior stance from one of those yoga-thing classes she took. Her long brown braid hung over her shoulder to her hips, taming the thick mass of hair that was so much like his. Her gaze flashed dark danger at him and her lips were pursed as if she'd just swallowed a mouthful of sour wine. Though she was two years older than he was, he'd always been the logical one and her protector when her slightly out-of-touch-with-reality beliefs got her in trouble. The thing was, so far she'd done pretty well for herself even if she did believe in a whole bunch of New Age, spiritual crap.

"I didn't do a darn thing other than walk into the store. I'm allowed to walk in, aren't I?" Darn it, he hadn't intended this meeting to get started with him immediately on the defensive. With this kind of a start there was no way in heck he was going to get an agreement to sell their parents' old house on the hill above Peachland.

She rolled her eyes at him and turned away, for a moment reminding him so much of their mother who had used exactly the same expressive histrionics when she was fed up with dealing with her children's antics. Sometimes it could take his breath away how much Chloe looked like their mother—not unexpected given genetics, but still unnerving.

"What now?" She stopped replacing a pair of earrings in the Regulus case.

"You're staring," she said when he looked at her blankly.

He shook himself. "Sorry. Just thinking. Did I really wreck a sale?"

"Nah," she relented. "Just a little window shopping while she was waiting."

"Waiting?" There had been something so vibrant and—real—about that slim female figure.

Lila locked the glass case and glanced up at him. "She said she's a school friend of Lila's and just popped in for a visit." She frowned, her lips pursed, and shook her head. "That's not the whole story, but I don't think she's one of those fan girls and boys who've come looking for Lila because of that stupid cult movie. She's looking for something, that's for certain, but I'm not sure what. Lost now. And a little lonely."

Brett managed to stop his own Main family roll of eyes. "She tell you that, or is that one of your hunches?"

She crossed her arms again. "So just what got you to leave the hallowed halls of Elkhart Winery. Surely there must be a wine barrel to check or an admiring tourist to instruct on the art of wine tasting? I hear that can be quite the sensual experience.

Or perhaps there's a new intern? Female of course." She said it sweetly but there was an unsheathed barb underneath that he'd experienced ever since they were kids. Definitely not the time to discuss disposition of the house. Chloe had never approved of his slightly wild way with the ladies, but she didn't usually bring that out unless she was really looking for a fight.

He glanced out the window, but the attractive blond was marching it quick time back the way she'd come down the promenade. But his neck burned from Chloe's pointed little tirade. "I've told you—I've changed my ways." He stopped himself. Words were cheap and Chloe had pointed it out enough times. "Listen, let's start again. I'm sorry about the girl. Do you want me to go get her? I'll apologize. I mean, I'd hate to wreck a reunion for Lila. Where is she, by the way?"

"Out. For the day. Why? You fixing to smart mouth her, too? Maybe ask her out on another date?"

At that he did roll his eyes. "Ancient history and you know it. Lila and I—not going to happen. I got that. Besides, she's not my type. And if you'd just give me a chance I'd show you that I've turned over a new leaf, remember? What I'm trying to do is make things right between us. Now do I go get her—whatever her name is—or not?"

"Kylee. Her name's Kylee." Chloe said and went to peer out the window next to a display of ice-cream pastel shawls that he'd been told last time he was in were real pashmina and silk, worth a small fortune.

"So that's a yes?"

She glanced up at him impatiently. "If you're serious about making amends, yes."

In the interests of selling the house, he went. Back out into the Okanagan heat and glare of sunshine. He fished his Raybans out of his pocket and put them on, then headed after the blond— Kylee. Given she'd headed back the way she'd come, there was a pretty good chance that she had a car and if she left that would be a disaster, not only because he'd have failed his sister, but also because he wouldn't mind meeting her.

She *was*, after all, attractive, and the dancing way she moved said that even if Chloe was right that there was something going on with Kylee, she had the potential to be happy. It was an unusual trait given all the depression and anxiety in the world. Maybe that was why he made wine—take the edge off the world's cares for a while. Right at the moment he could use a little happy. Even if it was just a little roll in the hay.

Belay that thought....

At an easy lope, he headed down the promenade after her, but the flocks of tourists blocked any chance of spotting her. He lengthened his stride until he was almost running, down past the small string of stores and coffee shop, to the picnic area under the trees and the long line of parked cars edging the road. No sign of her by the water and no car pulled out, so he'd either missed her or she hadn't gone this far.

Turning back, he caught a glimpse of bright color amidst the coffee shop tables. Maybe—yes! The shock of bright sun-blonde hair confirmed it was her.

She sat alone at a wrought iron table in the shade of one of the store-front's brick pillars, staring out at the lake. In profile, her back was straight as a ramrod, her neck fine and long, her chin up as if she was defying the day. But the way she cupped her hands around a plastic glass of water gave an impression of sadness. Or maybe prayer. The breeze seemed to love her hair, tossing the long bangs in her eyes and shifting the longer strands over the crown of her head. Lovely. Beautiful, even, in an unconventional way. That hair would be fine as silk when he ran his hands through it to brush it out of her eyes.

She took a sip from her drink and set the plastic cup back down. Nursing it, as if it was an excuse to sit here.

Water. She drank water and free water at that, sitting in a coffee shop known for its superb coffee. Something wasn't right.

"Excuse me? May I join you?"

Startled blue eyes glanced up at him and he caught a brief glimpse of recognition—and fear? She looked back at the lake as if checking with someone and just that small movement released her scent.

Like an old fashioned Viognier she had a floral aroma—it reminded him faintly of lavender.

§

Standing amidst the grouping of iron tables and gathering patrons, the man was tall enough his broad shoulders actually blocked out the sun, so a golden corona glowed around him. It left his figure black, his features indistinguishable, but she still knew who it was. The faint, unexplainable scent of wine arbors and sun-heated earth made sure of it. She would prefer to be left in peace. She could consider her options while she stared out at the deep blue water of the lake and the undulating gray-green mountain beyond and all the people having summer fun. But the day was too beautiful to be all doom and gloom about things and her mother never brought her up to be rude.

"Fine." She nodded at the lone chair across the table and he settled himself in one simple economical movement. His hands lay palm down on the table. A sign he was hiding something?

"You're Kylee, right?" He had a nice square jaw and strong chin that went along nicely with his straight brow and clear green eyes. "I'm Brett. From *This & That*. Well I don't work there, but my sister does. Chloe. I mean Chloe works there. I'm sorry about the little scene in the store. I guess it made you uncomfortable. We don't usually do that. Fight, I mean. At least not in the store. I mean we're brother and sister so we *do* fight, but not all the time, right?

She raised a single brow at him, charmed for the moment by the way he seemed to be babbling which didn't fit the confident masculine exterior. Probably not hiding something, then.

His short sleeved brown polo shirt seemed meant to expose tanned arms with a nice cording of muscle—the kind that came from tennis or golf or swimming rather than weight lifting or hard labor.

" So," he said, finally stopping for a breath. "You're an old friend of Lila's. How do you know her?" A light dusting of sun-bleached hairs dusted the backs of his arms and his hands were long and refined, with close-clipped fingernails as if he didn't brook any nonsense from them. The neatness of his hands made her curl her own chipped nails under her palms. In the last few months, giving herself a manicure had been about the farthest thing from her mind. Compared to his hands, hers made her look neurotic—which she was pretty sure she wasn't. At least most of the time.

His sudden question left her momentarily at a loss. Were Chloe and her brother checking out her story, now? What would it be like to have a sibling you could fight with and still care about?

"I told your sister. I knew Lila in high school. We were best friends—until her family moved away and she did her fame thing. We sort of lost touch then, except by mail and then e-mail." She shrugged. "Life got in the way, I guess. I know we tried to get together while she was doing her movie, but she kept getting pulled away and then I got busy with university and travelling and the next thing you know, years have passed." She met his gaze. Shrugged. "You know how it is."

"So what brings you here now?" He was looking at her so hard it was uncomfortable—almost as uncomfortable as the thought of answering his question.

What was she supposed to say? That she was broke and at loose ends and looking for a friend? That she'd put all her eggs in one basket with Kevin and when he dropped her like Humpty Dumpty she fell a long way and there didn't seem to be anyone around to pick up the pieces? Heck, she wasn't even sure she could find them.

"It just seemed like the time. I was headed this way and thought I'd drop in. I didn't think I'd have to get through a screening team, though." She managed a smile. "That's what you and Chloe are, isn't it? A screening team, double-timing me?"

§

For a moment he was nonplussed that this small blond woman had caught him out. She looked so small and vulnerable with her froth of tousled hair and her big blue eyes, but there was clearly nothing vulnerable about her mind. She'd seen right through the both of them. He sat back in his chair and wasn't sure whether he liked that about her. It made her totally different than any woman he'd ever dated. It made her harder to figure out when his perception said she was one thing, but her actions said another, like a flawed cluster of grapes that was still bursting with flavor. It would take a research project to figure her out and categorize her, but it could be an interesting process.

Hell, what was he thinking? He had more than enough on his plate what with dealing with his parents' estate and running the winery. The last thing he needed to do was live up to Chloe's very low expectations and chase the new skirt in town again, even a flirty floral one that came with a set of great legs. That was Kylee, all big eyes and long slim legs. Just how did someone so small have legs that seemed to go on forever? An optical illusion?

"Okay. So you caught us. Lila's been stalked a time or two by adoring fans. We sort of run interference for her. We all do."

"We all?" she asked.

"Her friends. The old timers in town. People who've known her a long time." He saw her frown, saw something click in her brain as her eyes narrowed.

"Are you by any chance the guy that used to be the lifeguard at the old Peachland swimming beach years ago?"

What the hell? Don't let her have been one of his past conquests. Please don't. "How'd you know that?"

Her lips curved in a most attractive grin and she gave a little laugh that set off a soft chime inside him.

"Well, I'll be darned. I came up one summer with Lila. She introduced us. We were fifteen and feeling the stupidity that comes with hormones. I think we might have taken turns almost drowning and being rescued by you until you caught on."

A charming rose-colored blush ran up to her cheeks from her shoulders and he frantically wracked his brains for a memory of this woman—girl then. He leaned forward conspiratorially. "I don't remember, but if it's any consolation, I was pretty much a jerk that summer. My head too big for my shoulders, my mother used to say. Chloe, too, for that matter."

He glanced down at her water and her hands twitched again. She had small, delicate hands with slender fingers, but she seemed intent on hiding her fingernails from him. "Listen, can I buy you a coffee? The *Peachland Bean* has the best coffee in the Okanagan Valley. Or we could head back to the shop. They usually have some pretty good coffee in the back and we could sit on the porch and wait for Lila together."

She hesitated and pulled her hands down into her lap behind the table while she did one of those small usually involuntary head-shakes. "I thought—I thought you needed to have a conversation with Chloe. I don't want to intrude. No, I'll stay here and check in at the store later. Thank you for the invitation, though. It was kind of you to come and ask."

And just like that he had no more excuse to stay even though he wanted to. Because actually, she looked like the kind of research project he could really get into. The kind that ended up with a palate pleasing new blend of grapes.

There'd been that laugh and frankly, if he was honest with himself, he did remember cool water and rescuing a slim white body—more than once. Layers of woman to uncover.

He liked the thought of that.

CHAPTER 4

IT HAD BEEN A LONG DAY FOR LILA WEBER. Six o'clock and the sun had finally fallen over the hills that backed the western side of Okanagan Lake. It bathed the town of Peachland in welcome shadows after the long heat of the day. Now was the time that she loved this town most of all, especially in summer. From the somnolent, suntan lotion scented days, the late afternoon returned to a time when people actually talked to each other, instead of grunting in the heat. The scent of charcoal briquettes and barbecue joined with the tinkle of gin and tonic or white wine drunk on the patio. On the lake the power boats had largely docked for the night or were farther out from shore so their rumble was less annoying. The last kids were being hauled up on shore.

The locals could almost enjoy their town again. As long as you didn't want to get space in a restaurant. Fat chance of that happening without a reservation or a heck of a long wait.

She turned her red Ford Escape off the highway onto a road mostly used by locals and sighed as she followed it through what had once been an area of small cottages and mom-and-pop resorts. No longer. Now it was million dollar homes, condos and B & Bs and the last willow-and-poplar shaded campground was holding on by a thread. Change. She was so frigging tired of change.

Okay. Let's rethink that, given change was part of her business. She was just tired because actually it had been a long *couple* of days. With the load of stuff she's picked up at the various estate sales in Kamloops, Vernon and Kelowna, it was going to be even longer.

Beach Avenue crossed the bridge over Trepanier Creek and curved into the wide bay that held Peachland proper strung along its shore. Tall cottonwoods swayed in the breeze off the water. At this hour there were gaps in what would have probably been wall-to-wall campers, motor homes and cars parked along the water. She slowed for the corner next to the coffee shop, inhaling the scent of coffee and baking. At this hour most of the outside tables were empty and the place had seriously emptied out. It was the hour when both the summer people and the residents agreed that it was time for dinner. The bakery staff would be getting ready for tomorrow.

Amongst the cast iron tables outside sat a lonely-looking figure in a blue and turquoise floral dress. The blond woman's hands were clasped patiently on the table before her. As Lila watched, one of the café staff came out to her and said something. Lila checked her watch. Six o'clock. The shop was closing. The woman stood up and took an uncertain step toward the park benches next to the water, then glanced down the street as if looking for someone.

There was something about the slim figure and Lila slowed her SUV to let the woman cross the street and maybe get a better look. It was something—familiar. The impatient flip of blond bangs out of her eyes. The way the blond hair clung to the head and how the woman lifted her chin. Almost as if she was steeling herself for a blow. She raised a hand in thanks for Lila stopping her car and that was also something familiar.

It couldn't be. There'd been too many years since they'd last seen each other for Kylee Jensen to look so much the same. Besides, Kylee was somewhere else in the world according to the e-mail she'd sent out to her list before she left. Off on a grand adventure with the love of her life. When Lila had read that, she'd sat back in her chair and felt a momentary envy.

So this couldn't be Kylee, and yet…

The woman walked over to the park bench and sat down, her dress fluttering prettily around her.

Darn it, it *looked* like Kylee!

She swung her car to the curb and climbed out, feeling foolish as she strode across the street and up behind the lone woman. From behind there was no question but that it was her friend. From the side, though…

She came around the bench and the woman looked up at her. "Kylee?"

The woman's eyes were wide and blue with so many worries in them, but then all of a sudden they cleared like the lake on a summer day and a burst of joy spread over her face.

"Lila! Lila, my God. It's you!"

She was up and thin arms came around Lila's shoulders so fast she was almost bowled over. They embraced and then Lila held her old friend away. "Kylee Jensen. I don't believe it. So what wind did you blow in on? I thought you were in Europe or Africa or Thailand or something. Out seeing the world on an extended trip with some grand paramour."

The joy seemed to crumple a little. A heavy sigh lifted Kylee's thin shoulders. "Let's just say it didn't work out. So I came home." She shrugged, but her throat worked as if the nonchalance cost her.

And came here of all places. The unspoken words stretched between them. "Well, you're better off here, given the state the world is in," Lila said as she caught her friend's arm. "What I'm wondering is what you're doing in Peachland?"

Blue eyes looked up at her from the fringe of long bangs. "Honestly? Would you believe looking for you? I had this need to reconnect with my past, I guess. Sounds lame, but it was like a compulsion to get here and find you. Sort of reclaiming my youth." A wry smile.

This Kylee was thin compared to her friend in high school, but maturity could do that. But the fine lines at the outside of her eyes and the dark circles under them both suggested that something else was going on. Kylee had a long history of falling deeply in love and then being devastated when it wasn't fully reciprocated. Back in high school she'd seriously struggled when she'd had to get over her first boyfriend. But then she'd done it all over again when she met the next guy. Kylee was a serious case of the heart being too big for such a small person.

"If you were looking for me, what are you doing out here? My shop's just down the block" A gust of wind picked up dust off the beach and swirled it toward them. "Come on. It looks like we've got a little thunder cell coming up."

It did. Above the western mountain a single huge black cloud glowered down as its white heights towered into the sky.

"My car. I left it down the street."

Lila caught her hand and shook her head. "It's fine where it is as long as the windows are closed. We can get it later. Now come on and hop in mine."

Against Kylee's protests, she dragged her into the Escape and then drove down and around the corner to get into the back carport of the refurbished old house. She turned off the car and just sat a moment. It felt good to be home. It always did. She might like to travel, but she was a homebody at heart. She glanced sideways at Kylee and found her old friend studying her.

"I've come at a bad time, I can tell. You're tired." Kylee climbed out of the SUV as if she had to get away and Lila climbed out her side.

"You try to leave and I'm gonna tackle you and drag you inside." She frowned over the top of the car. "Don't make me do that. It's much too hard on the clothes." She motioned down at the flowing knit tunic and trousers in a cream color, her absolute favorite outfit.

The resolution on Kylee's face faded. "Well, maybe I'll come inside for a moment. I did come earlier, but Chloe said you weren't here and I didn't want to get in the way."

"So. What? You waited all afternoon for me at the coffee shop."

Kylee looked down at the daypack she carried. "Sort of."

Lila looked heavenward. "I swear you're even worse at taking care of yourself than I am. Now, make yourself useful and give me a hand with these boxes." She opened the rear of the car and grabbed a small moving box and placed it in Kylee's arms, then grabbed another herself. Three more boxes, an ornately carved antique clock, a copper kettle and a lovely old ceramic butter churn could wait until later. Closing and locking the car, she led the way inside.

The carport sat along a lane that ran behind *This & That*. Between it and the house was a small workshop on the left and a lawn-and-garden-filled yard with wicker furniture with bright yellow, turquoise and cranberry cushions that were going to get wet in the coming downpour. Thankfully they'd dry easy enough. Next to the broad kitchen windows stood her well-used barbeque. She pushed open the door into the kitchen that filled the rear of the house just as a gust of rain fell across the yard.

"I'm back," she called and set her box on the counter.

"About time," said a male voice and Lila swung around.

Chloe's brother, Brett, stood up from reading a book in the old kitchen nook at one end of the room. He was always a good looking man, but more so now that he'd gotten over himself and quit treating women like a used car salesman.

His gaze caught on Lila's companion and locked. "I see you found Kylee. I tried to get her to wait in the shop, but she preferred the café. I was just getting ready to go find her, given the threat of rain and that the coffee shop would be closing."

Almost too casual, Lila thought as she looked at the way Brett studied her old friend. Interesting. Chloe would be amused. Lila shook out her tumble of auburn curls and, with hands on hips, turned back to Kylee.

"See what you did? You made this handsome man hang around waiting to come and rescue you, and then I steal his opportunity. You are going to owe him a big one, I'm thinking." She shook her head, because Kylee's face said she wasn't ready for anything to do with this man. Nope, better to let her get comfortable first. Then she and Kylee could talk and maybe Brett and Kylee could get to know each other. "I'm thinking Rooibos tea. You like?"

§

It had all happened so fast, Kylee didn't know what to say. She'd forgotten that aspect of Lila. Even when they used to hang out together, Lila was a force of nature just like the storm cloud that was currently blowing a sheet of rain against the kitchen window and roughing up the rose bushes in the lush backyard garden. It had often made her uncomfortable, because it pointed out everything she—Kylee—was not. Not tall, not forceful, never knowing what she wanted and certainly ignorant of what was good for her. That was about the farthest thing from Lila.

"Uh, yes?" she answered Lila's question as she took in her surroundings and tried not to be so aware of Brett Main who stood beside the kitchen table.

The kitchen was a room to die for, just like she remembered—an old-fashioned kitchen with white walls and yellow cupboards. Now, though, it was updated with a gleaming steel gas stove, and other appliances. The stove was a work of art, set back in a black and white arched alcove holding a professional-looking steel range hood, with copper pots hung on the wall. White marble countertops ran almost the full length of the room under a wide set of wood-shuttered windows. They would let in the sun or could be closed on too-hot days. At one end of the room sat a cozy nook with an old, round, blond-maple table. The bench seating around it had colorful turquoise and cranberry cushions that tied into the patio furniture outside. The same two accent colors were splashed around the kitchen in cooking tool holders by the stove, and cute sun and moon decorations on the walls. Small paintings of tropical shorelines and sailboats filled other niches. The whole effect was one of comfort and welcome. It also screamed that the owner of this kitchen was someone who loved cooking.

In addition to being one of the most beautiful women Kylee had ever known, Lila Weber had always had a way with anything she decided to turn her mind to. Food was one of those things. She could make canned corn and fried Spam taste like food of the Gods when they were kids. She had introduced Kylee to such esoteric dishes as pickles and ice cream, and pad thai. Now she moved around the room with the same old grace, her long curls of bright auburn hair tumbling down her elegant back.

She swiftly put the kettle on a lit burner and efficiently used tap water to warm a slightly off-shaped tea pot in bright Alice in Wonderland colors. By the time she had the loose tea in a little tea ball, the kettle was starting to boil. She made the tea, placed the pot and four cups on a tray and carried it over to the table. On her way past a swinging door she bumped it with her shoulder.

"Chloe! Tea!" she called.

"Come. Sit." She commanded and motioned Kylee to the table. At six feet tall in her stocking feet, Lila always towered over Kylee. As kids walking to school together they had composed a poem to capture how silly they looked together. *The Tall and the Small of It All*, they had called it and their rhyme had channeled Dr. Seuss.

She sat in the nook and found herself trapped in the back between Lila and Brett. When Chloe joined them from the store, it seemed even worse, though Chloe took the lone chair at the table.

"So how was it? Chloe asked as Lila played mother and poured the tea.

Lila nodded toward the boxes on the counter. "That, three more and a few larger pieces in the car. I picked up a couple of antiques that particularly caught my eye. I know, it shifts outside of our original vision, but if we don't sell them, they'll make lovely display items." She shook her head. "It was a heck of trip, though. The Explorer's check engine light went on in Vernon so I ended up spending half a day at the garage. By the time I made it back to Kelowna for the Bristol estate sale, it had largely been cleaned out and I still had to make it back to Kamloops for the sale there. Thankfully Moira had basically thrown the pieces she thought I might like, and junk she couldn't sell, in a box and let me have them for a song. I'm not even sure what I've got. The second sale I arrived bright and early the next day so I had my choice. I picked up a few nice pieces, but they were mostly selling furniture. In Vernon I picked up the clock and the copper pieces that are still in the car." She shook her head. "Not much to show for three days on the road, I'm afraid."

She took a sip of tea, and then turned too-intent hazel eyes on Kylee. "So. I thought you were off on the adventure of a lifetime? Don't tell me Peachland was on your itinerary. And where's Kevin?"

Kevin. A sharp pang of loss hit Kylee square in the heart. She swallowed and caught the slight rise of Brett's and Chloe's brows as three sets of eyes settled on her. Any pleasure at finding Lila disappeared at having to bare her soul to these strangers, because the question seemed to tear open the spurting wound of hurt and anger she'd been trying so hard to contain these past three months. How was Kevin? It was like she'd hived off a part of herself—the part with her heart. She blinked. Blinked again and finally sighed, trying to loosen up the tight band that constricted her chest.

A little shrug. "That was what didn't work out. That, and I discovered that I don't like travel." At least travel was not her friend when it came to relationships. How many times had she run after someone only to have something like this happen? She tried for a smile.

Lila seemed to study her for a moment, then her full lips curved kindly as if she'd read the story behind Kylee's smile. "Well, Kevin's loss and Peachland's gain, I say. So you decided to come see me instead?"

Kylee felt a worm of discomfort. She'd really just assumed Lila would be happy to see her. "I hope I didn't come at a bad time. Maybe we could just make a plan to meet for coffee or something if this doesn't work for you." It sounded lame, lame, lame. She looked down at the fragrant tea she was drinking out of a pale green and cream colored checkerboard mug that seemed to fit perfectly into her hands. Too perfectly. As if Lila's place was exactly the place she'd wanted to be all her life. But she was *not* going to impose herself. Besides, she wasn't exactly the kind of person with deep roots anywhere. "I won't keep you from your work. I really do need to get going, but I wanted to reconnect."

"Where are you headed?" Brett asked and she saw the look that his sister and Lila shot him.

Oh God, they knew. They'd seen right through her ridiculous bravado. But not Brett. At least there was that, because for some reason she didn't want him to see just how pathetic she was, running to a friend she hadn't seen in years for help because she didn't have anywhere else to go.

"I'm not really sure. It's all an adventure isn't it? Life I mean. I'm on the road. I've found that it's better to live your life unencumbered so you can just do or be anything." It was the same horrible, silly speech that Kevin had used on her, except he'd added in the clause 'be with anyone.' *Anyone else, was what he'd meant.*

It felt like a knife carved out her heart, because Kevin had been *the one*—she'd thought. She plastered a smile on her face and hoped it worked. "I've seen a lot of wonderful places and met wonderful people. Why not keep on doing that? Maybe I'll write a book or something."

Brett's green eyes carried disbelief, while Chloe's had softened as if she saw the cracks in Kylee's story and knew she needed to be gentle. Darn it, she didn't want pity.

Lila though, just placed her cup down on the table.

"Good. Then it's settled. You'll stay here a while so you can put Peachland and the shop in whatever you happen to write. I could use the advertising."

So totally *not* what Kylee'd expected that for a moment she didn't understand what she'd heard. "But... No... I wasn't looking for an invitation."

Lila held up her long-fingered, many-ringed, elegant hand. "Of course you weren't. But we're old friends and we haven't seen each other in a very long time. What better time to catch up, than when you're not in a hurry to be moving along. You could even help me out a little. Chloe has better things to do than man the store while I'm gone looking for stock. Maybe you could watch the store for me a time or two. " Her brow rose in two perfect arches as Kylee hesitated. "I'd pay you of course."

Gratefulness warred with mortification and broke through all Kylee's defenses. They roiled up through her and suddenly she was sliding along the seat elbowing a protesting Brett out ahead of her. "Stop it! This is all too much."

She shoved out of the nook and stumbled for the door. Silly tears half blinded her and she shouldn't be crying. She should be down on her knees thanking Lila for being so kind. But it was all too much. Had all three of them seen how desperate she was? How hopeless?

Oh God, kill me now.

"Kylee, wait." Lila's soft voice.

She fumbled for the door and staggered out into the rain. Her dress instantly plastered itself to her and her stupid shaggy bangs half-blinded her. Just get away from this place where she was an object of pity.

Down the three steps to the garden and the wonderful scent of wet, heated soil and warm roses. Down the path to the carport and the shiny SUV that she could never afford. She came out to the lane. Left or right? Which way was her car?

A hand fell on her shoulder. "Don't do this, Kylee. We really haven't seen each other in such a long time. I meant what I said." Lila's soft voice cut through the panic.

She stopped and took a deep breath, but couldn't face Lila's understanding grace. "Well, I didn't. I didn't tell you the truth, did I? It's just like way back when we were kids, Lila. Just like all those other times. I fell in love and Kevin dumped me and I fell apart. He...he..." she tried to get it out, but the flooding emotions froze her throat closed so all the clammed up feelings welled up in her eyes. She shook her head.

Two long, knit-clad arms came around her shoulders. "I sort of figured. And I'm here for you, my friend. Just as I always would be."

Lila gently turned her around and looked down at her from too-kind, too-understanding hazel eyes. "Your heart told you I always would be. It was right. We swore all those long years ago that we'd be BFFs. I didn't lie. Did you?"

Kylee swallowed back a hiccough and palmed the tears off her cheeks. The comfort of human warmth was so what she needed. She still couldn't meet Lila's gaze, because if she did, she might start crying again. "I'm just so darn silly when it comes to love. I hate that about myself."

Lila shook her head and eased her around back into the carport and toward the garden. "You shouldn't hate yourself for that at all. The fact you fall in love so deeply means that you have a great heart. It gives me hope that people can love so deeply. Now I happen to have a spare bedroom that's all made up and waiting for you and I won't take no for an answer, so it's settled. Besides, I'm bigger than you so you have to listen to me, or else I'll strong-arm you into the house." She grinned.

The rain slackened as they stepped into the backyard. Westering sunlight sent beams around the edge of the storm clouds to catch in the drops on the leaves and the blades of grass. The door into the little building to the side of the yard swung open and out stepped a woman with kohled eyes and shoulder length black hair cut in geometrically uneven bangs. She wore a black singlet t-shirt and baggy black cargo pants that suited the Celtic knot tattoo that encircled both upper arms. Tough chick. The kind Kylee'd cross the street to pass around because she reminded her of a certain German girl she'd met on her safari.

The woman had long bare feet and leaned against her door frame with her arms crossed. *Did she live in Lila's shed?* By the unkempt look of her, Kylee wouldn't put it past her.

"Look," the woman said and hefted her chin southward. Her voice was husky, like a drinker's, and Kylee shivered.

Kylee and Lila turned to follow the black-haired woman's gaze. Southward, out over the water, a vivid rainbow had formed with one end on the mountain bluffs across the lake and the other magically set down at their doorstep in Peachland's bay.

The pain in her chest eased.

CHAPTER 5

THE NEXT MORNING BLOOMED EARLY WITH LIGHT seeping through the blinds and sheer curtained window of Lila's guest bedroom. It was a good room. A very good room, in fact, though it had changed a lot from when she was a teenager. Previously it had been a little run down with white walls and an over-soft quilt-covered bed. Now it had pale mauve walls and a tall brass bed with a gray and purple duvet. Darker gray sheets made her feel like she was sleeping in lavender-scented mist, instead of at summer camp. The dresser was the same one she had used, but someone had chalk-painted its dark wood so distressing allowed bits of dark to shine through the pale surface paint. A low armchair with deep aubergine cushions sat in the small alcove caused by the dormer window and looked northeastward toward the lake. Best of all there was now a small bathroom attached.

Kylee bounced out of bed and went to the window, padding across the gray sisal rug and the dark-stained hardwood flooring. The window catch opened easily and she drew up the sash and inhaled—morning. The lake was a still mirror that caught the mountains' refection in its embrace and the sky was the same mauve as the room's walls. The air smelled clean from the thunder showers last night that had rumbled overhead and lulled her back to sleep the few times she'd woken. Somehow the night and the afternoon before had left her cleansed as well.

Compared to yesterday the beach was abandoned—just a few dedicated joggers out this early on the damp pavement. Early? She checked her watch. Hell, yes. Five thirty a.m., she hadn't woken this time of day since the African wild doves woke her each morning on safari six months ago. A knife jab of pain made her wince. She turned away from the view and the memories of what should have been a magical time. Maybe she should just go back to bed. But she'd come up here to get her head on straight, hadn't she? If that was the case, then she needed to quit wallowing in her grief and get on with fitting herself into a new relationship with the world. She might not have anything left of her old life, but she could start a new one wherever she decided. One without men, preferably. It might as well be here as anywhere.

She quickly showered and dressed in yesterday's dress and underwear that she had washed out last night. Then she crept down the stairs. If she was starting a new life she might as well start with a new routine and go for a walk. She could decide what to do next while walking because movement always gave her inspiration. On the way back she could pick up her car.

She snuck out the kitchen door, pristine, so someone had cleaned up after the luscious dinner of pesto-baked chicken and pasta Chloe and Brett had prepared. It had been a lovely evening with wine, food, discussion of the store and laughter. No one had plied her with anymore questions. She had laughed at the jokes and felt welcomed into their circle of friendship—Lila and Chloe and the strange, black-haired woman, Reggie who turned out to be Lila's third partner. But Kylee still wasn't sure about her. And of course there'd been Brett.

She smiled, thinking about sitting squeezed together around the kitchen table, and then pushed open the back door to step down into the yard. It should be rain drenched, but it looked like only a heavy dew had fallen to leave crystal droplets on the roses.

The door to Reggie's shed was slightly open and she could hear someone moving around, so someone else was up and around this early. She tiptoed across the yard to the carport and then struck out down the street to the corner and down to the beach. It felt good to move and, frankly, almost good to be alive after a good night's sleep.

Even if she didn't have any prospects—no job, no home, no nothing.

Don't go there, Jensen. That kind of thinking could seriously get her standing at the edge of a bridge and she wasn't that kind of person even if she was a wandering soul. Besides, she had a connection to someone. Lila. And that was definitely worth something.

She set off toward what would always in her memory be the sleepy central part of the village of Peachland. While the *This & That* sat toward one end of the long shallow bay, what used to be the commercial heart of Peachland sat a mile away at the other end. The white spire of the odd octagon-shaped church-come-museum sticking up through the leafy trees, her destination.

Last night had been a wonder. First of all that Lila had even remembered her after all these years and had invited her in just like she'd hoped—no, more like wished-hoped-dreamed she might. But it had been so much more. The warmth of all those people— even Reggie—Reggie Lewis—was nicer than she'd expected. Lila so supportive. Chloe and Reggie who, according to Chloe, was an artisanal jeweler and had her workshop in what had once been Lila's grandmother's old gardening shed. The three women were almost perfect foils for each other. Lila tall, willowy and beautiful like the Goddess she had once played in her one movie role. Chloe more Earth Mother with her Indian cotton clothing and her slew of necklaces that seemed to whisper around her whenever she moved. Reggie who looked tough, with her black clothing, severe haircut and her tattoos, but who had actually seemed okay during the dinner last night.

And then there'd been Brett with his thick dark hair and his pale green eyes that she'd felt looking at her too often last night. Sure he was good looking, but that first confrontation with his sister had been enough to warn her away. As if everyone should just agree with him, and if they didn't there'd be hell to pay. Kevin had been like that at the end. Certain she'd understand the logic of his position that he had to leave her because there were other fish in the sea of women. She shivered because Kevin had left her not even trusting her own feelings. Her heart was a faulty thing and always had been, no matter what Lila said. Why else would she always end up feeling like this?

Sighing, she looked out at the lake.

But last night Brett had been different than Kevin, too. Getting into the kitchen with his sister and cooking together like a well-oiled machine, no matter the conflict she'd seen, so maybe there was something to what he'd said about the brother and sister thing. She just had nothing to compare it to, given she was an only child.

It had been a pleasure to watch them sipping wine with Lila and Reggie that Brett had picked out. Not like Kevin and not like that afternoon at all. Brett had a nice smile and a better laugh, too. Like a kid when his hair fell into his eyes as he raised a toast to Kylee's arrival. He'd grinned and looked right at her then and she—silly fool—had blushed.

She felt the blush roll up her shoulders again and shook her head, her hair—dry now—flopped across her eyes.

Yup, Brett was good looking and he'd made her blush, but there was no way she was going through what she'd just been through again. Brett was—well, that was the problem. She didn't know him except that he was good looking, he could cook, and he had a nice sister. That was not enough to let her guard down even if she'd been flattered just the tiniest bit when he'd paid her the attention. Nope. Men were *verboten*—a word she'd picked up with Kevin in Germany.

She couldn't risk her heart again. *Heck, one more time and I'll end up a street person.* And that was incentive to remain uninvolved if anything was.

With that load off her shoulders, she stretched her legs out and almost felt like she could run the path along the water. Fifteen minutes later she reached the center of the historic town which cuddled up against the lakeshore, though it had changed since she was last here. Now it looked greener, tamer, more gentrified with outdoor restaurants in what had once been service garages along the broadened sidewalk, though the tables were vacant at this early hour. The old post office was gone, turned into an accountant's office, but the pharmacy and the old Peachland General Store still stood, complete with faded posters of ice cream treats and a hand-painted *Help Wanted* sign in the window. The old, iconic church still stood, its odd eight-sided white spire against the glowing blue sky with the pine and poplar climbing up the hillside behind it. It still all just fit together, each piece a part of what made Peachland itself.

She just stood there studying the place when a shadow fell beside hers. She looked up and found an older, gray-haired woman considering her companionably.

"You okay, dear? You look a bit lost."

The woman was dressed in khaki shorts and a neat blouse. She had short curly hair and tan, muscled limbs as if she walked or swam a lot. A circle of keys jingled in her hands.

Kylee smiled. "Nah. Just taking the old town in. It's been years since I've been here, but it still feels the same even though some things have changed." She waved out at the fancy flowerbeds by the old town cenotaph and the broad promenade sidewalk. It had been a gravel path last time she came and the flowers hadn't been there then. At least that was what she remembered.

"It's a good town. I've been here thirty-five years and I haven't regretted it. It's a place you can put down roots and call home. If you're waiting for the museum to open it won't be for a few hours, but if you like I can let you take a peek inside." She jingled the key ring.

"Really? I know I'm too early, but I'd love to see inside. It was something I never did as a kid. Not exciting enough, I guess."

"My name's, Nora," said the woman as she led the way up the sidewalk and stairs to the old church door. She unlocked it and held it open. "Nora Kallaher. Welcome back to Peachland, a good place to call home."

It was then the feeling enveloped Kylee and it was strange and wonderful in its unfamiliarity.

Home. She was home, or she wanted this place to be. It was silly because she'd only been here one night, but she had friends here. She liked the town, the honest simplicity, and welcome it seemed to offer.

Typical, Jensen. One night and you've fallen in love.

She stepped through the old church door into darkness illuminated by light through eight stained glass windows. Shadows filled the open space, and wood-sided, glass-topped displays, as well as a model of a large boat. The walls between the windows held what looked like an antique map of the lakeshore. At the rear of the room a set of stairs led up to a hidden second floor. The place smelled of old wood, varnish, dust and, well, age.

"I guess I'll have to come back another day and take a real look around," she said.

"I'll watch for you then, dear." Nora let her out again and they stood in the sunshine chatting.

§

Lila heard the soft click of the kitchen door as she finished her meditations in the small room she reserved for her morning yoga. It was a pretty room, once her grandmother's sewing room, but now every inch filled with orchids, ferns and kitchen herbs, with a hardwood floor and just enough space for her to spread her yoga mat. She finished her last Natrajasana pose and settled both feet on the floor, arms at her sides and breathed in deeply. Yes, all the stress of the past few days was gone, even if she hadn't gotten to sorting through her purchases last night as she'd originally intended. Supporting Kylee had been more important.

She toweled off, padded into the kitchen to turn on the coffee, and then went for a quick shower. Then she dressed in a simple shift of orange cotton that fell to her knees and a pair of Roman sandals that laced up her calves. Her hair she left wet, because it would dry fast enough in the dry Okanagan air. Then she went back down to the kitchen, poured herself a cup of coffee in a bowl-shaped mug of celadon green and carried it out through the shop to the wicker seating on the broad front porch.

It felt good to be home again and to get back to her routines. She settled in a wicker armchair with a high back and russet and yellow striped cushions and inhaled the warm lake smell. After all the years here, she still wasn't bored with it. She doubted she ever would be. The lake this morning was a dazzling flat expanse, but as she sipped her coffee light ripples across the water presaged a change. Kylee's arrival perhaps—that's what Chloe would say. More logically it was likely just a wind coming up from the south.

"Penny for your thoughts?" Reggie's husky voice disturbed her reverie.

Lila looked over her shoulder to where her friend stood just outside the door cupping her own mug, a misshapen purple hand-built cup that had been lovingly made by her ten-year-old daughter who was currently off on a holiday with her father.

"Join me. I was just thinking about Kylee turning up after all these years. We were such good friends back then. It's hard to see her so sad now."

Reggie ignored the other chairs and perched, like always, on the veranda rail. "This is all because some guy dumped her?"

"She's gives up her heart every time she falls in love, but it looks like this time she gave up everything, including her sense of herself when she went off with him. Kylee was always a sweet person with too big a heart. She was continually falling for strays—dogs, kittens, men. It's part of what I love about her. Once she was your friend you knew she'd always be there for you. The kind that bonds for life, I guess. If they can find the right one."

"You're thinking about letting her settle in with you, aren't you?"

Lila glanced up at her. This morning Reggie had eschewed her black work-clothes for a slim-fitting brown sleeveless shift and brilliant peach scarf that set off her tanned skin and well muscled arms. She looked artsy and beautiful and exotically different. Something was up.

"I guess I am. She needs a safe place and people who care about her. Now what's got you all dressed up today?"

Reggie looked down at herself and gave a charming crooked smile. "I had a call from a couple of Vancouver designers wanting to see my jewelry for possible inclusion in the spring shows. They're up here on holidays but wanted to meet to discuss it. I thought I'd look a little more human like this. Maybe fool them into thinking I am, anyway."

"Oh get over it. Just because your ex told you that you weren't normal, doesn't mean it's true."

The noise of a car disturbed the quiet as an older model Silver Civic pulled into the curb. Kylee climbed out and lugged a backpack out of the trunk before turning toward the house and waving. Lila waved back, but Reggie eased up from her seat.

"Listen, before you get all distracted with your friend, I thought you should know. I was listening to the news this morning and Moira Burns was killed two nights ago—a hit and run. They just released the name. Isn't that the agent you dealt with in Kelowna at the Bristol estate sale? You had her down here for a Christmas party last year or something."

"Moira? Dead? That can't be right. That's the night I saw her." She sat up so quickly that she sloshed coffee over the russet seat cushion and leapt to her feet, spilling more across the pinewood decking.

Kylee came bouncing up the front stairs looking breathless and happy, her sundress fluttering around her body as the promised breeze picked up on the lake beyond.

"Guess what? I've found an apartment and I have a lead on a job!"

Lila looked from Kylee's flushed face, to her spilled coffee, to Reggie quietly waiting with her news. Maybe Chloe was right and change was coming. The question was whether it was bad or good.

Either way she couldn't very well go charging off to find out about Moira when she had Kylee standing here like some bright-eyed child waiting for approval. She pushed the news aside and glanced up at Reggie. "Could you...."

"Stay put. I'll bring out some coffee for Kylee and then I'll make a few phone calls."

"Sounds like you've had a busy morning and it's not even eight thirty. Come sit and tell me all about it." She brushed the coffee off the chair pillow, turned it over and sank back down. Kylee settled on the wicker couch beside her. The woman positively perched there as if she would take flight at any time.

§

The morning felt so wonderful and Kylee was so excited she felt like she positively vibrated on the thick cushion of the wicker couch. Across from her, Lila looked as cool and composed as a Goddess, especially with the strappy sandals that wound up her long slim calves. A light, lake-scented breeze picked up her curls and they seemed to wave and move of their own accord as if they loved to play around her shoulders.

Kylee shook her head. "It was all so simple. Like everything was just meant to be. See? I knew coming to see you would change things." She told Lila about going for a walk and meeting Nora Kallaher at the museum. "She showed me around and we got to talking and she told me they've renovated the Beach Hotel to provide apartments. I can move in almost immediately." She grinned, feeling a little triumphant, but also a little sad at leaving

Lila when she'd only arrived so recently. She hoped Lila wouldn't see her as ungrateful. "I'll be out of your hair, but still living here. Isn't that great?"

Lila went still and for a moment seemed confused as if her thoughts were on something else. Then she managed a smile that didn't quite work. "That's super, Kylee. But it makes me kind of sad, too. I was looking forward to having you around for a while."

"Oh I'll be around, alright. But I need a job. I noticed they need someone down at the old General Store. I'm going to check it out when they're open."

Lila looked away to the lake as if she didn't want Kylee to see what was in her eyes. What was this? Didn't Lila approve of her standing on her own? Or had she really hurt Lila's feelings? Kylee was considering apologizing when the bell rang above the front door. Reggie elbowed her way out with a tray full of coffee cups, a carafe of fresh coffee and a platter of English muffins with little blue ceramic pots of fresh jelly. She set the breakfast down on the wicker coffee table.

She looked nothing like the Reggie Kylee had seen the night before, now in a neat brown dress and peach scarf, but if anything she looked even more like the German woman Kevin had left her for. Claudia.

"There. Now enjoy," Reggie said and cocked one sculpted black brow at Kylee. "If I didn't know better, I'd say you met a man the way you're glowing."

"Kylee was just telling me about an apartment she's found at the Beach Hotel," Lila said.

Reggie's dark eyes widened. "What? You set her straight, right? I wouldn't let my worst enemy stay there the way that women get hassled. And the noise! Shoot, that bar is open until two in the morning. When are normal people supposed to sleep? There's a reason that place is in the downtown section—because no one lives there."

Kylee felt like a helium balloon two weeks after the party. All the excitement dissipated. She turned back to Lila who had to look away. "She's right, isn't she? You know she's right, but you didn't tell me."

Sighing, Lila nodded. "I thought I'd let you enjoy the excitement and then I'd try to ease you into that information."

She was *so* stupid. There she'd gone again, throwing herself into something with her eyes willfully closed. She sagged back on the couch, her fingers clenched on her legs. "I am such a mess. You know, when I think about it, I should have twigged to all those problems, but I just can't seem to help myself. I fall in love with something and throw myself at it too quickly, and then end up floundering around grabbing for anything." She raised her gaze to Lila and then Reggie. "Thanks for saving me from doing something stupid."

"That's what friends are for, and it's not stupid. You're just trying to get your life back in order, but sometimes you need to take a little time to sort things out in order to do that. So relax and be my guest for a few days, will you? First order of business is to drink some coffee, eat these muffins with the jelly we made last summer and enjoy this view."

Easy for Lila to say. *She* wasn't an emotional bruise trying to prove to herself she deserved to live.

Reggie excused herself as Lila poured the coffee and settled back in her chair. She seemed preoccupied with something. Kylee just hoped it wasn't her. The last thing she wanted was to cause a problem for her friend.

Kylee covered a half an English muffin with jam and took a cup of coffee and sipped. Then she crunched into her jelly-laden muffin, looking out over the lake. A medley of sweet and tart burst in her mouth.

"O.M.G. This is so good. What is this jelly?"

Lila smiled and seemed to pull herself back from wherever she'd been. "Saskatoon berries, or service berries as some people call them. They grow wild all over this area. They sort of look like blueberries except the bushes are bigger and the berries are a lot dryer than a blueberry. The Indians used to pick them, mash them, and then dry them into bricks. During the winter they'd just cut off pieces to use in stews and such. We make jelly out of the berries, but apparently the Indians used other parts of the plant for medicine, too. If you want to know more, ask Chloe. She's the queen of esoteric information, though most of it involves stones and crystals."

"Lila, are you sure you don't mind if I stay with you awhile? I know I'm not good for much right now, but I promise I'll get better."

"Stop it right there." Lila caught Kylee's wrist as it brought a muffin to her mouth. "You have to stop talking like that because you're smarter than that. Smart enough to know that this was the place you needed to be right now and to come here. So let it be, try it out and let's see what happens, all right?"

Kylee hesitated, not quite able to believe, but she nodded at her friend. She was so lucky to have Lila. She set her muffin down and gave Lila a quick hug. "Thank you. I'm going to quit being so manic and give myself the chance to figure things out, but on one condition. You have to be willing to tell me to get out when I've worn out my welcome, and you have to put me to work so that I'm not just freeloading. Oh, and you have to stop me if I want to run off and fall in love again."

"Technically, that's three conditions," Lila said with a grin. "But I'll give you that."

"Deal." Kylee stuck out her hand and they shook, so the problem had blown over with the breeze.

"Then as soon as we get this lovely breakfast finished I'm going to put you to work. You are going to help me unload and unpack all the stuff from my car."

Kylee made her eyes round with mock horror. "I've made a deal with the devil."

Lila gave a nefarious laugh and wiggle of her brows as she spread jam across an English muffin.

The front door opened again just as she bit in and Reggie stepped out. She said nothing, but nodded at Lila and all the color seemed to leave Lila's face.

"Oh my God. Moira," she said and turned to Kylee, her coffee and English muffin apparently forgotten. "One of my friends is dead."

CHAPTER 6

Kylee stood in the open kitchen doorway, the breeze at her back as Chloe and Lila shifted around the room like dancers in a well-rehearsed routine. It was mid morning, and Lila's yellow and white kitchen had been transformed into something more like Scheherazade's closet. That or maybe a dragon's treasury. Lila and Chloe organized Lila's finds into small piles of what they could clean and sell as is, what needed new stones, what might sell if it was redesigned or incorporated into something else, and what Lila had perhaps been mistaken in purchasing. The first and last piles were extremely small.

Bits of silver and occasionally gold spread across the black cloth laid over the counter and caught the sunlight through the broad kitchen windows. Gleaming copper pots and the old clock sat on the kitchen table. Chloe, once more dressed in a flowing Indian cotton tunic—this time a deep indigo—was bent over examining the stones of an ornate necklace of heavy silver. A medley of silver necklaces gleamed around her neck along with one of turquoise and coral. She had a concentration like an ancient crone—almost as if she could feel the vibrations which she said came off each stone. Lila, on the other hand, looked lost in thought—probably of her lost friend. Though she still moved like a business Goddess, efficiently taking inventory of everything on a list in her precise handwriting, it was clear the woman's death still bothered her. She'd already spent a few minutes sharing her regret that she hadn't been on time and how that might have impacted the woman who had waited until Lila arrived before closing down the estate sale.

Kylee went to Lila as she ran an elegant French manicured finger down one of her lists. "You okay?"

Lila glanced up at her and from somewhere found a smile. "Okay. Just sad is all. She was a good woman." She sighed and scanned the room. So far they'd finished three boxes. One more box waited on the kitchen floor.

"Kylee, would give us a hand? Could you help with that box? Maybe set it on the table and start taking things out. Call them out to me so I can inventory them and tell you what pile to put them in. Sound good?"

Up until now Kylee had basically provided an extra set of hands and a strong back. She'd followed Lila around some, watching what she was doing, but realized that she was just underfoot. These two women could almost finish each other's sentences. Lila would hold up a turquoise pendant with a question in her eyes. She'd open her mouth to say something and Chloe would look up. In unison they'd say Reggie and that would be that. The pendant would go on the pile for Reggie to examine and potentially transform.

Thankful to finally have a task of her own, Kylee hauled the box to the table. It wasn't that heavy, but there was definitely weight to the contents. She slit the packing tape, opened it and stopped.

"Holy cow."

That brought Chloe's head up and Lila to her side.

The box was full to the brim with jewelry. There were old lady broaches and long thick gold chains and strings of pearls and even a tiara all tangled together as if whoever had packed the box had simply taken the items and heaped them in.

"My God," Chloe said. "Where'd this lot come from? If those stones are real, there's got to be a fortune here."

Lila was shaking her head and—was that a tear in her eye? "This doesn't make sense." She ran her hands through her hair. "This was the box that I got from Moira. She already had it all packed and ready to go. She charged me two thousand and said she'd made it worth my while to take it sight unseen. She said she had orders from the family to just get rid of everything by the end of the day."

Frowning, she picked up a long string of pale pink pearls and laid them across her long palm. "Two thousand dollars would barely touch this alone if they're cultured pearls." The pearls clacked together softly as she ran them across her teeth. "Definitely real."

"Okay, here's what we're going to do. You pick up an item, you call it out. If it has stones in it, it goes to Chloe for sorting. If no stones, I'll tell you where it goes."

They set to work.

It was like a dream, really. A box of other people's dreams. Dreams that she could never have. Burrowing her fingers in the antique gold and silver, she held up a gold chain in the finest weave she'd ever seen. It was long—almost twenty-four inches.

"Gold chain. By the color I'd say fourteen carat or more. It's sure not the pale gold of most chains you see these days. The clasp is broken."

Lila arched a brow at her. "Very good. Put it in the pile over there for needs mending."

A broach of pale purple stones made up to look like a spray of flowers. She handed it to Chloe. "Broach. Amethyst, maybe?"

Chloe nodded and took it from her.

And so it went. Half way down the box, Reggie returned from her meeting with the man and a woman visiting from Vancouver. Her face was flushed and lovely compared to the severity of her hair and for a moment Kylee winced, she reminded her so much of Claudia, and Kevin's departure.

"So?" Lila said. "What gives?"

Reggie's full mouth curved in a too-brilliant smile which made Kylee feel insipid and bleached out.

"I just can't believe it. The woman is a Vancouver designer, but what they didn't tell me is that the guy is a buyer for Valentino. *The* Valentino. And they want my designs. Not just for Vancouver, but they're talking shows in Milan and Paris. Regulus jewelry might actually be shown on European runways!" She slumped down on the nook bench by the table, her faint smoke and roses scent filling the space around her. "I just can't believe it. I mean New York a few years ago was a lucky fluke, right, and with a nobody designer. But this is Europe. This is one of the grand old houses." She looked up at each of them, her expression one of wonder like a little girl. Not like Claudia, and Kylee softened a little.

"Regulus?" Kylee asked, thinking of the earrings she'd admired in the shop. "*You're* Regulus? You make that beautiful jewelry out front?"

Reggie gave a bashful grin. "Of course. Who else? Reggie Lewis—Regulus."

Kylee felt a little dazzled. Then she grinned. "First time I ever knew someone who might be famous. Besides Lila, of course. Congratulations!"

Lila checked her watch. The wall clock said it was almost eleven. "Listen, we're going to have to open the shop in a few minutes, but first I think we have time for a little celebratory refresher of orange juice and champagne."

Leaving her inventory list, she found space on the counter to set out four fluted glasses and pull out a bottle of what must be champagne from the fridge. Reggie was busy telling Chloe all the gory details of the meeting leaving Kylee to turn back to the box of jewelry. She started picking out pieces with stones and putting them in a little pile to hand to Chloe, but the slim silver bracelet she'd bought in Morocco caught on something in the box and wouldn't pull loose. With her free hand she started digging around her hand. Whatever had snagged her bracelet was hidden under a mass of also-snagged silver and gold chains that had, in turn, snagged on more broaches and earrings.

She tugged the whole mass out onto her lap and began to gently untangle each piece, setting them aside into a Chloe pile or an inventory pile as she went. She accepted the champagne goblet and drank the toast, but kept on working. She had to do something to give back to her host.

Finally she spotted what looked like a little key and a bit of chain that had tangled around her slim bangle. "Well, there you are, you little dickens."

She looked up and realized the kitchen was empty.

Where had everyone gone? But the sound of movement from the front of the house and a flicker of movement from the back yard gave her the answer.

Gently she unhooked the culprit from her silver bangle.

The key was silver, about one inch long, ornate with a head of carved scrollwork and a simple bar shank with small, perfectly made teeth. It was attached by two fine silver chains to a series of small, inch-and-a-half high doors that were the most ornate, perfectly formed miniatures she had ever seen. Each door was different, and yet all were intricately made. One looked like the iron-clad doors she had seen in North Africa and Zanzibar. Another looked like a farmer's door with separate upper and lower panels like you might see in Holland or France and still another looked like it was made of wood with a curved top and tiny Fatima's hand knocker like she'd seen in Morocco. There were others, but the last of the six doors was made of tiny silver slats made up to look like wood. It had what looked like a leaf-shaped knocker and door handle, and tiny silver grapes around the edges as if surrounded by an arbor. Next to it, connected by two slim silver chains was a filigreed keyhole that she just bet that the little key fit through.

It was without a doubt the most beautiful and charming bracelet she'd ever seen. Amazing because this wasn't something just made out of pressed metal in molds. No, someone had taken the time to make each door individually and lovingly—from the back it looked almost as good as the front.

She lay the bracelet across her wrist.

Put it on. It was as if someone whispered just behind her. She jerked around, a cold chill up her back, but of course there was no one there. She draped the bracelet over her arm. The silver looked wonderful against her golden tan. Perfect, almost. Like it belonged there. On a whim she fumbled the key through the lock so it formed a perfect circle around her wrist and shook her arm so that the bracelet could just settle into place. A shiver ran through her, almost of excitement.

It was surprisingly light and the small series of doors fit like a loose cuff down over her wrist bones, but almost seemed to meld to her arm as if it was made for her. Someone was sure to love this bracelet, because she did. If she had the money she'd buy it right now. Maybe she could make some sort of arrangement with Lila. If she did, she'd never take it off.

And there she went again, falling in love. She sighed.

Who was she kidding? She already owed Lila money just for the kindness she was showing her.

"Kylee? Could you come give us a hand out here?" As if her thoughts had materialized, Lila pushed her head into the kitchen.

Caught red handed, Kylee stood mortified. She was tempted to hide her wrist behind her back, but that was a coward's way out. "Uh... Just give me a minute. I tried this bracelet on and I can't get it off." She couldn't either. The darn miniature key she'd threaded through the lock just didn't seem to want to unlock.

Lila stepped into the room for a closer look and caught Kylee's fluttering hand to study the bracelet. "That has got to be the most amazing piece of jewelry I've seen in a while. It looks great against your skin."

"Lila!" came Chloe's voice from the front of the house. It sounded a little panicked.

Lila dropped her hand. "Listen. Just leave it on and come on out front. Seems there's a tour group in town and they've all come in to the shop at once. We could use a hand."

"But I don't know anything about anything out front and I'm still windblown from my walk." Kylee shook her head, suddenly taken with stage fright.

Lila grinned. "You look great and you'll know plenty about the store by the time the next hour is over. Just enjoy the bracelet and brace yourself for a bumpy ride."

Feeling immensely windblown and foolish and with not just a few trepidations, Kylee followed Lila down the wood-floored hall with its gallery of photos of friends and family, to *This & That*. Madhouse came to mind. There were actually people pushing and shoving to get a look at the jewelry cases and the displays on the walls. Lila immediately stepped into the crowd, graciously apologizing for being unprepared for so many customers at once. Kylee hesitated, then, what the heck. She wanted to help where she could. Taking a deep breath, she stepped up to a couple dressed in expensive-looking resort wear who were considering the Regulus jewelry display. Here goes.

"May I help you?"

The woman had artfully applied makeup and carefully coiffed blonde hair in a pouf that might be just a little too young a style for the years she wore around her eyes. She pointed a perfectly pink lacquered nail at the same pair of earrings Kylee had admired.

"I'm quite taken by those."

"Aah, yes. Lovely aren't they. Kylee slid the, thankfully, unlocked display cabinet open and gently eased the earrings out. "This display is all made by the designer, Regulus. The jeweler's designs have been seen on the runways of New York and I understand may be coming to Paris and Milan in the near future. Would you like to try them on?"

The woman's eyes had flashed when Kylee had mentioned New York and Europe. A couple of other women had crowded around to see the jewelry and were now oohing and aahing over a slim bracelet of interlocking silver leaves, and a necklace that looked like it was made of fish scales and pale translucent stones.

The blond woman removed her diamond studs and tried on the earrings. They hung perfectly as if made to show off a woman's fine neck.

"They look good. If you wear your hair up, those will be perfect," Kylee said.

The woman preened a little in the hand mirror Kylee held up for her and turned to her companion. "What do you think, Harry?"

Brown-haired Harry dutifully nodded.

The woman turned back to the case and pointed. "That necklace goes with them, doesn't it?"

"Yes, it does." Or it sure looked like it did.

"Excuse me, may I see that bracelet. I'd like to try it on," the dark-haired woman who had been admiring the bracelet interrupted. She wore a sleek, sleeveless body suit with a cape-like vest with wide pockets over top.

Kylee nodded and pulled out both the necklace and the bracelet. The blond woman held the necklace up and Kylee came around the counter to do it up for her. When she turned around the dark woman was headed for the door—and the bracelet was gone.

As the blond woman checked herself in the mirror, Kylee checked the floor. Not there and not in the cabinet. That left either the blond and her companion or the dark woman. She was betting on the dark woman.

"Excuse me for a moment, would you?" She asked the blond and her husband/lover/companion. Who knew these days?

She eased through the crowd milling around the scarf display and earring cabinets on the wall, and had almost caught up with the dark woman when Lila blocked the woman's passage at the door.

Kylee caught up to them and glanced at Lila. By the expression on her face, she knew that something was happening. Kylee looked back at the woman and made eye contact.

"Madam," Kylee said. "I'm sorry to stop you, but I think you accidently must have knocked the bracelet of silver interlocking leaves into one of your pockets. Your lovely cape probably caught it by accident. When you turned to leave."

There. She'd given the woman a graceful way out of this, because by the straight set line of Lila's lips, the woman wasn't getting out the door without pulling out her pockets. She must have seen the look, too. She swallowed.

"Of course." Her hand dove into one pocket and came up empty. In the other, though, she stopped and her face took on a shocked expression. "Oh my goodness! I am so sorry. She relinquished the bracelet and quickly left the store, Lila looking after her.

Kylee hurried back to the Regulus case and thankfully the woman and man were still there with the necklace. The woman still preened before the mirror and the man just looked bored.

"I love your bracelet," the woman said. "Do you have anything else like it in the store?"

Kylee's hand went to her wrist feeling momentarily protective and knowing that she really should tell the woman it was for sale, too. "It is lovely, isn't it? But no. It was found in an estate sale."

The woman nodded and checked herself out again. "I quite like this set, but the price is a little steep. Is there any chance of a discount if I purchase them together?"

Oh my goodness. A sudden sense of déjà vu came over Kylee from all the markets from Marrakesh to Zanzibar. Haggling. Haggling she knew and frankly she's been pretty good at it. The problem was, she had no idea what Lila's stance on it was. She glanced in Lila's direction, but she had left the doorway and was now deeply involved with another customer. Chloe was busy, too. That left her to make the decision.

She shook her head. "I'm sorry. They are meant to be a set and are priced to be sold as such." State your opening gambit and see what your opponent does.

The woman pouted her disappointment. "So I suppose if I took the bracelet of the set, too, that wouldn't help either?"

"I'm sorry. No. The price is set. But I'll tell you what." Kylee leaned in close. "If you take all three, I just might be able to arrange for you to meet Regulus herself. She happens to be here."

"Really?" The blonde's eyes grew round and even her companion looked a little impressed.

"Stay here a moment." Kylee caught Lila's eye and then headed for the back of the house and out to Reggie's workshop. She knocked on the door and heard stirring from inside.

Reggie came to the door, releasing a puff of heated air when she opened it. She had returned to her black singlet and cargo pants and had a heavy leather apron over everything. Her black hair had been tied back in a pony tail and she wore goggles on her sweat-beaded forehead and heavy gloves.

"Yes?" She looked distracted and like she really wasn't happy about being interrupted. "I'm just in the middle of messing with some designs for Milan."

Exactly what the woman would eat right up. "Hold that thought! I've got a customer who wants to meet you."

Kylee dashed back into the house and through to the shop. She took the bracelet from the cabinet, locked it, and with the blond still wearing the necklace and earrings and her "husband" in tow, led them down the hall, through the kitchen that still looked like an explosion of jewelry, and into the backyard.

"You'll have to excuse the mess. We've just received a new shipment." She stopped in front of Reggie. "I'd like you to meet the designer of those lovely pieces you are wearing. This is Regulus. We can't keep her long, because she'd just working on the designs for Milan show."

She caught Reggie's sharp glance, but then she was all graciousness. Reggie approved the look of the earrings and necklace on the woman and agreed that the bracelet would be a nice addition.

"Just a moment," Reggie said and disappeared back into her workshop. She returned with another set of earrings, these ones made of what looked like woven silver strands with small rose-colored crystal stones set in each gap of the weave. "These would look lovely with your coloring. I plan to make the necklace to match, but right now other commitments have gotten in the way. You understand."

The woman tried on the new earrings and Reggie was right. They sparkled and somehow the pink seemed to light up the woman's face.

"I have to have these. And can you complete the necklace for me as well?" the woman said with only the briefest glance at the long suffering Harry.

"But you don't even know the price. I don't even know the price yet," Reggie protested.

The blond woman caught Reggie's hand. "You figure it out and let this one know." She nodded at Kylee. "Harry and I will be out front paying for everything."

She took off the necklace and earrings and replaced her diamond studs, then caught Harry's arm and started for the house.

"What the hell's going on?" Reggie whispered.

"How the heck do I know? Just give me a price." Kylee whispered back and started after the couple.

Reggie caught up to her with a small slip of paper while she was in the hall.

By the time the surge of customers had left the shop Kylee was exhausted. It seemed the crowd from the tour had drawn others in as well, and it was two o'clock before the customers began to thin out. The early afternoon sunlight placed a glare on the lake that was softened by water evaporation, but it was still bright and hot in the shop, except for the fans Lila had blowing at every open window. In the breeze the scarves fluttered prettily, but it tended to make the display a mess. She busied herself fixing the display and creating a simple braid effect by linking the scarves through each other. When she was done it was like a rainbow of scarves were plaited across that wall. When she stepped back, she found Lila beside her.

"That is masterful. It makes the scarves more secure, but the effect is truly lovely."

"Uh, thanks. I guess. Sorry about the bracelet thing today. I just didn't expect it to happen. All those people looked pretty well dressed."

"The shoplifter, yes. They come in all shapes and sizes and with all levels of social advantage. What that woman did to you is a ploy as old as the hills. Find a busy, less experienced clerk and take advantage. I saw it, but you caught it so fast I didn't have to do anything. You handled her just right, given the situation. If there'd been a scene it would have scared away all the rest of the customers."

"Well. I'm still sorry it happened. It won't happen again."

Lila looked at her strangely. "I don't suppose it will. Did you know, you outsold both Chloe and I today, at least in value of goods sold? You have a real way about you with the customers. You're open and you tell them what works and what doesn't. That brainwave of taking that woman back to meet Reggie—that was inspired!"

"It was?" In all her years of work as a junior marketer in the corporate sector she'd never received compliments like this. She felt a little uncomfortable. "I just wanted her to pay full price for the necklace and earrings and bracelet set. I had no idea that she'd find another set, too." She grinned up at Lila. "Beginner's luck, I guess."

Lila put her hands on her hips. "Kylee, I'm trying to give you a compliment. Learn how to take it, okay? And while we're on the topic of how well you did in the store, Chloe and I have been talking and we've agreed that if you're interested we'd like to offer you a job here. Chloe needs time for the stonework, she's trying to establish a healing center, and I've got a list of estate sales to get to. That means we need someone to take care of the *This & That*. Would you be interested?"

"Interested...?" She'd be over the moon, but there went her heart again.... Still, she'd discovered she really liked working amongst all these beautiful things. It felt more like playing—like when she was a little girl playing dress-up with her mother's things. She scanned the room. "Of course I'd be interested," she said, trying to quell the desire to dance. "But as long as I'm staying with you, I'll just do it to pay for my keep. When I find a place to stay, then we can discuss being an official employee. Okay?" It was only right, given Lila was giving her free room and board. She had to earn her keep somehow.

Lila's eyes narrowed as if she was going to argue, but she finally nodded. "Good enough for now."

That settled, Lila went back to Chloe at the counter, and Kylee grabbed a broom and set about sweeping the store's rich honey-oak flooring. If she did it with a little more flourish and twirling than was needed, well no one needed to know it except her. She was in the far corner where it seemed as if someone had cleaned all the lint out of their pockets, when the front door tinkled open and heavy footfall announced a man had entered. She glanced up and paused in her little broom-dance.

Definitely male. Tall, but then most everyone seemed tall compared to her five-foot two height. He wore a well-made dark gray suit that somehow didn't seem to fit him exactly right—as if it was too restraining for his broad shoulders or was something he usually only wore for funerals. He had russet colored hair like a fox and blue-gray eyes that seemed to take everything in and never let it go. His hair was cut short over his ears and he moved with such physical strength that she wanted to take a step back.

His gaze seemed to settle on Chloe, so Kylee eased back, suddenly not wanting this man's attention. Definitely not.

"Can I help you," Lila asked, drawing his attention before his gaze found Kylee.

"I'm looking for Lila Weber," he said in a deep rumble that spoke of power.

Lila visibly straightened and the corners of her lips drew down in apparent concern. "I'm Lila Weber."

The man nodded. "I'm Corporal Danny Forester with the Kelowna RCMP. I'd like to talk to you about Moira Burns."

§

To Lila, the comforting space that was *This & That* seemed to suddenly be too small and vulnerable. All its too-easily shattered glass cases, easily accessed open windows, and breezes fluttering the dust Kylee had raised across the floor could be destroyed in a moment of destruction. For a moment everything she'd worked so hard to build with her friends felt frivolous and lacking compared to what this man must deal with every day.

It was so jarring to have this man—this *police* man in front of her—that she had to stop herself from grabbing the glass cabinet next to her. Instead she nodded and straightened. "So it's true, what I heard on the news."

He nodded and glanced at Chloe who had stopped what she was doing at the counter. One of her hands white-knuckled the mess of chains she wore. Kylee had seemed to shrink back against the wall, the broom in front of her as if she were trying to hide behind it.

"Perhaps we should find some place more private?" the corporal asked.

Lila shook her head, although she really didn't understand why she didn't want to be alone with this man. Maybe it was just that she didn't want to hear about Moira's death or maybe it was that there was something about him. She couldn't put her finger on it, but something seemed off. Maybe it was the way he didn't seem to blink that often. Or the slight smell of iron and something burning as if he had a furnace within. "Here is fine. I have no secrets from my friends." And they'd be witnesses and *what a strange thought...*

Corporal Forester's expression seemed to twist and flow as if he had some inner struggle, but then he shrugged.

"Have it your way." He pulled a notebook out of his jacket. "What can you tell me about Moira Burns?"

Lila met his gaze and almost wished she hadn't. It was like looking deep into a cave and seeing a creeping, crawling, dark creature gazing back. She swallowed and looked down at her hands.

"That I heard on the news that she'd been killed. That I can barely believe it. I saw her just two days ago. Moira was an estate lawyer I'd dealt with many times. She'd built her business reputation on doing an excellent job of arranging and managing estate sales. That's where I met her because I go to estate sales to purchase heirloom jewelry that we can either clean up and sell directly, or repurpose into more modern pieces. She had a sale two days ago in Kelowna that I was supposed to attend, but my darn car broke down coming back from Vernon, so I only got there after everything was pretty well gone. She had a box of odds and sods that I purchased. Then I left to head back to Vernon and Kamloops for some sales planned for the next day." She shrugged. "That's about it. I didn't know Moira well, though we'd done business together many times and had had drinks a few times over the years. She'd even come to a party here at one time. I believe she was divorced, but amicably. There might have been someone new in the picture, but I really don't know."

The corporal was taking notes and when he'd finished, he looked up at her again with those creepy eyes. They had gone gray like tarnished silver, and a little yellow at the edges. It felt like he could read right down to her soul as if she had something to hide, and that was a truly unsettling thought given she didn't really think about souls a lot. That was Chloe's department.

"So tell me about the last time you saw her?"

Her knees suddenly weak with guilt, Lila leaned back against a display case and wished she had taken him some place she could sit down. Even the kitchen would be better. But the kitchen was still a disaster from the unsorted jewelry, so she might as well talk here.

"Well… my Explorer started giving out on me on that stretch of new highway over the lakes. I ended up pulling over to the side of the road and calling Triple A and then waiting three hours for someone to arrive. It was dark by the time they arrived and told me they thought I had a blocked fuel line, and blew it out." She remembered the dark—no street lights for miles and the yip of coyotes over the hills when they weren't drowned out by the rumble of highway traffic. "So I made it to the estate sale address. I was only there maybe thirty minutes. I'd phoned earlier to let Moira know I was still coming. When I got there Moira had pretty much cleaned up after the sale. There were a few larger pieces awaiting pick up and a few for Goodwill and she had a box pulled together for me—leftovers mostly, she said. Stuff that she sold to me for couple of thousand dollars. Over the years Moira had come to know what I looked for. Anyway, I pulled in feeling like I'd been run over by a truck, took the box sight unseen and headed out. Moira was just going to lock up and be gone herself—at least that was what she said. At the time she looked tired, but she said the sale had been a success."

She shrugged and shook her head. "I'm sorry. That's all I can tell you."

Corporal Unfriendly's strange reflectionless eyes met hers and this time she didn't—couldn't—look away. It was—like something was sniffing its way through her brain, even though his face was neutral, noncommittal. "So where did you go when you left?"

She inhaled and the fatigue of that night seemed to settle on her. "Oh my goodness, where did I go? Frankly, I was so beat, that I really wanted to just come home or curl up in the back seat of my car, but I headed right back to Vernon and got a room at the Vernon Overlook Inn." She frowned. "Am I a suspect or something?"

He eyed her again and his glance chilled her skin. She wished she had a sweater on instead of this thin summer tunic that left her arms bare.

"Not a suspect, no. But you are quite likely the last person to see Ms. Burns alive. Tell me, may I see this box that you bought?"

The box? "I thought she was killed in a hit and run."

It seemed strange that he wanted to see a box of jewelry, but then maybe he just wanted to confirm that she really had picked up a box from Moira.

"I will want to see your vehicle as well," he said, gaze never leaving her.

She nodded, and was aware that Chloe and Kylee were watching. She led him back to the kitchen and the mess of jewelry therein. He stopped at the entrance.

"You got all this from Moira Burns?" he asked, his gaze roaming over the counter in a way that made her uncomfortable. Almost as if he was hungry.

"N—no." What the heck was the matter with her? Sure, there was something off-putting about him. That could be just the fact he was a cop in the middle of an investigation. But that didn't explain the way she just felt unclean. "As I said, I went to another two estate sales in Vernon and one in Kamloops. This is everything I purchased. You caught us in the middle of going through it." She went to the table and motioned to the half-empty box." This is what was obtained from the Bristol estate. We hadn't quite finished with it. The jewelry with stones is right there. "She motioned to Chloe's pile. "The rest is mixed together with everything else." She motioned around the room.

Corporal Forester shifted to the table, looked at the label on the side of the box and pawed through the remaining jingling contents. Then he moved to the counter and studied Chloe's pile and the other small clusters of sorted jewelry. "Anything of particular value or uniqueness that you've found?"

"No? At least nothing that I can think of. Not that I've examined everything yet. It's just old jewelry—material we use in making original new pieces. We have a designer on site."

He turned back to her expectantly.

"My vehicle's out here." She led him out through the yard, the heat of the sun strangely ineffective in warming her. She ushered him into the carport and rubbed her arms trying to get rid of her gooseflesh while he inspected the front grill. Finally he stood up and faced her.

"Was there anything different the night you met with Ms. Burns. Anything at all you can think of?" he asked, studying her with those pale eyes.

"I'm sorry, no. Moira was a little harried trying to get everything labeled and ready to move out the next day. We spoke only briefly and then I gave her a check and took the box and left. She waved me goodbye and that was it. I left and headed for Vernon."

For a moment he looked as if he could snarl, but then he nodded. "Then I'll thank you for your time and be on my way."

He led her back to the house and down the hallway to the *This & That*, where Chloe and Kylee both looked like they'd barely moved. Corporal Forester stopped at the door and turned back to her, for a moment looking like he was actually sniffing. Then he stuck out his hand. "I thank you for your time."

Lila simply inclined her head, not wanting to touch that outstretched palm. "Thank you for coming."

She held the front door open and he stepped outside and clumped down the stairs without looking back. When he reached the sidewalk it was like she could suddenly breathe again. She inhaled deeply of the lake-scented breeze and wished for the sun on her face.

A hand on her shoulder made her jump. "What a weird guy. What was that all about?" Chloe came up beside her and placed a warm, reviving arm across Lila's back. Kylee stood right behind her, her blue eyes wide and concerned.

"I—I don't know. You heard him asking. I showed him the box. The weird thing was, it was almost as if he were looking for something. He looked over all the jewelry." She shook her head. "Odd. They usually leave a card and ask you to call if you think of anything else. At least they do on TV"

"I wonder if it was this he was looking for?" Kylee said. She held up her wrist, the bracelet she had found flashing in the sunlight through the window. It really was a lovely thing with its intricate silverwork.

"Maybe... I doubt it. I totally forgot about it with everything that was going on. It's just a bracelet, and it was a car that killed Moira." Lila patted Kylee's shoulder. "But let's get that bracelet off and see what you've found, shall we? Chloe, we'll make lunch if you'll hold the fort up front here."

§

Kylee glanced back out the window at the police officer. He sauntered down the street, but Chloe was right. There *was* something about him. For a moment, when he'd walked into the store she'd felt like a cornered mouse, but then the guy had focused in on Lila. Now she seemed to be throwing off whatever had her rattled. Her own reaction had to just be her reaction to any man these days. The guy was just a cop—tall and athletic and to be avoided.

Chloe tipped her head at Lila's suggestion and went back to straightening the displays after the mass exodus of the tour. Kylee followed Lila back to the kitchen where, in the pooling sunshine, Lila tried to figure out the bracelet's unique clasp. It wouldn't open. Reggie came in wearing her workshop attire when they were on the third frustrating try at fitting the tiny key through the bracelet's lock.

"Good," Lila said throwing up her hands. "The expert is here."

Reggie's dark brows arched in question.

"Kylee found a bracelet in the box of stuff from Moira. She tried it on, but if you think I can get the darn thing unclasped you've got another think coming." She motioned Reggie closer. "See what you can do, would you?"

Reggie caught Kylee's wrist and Kylee was surprised at her strength. It wasn't that Reggie was a big woman. In fact she was actually slight and looked slimmer in her baggy trousers, even if her shoulders and arms were well muscled. With the sheen of sweat on her forehead and her dark hair she looked like some exotic warrior woman. Her hands were even callused.

She hauled Kylee next to the brushed-steel sink where the light was even better. Then she whistled softly. "This is really beautiful work. I love the design. This was in Moira's box?"

Kylee nodded. "My bangle snagged it somehow and it was a beast to untangle it from all the chains, but when I saw it I just had to try it on." She sighed, "Now I can't seem to get the darn thing off. Sorry." She glanced an apology at Lila.

Reggie flipped her arm over to expose the bracelet's closure and smiled with delight. "This wasn't just made by anyone. This guy was an artist. A lock and key to hold a door bracelet closed." She glanced up at them. "The key just slips through the hole of the lock. Simple."

Lila had leaned back against the counter, her arms crossed. "That's what I thought."

"Well you just go like this." Reggie pulled the little chains holding the key further through the lock hole and then tilted the key down so the blade could go athrough. "Easy-peasy," she said.

Then the lovely ornate head of the key snagged on the metal lock and was too big for the keyhole. She jiggled the key. Frowned.

"That's what happened when Lila and I tried."

Reggie's delight faded as she tried again. "It's almost like it's a trick. An optical illusion that the key fits the lock. Actually the key looks way small for the lock." She tried it three more times, each time ending with the same frustrating conclusion, until she finally turned the bracelet over and patted Kylee's hand. "It looks great on you, if it's any consolation."

Kylee rolled her eyes. "Gee thanks. I guess I'll just amputate my hand so Lila can have her bracelet back."

"Now don't be hasty. Maybe you and Lila can work something out in kind. I can see it now: indentured servitude," Reggie said straight-faced. Then she grinned again and when she smiled she really didn't look anything like Claudia at all. "It really is a beautiful piece. And so intricate. I wish I'd thought of it."

She leaned in to study the workmanship. "You don't see work like this much today. Today it's all about molds and pouring instead of the craftsmanship of this work. If someone tries to do something like this it usually comes out looking a lot rougher. The silver has a certain patina, too, as if it's purer than most jewelers work with."

Reggie shook her head and gave an evil grin with too much teeth. "I guess you're just going to have to sell it to her, Lila. You know the rules. Someone starts wearing jewelry from the shop and they have to buy it. No loansies."

Kylee groaned. She'd just been offered the job. She couldn't pay for an expensive piece of jewelry even if it felt like it was made for her, all warm and fitted to her arm. In fact, it was the bangle that felt out of place, even though she'd worn it constantly it for almost a year since buying it in a Moroccan market.

"There has got to be a way to get this thing off." She flipped her wrist over and tried the lock and key once more—in vain. She tried to narrow her hand and pull the darn cuff over it, but all she succeeded in doing was scraping her skin on the small locks and grape leaves around the door she's been admiring. The darned bracelet apparently wasn't going anywhere.

She sagged against the counter and looked ruefully at Lila. "I am sooo sorry. I won't try on anything else ever again. But I will get this off and back to you. I will."

Lila threw a long tawny arm over her shoulder and pulled her in close. "She's pulling your leg, Kylee. That's Reggie."

The black haired woman was busy pulling some cold cuts, bread, and a bottle of beer out of the fridge. "Heavy in the middle of design and mockup. Need food." She glanced at Kylee like some kind of cavewoman as she slapped layers of meat onto bread she'd slathered with Dijon mustard, then slapping the bread together. No butter, no mayo, no plate, she took a big bite and turned for the door. "I'll want to look that bracelet over more thoroughly when I'm finished."

As if the fact the bracelet still sat on Kylee's arm had nothing to do with it.

And then she was gone, back to her cave workshop.

"Is she always like that?" Kylee asked.

"When she's in the middle of something, yes. But she's harmless. And good at what she does. She'll get the bracelet off for you."

Kylee wasn't sure she wanted Reggie touching it again. Or anyone for that matter. It really did feel like the darn thing belonged where it was.

Together she and Lila sliced fresh tomatoes and cucumber and sautéed fresh asparagus from the garden—anything grew in the Okanagan soil. They sliced yellow cheddar and fresh crusty bread from the bakery and set out a bowl of garlic-stuffed olives. Lila made tea and then they carried two trays with their bounty out to the front. *This & That* was empty, so they took the trays and out to the front verandah and settled themselves on the wicker couch and chairs where they could enjoy the view and still be available to help any customers.

With a cup of tea in her hands and a piece of bread and cheese topped with sweet fresh tomato on a plate beside her, Kylee toed off her shoes and curled her feet under her. "Do you do this often?"

"Whenever we can," Chloe nodded, her dark braid draped over her shoulder as she watched the passing joggers, and the boats on the water.

It was just so darned idyllic. "No one should be so lucky."

"Why?" Lila asked as she thoughtfully chewed on the end of an olive. "My grandparents worked hard for this place. To hold onto it, I have to work hard to make the place earn its keep and support me, and my partners. It seems only fitting that I take time to appreciate what I'm working for. Otherwise why do it?" She reached over to pat Kylee's hand. "Relax. You deserve it, too. To be happy. To have a life. A love. A home. It'll happen."

Kylee frowned. It was a different way of looking at things than her corporate employers had had. They never cared about quality of life, just about getting the job done as well and as quickly as possible. Stopping to smell the roses never entered into it. And as for love, after all her years of searching and following after the men she'd thought were Mr. Right, well she'd pretty much given up on that. It apparently wasn't in her makeup to be successful in love. She was flawed—too needy—because she apparently had a heart that couldn't be trusted. She'd fall in love with a man who didn't end up loving her and to keep him she'd give up everything good about herself. But Lila had somehow found more balance in her life. She was offering to bring Kylee into that comfortable place.

Her heart did a little ba-bump in her chest. She wanted what Lila had so badly, but that was the trouble, wasn't it. She threw herself into things she thought she wanted and it never worked out. Maybe she just didn't deserve it or maybe she just wasn't cut out for this kind of bliss. Because it was blissful sitting here just immersing herself in the sharp tang of the cheddar, the sweet tartness of the tomato and the crunch of the crusty bread. Sipping her rich black tea, she chewed and contemplated the view and the opportunity.

The lake was a rich cobalt blue which carried reflected white clouds woven in by the waves and the wakes of the boats cruising the deep water. The breeze smelled of water, suntan lotion and a hint of cinnamon from the café as well as pale purple heliotrope from the cascading copper pots on the verandah. Cars rumbled past, but slowly enough they didn't disturb the sleepy, summertime feeling of the town. It was like she'd somehow stepped back about fifty years and she could almost imagine the legendary Ogopogo lifting his horse-shaped, sea-serpent head above the lake, his sinewy three humps trailing behind him.

Someone had once told Kylee that the lake was over 760 feet deep and that the water off Peachland was some of the deepest. That was why there'd never been any success in trying to find the creature that the local Aboriginal tribes said lived across the lake near the barren hump of Rattlesnake Island. That island cuddled up to the mountain shoreline. Ogopogo had been sighted on and off over the decades and there'd even been a photo, but just like the Loch Ness monster, nothing had ever been proven for sure.

It was sort of like her love life—there were tales it might exist, but reality said otherwise. Nope. She was better off single and getting her feet under her and this darned bracelet off her arm, before she set off wandering again. Because she would. She always did.

A cyclist in dark green and yellow lycra and racing helmet cruised down the street toward them, thickly muscled thighs pumping, a thatch of brown hair escaping the helmet. The rider's handsome profile made her pause mid-chew. Chloe's brother.

"Aah, nuts," Chloe said, catching a glimpse of him. She half-rose and then sank back into her chair and into herself until she looked small and uncertain. "What am I going to do, Lila? He's pushing me to sign the papers so he can put Mom and Dad's place up for sale and I don't want to do it."

CHAPTER 7

THE FRONT OF *THIS & THAT* LOOKED JUST A TAD daunting with the three of them sitting there on the white house's wide front porch, but he was darn well not leaving without the signed papers. Lila sat like a queen, ever glamorous, even in a simple orange shift that likely would have looked like a sack on anyone else. Chloe, with her perennial braid and square shoulders, looked like she was ready for a fight. And the new girl with her fly-away tumble of white-gold hair looked like a bit of dandelion fluff that had just touched down for a moment before lifting away again—Kylee, that was her name.

Who was he kidding? That sure enough was her name because it had run through his brain all night and he was pretty sure he didn't want her to lift off again. She was dressed in the same floral dress as yesterday, but still looked fresh-faced and pretty with the ends of her blond hair playing in the breeze. Her heart-shaped face showed off her bright blue eyes and delicate mouth and chin. She looked up at him with a long-suffering gaze almost as if she was waiting for the other shoe to drop—or like a puppy waiting to be kicked—which made no sense given he'd never done anything to this woman and never wanted to, either. She was—almost fragile. Like she needed protection.

Yeah, right. With Lila and Chloe by her side, she was part of a triumvirate of valkyries, with Reggie in reserve. Still...

"Hey," he said, leaning his bike against the porch rail. He climbed the stairs with the small backpack that carried what he needed and nodded a smile in Kylee's direction. Her lips curved in response. Nice smile. Real nice. See? He wasn't someone frightening. "I was working from home today and thought I'd swing by with those papers. You got a moment?"

It was going to be pretty obvious if Chloe brushed him off again today, given she'd been sitting with her feet up until he started up the porch stairs. Still, her hands tightened on the arms of her chair and Kylee stirred, shifting her bare legs from where they'd been curled under her on the wicker settee almost as if she was going to rise to Chloe's defense. Or run again.

Chloe shook her head, her infernal multi-strands of necklace shifting together like some flipping shaman's rattle. "We can talk, but I still don't want to sign, Brett. I feel... I'm not going to deal with Mom and Dad's stuff like all those estate sales that Lila goes to. I can't let go yet. They passed too suddenly in that car accident. Their spirits are still around here and we have no right to sell their stuff and their house on the hill out from under them. You know that if you sell it someone is just going to mow it down to build one of those monstrosities springing up everywhere. That or condos." She shook her head. "It would break their hearts and I couldn't do that to them."

A little defeated before he started, he sank down on the edge of the verandah railing, but left the sheaf of papers still in his bag. Hauling them out now was just going to send Chloe further into her woo-woo talk about spirits. Her and her belief in chakras, spirits, healing stones and, hell, astrology and palm reading for all he knew. It certainly wasn't the careful science of wine making.

"Chloe, it's been six months. The security fees, the heat and electricity bills, the gardeners because neither you nor I have the time or interest to keep the place up—it's all eating away at both our savings. We can't keep doing this. You have your apartment along the beach. I've got my place up at the vineyard. We don't need mom and dad's place anymore. We need to let it go—let them go."

But she was shaking her head and darn it, he needed to get her to understand.

"Maybe—maybe the house still being there is holding them back, Chloe. Maybe they need the house to be taken down to set them free."

His sister looked heavenward. To roll her eyes? Maybe, the way she blinked, she was trying to get emotions under control. "Give it a break, Brett." Her voice was husky. "Don't try to use my arguments against me. I don't want to sell and that's it. Period. End of conversation. Not now."

"Well that's a real fine way of negotiating, sis. I thought we were going to be a team to get through this and deal with the estate—but no. You've left all the hard stuff to me and now you're refusing to take my best advice *and* the advice of the lawyer."

"The lawyer didn't know them like we did, Brett. He can't feel them like I do—like you should!"

"Damn it, Chloe, I hurt, too. But we've got to be logical. You don't feel them because they're dead. For once in your life, would you just forget your spirits and think with your head!"

He knew he'd gone too far by the way Chloe winced and when she closed her eyes a gleam of tears squeezed the rim of her lids. His sister might be strong, but she had her vulnerable spots, too. Beside her, Lila had gone still as stone and Kylee looked ready to run just like she'd run out of the store yesterday. Damn.

With a sigh he climbed down off the rail and crouched in front of a sniffling Chloe, hating that he'd done this to her. Chloe always tried to be so strong and together, like a peaceful mother Goddess who floated through life.

He caught her hand. "I'm sorry. I know you miss them terribly. I do too. We didn't even have a chance to say goodbye except at the funeral." Darn it, his voice sounded thick and clotted with emotion, too. He caught her in a hug. "But we need to do something, Chloe. I don't think we can keep going like this, with the house chewing up our savings."

"Perhaps you should think about renting it," Lila said.

He and Chloe pulled apart and looked at her. "What?" Said in unison.

"Maybe, if you want to give yourself some breathing room, you should consider renting it."

Brett glanced at his sister. "There's a bit of a problem with that idea because the house is old. Not too many people are going to want a place with all its quirks. At least not people we'd want to rent it to."

"What about someone like me? I like old and quirky."

Kylee's voice wasn't much more than a tentative whisper and when everyone looked at her a bloom of beautiful pink ran up over her shoulders to her cheeks.

"I-I'm sorry. I didn't mean to be so forward, but I'm sponging off of Lila here, when I really need to get my life in order. I have a job—at least I think so...." She glanced at Lila who nodded. "So I just need a place to live. It would be great for me to be out of Lila's hair and have my own space and if it would help you out...." She shrugged, but her voice had gotten stronger as she spoke, so she wasn't just some timid mouse. Just timid around men? Or just around him?

"That's a really good idea, Brett," Chloe said, brushing tears off her cheeks. "Kylee's good people. Mom and Dad will like her— would have liked her. And the house isn't too big—in fact it's probably best for just one or two people. The more I think about it, the better idea it seems. Brett?"

It wasn't what he'd intended. Hell, it wasn't even close. There had to be something wrong with the idea. It wasn't logical that he'd missed another way out of this mess when it had been staring him right in the face. It would at least be better than pouring money into an empty house. The rental income might even cover the costs. And the taxes. He couldn't forget about the taxes. Or the gardener, for that matter.

"Wellll." It looked like the three women all held their breath. "It could work. If Kylee even likes the place and we can come to a mutually acceptable agreement. Tell you what," he stood up, his knees cracking from couching with his sister for so long. "How about I cycle home and pick up my car. I'll come back, pick up Kylee, and take her up to the house to show her around. It she likes it, then we can discuss the possibility. Otherwise it's silly to get everyone all hopeful about it. That work?"

There were nods all around.

"Good then." He felt mighty out of place and started down the stairs, but Chloe followed him right out to the sidewalk where she stopped him.

She clasped his hands and looked up at him with her deep blue eyes almost purple in the sunlight. "Thank you. Thank you for being willing to consider this option."

He shrugged knowing he was being a coward and really only putting off the inevitable. "It was only logical given you don't want to sell right now. Far better than getting in a big fight, and if it helps out Kylee...."

Chloe's gaze narrowed and she looked at him with the unfortunately astute laser vision she'd had since he was a kid. He'd never been able to pull anything over on her like other brothers had on their older sisters.

"What? What'd I do now?"

She cocked her head and smiled that small secret smile she had. "Oh nothing. I won't get my hopes up until we see what happens with Kylee. About the house." She gave him a quick pat on the arm and then left him and the brilliant sunshine for the shade of the verandah.

The damned women were laughing as he mounted his bike and took off down Beach Avenue. When Chloe laughed like that, it always made him nervous

§

With the sun reflecting off the lake, Chloe's face was in shadow as she returned up the sidewalk to the broad front porch. When she reached the shadow of the stairs, she had a small, self-satisfied grin on her face. She plunked herself back down on her seat, glanced at Lila and then turned to Kylee.

"That, my dear, was very well done. Shut ol' Brett right up you did. I've never seen that man stop worrying a bone so fast in my life. I'll tell you, if you can get him to back off on selling the house, you can probably get him to do just about anything else." She raised her brows slightly as if to suggest that the sky was the limit. She laughed and Lila seemed to catch it from her until the two of them almost cackled like a pair of plotting old crones.

Kylee frowned and rubbed the bracelet. It had seemed warmer a moment ago. "I was just trying to help you two out. Family shouldn't fight like that. People shouldn't make each other cry. It—it hurts to watch it."

"But it hurts worse to live it, doesn't it, Kylee," Lila said softly.

The warm, lake-scented air seemed to catch in Kylee's chest so all she managed was strangled squeak and a quick nod. She looked away. She'd caught the way that Chloe and Lila looked at each other. Lila leaned forward and caught her hand.

"Kylee, honey. You know you can unload on me any time."

Kylee bit her upper lip to hold back the torrent of threatening emotions. It would be so easy to just let it all come spilling out in a horrible tidal wave of pain. Instead she lifted her chin, drew in a deep breath and blew it out again. "I don't have time for that, do I? We've got the shop to run if I'm going to earn my keep and I've got a house to go see." She glanced back at her old friend and her new one and smiled. "Besides, it would so not be pretty. Better to focus on things we need to do right now, like getting this bracelet off my wrist."

She held out her arm and the exquisitely shaped silver doors gleamed in the shadowed sunlight. It looked like it belonged on her wrist, and frankly she really didn't want to ever take it off. If she was honest with herself, all morning, her fingers had kept travelling to it, exploring the finely wrought doors, and always coming to settle on one particular door—the little arched one made to look like wood, with tiny grape clusters around the edges. She ran her hand over the links again, and once more her fingers smoothed that certain door. It was hard even turning over her arm to expose the key and lock for Lila and Chloe's examination.

"So free me, will you? Please?"

A total change of subject and no one even noticed. She could breathe again, too.

Chloe peered at the closure. "That should be easy enough."

Lila said nothing and just watched as this time Chloe tried to get the little key through the lock. "That doesn't make any sense," she said sitting back to just look at the clasp after three unsuccessful tries. "The key is sizes smaller that the keyhole, so why won't it fit through?"

"Maybe it's magic," Lila said with a quick up and down of her brows. "It chooses its owner before someone can choose it," she said with a spooky voice and grinned at Chloe. "Sorry. I just thought I'd say it before you did. I mean it *did* come to us under mysterious circumstances."

Kylee tensed at the cutting words. Kevin had done things like that to make fun of her in front of other people.

But Chloe didn't seem upset. She rolled her eyes again. "Is that nice? The circumstances weren't that mysterious and I would not have come up with a silly story like that. I study the powers of crystals. I don't write fantasy novels. And speaking of fantasies, my big ol' brother is pretty fast on his bike. You've got maybe thirty minutes if he has a shower. You should go get ready, Kylee."

Kylee looked from one woman to the other. They weren't fighting. It was like this was a long-time act they had together and from what she'd seen they got along really well.

She looked down at her little sundress. Sure it was a little worn from travel, but the colors were still bright and fun. "I know I wore it yesterday, but I washed it out last night. I'm only going to look at a house."

"So put on something more casual. Enjoy yourself," Chloe said. She practically pushed Kylee up out of her seat and into the house.

A little confused, Kylee hurried upstairs to her room and checked herself out in the mirror over the lovely old dresser. The age-smoked glass made it hard to see the details of the travel fatigue she knew she wore in her face. Instead, her figure looked misty and distant—like some Greek-era heroine who might have walked the Peloponnesian beaches waiting for her warrior to come home. She could almost imagine the figure of a man trying to reach her. A sense of movement startled her and, she jerked around to check. There was no one there.

Silly imagination.

But Chloe said she should dress down, so she hiked the backpack she'd dragged up from her car this morning up onto the bed and opened it up. Doing so released so many memories, that for a moment she couldn't move. The faint scent of the beer Kevin had spilled on the pack at a small pub in Dublin when they should have been looking for a guesthouse, a lick of salt and sweet Port from a week spent along the Algarve where the Mediterranean melted into the Atlantic, a licorice scent of ouzo from one of their many nights in Athens. Boozy, yes, but Kevin was all about the booze. Almost as if right from the start he'd been drowning his sorrows at being shackled with her.

She closed her eyes against the pang of hurt and yanked clothing out of the bag. Shorts and tees mostly. Two pair of trousers, a few leggings, and a couple of sarongs. Her bikini. Not much of a wardrobe for a woman in her thirties. She had the shoes she had on, a pair of runners and a pair of athletic sandals. Not much to build a life on. Just what had she been thinking when she sold everything and went with Kevin?

There hadn't been a lot to sell even then. Not much of a life I'd been living. And she'd so hoped and prayed that Kevin was the one. When he'd said he wanted to dump everything and go traveling, it had seemed like a match made in heaven. She'd gladly sold her stuff and gone with him in the belief that this time it would work. No, she amended. She'd hoped it would work. She'd blinded herself to who and what he was because of that hope. She scanned the debris of her life spread on the bed.

"Well, you had a damn sight more than you've got right now, so quit your moping and get on with it. You got yourself into this. Now get yourself out. It's bad enough you come running to friends for help."

Still grumbling at herself she pulled out her best pair of khaki shorts worn soft from months of daily hand washing and a pale blue t-shirt of Egyptian cotton that she'd tried to keep for special occasions on the trip. The cotton felt like silk against her skin and set off her eyes nicely. When she brushed out her hair and checked herself in the faded mirror she could have been an intrepid explorer. She felt tired just looking at her image. There were circles under her eyes to prove it.

With a dab of lipstick and her daypack over her shoulder, she returned downstairs to find Lila and Chloe back in the store and Brett prowling around the cases.

"Whoa!" Brett said after she stepped through the curtain into the shop, the beaded curtain clicking behind her. His gaze seemed to widen and do a slow glide down to her bare legs and back to her face. "You look like you're ready to go visit the pyramids or climb Mount McKinley or something."

She looked down at herself not sure whether to take his reaction as a compliment or not, and flicked her bangs aside. "Sorry. When you live out of a backpack, your wardrobe is sort of limited to the lowest common denominator."

Darn it, she wasn't going to let him make her feel nervous. She cocked a hip and set one long leg in display. "So are we going to see this house or not?"

Was that a little gulp on Brett's part, because he was sure enough looking at her legs again. Darn it, she didn't want to lead him on, but she couldn't remember a man reacting to her like that in... well, ever, really. But she wasn't interested in a relationship with anyone. Not now, not ever again. She'd finally learned her lesson. Relationships just hurt too much when they were over and they *always* ended.

He swept his hand toward the door. "My chariot awaits. Ladies." He tipped his head at Lila and Chloe. "I promise to get her back here in one piece in just a little while."

She recognized his racing green older-model Miata that was in mint condition. He held the car door for her in a gesture so foreign and gallant she only stammered out a thank you, before he carefully closed the door behind her. Just trying to take care of his baby, probably. So many people climbed into a strange car and slammed the door.

He opened his door and leaned in to her. "Top up or down?"

She'd never driven in a convertible before. "Uh... down?"

He grinned like a kid just told he could have whatever he wanted in a candy store. Quick as a wink had the top down and packed away behind them. Then he settled, grinning, beside her. A slight tingle ran through her as his gaze glanced over her face.

"This's going to be fun."

Fun? They were just going to look at his parents' house.

Weren't they?

The car vroom-vroomed on command and they pulled away from the curb and cruised the lake shore down through town, with the sun beating down on their heads and the breeze in their hair. The heat felt good. She relaxed back into the brown leather seat even though Brett's gaze kept slipping from the road to her legs. She almost wished she had a blanket to hide them or had worn her leggings. And then they were through town, crossed the highway and zoomed up a long curving hillside with old orchards and pine trees and heritage houses. They turned right on a street called Somerset and followed it up higher, then turned again to drive through a subdivision. The road turned again, before Brett pulled into a driveway at an older, stucco-sided, white house. It had faded blue trim that reminded her of blue and white Aegean towns.

The house had a small porch with one of those old fashioned arched porticos and room for one chair by the door. A small postage-stamp sized lawn ran around two sides of the house, with a larger expanse of lawn, an actual garden plot and two ripening cherry trees that would be ready to harvest in a week or three. A faded wooden picnic table sat in the shade of a giant willow. But it was the fourth side of the house that almost made her say she'd take it before she even saw the inside. The fourth side of the house looked out over the tops of pine trees to a magnificent view of the lake both north and southward for miles.

"Oh my God!" she said walking to the edge of the grass, a kaleidoscope of views running through her head—the ends of the earth from Cabo Sao Joseph in Portugal, the Indian Ocean from the heated Zanzibar beach, the blue ocean from a Santorini cliff top, the North Sea from the highlands of Scotland. So many views she'd fallen in love with and they all seemed to culminate right here. The constant need to shift, to run, to move, eased a little. "You mean I could live here?"

Brett came up beside her and stuck his hands in his pockets. He stood close enough she felt his presence like another sun. "It's a pretty good view. Mom always loved it."

"I'll just bet she did. It feels like I can see forever." And breathe. Really breathe in the pine-scented air and feel alive for the first time since Kevin—since forever.

She shook her ex and all the others she'd thought she'd loved out of her thoughts and grinned up at Brett. "With this view it's going to have to be a pretty bad house for me not to take it."

"I guess we'll see. Come on." With a cock of the head, he led her toward the house.

§

The flash of silver in sunlight was enough to make Corporal Daniel Forester sit up in his nondescript brown Marquis parked just down the street from the *This & That*. The sun was hot and the damned car had no air conditioning so that even sitting here with all the windows down and the breeze off the lake, it was like he sat in an oven. A fucking old hamburger-wrapper-scented oven. He hated fucking stakeouts—avoided them like the plague—and yet here he was. His shirt stuck to him and he hated that, too. And the fact that the woman he'd interviewed had been like some ice-fucking-queen.

He hadn't believed a word the Lila woman had told him. She knew—something. Something she shouldn't know because she might have been late, but for his purposes she'd come just too soon to meet with Moira Burns and had taken away the box with the precious contents he'd been waiting to claim.

No, that wasn't right. He winced and squeezed the bridge of his nose against the headache that was frigging eating his brain. The world seemed to ripple around him.

The woman had been a cooperative witness... hadn't she? He kept rubbing the bridge of his nose and the spot between his eyes because his head had been killing him since he'd interviewed the homeless man near the accident scene. The man had been less than helpful, yelling that the ghosts in his head made him do things he didn't want to. When Daniel had questioned him about the Burns woman's death, the man had broken down into incoherent sobs until they'd finally had to hospitalize him. But ever since, this damned headache had raged.

But *he* hadn't been waiting to claim anything. *He* had never heard of Moira Burns until the morning when he got the call to assist with the hit and run investigation on the quiet suburban street of heritage homes. He'd been helping out Kelowna detachment with vacation coverage when another detective had gone off on sick leave. At the scene, he had been greeted by a lawyer named Jack Lutz who had found Moira Burns' body tossed beside her car hood, her briefcase pried open as if someone had been looking for something. The uniformed traffic constables had cordoned off everything tight as a drum and he'd come in to take over the investigation. The world rippled again.

He'd looked through her personal effects and found her timetable and organizer. And that brought him here, on the tail of something he'd been waiting eons to find.

Damn it, would the world quit running like a bunch of flipping water colors? Because he hadn't been looking for anything other than who killed Moira Burns. He was here, sure. But on the tail of something…? What the hell was that all about?

He scrubbed his short nails through his hair again and watched the leggy little blond climb into the green car and the man take down the top of the little convertible. Nice ride, even if it was a little small. The silver flashed again as the woman touched her hair when the car started down the road.

Corporal Daniel Forester climbed out of his car and inhaled the wind. Another ripple in the Okanagan daylight.

Water, sand, suntan lotion and heated bodies couldn't disguise the incense scent of ancient silver.

And power.

He climbed back in his car and turned the engine on.

CHAPTER 8

It was a little disconcerting, this powerful attraction to someone he'd barely met, but just sitting beside Kylee Jensen in the car on the way over had made him aware of all the reasons he shouldn't be interested in her. She was too pretty, too vulnerable and her skin was the smoothest silk he'd ever seen. Here on the lawn of his parents' house, she reminded him of young wine—full of promise. She looked long-limbed and coltish in the shorts and blue t-shirt. Yet even with the wind blowing her hair and her bright blue eyes glowing at the view from the yard, there was a fear. No, fear was too strong a word. It was uncertainty like wine that could either become bitter and undrinkable, or an award-winning vintage of elegance and complexity. That uncertainty radiated off her now, yet it wasn't there when she was with Lila and Chloe. It was almost as if it was because of him. That wasn't good.

But there was something else in her, too. He spotted it as soon as she stepped up to the view. Longing. A basic, primal hunger for something that positively radiated off her. And then it was gone with slightest shake of her head as if she consciously forced whatever it was, away.

They stood on the lawn that ran out from the side of the house. Under the shade of the willow the grass was too long. He hadn't had time to get up here and mow due to demands at the winery. The unshaded areas were already browning because the darn sprinkler system was temperamental and he hadn't had a chance to fix it himself or get someone in to do it. Who knew what else had gone wrong inside the house sitting empty all this time. About the only thing that hadn't faded into a repair problem was the view. The view was worth a lot, though—if he could only get Chloe to sign the papers. Maybe—just maybe—Kylee living here and all the demands of dealing with a tenant would change her mind, because everyone knows that renters are notorious problems.

Even cute blonde ones.

"Come on," he said and led the way to the front door, pulling a set of old keys out of his pocket. He unlocked the door and held it open for Kylee, but she hesitated and looked up at him. Then she eased past as if the last thing she wanted to do was touch him. He frowned.

Inside he inhaled the old bouquet of his childhood home—furniture wax and pine floor cleaner. Somehow it lingered in the nose and on the back of his tongue. Everything still looked the same, because Chloe had refused to get rid of most of the furniture and even the knickknacks. They'd each taken a few treasured keepsakes home—antiques mostly, or photos, but otherwise the place was a damned museum—or mausoleum—to the memories of his mother and father. He hated it. Hated that they were gone and that this place caused a pain right next to his heart that had no reason to be there. They'd been gone six months. He should be over it. He was a man who lived in the present, not the past. The present and what the future could bring with a little work and time—like fine wine fermenting.

Like maybe, with a little time, Kylee could stop being so uncertain around him?

She was wandering around the living room, the muted light through the closed sheer drapes placing an ethereal patina on her skin. Her fingers skimmed the tops of the worn armchairs that flanked the fireplace. She paused at the mantel to look up at the family photo that hung there: Brett, Chloe and their parents with wide white smiles in suntanned faces. It had been taken at a beach vacation they had shared in Hawaii two years back.

"Your parents look like they were pretty vibrant people," she said glancing over her shoulder at him.

"They were." He moved up behind her, aware of the way her shoulders stiffened and of the way the pale hairs on the back of her neck formed a faint line that led down under the neckline of her t-shirt. In the closed space he caught her scent of lavender soap and sunshine and almost closed his eyes to savor it. "They got the travel bug late in life and were always running off somewhere together. A cruise around the world. Three months in Australia and Bali. They'd rent an apartment and just live in the place and get to know it. They loved other cultures and seeing new places."

She nodded.

"I guess you'd understand that what with all your travels."

Another nod. "I guess it would be a better time if you were with someone you loved."

Her voice was strained and he didn't want her to feel that way around him. He stepped back a pace. "Well this is the place they always came back to. Not glamorous, but it was home."

She seemed to wince and eased past him to the front window that looked out onto the lake.

"From this room you have the same view as from the yard," he said. He used the drawstring to pull the curtains open and daylight filled the room with sudden color. The couch was a warm floral with cream background and rich burgundy flowers and green foliage. His father's favorite chair stationed so he could watch the old television in the corner, was a matching green and the chairs by the fireplace picked up the burgundy. The colors always reminded him of a vineyard when the sunlight gleamed through the leaves and ripening red grapes.

Like a cloud in a glass of wine, she shifted around the room still touching things as if committing them to memory. "It's very nice. I like it."

And suddenly it was important that she did. He wanted her to rent this place, to feel the safety he always had here. And maybe, just maybe, she'd see where he came from and be a little less uncertain of him. He wanted to see the elegant woman she would become. He couldn't imagine her turning out otherwise.

"The kitchen's this way," he said, leading her through a short hallway to the other side of the little house. "Mom had the place renovated about ten years ago—much to my father's horror. She said if she was going to be retired here, she wanted to be able to cook meals that would bring people into their home. Lila and Chloe helped design this space."

He flipped the light on and pot lights illuminated a room done in shades of green that seemed to flow from the colors in the living room. A white stove, fridge and dishwasher matched the white counter and cupboards, while the floor and backsplash were done in pale green and white. He opened a louvered cupboard to reveal a full-sized washer and dryer and another set of doors that showed a full pantry. "Dad and I did the tiling." He smiled.

"You sound proud," she said and for a moment she stood close by him and the uncertainty was gone.

"I am—that it came out as good as it did. If you'd seen the mayhem and heard the arguments—all in good fun, of course. It's amazing what it looks like now. But Dad was always pretty good with his hands." He looked down at his own, long-fingered and tanned. "I hope I got some of that from him."

"I'll bet you did."

Her blue gaze met his. For a moment it held and the room disappeared. The clarity of her gaze was like a fine unoaked Chardonnay. Her flawless skin seemed lit from within like grapes in sunshine, yet she appeared to wear no makeup except, perhaps, for the smudge of her dark lashes. A strand of her bangs was perilously close to her eyes, and with his thumb he gently nudged it away and pulled back before she could freeze. The soft touch of her skin almost made him groan. Damn it this should not be happening, but he wanted her to notice him in a good way, not in a way that made her afraid. And not just as a summer fling like all the other summer women had. He'd have to figure her out and then carefully coax her into revealing herself to him. He could do it. He did it all the time with grapes, coaxing them into the flavor they had the potential to give.

What flavor are you? He gave himself a mental kick. This woman was not his type.

Was she?

§

"Well then." She saw him swallow as he stepped back to give her space. To recover? Because she needed that space the way her body was trembling. Heck, just sitting beside him in the car had set her whole body tingling from her wrist, her hands, right down to her core and that was a bad sign. The touch had set off a wave of heat that even the bracelet seemed to have caught. It was a very bad sign given once upon a time she'd had a similar reaction to Kevin and every other man before him. Or she'd thought she had.

She fell for guys too quickly. She was *not* doing it with Brett.

But Brett simply nodded like a gentleman and maybe that was all the touch had been. But she didn't think so. She'd caught his glances at her legs and seen the way his pupils had dilated when their skin connected. She was not going to be just a fling, either, no matter what Mr. Brett Main might think.

"Let me show you the rest of the place," he said and led her off down a short hallway to the back of the house. A small bathroom and what looked like an office with an easy chair and small flat screen TV gave onto the street side of the house.

"This was where one of them got banished when the other one hogged the main TV Mostly it was Mom, escaping Sunday golf and football." He gave a small wistful grin, "Sometimes I'd drive up here and take her out for a drive so she could really escape. She loved to drive with the top down."

He'd clearly loved his parents and she liked that about him. "She probably loved her son's attention, more."

His green gaze clouded a moment as if old emotion roiled up from within. Still, grieving then, regardless of Chloe thinking he was just pushing to get rid of everything his parents represented. No, this man was clearly hurting and trying to deal with it in the best way he knew how—by trying to move forward. It was something she could understand.

"I'm sorry. It must be hard coming up here. So many memories. I think I understand why you want to sell, but I'm glad you're considering renting. It really is a lovely place."

Brett shrugged. "Yeah, but the water's hard and the plumbing creaks and groans and there's ants. They continually had to fumigate as if this whole mountain is nothing more than an anthill."

Ants. Her skin crawled. Insects weren't exactly her favorite thing.

"The bedrooms are upstairs," he said and led her away still looking for signs of ants on the floor or wall or, God forbid, the ceiling. On the other hand, at least they weren't spiders.

At the end of the hall a narrow staircase rose four steps and then took a sharp turn before running up to the floor above. A single octagonal window above the stairs let in a long beam of light that illuminated the entire hallway. The wooden stairs showed the honor scuffmarks of long use, and creaked as Brett led her up them. At the top she came up behind him and gasped.

The entire upper story was the one master bedroom, with dormer windows on the four sides letting in the light. A queen-sized bed draped in a thick cream-colored duvet had been set across one corner, with a poof of cream cloth coming out from the corner to drape over the bed's iron headboard. She could imagine a couple reading in bed together. A dresser and highboy mirrored each other from against opposite walls and a lovely old wooden trunk sat at the foot of the bed. Underfoot lay a thick cream-colored carpet as counterpoint to dark oak hardwood. With the pale blue walls the entire room gave a sense of peace, contentment and coolness.

"So much space," she said, because otherwise she was lost for words.

"It used to be three small bedrooms and the bath up here. After Chloe and I moved out Mom had this done at the same time as the kitchen, but the stairs were getting harder for them."

She hesitated to step further into the room because it still felt like a sanctum of the living, but Brett led her in. "The dressers and closets are empty. That was one of the few things Chloe and I did together. We took their things to Goodwill and went through the jewelry and so on. Most of the old stuff ended up getting taken to *This & That*. He opened the door to a closet built in one corner to expose a luxury of closet space she didn't think she could ever fill. The other door in the other walled-off corner, gave onto a bathroom with a big old clawed-foot bathtub that could fit two people. It was equipped with a hand held shower, and a double sink counter with retro fittings. The room was painted the same pale blue as the bedroom and head-high shelves around the bathroom held an array of pale candles, all half burned. Overhead was a skylight and she could imagine evenings chin deep in the bath with the candles lit, a glass of wine, and stars overhead. She had a sudden warm surge of *home*. This was home and she wanted to wrap herself in this place so badly the thought of leaving it was like a blade in her heart.

Stupid. Silly. Stupid heart. This was not her place. She was only a maybe tenant.

She looked up from her study of the bathroom and found Brett watching her with a slight smile, quickly smoothed away. She swallowed and her hands fluttered up to her hair. My God, she was acting like a stupid school girl and she was *not* that and she was not interested in this man. Not ever again.

She turned on her heel and marched out of the bathroom feeling his presence like a force behind her that willed her to turn around. She wanted to, but her heart was a silly, foolish organ and this wasn't even her heart. More like her gonads.

It *had* been a while since she'd had sex. Belay that thought, Kylee Jensen. That way leads to insanity and you're just getting your sanity back. Because losing Kevin had left her wild and unmoored, like everything in the world was out of control. She'd felt like that all through the remainder of the safari and had barely slept most nights because her heart wouldn't stop racing. When they'd reached Capetown she'd run—right back to Vancouver via India, Thailand and Bali. That had been another fiasco because she hadn't been able to concentrate and had lost her job—actually three jobs. Until she took the hit of losing her damage deposit on her rental apartment and escaped to Peachland. This was the sanest she'd felt in months.

She clattered down the stairs and down the hallway until she was safely in the kitchen. There she turned to face him. "It's a really nice house—I like it. I guess what we need to talk about is what you want to rent it for and whether I can afford it." She tried to keep her shakiness out of her voice.

Because she really did want this house even though she knew she shouldn't. Each of the rooms as Brett showed them to her, had offered her a piece of normalcy she'd lost somewhere. A place to eat and nourish herself and break bread with friends. A place to warm herself by the fire and fill herself with all the books she hadn't been reading. A place to rest and recover from all the mistakes she'd made. She'd envisioned what she could do to make each space her own, while still honoring the people who had been here before.

Brett looked thoughtful and shook his head, but his consideration was far too intent, as if he was sizing her up or something. "That's something Chloe and I will need to discuss if you really want to rent the place." He hooked his head toward the door. "Come on. It's far too fine a day to spend it inside an old house."

They stepped out from the cool, comfortable shadows of the empty house into the sunshine and heat of the day. They climbed into the waiting Miata and it started obediently as Brett turned onto the road away from the direction they had come in on. "I'll show you a little of the neighbourhood."

The little car followed the road as it swept up onto bench land with orchards and small hayfields going golden in the sun. Horses lounged in maple tree shade.

"Look! Quail," he said and slowed the car in time for a mother and a whole gaggle of tiny little chicks to hurry across the road. "That's a big covey. I wonder how many will make it to adulthood. Too many cats and dogs in the neighborhood, along with the coyotes. The crows and ravens and magpies too. I hate magpies. I used to take my slingshot after them when I was a kid. It's hard growing up quail." He grinned, his thick brown hair falling charmingly in his eyes so she could imagine him with a slingshot taking aim at the long-tailed pesky birds.

He pointed out an orange and black oriole and a bald eagles' nest perched high in a tree, then spotted a doe and fawn as the Miata wound farther up the gravel side roads that snaked up this side of the lake. There were subdivisions of new houses that set him shaking his head and lamenting some lost orchard. He mainly kept to roads that, when he shut the Miata off, were filled with the sounds of the poplar leaves, the wind in the pines and the scent of heat and dust.

And Brett's faint herbal aftershave.

"I love the silence up here," she said. "You can actually hear yourself think."

Brett sat with his hands on the brown leather-clad steering wheel, his head slightly bowed. Finally he looked up at her sideways. "You're right. I remember as a kid there were times in the early morning that there wasn't even a sound from the highway. Now there's always a rumble in the background. I sometimes wonder whether there's any place near this lake that you can really find silence—especially with people around. You seem to be the exception."

Was she imagining it or had his smile gone vulnerable as if he was baring a part of himself he wasn't used to sharing? "You really love this town don't you?"

"Love it?" he looked away from her again. "I'm not sure. Sometimes, I guess. Sometimes I hate it, too. It's a small town after all, with all the cliques and all the rumors. Most of the kids I grew up with moved away."

"And you didn't."

He looked sideways at her, over his arms, his hands still fisted on the wheel. "I guess when I had the chance to move away was one of those times when I loved the place."

"And now you work at a winery."

He nodded. "That's right. I went to vintner's school at University of California and then came home and found a job with Elkhart. The owner was an old friend of my Dad's."

"But you've never settled down, even though you're here."

He straightened then and released the wheel, grinning. "Is it that obvious?"

Kylee waved her arm at the car. "This. Your looks. Pardon me for saying it, but you must have women falling all over you."

There. She'd set him straight that she could see right through him. She wasn't going to subject her heart to breaking again. Not even if there was something about this man that attracted her immensely. Especially those moments of charmingly real vulnerability. In those moments he seemed like someone she could hold onto and that would hold onto her. But that her heart was about as reliable as Kevin had been. She knew better.

His brows rose in a momentary surprise. "Once upon a time, maybe. I've mended my ways."

She laughed. "Sure you have. Just like I've stopped falling for good looking guys who throw me away like yesterday's garbage."

The bitterness in her voice surprised her. She'd heard bitterness in other women's voices before and it hadn't been pretty. In either the lives they lived or the lines on their faces. Her hand came up to her face, the bracelet sliding up her forearm. Was that what she was going to become? One of those pruned women she'd met in the workplace with the frowning mouths? But she *wasn't* about to be vulnerable again.

"I wouldn't throw you away."

She yanked her gaze away from his green-as-forests-she-could-get-lost-in eyes and stared straight forward through the windshield. All her muscles had stiffened, yet a nice little tingle ran through her body. The way he looked, he might try to kiss her, and she might even want him to, but no!

She was not doing this again—getting lured in and then running herself ragged chasing after him.

"I don't know what to do with that comment," she said, fighting to keep her voice cool.

Beyond the car, robins were calling in the trees and a light pine-laden breeze played around her shoulders. The road was dappled with tree shadows. He was silent a moment and the car shifted as he turned to her and sighed. "That's a lovely bracelet. It looks good on your arm."

The moment of fear passed and she could breathe again. "It is, isn't it?"

She held up her arm to admire it and in the sunshine its workmanship was even more amazing. "It's not mine, unfortunately. It was in the last batch of stuff Lila brought home and I tried it on, but I can't seem to get the darn thing off. Lila and the others haven't figured it out either."

"Well let's see, then. Maybe it just takes a masculine touch." He waggled his brow. "Turn your wrist over."

She obeyed and momentarily felt vulnerable with her inner arm exposed. He studied the closure for a moment without touching. "Looks simple enough. The key slips through the lock, right? May I?"

She nodded and he caught the key and lock in his hands, then twisted the key to slip it through the small ornate lock. It was all Kylee could do to hold her breath, because beyond the light brush of his skin and the sun-bleached hairs on the back of his hands, an electric shock seemed to run through the bracelet and right up her arm. Enough like lightning that she expected to smell ozone.

Instead she inhaled the suddenly potent scent of Brett's personal scent of freshly pressed grapes, sunshine and man. Did he shudder for a moment, because she was sure enough shaking inside? It had to just be the fact that it had been six months since she had been with a man. That was all, surely. She bit the inside of her mouth as he gently twisted the key this way and that trying to get it through the lock.

"Well, I'm stymied," he said and caught her hand, turned her arm over and studied the bracelet. "Doors. For new beginnings," he said softly and looked out of the tops of his eyes at her. "That suits you."

"It could be for things ending, too," she said too quickly because she wasn't sure she liked the insight of her that he seemed to gain.

He smiled, "When one thing ends, another begins. Life's like that. I like you Kylee Jensen; I intend to show you that until you believe." And then he did the strangest thing: he lightly kissed the back of her hand.

CHAPTER 9

Six kinds of fool. Ten times an idiot.

Brett steered down Princeton hill under the late afternoon sun, allowing the little Miata to pick up speed. Orchards and housing developments pressed in from either side and huge scars showed on the hillside where more pine forest had been mowed down to allow more houses to be built. Peachland wasn't the sleepy small town it had been when he was growing up. Now it was a bedroom community for the city of Kelowna and a final resting place for too many retirees from the prairies. Not any place he should be living in, and yet he was because he *did* have a love-hate relationship with the damn town and his parents' house and—now—the woman seated beside him.

Just what the hell had he been thinking, making a pass at Kylee, even if it was the most gentlemanly thing he'd ever done? Someone had obviously hurt Kylee badly—her comment about being thrown away had been about the most bald-faced clue he'd ever been given, and a clear warning that she didn't intend to be tossed away again. If he was really trying to get a read on her, well he had it now. It was like she was one of those precious clear Chardonnay varietals that could be overwhelmed just walking past an oaken cask. So he'd gone and ruined the rather fine intimacy that had been forming between them by, if not kissing her, then the next best thing. And maybe it was a good thing because he didn't want to want her. He had no time for a vulnerable woman, but damn it, there was something about her.

And the more time he spent with Kylee Jensen, the more clear that was to him. Even just sitting silently in the car.

They crossed the highway and turned onto Beach Avenue, then cruised too fast for the speed limit down to *This & That*. He was tempted to just drop her there and burn rubber to his aerie at the winery, but that was illogical and, frankly, a cowards way out. He'd taken her up to see the house and now he was going to have to discourage her from renting it. Maybe make the rent too high or something.

With the engine shut off, the sounds of the summer people drifted in around them, but he didn't know what to say.

"Thank you for the tour of the house and the area," Kylee said and slipped out of the car, stealing the moment from him.

He climbed out too, against his better judgment and went around to her. She looked out at the lake with an expression of longing he'd seen too many times at the end of someone's holiday. They were letting go of Peachland, which meant that Kylee was thinking of leaving.

"We'd better go in. They'll be waiting," he said and she sighed and nodded, just like all those summer girls he'd promised to write to when he was young. He never had.

She followed him up into the waiting white and red house, into the bedlam of women that was his sister's domain, but surprisingly Chloe was alone in the store and everything was quiet.

"We're back," he said.

"So I see." She checked her watch, a slight smirk on her face. Her bevy of necklaces whispered around her "That was a long house viewing."

"We went for a drive. Brett was showing me the sights," Kylee said with a primness and finality that said that was all she would divulge.

Chloe came around the counter. "And? What'd you think?"

Kylee blinked as if for a moment she wasn't sure what Chloe was talking about. "The house? Oh, it's lovely. Listen would you excuse me a moment. I need to talk to Lila about something."

She disappeared like a sprite through the beaded curtain into the back of the house leaving Brett dangerously alone with Chloe.

Gaze narrowed, she placed her hands on her hips. "Well?"

"Well, what? I didn't do anything." Okay, so he lied.

"And I'm tall and blond and beautiful. So now that I've got that out, let's cut the lies. What happened? She's like a scared little rabbit, running back to its hole."

His shoulders slumped as he nodded. "She is, isn't she? But I really didn't do anything much. I took her to see the house. She seemed to like it and we seemed to be getting along so I took her for a drive is all."

She still looked at him with those blue eyes of hers, now gone black and steely. "And you did what?"

"I kissed her hand, okay? I kissed the back of her flipping hand and since when have I ever done that? No, Brett Main goes in for the kill. He doesn't kiss a flipping hand, okay? You happy?" He didn't need this. He headed for the door.

"Hold it right there, Mister."

Damn it why did he hold? She was his sister, not his mother. But he'd always listened to Chloe, first as a little brother, then as a confidante and then as a friend. She'd put up with his screwing around with just a resigned nod and few pointed questions about whether he really liked himself when he was playing Casanova and leaving a long string of broken hearts behind him. That, and his parent's death and made him rethink his approach to women. After all, his father had always honored his mother.

"You're right." He swung back to her with a deep breath. "We need to talk about the house. What do we charge for rent if Kylee decides to take it? The conditions of the rental agreement, etc."

They could go through the motions and let it be Kylee's decision that she didn't want it.

The damn woman looked like she was still angry except for the telltale laugh lines quivering into existence around her eyes. She thought his discomfiture was funny! Then she shook her head.

"For your sake, I really hope you haven't screwed this one up, brother." She went and retrieved a piece of paper from the counter by the cash register. "Here. While you were out flirting I turned my mind to more practical matters. Take a look and see if the agreement I propose makes sense. That is, if she isn't intent on running for the hills."

She patted his cheek and went back to her counter, leaving him a little nonplussed—not that today she'd been the practical one, which was so unusual he should mark it on a calendar, not even that she'd patted his cheek when she knew he hated that action, but that she knew.

Somehow she'd sensed his attraction to Kylee even before he'd known it was there.

§

"I—I'm not sure I did the right thing coming here." Kylee choked the horrible words out as she perched on the edge of the nook bench, her hands clenched between her knees to stop the shaking.

Lila faced her across the table, still clad in her fitted orange cotton shift looking far more like Jackie Kennedy than Kylee could ever hope to be. Nope, inside she felt more like the jumble of glittering jewelry spread across the kitchen. It was clear that Lila had made a more serious dent in the kitchen disorder than Kylee had managed internally in the long months after Kevin. Small piles of jewels were labeled and in small plastic bags, ready to be taken out to the store. Others had been placed in a neat wooden box with *Reggie* stenciled on the side. The glitter of amethyst and topaz spoke of some of the precious stones destined to become part of the jewelry maker's creations. Others were in a box marked for Chloe, probably for her to examine the stones. The copper kettle had been shined to a glowing patina and sat by the sink with a lovely crystal vase that broke the sunlight into a thousand rainbows which caressed the kitchen's white walls. Heck, even the kitchen mess wasn't as messed-up as she was inside.

The table still had the half-unloaded box of treasures bought from a dead woman, and the long rat's nest of chains that had hidden the bracelet still on her arm. All in all, it was like returning to the scene of the crime.

She looked up, meeting Lila's green-flecked hazel gaze. "I think all I've done is run away from my problems and set myself up to fall again. I shouldn't have come here. I've caused more trouble for you and your friends. I think before I overstay my welcome I should pack up my things and head home."

There. She'd said it. Because she might think she'd love it here, she might even think she'd dream her whole life for a chance to live in that little house up Princeton Avenue, but she was not going to put herself in the position of making another horrible mistake with her heart. It was too easy to fall in love with the house and too easy to fall into old ways with men. Her heart had been broken enough already. She didn't think she could stand being someone who ran men only to have them grind her heart under their heel every time. She hated herself enough for her failings as it was.

Lila just studied her a moment and then stood, the shift settling to skim her body.

"Wow." She filled the kettle and put it on the stove. "That's a lot to take in at one sitting." She put hot water in her Alice in Wonderland teapot and tea leaves in a tea bulb. "You fit in here so well." She turned back to Kylee, leaning against the counter. "You did so great here this morning. I was really hoping that you'd stay on and eventually take over the shop so that I could spend more time travelling to find unique jewelry."

She shook her head and shifted around the kitchen. "As you can tell, there's a lot involved in the care and feeding of a store. And I know Reggie is going to be travelling more now that her jewelry is catching on. And Chloe—well one never knows what Chloe's about to do, does one?" She said the latter almost to herself. Then the kettle started to boil. She made the tea and brought it back to the table along with two mugs, including the one Kylee had liked so much earlier. Almost as if Lila'd known that it fit Kylee's hands perfectly. Or maybe she'd known it was the kind of thing Kylee would like.

She sighed. "I'm so sorry Lila. I swooped in here as if I had a right to come in and disturb your life."

"Kylee, you've always been welcome here. You were when we were kids, you are now, and you always will be in the future. How many people in our lives can we not see for years, but we can pick up exactly where we left off. We still laugh together. We understand each other. We help each other."

"You help me, you mean. You've been my rescuer twice now and that's not fair to you. You shouldn't have to be the one who picks up the pieces of Kylee every time I come chasing after you for help. What have I ever done for you?"

"Wow. You really are determined to be down on yourself. Did you ever think that friends do things for each other? I have the utmost faith that if I was in need, you'd be there for me." She poured the tea and set the cup before Kylee. "Drink. Then I want you to tell me what this is really all about. You liked the house, didn't you? It's exactly right for you."

The tea smelled amazing—like mint and berries and rosehips. It seemed to steady her nerves so her hands didn't shake like they had been. She felt safe pulling them up from her lap and took a tentative sip of the tea. "It's good. What is it?"

"A little local concoction. Mint from the sinks in the hills, rosehips and Saskatoon's from local bushes." She cocked her head. "So? Spill. Everything. And not the Cole's Note version."

And just like that she was a kid back in the high school cafeteria when Kylee had turned into a basket case.

Kylee shook her head suddenly feeling incredibly stupid. "Today? My whole incredibly sorry little life?"

"Well how about we start with what happened with Kevin. Tell me about him. We can get to what happened this afternoon after we've had a chance to work out the context." Lila took another sip of tea and checked her watch. "And just so you know, it's late enough I have no qualms about shutting the store. We can stay here all night if you want to."

She laughed, but it came out shakier than she'd expected. "I don't think my sordid little life will take that long."

"Maybe. Go on."

So she told. All the pathetic details of her taking a new job at a marketing firm in Vancouver and how she'd met Kevin at one of the business parties. He was a junior associate, but brilliant and with strong prospects for advancement. He was handsome, charming and with a sense of adventure that she wished she had. They'd been friends at first. She had tried out wind surfing and paddle boarding with him. They'd gone hiking on day trips at first, but then they took a longer, weekend trip and that had led to their first intimate encounter. It had been in a tent in a rainstorm high on a mountainside. The lightning had flashed and the thunder had rolled through them both as they made love. She had thought it was the most romantic thing in the world.

"We became an item then," she air quoted item. "We were inseparable, but Kevin was getting restless. He started talking about how his job was a dead end and didn't fill up his soul. So we started plotting together how to find the adventure in our lives, even though I'd thought we were doing pretty well. Heck, I even tried rock climbing though I disappointed him by not wanting to scale the cliffs of the Chief with him. He seemed so disappointed— as if I'd failed him. I realize now that was the beginning of the end. So we made plans to sell everything and go around the world. It was the right thing to do—everyone agreed, at least to my face. We loved each other and were the next thing to engaged. Or so I thought."

She looked down at her mug. In the real world the tea had gone cold and the sunny backyard of the house was in shadows, the sun having disappeared westward over the mountains. For a moment she felt more cold and alone than she ever had. She'd been such a fool.

"So we sold everything including my apartment and put it all toward the trip. At least I did. I didn't even think about how the money was so one-sided. It was our future, wasn't it? We backpacked through Europe. When I think about it now, I realize I was the just the means to an end. For all his high-powered job, Kevin barely had the proverbial pot to pee in and no window to throw it out of. He was too busy being a high roller to save any money."

She took a steadying sip of the cold tea, but still couldn't meet Lila's gaze. The woman sat so silently, was so nonjudgmental, it was like talking to herself. Yet Lila's hazel gaze held encouragement to keep going as if by talking she was lancing a wound. She *hadn't* had the chance to really tell her story to anyone before. She swallowed back the cool berry and herb tea and took a deep breath.

"So we headed out and backpacked around Europe, except Kevin wasn't content to stay in the low rent district and he liked to go out drinking with people we met. A lot. Anyway, we blew through almost a third of our money by the time we hit Morocco where we joined a tour group trucking across Africa.

"At first it was good. We were back in a tent together and treated as a couple, but there were a lot of single girls on the trip and Kevin seemed to make a point of cultivating them. When I think back on it, a lot of the people we met and hung out with in Europe were women, too, but I kept telling myself we could overcome it. I stayed with him and went where he wanted to go. Anyway, on the Africa trip about a third of the trip in, I finally found the guts to confront him about it. He said I was just being silly and had nothing to be jealous about. I felt foolish and threw myself into keeping him happy. But then he started staying up really late drinking with some of the singles even though it was way past the time we usually went to bed together. I tried to stay up with him, but the travel was exhausting and the conversations were inane. By the time we got to Kenya the group on the truck had pretty much split into two groups—the older thirty somethings and the younger twenty somethings. Kevin hung with the younger group and I, unfortunately, found myself with the older ones."

"Not unfortunate at all. It sounds like you were two very different people," Lila said. "Go on."

Now came the hard part. She wasn't sure she could go on. Her chest felt tight and her eyes ached with all of the hurt the next three months of her life had brought. But she'd gone this far. She might as well tell the rest.

"So Nairobi is a dangerous city, right? I think at one time it was ranked the most dangerous city in the world. We were put up in a hotel because camping wasn't safe, but the shopping area was a good walk from the compound. So one afternoon Kevin says this German girl in our group, Claudia, wants to go into the market to buy a Baobab purse. He's going with her as escort for safety reasons. It's like he's asking if anyone else wants to come, but like an idiot I decided to stay by the pool. It was such a luxury after the months of travel. So they leave. At six o'clock the sun's sliding toward dark and we're all going to dinner and there's still no sign of them. I send the others on their way and wait. At eight o'clock I finally got frantic and hired a taxi to take me around Nairobi to look for Kevin and Claudia. By nine o'clock there's still no sign of them, and I had the taxi drop me off in the center of town. I didn't realize how stupid I was being. Pretty much anything for tourists was closed up by then. The taxis were gone, too. It was terrifying, but somehow I managed to make it back to the hotel. The whole group was back from dinner and Kevin and Claudia were with them, but it was like those two were a couple. They had their hands all over each other, and hadn't even noticed I was missing. The tour leader had asked where I was, and Kevin had told him I was in the room. He hadn't even checked. I was shaken and upset, and more upset when I saw him. He came back to our room with me and had the nerve to tell me I had no reason to be worried. They were just friends. They got caught up at the market and just went directly to the restaurant to meet the others. And as for me choosing to wait for him at the hotel and then risking my life to look for him, that was my choice. No fault of his.

"I should have seen it then, but I'm an idiot about men. We made love that night and I thought everything would be okay when we left on the long overland route to Capetown the next morning. It wasn't. It only got worse over the next three months and more blatant. Like a fool I kept running after him and holding onto hope that it would be over, because Claudia would go back to Germany and we'd head for India. It was over, all right. For me. The last night of the trip, he officially dumped me in front of everyone and left with her, taking half of the money that was left and there wasn't much of that. Unbeknownst to me he'd been buying the beer for the whole trip and had used a bunch to buy a ring for Claudia.

"So I took what was left and I already had a ticket to India, so I left Africa, but I just couldn't do it. I spent a short while in Northern India, stopped in Thailand and thought I might recover in Bali. Didn't happen. I came back to Vancouver to try to start over and rented an apartment, but how do you start over when there's nothing of you left? So after three months of struggle to finally realize that my trouble is that I always throw my heart out there and hope that some guy will catch it, I came here. It was either that or find a cliff." She managed a weak smile.

Lila reached across the table and caught her hands. "Feel better?"

Kylee thought a moment. Her throat still felt thick, but the tight band around her chest had loosened. She hadn't cried when she told the story, and all the other times she'd even thought about Kevin, she had. "Actually, yes. It does. Sort of like letting the puss out of a wound. The pressure eased somehow."

Lila nodded, her beautiful sculpted face softened in the softer light. "It's why women need to talk about their problems. Somehow it sets the problems free, and when they are shared they aren't so big anymore." She sighed, "You're not an idiot, Kylee. You loved a man and he wasn't good for you. It happens. It happens to all of us at one time or another, I think."

"To you?" It was hard to believe that beautiful, smart Lila could ever be so ensnared.

Lila gave a soft laugh and shook her head. "I am human, you know. I do make mistakes and in the man department, I've made some doozies. But this little conversation isn't about me. What happened today that makes you think you should leave? If you leave we can't have more of these girlfriend conversations..."

The squeeze of her hands was so reassuring and warm, but Kylee wasn't sure what she should say. She shook her head. "It's stupid and it involves Brett and I am not going to cause problems between you and a friend." Kylee went to strip her hands free but meeting Lila's gaze somehow made her leave them where they were.

"Tell me what happened. Did Brett make a pass or something, because I'll kill him if he did. He's got a long habit of being a ladies' man, but I thought—make that hoped—he'd turned over a new leaf."

Kylee told: about the viewing of the house and how Brett seemed to stand close; how he'd brushed her hair off her cheek, and about their drive and what he said. "And then he kissed my hand like he was some kind of ancient chivalrous knight and I just about lost it right there. I—I wasn't ready for it. I'm not ready for it and I don't know if I'll ever be ready for it after Kevin. I don't trust men anymore."

"It sounds more like you don't trust your judgment."

"Maybe." For some reason now was the time when the tears broke free. The silly things ran down her cheeks and her nose went all snotty. She palmed the tears away and sniffled until Lila grabbed a box of tissues and placed them on the table beside her. Kylee blew her nose. "How can I trust myself when I've made such bad decisions? I give men my heart and everything else and then chase after them when they don't want me. I've lost everything."

"There are those who say sometimes you have to sweep everything away to see new possibilities. Around here each spring some people will burn off last year's dead field grass because it allows the new green shoots to come in thicker and faster. Nature does the same thing with forest fires. It burns off the old growth, but it also incites dormant seeds to grow. The worst fires are always where there's the most old stuff to burn away."

Kylee blinked through the tears. "You mean I needed to lose everything to get to a place where I could realize the destructive pattern I was in. How did you ever get so wise? I mean we're the same age and all, and yet you seem to be able to cut through to the heart of things."

Lila shrugged and for the barest of instants seemed to look sadly away. "Let's just say that spending your teenage years in the spotlight can age you prematurely."

Kylee blew her nose on a tissue. "You are about the last thing I'd think of as prematurely aged." She waved her hand at the silliness of the idea, and the bracelet caught the light. "You know, Brett said the same thing you did—that maybe this darn bracelet was fitting for me because doors symbolize new beginnings. I told him they might also mean things ending. And just so you know, he couldn't figure out how to get it off, either."

Lila was silent for a moment, her gaze intent on Kylee's. "It sounds like Brett was trying to be a friend." Silence again and Kylee felt laid bare under Lila's knowing gaze. "You like him, don't you."

Oh crap. Was it that obvious? "I figure it's just physical attraction and the stupidness of my brain. It's a long time since I've been with a man."

"Uh huh."

Kylee sat back in her chair and this time Lila released the grip on her hands. "You sound like you don't believe me."

The barest of shrugs lifted Lila's bare shoulders. "Would you be so afraid if it was just physical attraction? And while you ponder that, think about this: Brett Main is the vintner for Elkhart Winery. He has far better things to do than waste an afternoon showing a woman around the back roads of Peachland."

"But you said he's a womanizer.... Exactly the kind I'd probably find attractive."

Lila shook her head and slid out of the nook. "No, I said he used to be womanizer. Not the same thing. No womanizer I know would have had you alone and only kissed your hand."

CHAPTER 10

BRETT SPRAWLED IN A WICKER CHAIR IN A CORNER of *This &
That* letting the store fans wash over him and tried to fathom
what had happened with Kylee. From his perspective things had
been going pretty good. He was pretty sure there was something
complimentary about them, he just needed to figure out what it
was. Being with Kylee would be just like pairing a good wine with
a special meal—if he could just figure her out. What the heck had
set her off?

The spotlights above *This & That's* displays had been
turned off so that natural light through the windows didn't
quite relieve the gloom. The room smelled of Chloe's incense
and patchouli. She sat behind the till with a small desk lamp
examining a group of creamy white stones—moonstones,
maybe, if he remembered anything from when she'd tried to
educate him about her woo-woo stuff. For some reason the
woman wanted to establish a healing center based on the use
of crystals and was gradually collecting the stones for her art.
A stone healing center. I mean, come on. Who believed in that
stuff?

The beaded curtain clacked and Brett gripped the chair arms
and pushed himself up to sitting, but it wasn't Kylee. Lila pushed
into the room and he slumped back. Was Kylee behind her? He

leapt to his feet and caught his sister raising a brow and nodding in his direction. What? So they figured they knew what was going on? Had Kylee said something? If so he wished they'd fill him in.

Maybe Lila was, the way she crossed her arms and faced him. He looked around the room, but couldn't avoid her hazel consideration. She'd looked just that formidable when he was seventeen and he'd tried to kiss her. She'd punched him in the nose. End of story. "So just what got into you this afternoon?" she asked.

"What got into me? What is this? First Chloe and now you..." He shook his head and blew a sigh up over his face. "Hell if I know. I can't even use the excuse that I think with my gonads. Kylee's nice. She's obviously been hurt. I guess I was trying to be gallant for a change." He scowled in Chloe's direction. "Look where it's got me. I feel like I'm in friggin' detention here."

Lila looked like she could barely swallow her smile as she leaned back against the counter. "You scare one of my friends and this is what happens. You scare her again and it gets worse."

"God save me." Brett looked heavenward, but shook his head again. "Like I said. I had no intention of scaring Kylee. I just took her for a drive after showing her the house. I admired the bracelet she wore and I complimented her about it. If it's any consolation it—it won't happen again."

Because maybe this girl was too much work? Who was he kidding? He was working with flipping Viognier grapes at the winery and they were a finicky old fashioned lot. It was a challenge to bring out the best of them. Maybe he was just drawn to the challenge of Kylee, to try to do the same.

"So you won't scare her. Good." Lila eyed him like a grade school teacher when he glanced toward the curtained doorway again. "Because I can't imagine how we'd make it work with her here and you scaring her every time you come to see Chloe. Now did you two come up with a rental price? I think Kylee's really interested."

Was that an actual smirk on her face?

He glanced at his sister but she seemed to be enjoying this far too much. They'd talked about Chloe's rental recommendation and it really wasn't good business, but on the other hand, it was the farthest he'd been able to get Chloe to even think about moving on from the house. Brett nodded.

But Lila seemed momentarily distracted by something beyond him, outside. She shivered and Brett turned to follow her gaze.

"What is it, Lila?" Kylee asked, the shivering curtain clacking softly behind her. She entered the room like a breath of fresh air and Brett realized that he felt like he'd been holding his breath.

Lila shook her head. "I don't know. But isn't that the police officer that came here about Moira Burns' murder? He seems to be watching the place. Or me." She rubbed her arms, gooseflesh had formed on them.

Brett peered through the window. There was a man. A cloud passed over the sun and the shadow settled over a dark brown sedan parked just down and across from *This & That*. A tall red-haired man leaned against the rear of the car and seemed to be looking in their direction. Brett frowned.

Lila shook her head. "He probably just forgot to ask something and came back. Nothing to worry about." She smiled down at Kylee. "So. What have you decided?"

Kylee hadn't yet looked in Brett's direction. In fact, she seemed to be avoiding acknowledging him at all. But at Lila's question she sent a brief smile in his general direction and then turned to Chloe. "I'd love to rent the house if I can afford it—that is if you and Brett will have me?"

At that she managed a glance in his direction and a lovely rose-colored blush flowed up her shoulders to her face. His mouth went dry and his knees went a little weak.

When Chloe remained mute, Brett finally jumped in. "Welll, Chloe and I talked it over and it really would help us out just knowing the place is taken care of and that someone is there in case a water main breaks or something shorts out. For insurance purposes etc. We sort of thought that if you'd pay the property taxes on the place and take over the gardening and upkeep, that would be enough."

"The taxes. How much are they?"

Brett glanced at Chloe again, as if asking again if she was sure. "About four thousand five hundred dollars a year given neither of us is eligible for the home owners grant."

"But... but that's less than four hundred dollars a month." Kylee was shaking her head. "The woman with the noisy suite over the bar was going to charge me twice that much. That's— that's highway robber—except I'm robbing you!"

Her concern and her excitement were so real and so charming he wanted to take her in his arms. Before he could make a fool of himself and really cause a problem, Chloe came around the counter and swung her arm over Kylee's shoulder. "Sweetie, you would be royally helping me out if you would be our renter because it will get this sod off my back about selling the house. Please say yes."

There was a look of such open longing on Kylee's face it was almost hard to watch her. Then she burst into tears and gave Chloe a big hug."Thank you! Oh, thank you!"

Then she hugged Lila. "And thank you for the job."

Kylee swung around to Brett. Stopped. Hesitated and then stepped up, stood on tiptoe and planted the lightest of kisses on his cheek. He inhaled her spring morning lavender scent and could almost get drunk on it—on her.

"Thank you—for being a friend," she said and met his gaze for a brief instant.

A friend was about the last thing his body wanted, but if that was what she needed, then he could go with that, too. For now.

When Kylee stepped back, Lila was gazing out the window again.

Down the street, the brown-clad man outside the brown sedan was still watching.

§

Something was happening and he wasn't sure what. The thing in Danny Forester's brain could sense it like a scent on the breeze that blew up the lake and placed small white crests on the glistening waves. The water was darkening with the afternoon and the deadening of the bright glare of sun was a relief to him. He didn't like the sun even though eons ago he'd been born in a place where the sun was like a hammer upon a man's head and could sear a man's skin in a delightfully short time. No, he preferred the darkness of the night or the cracks and crevasses of the earth. He'd dwelt there for a long time after taking refuge there after the untimely death of his first body. He hadn't realized for how long, nor how that cave had become a prison to him until the soldier stumbled in during what had turned out to be the Second World War. All that time and he'd lost the trail of the thing he had searched for the entire latter half of his original life. The bracelet. The most cursed of items in a most cursed world. He must reclaim both the bracelet and the curse he had infused in its metal. It was the only way he could reclaim his power and with that power nothing could withstand him. Not anymore.

Since he'd come back out into the world, he'd learned that those skillful in his kind of power had mostly passed away from this earth. Items of power were no longer known for what they truly were—to his advantage.

The body he wore inhaled deeply and he tasted the tang of silver and the dark-treacle sweetness of what these imbeciles around him would call magic. His magic. It called to him, like to like and he would reclaim it, before the curse could ever be undone by other means.

But not now. He'd wasted too much time following the little green car earlier, but it had not been for naught. No, he knew now who held the object he desired.

He checked the heavy diver's watch on this body's left wrist. No time. He'd been long enough in this body that if he stayed even a little longer, this would become his permanent host. Not a good idea given how long he had spent cultivating the man he called home. Time to go.

He would come back for the small blond woman another time.

CHAPTER 11

THE NEXT FEW DAYS SEEMED LIKE A BLUR TO KYLEE. At five thirty in the morning Kylee sat sipping freshly-brewed coffee on the broad front porch of the *This & That* enjoying the quiet before the day started. It was June and the committed joggers and dog walkers were already up and running or strolling down the promenade, pooches happily sniffing the breeze laden with the scents of fresh bread and cinnamon buns from the bakery down the block.

The lake was calm with barely a ripple and there wasn't a cloud in the sky. Across the lake, the rocky mountain slope retained glimmers of spring green, though the trees were mostly gone after the infamous Kelowna fire. Little Rattlesnake Island, the alleged home of the Ogopogo, the lake's version of Nessie, looked like just a lower lump of the same brown rock and low grass that would bake in the rising sun, as if the island and the mountain slope had become one. So far the air was still cool, but it was going to be a scorcher and would only get hotter as summer began.

Behind her, Lila was still asleep or else she was doing her yoga. Reggie's workshop was quiet and Chloe hadn't turned up from her apartment down the block yet. It gave Kylee a few moments of quiet to simply be.

When she'd driven up to Peachland she hadn't known what to expect, but certainly not this. At least not so quickly. A job that so far she loved. She was having fun with the customers and her sales from that first hectic day had continued over the last week until finally Chloe had relinquished control out front. She was back working on her stones and sorting through the ones that were best suited not as jewels, but as medicines. Chloe believed in crystal healing and while she loved working with the stones as jewelry, and was good at jewelry-making herself, what she really wanted was to begin consulting medicinally. She and Lila had even discussed using Lila's yoga room as consulting space. Kylee fingered the silver chain around her neck. It held a single crystal with glittering golden needles inside that Chloe had said was called rutilated quartz. It was supposed to help her find the truth about her negative thoughts. To either side of the crystal, were butter-yellow crystal beads that Chloe had told her was chrysoberyl and good for clear sight and positive thinking. If it really worked it would be great—not that she believed in this kind of thing, but it was thoughtful of Chloe to come up with the necklace to help her. More helpful than the darn bracelet that still stubbornly resisted all attempts to get it off.

Another sip of coffee and she admired it in the early morning sunshine. The light caught on the line of small doors and added to their already three-dimensional perfection. The little door with its grape leaves and tiny bunches of grapes seemed to almost glow; it was so compellingly complete she almost felt that if only her hands were small enough she could catch hold of the door handle and push it open, and that would be marvelous. When she thought of it, if was like something welled up inside her, like hope and happiness and a sense of place. As a child she might have imagined a world of incomparable delights beyond that doorway.

Silly, really, but she'd come to think that the darn bracelet was on her arm for a reason and it wasn't going to come off until she figured out what. Of course she kept *that* idea to herself because everyone would think she was nuts. Except maybe Chloe.

But Brett and Lila had seemed so sure that something good was out there waiting for her. She wasn't sure, but Peachland had certainly brought opportunities to her. The store. She had plans for it, too. On Friday she was going to reorganize the display, and she had a couple of ideas to run by Lila, too. Plus there was Canada Day coming up and they all had decided to be open that day to take advantage of the crowds of people for Peachland's big centennial celebration. But all that would come later.

Today was a bigger day in the whole scheme of things. After three days of spending her evenings cleaning the cobwebs out of the small house on the hill, today, on her one day off a week, she was moving in.

She had a *home*!

A shiver of anticipation ran up her back, even though she might be setting herself up for a fall again.

"Penny?"

She looked over her shoulder at Lila, slim as a reed still in yoga attire. She elbowed her way out the screen door with a large mug of coffee, a plate of toast, cheese slices, and a bowl-sized cup of fresh fruit in her hands. She settled into what Kylee had come to learn was her favorite chair—wicker of course, with a turquoise-flecked seat cushion. She smiled over at Kylee. "You had the most beatific smile."

Kylee sighed and shook her head. "It's almost too much. Like a dream. The job—which I love, by the way. The house. Friends. Making plans for Canada Day. In the space of a week you've given me the gift of a life, my friend. How can I ever repay you?"

She left out Brett, because she wasn't sure of what was happening in that department. After signing the rental agreement with Chloe and Brett, she hadn't expected to see him much, but he'd clearly been up to the house while she was at work at the store. Little things that he'd pointed out as needing fixing had been fixed when she showed up to clean and shift things around each evening. He probably didn't want to see her after the fuss she'd made over him kissing her hand.

"Okay, now you're frowning. Stop that. It puts lines on your face. You are supposed to be happy today because you have your own space. Now eat something, because you need to keep up your strength for the move."

"Yeah, right," Kylee laughed. "I have so much stuff to move and all. I might hurt myself carrying my pack to my car." Chortling, she picked up a ripe cherry off the plate and popped it in her mouth. The sweet dark juice was almost intoxicating and she closed her eyes. "I'd forgotten how much better fruit was up here where it grows. We never got fruit like this in Vancouver." She spat out the pit into a napkin and reached for a wedge of toast and a piece of cheddar.

"So do you want some help up at the house today? The shop's closed so I'm free."

Kylee thought about it a moment. Lila was wonderful, but today she really just wanted to settle in alone and feel herself in place. Finally she shook her head. "I think I've got things under control, but you could come up later and I'll make dinner if you like."

Lila chewed her toast, but then shook her head. "I think that's too much of an imposition on the day you move in. How about we take a rain check for later in the week?"

Relieved, Kylee agreed. She looked down at the bracelet again. "You know, we really need to do something about this. I know cutting it off is a last resort 'cause it shouldn't be damaged. Maybe you could take it out of my wages? I'm just terrified that I'm going to damage it in some way. When I was working on the house I wrapped a tensor bandage around it to keep it safe."

Lila reached over and caught her hand, pulling Kylee's wrist in front of her. "It really is a lovely piece, but I don't think it's cutting-off time just yet. So keep it and enjoy it in health. We'll figure it out eventually and in the meantime you can wear it and tell people it comes from the store. Advertising. Who doesn't need more? Chloe does it all the time with her necklaces and I do it with the rings." She held up her silver-laden hands. On her long fingers, even the heavy man-sized rings with their turquoise and amber and cat's eye stones looked spectacular.

Kylee finally nodded. "But if anything happens to it, I want to be responsible. Okay?"

"If anything happens to it, we'll see," Lila said with finality, but she was running her fingers over the bracelet. "I really have to wonder what its provenance is. It's clearly handmade, and it's the type of thing that's fashionable now, but something about it suggests it's very old, too. That doesn't make a lot of sense given the doorways look modern enough." She fingered the silver. "There's something about it. Something different in the silver."

An uncharacteristic shiver seemed to run through her and she released Kylee's hand as if it was hot. Then her eyes seemed to clear, but her gaze lingered on the bracelet. "Very strange indeed."

"So what have you got planned for today?" Kylee asked. "More sorting?"

Lila shook her head, her auburn curls a loose corona around her head as the low morning sun found its way onto the porch. She took a bite of toast and spoke around the mouthful. "Actually, I'm planning the next buying trips. We're getting low on some of our foreign inventory so I need to get back to Nepal and Israel and India and so on. That's not a trip I'll do on the spur of the moment. It takes some planning."

"Have you been to Morocco and Mauritania?" Kylee asked looking out at the water where a kayaker, clearly someone with experience, coasted by like a dragonfly on the water.

"Actually, no. I haven't been there. Would it be worth my while?" Lila's gaze had gone all business.

Kylee looked back at the water. "Well I saw some nice silverwork there and Mauritania has some of the most beautiful stuff I've seen. When I was in Senegal, Mauritanian vendors would try to sell necklaces and so on, on the beach and at the restaurants on Goree Island. There were Niger crosses and the like, but there were also filigreed silver beads that were the most beautiful thing I'd ever seen. I suppose Ghana and so on would be good for stuff, too."

Lila leaned back in her chair and looked thoughtfully out at the lake. "You've given me some food for thought."

Kylee glanced sideways at her friend. The sun caught Lila like a photographer's light, highlighting the beauty of the angle of her jaw, the arched brow, the lush thickness of her hair. And yet she was alone. Men should be flocking to her, and yet in the week Kylee had been here, there had been none and no mention of any. She'd heard some women say that they just didn't need a man in their life to be happy, but Kylee wasn't convinced she believed them. Of course, in her own instance, staying out of a relationship was the right thing to do. She didn't know how to do a relationship properly. Not to make it work, anyway.

Draining the last of her coffee, she stood. "Well, I should get going, I guess. I've already changed the bedding in the guest room and washed the sheets. They're in the drier." She leaned down and gave Lila a hug. She smelled lightly of sweat and spiced oranges. "Thank you so much for your hospitality. Now stay here and enjoy your day off and I'll just sneak out the back and get out of your hair."

She didn't quite get to sneak out the back because Lila forced a care package of new sheets and towels on her. A housewarming gift, she said. But she did avoid Reggie and Chloe, and set off in her little Civic chugging up the little brother hill to the hideously long one she had slid down to get to Peachland. She wound up through the houses and then turned into the driveway of her blue and white house, turned off the engine, climbed out and just stood there.

Hers. It was still early enough that there weren't any lawn mower noises or shouts of children from down in the housing development. No, the air was silent except for the chuff-chuff-chuff of the irrigation in the pasture up the road and the call of a crow or a raven in the pines on the hill. That and the wind blowing softly in the treetops and the maple leaves fluttering. She'd never heard such silence except maybe in Africa when she'd made a point of getting up to watch the sunrise before everyone else. Silence like this was a gift, almost holy, and she could feel it somehow seep into her and heal some of the places left broken by too many people and Kevin in particular.

Well Kevin was good and gone and a good thing, too. She'd at least figured that out this week. He hadn't treated her with respect and she hadn't treated herself with respect when she took that treatment from him. She deserved far better.

Like this house and this silence and this life she was living. She just needed to be careful she didn't give her heart too freely—to anything—because Chloe and Brett could decide to sell the house at any time.

Smile on her face, she did a little jig and headed for the house. She tugged her keys—*her keys*—out of her pocket and unlocked the door and stepped inside.

It was already different than the place she'd visited with Brett. One of the first things she'd done when she was cleaning was take down all the curtains for washing and wash all the windows besides. It let in the light and she'd decided not to put some of the curtains back up. Now she could close curtains on windows that opened onto the street and the driveway, but the windows that looked out onto the view would now forever be open. She'd shifted furniture around and taken the heavy lounger out of the living room. It gave the room a sense of space. Yesterday evening she'd stopped by the grocery store and had splurged on a bouquet of flowers as well as groceries. She'd found a blue glass vase under the kitchen sink and had set the flowers in the kitchen window. Now the whole room smelled of the sweetness of baby's breath and lily.

She smiled. This was home. Her home. Or she wanted it to be.

She took Lila's gift of bedding, washed the sheets and towels, then set them on the clothes line outside to flutter and waft in the sunshine to dry. She opened all the doors and windows to welcome in the breeze. She danced her way through reorganizing the kitchen and repapering the cupboard shelves as she went.

For a late lunch she had a small salad sitting out at the old picnic table—she'd have to paint it this summer because she could see herself using it a lot. With the shimmering lake view and the long strands of the willow falling around her, it was like she was in a different world. Kevin and Africa and all of that old stuff could just be a bad dream. She was so over it.

Yes, she was. She was over Kevin and his treachery and everything.

She was!

The leaden weight didn't sit in her gut anymore when she thought of him. Looking out at the view she felt like *going there* and better still, *being there.* And even better still, being *here*, now. Like an emotional limb had somehow healed in the few days she'd been here.

She lifted her fork into the air. "Thank you, Lila and Chloe and Reggie and everyone." And Brett. Don't forget Brett.

Like she could forget him and that kiss on the back of her hand. It had been soft and possessive and almost reverential. Of course that was probably just her attaching emotions to something that weren't there. She had a bad habit of that and she wasn't going to let it happen again. Nope. She was going to keep it real and keep control of her too-quick-to-fall-in-love heart.

That decided, she took her dishes inside and came back out to check her laundry. The sheets were dry and smelled of sunshine and fresh hay. She took them down and bundled them straight up to the bedroom. She was just putting the bottom fitted sheet in place when someone knocked on the open door downstairs.

"Hello? Anyone home?"

A voice she didn't know. She ran down the stairs to face a spectacled, narrow-shouldered young man with thinning blond hair and wearing a canary yellow polo shirt and jeans.

"Can I help you?" Kylee asked.

"I'm Tom Beaton from just up the road. Me and my wife thought we'd drop by to be neighborly. We brought you this." He handed her a foil pan wafting the heavenly odor of fresh brownies and—peanut butter. He stepped to one side to reveal a dark-haired woman in bright blue capris and white blouse standing with a baby stroller at the base of the stairs.

"Hi," she waved down at the woman. "I'm Kylee. Kylee Jensen. Are those brownies for me?"

"I'm Mary and this is Marica." A tow-headed toddler in cute frilled coveralls and a pink t-shirt waved her arms happily. "And yes, the brownies are for you. They're chocolate and peanut butter. I hope you like them."

Kylee accepted the foil baking dish and inhaled. Closed her eyes. "Anything with chocolate and peanut butter has my name written all over it. Would you like to come in? See the place?"

Tom shook his head. "Thanks, but we'll take a rain check. We've got errands in Kelowna, but we thought we'd be neighborly. If you need anything, we're in the first blue house down the hill in the subdivision." He headed down the stairs and Kylee followed after him to meet Mary and admire Marica.

"She's adorable," Kylee said, looking up from the little girl after playing peek-a-boo.

"Thanks," Mary said. "If only she was always like this. She can be a little hellion at times. The terrible twos they call 'em. Feel free to drop in for tea any time. Tom's away at work a lot and it would be nice to have some adult company from time to time."

"Deal." Kylee stuck out her hand and walked them to the edge of the property to watch them head down the hill toward the housing development and their house. She returned inside and forced herself away from the heavenly smelling brownies and back to the bedroom. By the time the bed was made, the towels were dry and she decided to have a long bath in the lovely big tub to wash away the grime from this morning. Then she just might while away the afternoon reading.

It was such a decadent idea she almost felt guilty as she ran the water, lit some candles, doffed her clothes, and climbed into a bubble bath courtesy of a little vial of lavender-scented bath salts she'd found tucked in the back of the bathroom cupboard.

Heaven. She stared up through the skylight at the jumble of clouds in the blue sky. She really had found a bit of heaven and she was going to hold onto this. All she had to do was do the best darn job for Lila and keep the house in good shape. It should be easy. She ran her fingers through the bubbles and admired the bracelet still on her arm, but now covered in water droplets that caught the candlelight like jewels. The grape arbor of the little door she had come to think of as hers actually seemed to have grown, the grapes hanging heavy around the door. Amazing what different lighting can do. But the lavender warmth eased away any tension she might have had. She closed her eyes and let herself drift.

A thump downstairs brought her upright in the tub, water sloshing around her. Another thump and then the distant sound of heavy footsteps. They were in her kitchen and walking through to the living room.

What the hell? She'd closed and locked the doors—at least she thought she had. Feeling way too vulnerable and incredibly stupid, she stood, her feet squeaking on the tub enamel. Below her, the footsteps stopped. Had they heard her? Were they coming for her?

She hurriedly wrapped one of the freshly laundered towels around her and silently padded out into the bedroom. So far there was no sound from the stairs. She grabbed a clean pair of underwear and bra and pulled on her dress—the quickest thing she had—pulled on tennis shoes and went to the bedroom door to listen.

No sound came from downstairs, though she could hear the breeze and the distant sounds of traffic through the windows behind her.

Silently, she eased down the stairs, listening the whole time. No sounds at all except the usual creaks of an old house settling. Was whoever it was, still here and hiding?

She made it to the base of the stairs and into the hallway to the main part of the house. She peered in the TV room where she'd stashed the heavy chair from the living room. Empty except for the furniture. Cautiously, she moved down the hall to the kitchen and living room, her heart beating so hard and fast she was sure it echoed in the silent house. Both empty. The bathroom? She checked. No one.

She checked the doors. Both still locked. All the little hairs on her neck and arms stood on end as if a cold wind ran over her still damp skin.

She stood there, in front of the door from the kitchen, not knowing what to do. The sun-filled room was ripe with the scent of the brownies, but at the moment the smell turned her stomach. That was when she noticed it.

A single slip of white paper sitting in the middle of the kitchen counter.

She went to it, but did not touch.

GIVE IT BACK, it read.

Kylee shivered. In a rush, she picked up the note and ran outside to the edge of the yard overlooking the lake. There, her legs gave and she sank onto the grass in the sun because she needed to get warm. Heck, she could be on the surface of the sun and she *still* wouldn't be warm, the way she was shaking. Someone had been in her house. Someone had left her a warning and she didn't know who or why or even what they were referring to.

She hadn't taken anything that didn't belong to her. Her hands ran up and down her frozen arms, but it didn't help anymore than the sun did. Her hand grazed the still-damp bracelet. "And I didn't steal you, either. I've offered to buy you. You're simply borrowed until you can show me how to get you unclasped."

And boy-o-boy she was going crazy now. She would have said she was going crazy about the sound of the footsteps, too, but the note proved someone had been inside her house *while she was naked and alone in the bath.*

It kept playing over and over in her mind. What if he'd come upstairs. He could have killed her and no one would have known. Maybe this was all a mistake. Maybe she should have stayed with Lila. Or taken the noisy apartment. The little house suddenly seemed so alone and isolated, even though there were houses around her. They just didn't press in cheek to jowl like they did in Vancouver.

The sound of tires on gravel and a car engine turned her around. Green sports car. Oh no. Not Brett. Not now. And yet he was the most welcome sight in the world with his tousled brown hair and wearing a cream polo that set off his strong tanned arms.

Still freezing she scrambled up to her feet and brushed her hair back from her face. Found a smile and strode forward trying to find normal in her gait. She couldn't let Brett see that something had happened.

§

"Hey, star renter. Enjoying your view?" Brett called as he climbed out of his car with his brightly-bowed bottle of wine and started toward the small figure sitting at the edge of the verdant green yard. While he'd avoided her the past few days to give her some space, today he couldn't find an excuse to stay away. He would simply visit as a landlord checking that everything was okay. And to celebrate. As a friend.

And if you believe that, Main, well...

But against the blue view of the lake and the late afternoon sky, even in the bright floral sundress, the way Kylee stumbled to her feet she almost looked like she might collapse. Then she caught herself, squared her shoulders and turned toward him. That was Kylee. Strong.

Strong enough that she'd try her best to look normal when something was clearly wrong. The bright sunlight even at five o'clock didn't add an ounce of color to her ashen face. The breeze through the willow shifted her hair like fallen leaves. Her blue eyes were huge and—frightened? What the hell—this was supposed to be a day to drink wine with friends and celebrate. He lengthened his stride and met her.

"Kylee? What's wrong? You look like you've seen a ghost. Or something." He glanced at the gleaming white and blue house, praying she wasn't going to say the damned thing was haunted. Chloe would have a heyday.

But Kylee just looked up at him and shook her head. She handed him a piece of paper she held crumpled in her fist and watched as he unfolded it. Read. Frowned.

"What's this?"

"A note I found on the counter." Her voice was so small and shaky he was surprised she was standing, so he caught her elbow and guided her to the picnic table, the trailing branches of the willow hanging around them like a curtain. He sure as heck wasn't taking her to the house given she kept glancing at it with suspicion. She sat hunched over, hugging herself as if trying to keep warm in the eighty plus degree weather.

Absently, he set his bottle down, then seated himself across from her. Her hands, when he caught them, were ice cold, and he cradled them inside his to hopefully warm them. "Tell me what happened."

She blinked and it was like his question actually brought her back to herself. She took a deep breath and nodded. "Everything was going great. I had everything done—bed made, towels laundered and hung, I even got the kitchen reorganized and met some nice neighbors—the Beatons—a young couple and their child."

She smiled and that was a good sign. "I had lunch out here and thought it would be such a nice place to have everyone over for dinner some time." She looked up at him and he nodded encouragement.

"I thought I'd have a bath and wash the dust off and christen that lovely bathtub, then relax a bit before dinner. So there I am relaxing in the tub when I hear someone moving downstairs. A man, judging by the heavy footsteps. So I grabbed some clothes and came downstairs, but no one was there, only this was."

Somewhere in telling her story her hands had turned in his and strong slim fingers had grasped his and held on—hard. He squeezed back.

"You're sure you had all the doors locked?"

She nodded, "I closed them all before I went up for my bath. They were still locked when I came downstairs."

But maybe, just maybe, she hadn't locked them to begin with and whoever it was had locked the door as he left. Regardless, the issue was that Kylee was clearly spooked. The footsteps in the house were bad enough, but the note...

"What's this talking about?" He tapped his finger on the note that sat on the table between them.

"I don't know. I haven't got anything, Brett. Nothing at all except this stupid dress, and the shorts and the t-shirts you saw. And the car. That's it. I lost everything last year."

She was shivering even though the late afternoon air made him sweat. The wine bottle beside him was sweating, too. She didn't deserve this. No one did, but Kylee especially. He looked up at the house bathed in the warm light of the slowly westering sun.

"Well this isn't right. The house was supposed to help you get on your feet, not scare you to death. Come on. Let's check the place out and make sure everything's safe."

Standing, he came around the table and helped her up, then draped an arm protectively around her as they walked to the house—to warm her up, that was all. Her body was tense under his touch and small shivers ran through her. He'd bet money it wasn't him causing the reaction though. It was the thought of entering the house again. The footsteps and the note had clearly terrified her. They climbed the porch together and went into the kitchen.

Today, the place looked sunny and lived in with newly-washed dishes drying in the rack in the double sink and a bouquet of flowers in a blue vase by the window. The counters and walls were all scrubbed of cobwebs and the tile floor positively gleamed. His mother would be pleased.

"The place looks great," he said. "So where was the note?"

She pointed, her gaze trailing over the pleasant room as if she didn't trust it. He went to the counter, but there was nothing to see, just as the note gave no hint what it was talking about. *Give it back*, meant nothing.

"I—I think it might mean the bracelet, but I can't figure out why and I don't know why I think that. Strange, right? I mean I haven't stolen it. Lila knows I've got it. I'm only wearing it until we figure out how to get it off." Her big blue eyes were haunted.

"Well, if it's the bracelet—and it's a huge leap to believe it—Lila will need to know. But in the meantime let's check the house out, okay?"

She nodded and he caught her still-frozen hand and led her into the living room—still his parents' and yet with subtle changes that made the place different and definitely Kylee's. Like he could breathe in the room and what he smelled was her fine scent of lavender and strawberries, like heady fruit wine.

Next was down the hall checking the guest bathroom and the TV room, but there was nothing except furniture she'd stowed from the living room. He made a mental note to offer to shift some of the large stuff out to the garage. Or maybe Chloe would let them sell it or give it to Goodwill. He hesitated at the stairs that led to her bedroom, but she crowded behind him, urging him on. He climbed to the second floor and the single large bedroom, because someone, if they had been in the house, could have come up here while Kylee was outside.

He left her by the newly-made bed and checked out the large walk-in closet in the corner of the room. Nothing except a pitiful couple of t-shirts and a pair of worn athletic sandals in the corner, just like she'd said. The woman really did have nothing and that was a crying shame because Kylee Jensen deserved all manner of beautiful things.

Last was the bathroom. Steam escaped out the door when he opened it, leaving behind a single candle guttering, nearly fully melted away. The tub of water had cooled and he flipped the drain open. Nothing moved. Nothing here.

"All clear," he said returning to her.

He caught her by her shoulders and ran his hands up and down her frigid arms. "I'm so sorry this happened, but it seems whoever it was is gone now." It seemed so natural he almost didn't realize what he'd done until he'd already pulled her into him and wrapped his arms around her.

To warm her up. To comfort her. That was all.

She felt small and yet vibrantly alive and he wanted to make sure she stayed that way.

"Come on," he said and set her away before she could think he was coming on to her—even if he wanted to. "I think I know a woman who could use a drink and I just happened to bring a bottle."

He led her downstairs and back to the kitchen, then went out briefly to retrieve the bottle from the picnic table. He found the corkscrew just where his mother had left it and uncorked the bottle. The crisp grapefruit and pear notes of Pino Gris met his nostrils. Just the way they should. He glanced back at Kylee who stood pale faced by the door to the living room. "Wine glasses are in the cupboard over there—or they used to be."

She seemed to come to life then and brought two goblets to him. He poured, checked the pale gold that sunlight would turn saffron, then swirled the wine in his goblet. The aroma broadened to include hints of almond and mineral. Tasted the clear pear and apple notes and savored as the almond settled on the back of his tongue. He knew he was showing off for Kylee, but couldn't help it. "Good," he pronounced. "Try it."

She did, and nodded as she picked up the bottle. "Elkhart Vineyard, Peachland. I didn't know there were wineries here."

"There's a few actually. You're going to hear plenty about Elkhart. We've got some great varietals, like this one. Pino Gris's popular, but it doesn't get a lot of respect. I plan to change that with wines like this."

"You work there?" She tasted the wine again. "It really is good." There was even color coming back into her cheeks, so the trick must be to get her thinking about something—anything other than what had happened this afternoon.

"Don't act so surprised. I'm the vintner."

"Really?"

He feigned mortal wounding. "I'm beginning to be hurt by your apparent disbelief that I could make something so tasty. Or maybe that I could be someone so responsible?"

That finally brought a smile to her face, and the tension in her shoulders seemed to ease a little. She sipped again. "Well...maybe. There is a certain boyish charm to the wine. A little overconfident, maybe, but verrry tasty."

Holy shit, she was flirting with him and for a moment his pulse beat a little faster.

CHAPTER 12

HAD SHE REALLY JUST SAID THAT? IT HAD SIMPLY slipped out, a natural teasing response to his pride in his wine, because it *was* good. Clear and crisp and full of Okanagan fruit and just dry enough it went perfectly with the sunny afternoon.

But Brett Main stood in her sun-filled kitchen looking just a tad too manly and protective and maybe just a little bit stunned, with his strong jaw and his green eyes watching her and the muscle cording his forearms—from wrestling wine barrels no doubt. Now there was a lovely thought—Brett shirtless and muscled and glowing with sweat. *Oh my.*

And yet he had swirled the wine and sipped and savored with a confident—not delicate—sensitivity that made her wonder if he was that way about other things in his life. Say relationships?

Careful, girl. You're doing it again.

The careful, yet confident way he held the wine glass and the way his eyes seemed to swallow her like moss-green shadowy pools all left her pretty much feeling breathless and like a fool. But she couldn't take her comment back. It hung out there. She shrugged and gently boxed his shoulder.

"Gottcha." Then turned away toward the counter. She checked her watch. "Wow. Look at the time. Listen, in thanks for rescuing me and showing me I was being silly worrying, how about I make you dinner?" She flashed a glance at him. He still silently watched her and she could feel the heat of his smoldering gaze on her skin.

She pulled some of her meager supplies from the fridge—fresh pasta—and fresh tomatoes from a bowl on the counter. "How about some pasta?"

Not waiting for a response, she had to eat sometime, she filled a pot with water, added a tiny bit of olive oil and set the water to boil. She grabbed a knife from the knife block and a cutting board, but before she could start slicing the tomatoes, she felt movement behind her, Brett's breath on her shoulder.

"There's some fresh parsley at the base of the porch, at least there always was. Why don't you go get us some and I'll chop these," he said softly, almost like a purr in her ear.

For a moment, just a moment, she imagined his arms coming around her and leaning back against him. Then she nodded. "Sure. Don't cut yourself. Your mom kept her knives sharp."

"So do I," he said and began to expertly slice the tomatoes.

Kylee scooted down the porch stairs checking the yard for any strangers, but there was no one there. She had to have imagined it all, and yet the note was proof she hadn't. One hand nervously twisted the bracelet on her arm. A tingle ran up her arm that reminded her of Brett's gaze on her skin, but then she found the parsley and cut a handful. In the midst of weeds, there was also what looked like rosemary and sage, and was that a volunteer of dill? She'd have to weed this tomorrow evening and see what she had. Maybe plant some basil. And there was that garden plot if she got ambitious, even though it was late in the year for planting.

Carrying the herbs, she returned to the kitchen and found Brett sautéing onion and garlic in olive oil. Just what she'd planned to do. He'd found his way around her reorganized kitchen. "I can take it from here," she said.

He glanced back at her. "No you can't. You've worked on the house all day. Now's the time to sit and sip wine and enjoy it. Let me do the cooking." He grinned and waggled his eye brows.

She *could* feel a little resentment at his intrusion, but frankly she just felt grateful that someone was here and she wasn't alone, still sitting out in the yard feeling so cold and afraid she hadn't known what to do. She slid into a spindle-backed oak chair at the kitchen table. Brett's arrival had at least got her moving again. And into the house. It felt like a lovely welcoming place again, especially with the heavenly scent of fresh tomato sauce cooking, and the fresh bouquet of the wine. She sipped a little more and it felt like she was sipping the distilled sunshine of this Okanagan town. It flowed too smoothly down her throat and she suddenly noticed that she was smiling.

Maybe it was just wine, or the homey feeling of the scene, or maybe it was the way Brett had a tea towel tucked into his jeans as he expertly added pasta to the water, stirred the bubbling tomato sauce and then grabbed his wine glass. He glanced out the window and then turned to her. He looked good enough to eat, with the sun catching in strands of gold in his thick brown hair, and catching at the angles of his face. He looked like he had something he wanted to say.

"You should set the table."

So not what she'd expected, but she scrambled up. "Okay."

"I expect for five. Lila just drove up and I suspect the others are with her."

Dismayed, she turned toward the door. "But we need more food. There isn't enough for five. We need to chop up the rest of the tomatoes and throw on the rest of the pasta."

Brett caught her shoulders again and turned her toward him. "Would you quit looking for the disaster in everything in your personal life? Knowing my sister and Lila, I'm laying money we probably didn't need to cook the pasta at all." His green gaze eased her silly panic and she nodded. He gave her a soft smile and released her, the warmth of his touch still on her arms. "Now go on, welcome your friends into your new home."

He was right. She nodded and went to the door to greet the voices and the sound of feet on the hollow stairs.

Lila was first. She wore white cotton shorts and a white sleeveless t-shirt with an abstract black cat swirling up the front. It showed off her broad shoulders and the long swimmer's muscles of her arms and legs. She handed Kylee a freshly baked loaf of artisanal bread wrapped in a fine cotton t-towel.

"Welcome," Kylee said and welcomed Lila's embrace.

"Bread, so that your home will always have food on the table." She sniffed the air, "Something smells heavenly." She caught sight of Brett. "Well, look who's here. Chloe, your brother's here." She gave a little chuckle.

Reggie came on her heels, bearing a bouquet of African daisies and lilies in a hand-formed pottery vase that had bits of metal in intricate designs down the sides. "A new home should have flowers and beautiful things. May this be just the first of many." Another hug and a peck on the cheek from the black-haired woman. So not like Claudia. She wore a short black skirt that showed off long tanned legs and a knitted sleeveless black top that showed off the twinned tattoos on her arms.

Chloe crowded up from behind. The cascade of necklaces she wore tinkled as she moved. She removed one long chain with a pale pink crystal set in silver. This she placed around Kylee's neck.

"For balance between logic and feelings. And this..." she produced a bottle of red wine—also Elkhart. "This is so your home will forever have joy and laughter." She glanced over at Brett and gave a cat that ate the canary smile. "Howdy, brother."

With her hands on her hips she gave the room a once-over and nodded. "I like what you've done with the place. It feels alive again. And loved."

Reggie had disappeared back out the door and this time reappeared up the stairs bearing a large casserole. She set it on the table, while Lila and Chloe busied themselves setting the table with bright red cloth placemats and napkins, cutlery, and salt and pepper. From the fridge they pulled butter, and from the counter they claimed the cutting board—washed and dried—and a bread knife and five plates. Brett drained the pasta, then poured the tomato sauce over it and tossed, then put the lot in a large bowl on the table.

Brett's wine was poured all around. The bottle of red was cracked and everyone slid into chairs at the table, Brett pressed in between Kylee and Chloe so Kylee's knee brushed his occasionally to send a little zing through her each time. Then the casserole top was opened to reveal a rich fettuccini vongole—pasta with a rich clams in cream sauce.

"It's my mom's recipe. She was Italian," Reggie said as she used pasta forks to toss and serve everyone heaps of the delicious smelling food. Brett added his pasta with tomato sauce to each plate.

Kylee couldn't decide which was better. Reggie's clam sauce was a rich delight counterpointed by a freshly grated goat's cheese. Brett's, on the other hand, was like tasting a bite of sunshine with the fresh tomatoes and herbs right out of the garden. She overate from both dishes, surprised she had an appetite after the day she'd had.

A little shiver of ill-ease ran through her and for a moment she felt alone amongst the laughing voices of her friends. But Brett was watching her. Lila and Chloe both caught her mood for they both stopped talking.

"What's the matter, Kylee," Chloe asked, Lila nodding beside her.

Kylee shook her head, "It's nothing. Really. Just a brief disturbing thought that I shouldn't be having."

She smiled and took another sip of Reggie's red wine, but Brett's gaze was narrowed and neither Chloe nor Lila had gone back to their conversation.

"I think you should tell them, Kylee. Especially given you think the bracelet might be involved." Brett nodded and caught her hand under the table. Squeezed.

All eyes at the table turned toward her and she shook her head and sighed. "At this moment it all seems pretty stupid, but I had a little scare today." She told them what happened, shrugged. "So it was probably all my imagination, right?"

Brett, the betraying bastard, rolled his eyes. "I arrived up here around five p.m. with a bottle of wine to celebrate and I found her sitting out on the lawn looking like she'd seen a ghost. She had this in her hands." He fished the note out of a pocket to flatten it on the table and hand it around. "Doesn't look too much like imagination to me."

She elbowed him in the side. "I don't need you to tell my story, Mister. I was frightened, not helpless."

But Reggie, Lila, and Chloe were leaning over the note like the three witches.

"I suppose this paper has been handled to death by you two and now us, there's no hope at all of getting a fingerprint," Lila said. "Her hazel gaze came up and met Kylee's. "And you can't think of anything it could refer to except the bracelet?"

Kylee shook her head. "Nada. You saw what I brought with me. That's everything."

"Let's see that bracelet again," Reggie asked.

Dishes were stacked and the nearly empty casserole dish and bowl pushed aside so Kylee could lay her arm on the table. In the white light from the frosted hanging light fixture over the table, the silver gleamed whitely, its tarnish only emphasizing the ornately detailed work. Each tiny door looked like it really could open if one just had hands small enough to work the clasps.

Reggie leaned in close, studying the bracelet. "I thought before that the bracelet looked old, but maybe I should revise that estimation. The sheen is all wrong for modern era silver." She glanced up from under her bangs. "You see pure silver is too soft for jewelry and so it's always alloyed with something. Usually it's copper. Sterling silver is an alloy of 92.5% silver and 7.5% copper. For something to be marked silver today, it has to be 90% silver at least. Sometimes modern sterling silver is coated with ninety-nine percent pure silver to give it the really brilliant silver sheen. This almost looks like pure silver, but I can't believe a bracelet would last so long if it were pure. It would show marks and twisting everywhere."

She ran a fingernail over an edge of one of the doors, but it left no mark that Kylee could see. Kylee still wanted to tear her wrist away.

"That just doesn't make sense," Reggie said. "I wish you could get the darn thing off so I could test it. The finish almost looks brushed, like it's been out in the elements or something. "

Kylee shook her head. "Believe me, I tried to take it off all afternoon. I tried twisting it and everything I could think of with the key and the lock. At times it was like I was just about to get it—I could actually see it about to fit through the hole and then suddenly the darn key would slip and the chance would be gone. I swear the thing *wants* to be on my arm." She shook her wrist in disgust. "At least it's nice looking, but I'd like to get it off."

All through the conversation, Lila had been looking at the note. "I don't really think the provenance of the bracelet is our chief concern. We don't even know if it has anything to do with the note. It could be some idiot just trying to freak Kylee out. A kid maybe. There's lots of bored ones in Peachland during the summer."

She was right. It could be just that. Maybe kids had seen her moving in and had come in a door she'd accidentally left open. It wasn't a nice thought that someone could be so cruel, but... "There's actually nothing threatening in the note. It's just the way it was delivered. What do you think, Chloe?"

Because so far Chloe hadn't said a word. She had sat back and was watching everyone, fine little worry lines between her brows, her silver chains and stone pendants softly clicking when she moved.

"I don't really know what to say. I understand why you were freaked out. I'd understand why, if you decided not to stay in the house."

Kylee shook her head. "No way. I'm staying. I made up my mind while I was sitting on the lawn. If I could last through Africa, I can last through anything. I've been moving around too long, chasing... things." She glanced at Brett. "It's time I stayed put."

It was true, too. Maybe it was being surrounded by friends, or stranger things have happened, maybe it was Chloe's healing stones, but she felt strong enough to do just about anything. She might have been here only a week, but she wasn't going to let anyone push her around or go chasing after someone who wasn't good for her again. Thinking about Africa, now, just left her angry at herself that she'd let Kevin ruin her trip. She hardly remembered half of what she'd seen and that was a crying shame.

She grinned when she saw the doubt on Chloe's face. "Really. I'm sure."

"Wellll, okay," Chloe said. "But it you change your mind, you have to say something."

"Of course."

Brett's warm hand enveloped hers on the table and she felt a flush of heat run up her shoulders to her face.

"Promise?" he asked.

"Of course." She yanked her hand away, but the damage was already done. Chloe had that darn knowing look and Lila and Reggie were pushing themselves back from the table.

"We should help Kylee with the dishes and then get going. The shop's open tomorrow," Lila said.

"I can take care of the dishes," Kylee said. "There's a dishwasher, remember? You guys head out. It's only fair when I didn't make dinner."

They still helped clear the table and made sure the remains of dinner were put away in Kylee's fridge before Lila, Chloe, and Reggie headed out.

"Tomorrow bring the bracelet around to the shop and I'll take a scraping to send in for analysis," Reggie said.

It was only after they'd gone that Kylee realized that Lila had taken the note. And that Brett was standing close behind her.

§

The crunch of gravel as Lila's car backed out of the driveway, and then there was only the insect sounds of evening through the open kitchen door. The light breeze played with the ends of Kylee's blond hair as she stood framed in the doorway. Outside, the sun had fallen and the sky was streaked pink. The mountain across the lake would be pink, too. It always was at this time of day.

Blushed pink like Kylee's cheeks. Or like her lips. He stepped up closer to her and inhaled her soft scent of lavender and strawberries, heady as the best of wines, and was aware when she stiffened.

Lightly he placed his hands on her shoulders. "Let's leave the dishes a moment and enjoy the evening."

He eased her out the doorway and down the stairs to the yard, then walked beside her out toward where the lawn fell away into the side hill of Ponderosa pine and poplar and sage, in undulating folds down to the lakeshore. The scrub grass on the hillside was gradually fading from green into brown, and white and purple wildflowers bloomed amid the sage. The air smelled of them and Kylee's sweet scent.

"This was always my favorite part of the day. I think it was my parents' favorite, too. Maybe all of us actually. The heat gradually fades away, the breeze off the lake dries the sweat on your neck, and all the buzzing motorboats and jet skis have gone away for the night. It was always a time of peace and conversations."

He scanned the lake for Ogopogo just as he always had as a kid, even though he knew it was illogical. A ripple of waves formed a dark ridge in the water. "Look. There. Ogopogo likes the evening, too."

He leaned down beside Kylee and guided her view with an extended arm. "Out near Rattlesnake Island, see?"

"That looks like just a ripple of waves."

"Nah. It's the monster cutting through them."

She half turned to look at him, her face with those incredible blue eyes and that so-soft mouth far too temptingly close to his. By the way her gaze skittered over his face, she felt it too—the tightness in his chest and leg muscles. The heat.

She swallowed. "I thought you were all Mr. Logic and Practicality—not someone who believes in sea monsters."

He grinned and the moment faded away. He wanted it back, damn it. "What can I say? I have my moments of whimsy. I believe in sea—er, lake monsters when I want to. We can all use a little magic in our lives from time to time." Like the fact she'd come strolling into Peachland right when he hadn't even realized he was looking for something more, something different. Her, or at least it could be her.

But Kylee shivered and hugged herself.

"What is it," he said softly, knowing he was taking a chance by once more lightly rubbing warmth into her arms. "You've disappeared again. Or at least your smile has."

"I'm just thinking about today and those footsteps in the house. They were like magic, too, the way they were suddenly there, but no magic that I want to know about."

"Well then we'll just have to find a different kind of magic to take your memory off that, won't we?"

Easing around her, he lightly held her shoulders and leaned down to kiss her.

Soft, was his first thought. Her incredibly soft lips molded to his; at first tense, and then yielding. Her entire body went tense like the deer he often startled in the vineyards when he went tramping in the early morning. She tasted of clam and tomatoes and good Okanagan wine. He slid his mouth over to her ear.

"Remember, this is all for a good purpose. We're making new magic here."

He felt the soft exhalation of breath around a smile, and he pulled back, to smooth her pale hair back from her lovely face. His thumb traced her lips. "If you don't want me to do this, you can say so."

Her blue gaze held his as if searching. Then she looked away and swallowed. He almost thought it was over, until a smile bloomed across her features.

"I want to believe in magic. But any I've met has always blown up black in my face," she said almost shyly.

A plea not to hurt her. He gathered her in his arms and she felt small, and delicate and yet also strong. She relaxed against him, her head fitting just under his chin.

"If it's any comfort I'm too much of a realist to let black magic in." He leaned down and kissed her hair, tilted her head back and kissed her again. This time she turned into him and her arms came around him just like they were meant to.

§

Aargh! Just what she was doing, she wasn't sure. The night was cool on Kylee's skin that had suddenly become too hot, by far. The sky overhead had dimmed and shadows filled the yard and the angles of Brett's face as he loomed large in front of her, warm and alive. A place of shelter for her just as the distant lake provided shelter for the mythical Ogopogo.

Brett's arms felt so strong around her, as if nothing bad could ever get to her, here. As long as he wanted her. That was the thing, wasn't it—what made her hesitate. Kevin had wanted her, too, at first. He'd also moved on when someone younger and more vibrant came along. And Brett did have an admitted history with women, even if Lila said he wasn't like that anymore.

She looked up to try to read his intentions, but his green eyes were faded black and unfathomable by the coming night. Trust him? Her heart was just barely starting to feel whole after Kevin.

"I'm safe," he whispered as if he knew what she was thinking. He leaned in to kiss her once more and her legs wobbled at the heat that surged up through her and seemed to settle in her core and—the bracelet that burned with an intense, but pleasurable heat. He tasted of red wine and made her think of oaken casks and all the treasures they contained. If the man made wine like he kissed he was going to make a million. Heck, the man could kiss her right onto her back right here and now, and that was a danger because her heart just couldn't take what came after. She wasn't ready even though kissing Brett certainly made her reconsider swearing off men. Oh yeah.

She pulled back and got her arms between them. Looked up at him. "It's late and I have work tomorrow as you probably do, too."

Across the yard, light spilled out the kitchen window. "I've still got a mess of dishes to do."

"They aren't going to wash themselves, are they? Come on." His fingers twined through hers, he led her across the lawn and into the house. He sighed as he scanned the mess in the kitchen. "I was sort of hoping house elves would have dealt with this."

She cocked a brow at him. "My, you really have decided to believe in magic tonight, but where I come from dishes get done with elbow grease."

Together they cleaned up the kitchen, Brett clearing dishes while Kylee rinsed and placed them in the dishwasher. When the stove top was scrubbed clean and the counter shiny again, she turned to him and found him waiting for her.

"All done and I should leave you to get some sleep." He leaned down and touched his forehead to hers. "Just so you know, Ms. Kylee Jensen, I intend to be back. Probably frequently."

"Checking on your property, I'm sure," she smart mouthed.

His lips grazed down her cheek to her lips again and she shivered in his hold. Then he was gone, stepping out into the cool night air on the porch. He turned back to her there. "You keep the porch light on and lock everything up. I'm going to go around the house and check all the doors and windows."

She swallowed, all her nervousness about the afternoon swooping in on her again. She almost asked him to stay so she didn't have to be alone, but that wasn't the right thing to do. Not with a heart as vulnerable as hers was.

"Thanks," she said and closed and locked the door after him.

She turned out the light in the kitchen, but didn't go upstairs. Instead she stood there listening to the soft jiggling of each door and window and eventually the vroom of his car engine. She shouldn't have let him go.

CHAPTER 13

FOR KYLEE, THE NEXT WEEK AND A HALF WAS A madhouse at work. Apparently the woman Kylee had helped that very first day had told all her well-heeled friends about the store. Groups of friends on holiday from Vancouver were making a point to insert *This & That* into their itinerary. All this while Lila had scheduled meetings out of town and Reggie was tied up with jewelry design. Chloe was there, but Kylee ended up having to take over more and more of the tasks, simply because there was too much to do. After three days Kylee was opening up because she was a morning person who reveled in the quiet, and Chloe stayed late and put the store to bed every night.

It was almost lunch time on another beautiful Okanagan day when Brett showed up at *This & That*. The last of the morning customers had left carrying their small white bags with silver *This & That* logo of a silver sea serpent devouring his tail in a perfect wavy ring.

"I've been thinking about Canada Day," Kylee said. "The house is set up perfectly with it being all red and white and all, but I think we need to do more if we're going to make it worth our while to stay open. I was thinking maybe we should have a sale on earrings or something to get people in. What'd'you think?"

Chloe blinked up from her examination of some lapis stones as if she was coming up from deep inside their deepest blue. Beside her was a small selection of amethyst waiting for examination. Today she wore a pure white cotton caftan and, in counterpoint, her cluster of necklaces all had black stones. Her single thick braid was wound like a crown around her head.

"Sorry. What was that? I'm trying to decide which stones would be better used in jewelry and which ones I can use for my healing work."

"I was wondering if we should do something on Canada Day like have a sale. Maybe of earrings or something? As an incentive to bring people in. Once they're here, well, the stuff sells itself, doesn't it?" Kylee said.

Pursing her lips, Chloe considered. "We did get that last shipment of earrings from Asia…" She looked distracted, but then her expression cleared. "There's going to be a lot happening on Canada Day at different venues in town. If we had a sale, it would give us an excuse to put out some flyers and maybe a poster or two at each venue." She nodded, "Good idea. The flyer and poster should just be something simple."

"Agreed. Something like "Fine artisanal jewelry. Canada Day sale. Twenty five percent off designated earrings. And the logo and the address, right? Done in white with black text and silver logo?" Kylee grabbed a notepad and sketched. "Like this?"

Chloe considered the little drawing and raised her gaze to Kylee's. "You are really getting good at this, you know?"

A warm flush ran through Kylee's skin. "Hey, marketing background, remember? And it's easy to be good at something you love."

As she consulted a small calendar that came complete with quotations from Khalil Gibran, Chloe cocked an eyebrow. "If only more people figured that out." A long tapered finger tapped July first and she frowned. "Not much time between now and then. If we want flyers, we'll have to get them into a printer today. Can you run them up?"

"Sure. But will you be okay here, alone?" Kylee asked.

Chloe rolled her eyes. "I'll manage. I might be planning on breaking off into my own business, but I haven't lost my touch for this one yet." She grinned, "Really. No problem. Just get the flyer into the printer. There's one in West Kelowna we've used before." She wrote down the name and address and handed it to Kylee.

"I'll get my purse."

The bell over the door tinkled as Kylee hurried back to the sundrenched kitchen to claim her purse and then duck out the back to her car. The kitchen smelled of fresh coffee, toast and cut tomatoes so Reggie must have poked her head out of her shop for lunch.

"Hey, Kylee," Chloe's voice floated back to her. "Come here a moment. I think I've got you a better offer."

Mystified, Kylee returned to the store. Jingling her keys, she pushed through the beaded curtain. "What is it?"

Brett was standing there. Since the night she moved in, he'd popped over to check on her a few times, and to check on some of the house's old aches and pains, but had been decidedly hands off. A good thing because it stopped her from doing what she feared the most—falling for him. Because there *was* something between them. Just the way her heart did a little drum roll when she saw him standing there looking all tall and handsome and tousled so she was pretty sure he'd been driving with his top down. Her skin still tingled with the memory of his touch.

"Hey," he said, not moving from his spot beside the counter where Chloe had her stones spread. "I was going to ask our star boarder out for lunch, but Chloe says you've got an errand to run. Care to run it together? We could maybe grab lunch along the way." He glanced sideways at his sister who nodded.

A little concerned at the flutter of pleasure his presence brought, Kylee hesitated. Two sets of eyes seemed to drill into her expectantly. "All right, but if we're going to get this all done in forty-five minutes we're going to have to go quickly. I was just going to eat something in my car."

"I'm sure if you take an hour instead, my sister isn't going to report you. You *are* using your lunch time on business for the store." He looked sideways at his sister.

"Take an hour. Just get out of here, would you?" Chloe waved them away, and Brett caught Kylee's elbow and steered her to the door.

Outside the day was—Peachland. Blue sky. Blue lake. The drone of power boats far out on the lake and the brightly colored clothing of joggers and summer people on the promenade. She inhaled deeply of the scent of warming lake water and grapes heating in the sun, and she realized Brett was standing too close beside her. She edged slightly away, trying to keep her distance more than physically.

"Thank you for doing this. You don't have to, you know. My car'll make it to West Kelowna and back."

"Yeah. It probably will, but it won't be as much fun as it will be if we go together in my car." He hitched his thumbs in his jeans pockets and gave her an aw-shucks grin.

She rolled her eyes. "Okay. Let's get this show on the road. Time's a-ticking and all that."

Leading him down the stairs, she spotted his sports car down the block. As she'd surmised, the top was down. Brett held the door for her and then climbed in beside her, as he slipped on a pair of sunglasses.

"You look good enough to eat, which I might do, if I don't get some lunch." He leered over the tops of the glasses at her.

Kylee shook her head and crossed her arms. "And Lila said you were changing your ways. Shows what she knows. I guess I'll just have to guard my modesty myself. Now drive on, Sir. And if you try anything, know that I will name you a cad before your sister and your friends."

A bark of laughter and a vroom of the engine and the little car swept out from the curb. They followed the lakeshore to the highway, passing a stretch limousine just turning onto Beach Avenue.

It was ten minutes to the address in West Kelowna, a small print shop in a nondescript strip of buildings. They fronted one side of the highway that had speared through the town and killed off West Kelowna's heart to make way for massive development of malls and big box stores. Still, Marjorie's Printing, continued to exist after, according to the shop's sign, twenty five years.

Inside, the shop smelled of dusty paper, acrid ink and the ozone of hot machinery. The rhythmic pounding of copiers and printers was a beat that quickly got in the blood. An old transistor radio blared a local news station and the sole occupant of the shop hunched over a computer as if her life depended on it.

She was young—in her mid-twenties probably—with almost black hair pulled back in an abundant pony tail that fell well past her shoulders. She had smooth, naturally tanned skin and wore shorts and a simple pale pink t-shirt. She looked up, saw Brett, and leapt to her feet.

Another sign of Brett's past, perhaps?

"Brett! Hiya, guy! How's it hanging?" She looked just a little too pert and attentive to simply be interested in Brett as a customer. Besides, they clearly knew each other.

"I'm just fine, Joanna. This is my friend, Kylee. She works for Lila Weber at her shop in Peachland. They need a rush order on some printing. Can you help?"

Joanna frowned, and darn it, what was Brett doing, taking on her task for her? She was not helpless.

"I don't think it's a big job. The colors are simple. Black on white and if you've got it, some silver." She pulled out her sketch. "We want to do some flyers and a couple of posters around town for Canada Day." She explained about her sketch.

Joanna took the sketch and went to her computer. She brought up a clean screen and began to play with it, then turned the screen toward them. "This what you're looking for?"

The white page held a small silver logo in the upper left hand corner. Then the black text that she'd jotted down was centered on the page with the word 'Sale' in a larger font at the top.

"That looks good, don't you think?" Kylee asked Brett and instantly regretted it. She was supposed to make the decision here. Prove herself.

He pursed his lips. "Well... can I get her to try just one thing? How about enlarging that logo so it's the full width of the page as a background?"

Kylee turned back to Joanna, but the woman had already highlighted the logo and enlarged it to fill the page. If the poster/flyer had been good before, now it was outstanding. The silver-shot emblem made the plain white paper suddenly stand out and acted as a focus for the eye, while the black lettering gave the viewer their content.

"OhmyGod. It's perfect." Kylee said.

"Where'd you get such a good eye, Main?" Joanna asked.

Brett shrugged. "Must be all the years hanging with you and your mom."

"So can it be printed in time?" Kylee asked. The poster mockup looked fantastic, but Joanna still hadn't committed that she could get it done.

"Well... if we didn't have the logo already in our system I'd say no, but I'll sneak you in at the end of the day. I'm thinking maybe twenty-five posters and a few hundred flyers? You could pick 'em up tomorrow."

Kylee wanted to reach across the counter and hug Joanna. Instead she nodded and left her phone number, and departed with Brett. She still had thirty minutes of her lunch hour.

"So. Lunch," he said, holding the car door for her again. "How about we pick up something from the deli and head down by the lake? They have the best pastrami in these parts. You *do* like pastrami, don't you? Otherwise, this whole possible relationship thing is off."

"Relationship?" she said weakly and suppressed a little shiver because wasn't that the thing she was trying to avoid by coming here? The trouble was, being around Brett seemed to weaken her resolve. She was not going to get all tangled up with a guy and go chasing pathetically after him again—especially when she was just getting over the last one.

She looked up and found him studying her.

"Well, maybe relationship isn't the best word for it... this... whatever this is," he said. "Because I feel something Kylee, and I haven't felt it before and worse yet, I kind of like it. So maybe it's not a relationship. Maybe it's a more-than-friendship, right now. And what it will be in the future is anyone's guess. Okay?"

A light twitch of his fingers nudged a stray hair away from her too-dry mouth. She nodded.

"Okay, then. About that pastrami..."

"I've never tried it before, so you shall be my guide."

The sandwiches he bought from a little hole-in-the-wall shop that couldn't possibly have held anymore than one section of cured meat and one of cheese, were far more than she could have ever expected, full of thinly sliced pastrami, piled high, topped with havarti cheese and thinly sliced red and yellow peppers and lettuce for crunch. All of it was piled on thick slices of light rye bread that was practically perfumed in her mouth.

They sat on the end of a blue-painted wharf at a curve of the Peachland beach that was less frequented by people midweek. Both of them had kicked off their shoes and Brett had rolled his pant legs up to dangle their feet in the cool blue water. Out on the lake, the water was hazed with heat, but the breeze that rippled the lake kept it bearable.

Kylee took a swig of root beer that Brett had recommended as a perfect accompaniment for the pastrami.

"Is this not the perfect meal?" he asked as he chewed beatifically.

"There is a pretty good melding of flavors," she said around her own pastrami. "But then, of course, I've always been partial to grilled cheese."

One beat. Two. Three, and Brett turned an incredulous face toward her. "Are you telling me that a grilled cheese..."

"Are you saying that my home-made grilled cheese couldn't be?" she asked innocently.

"No. Well, yes. Well, dammit, Kylee, this is my favorite sandwich."

She burst out laughing. "Nice to see you're a man of strong loyalties. Just so you know, I do make a pretty mean grilled cheese though. I use three kinds of cheese and crusty bread and sun-dried tomatoes. To die for. But this might be better. Certainly the ambiance is, compared to a cramped bachelor suite on the seamy side of Vancouver."

"Nah," he murmured. "It's the company. It's totally the company."

He slid an arm around her and pulled her into his side. Instead of freezing, she went warm inside. As if the electric current that kept her alive had only been receiving half the power it was supposed to all her life—until now.

§

In the silence of *This & That* Chloe breathed in deeply of the scent of oiled wood and Windex they used on the glass cases, and watched Kylee and Brett clattering down the porch stairs and down the block; the bright shock of blond hair followed by the intent clot of darker brown. Had she ever been as young? Or as clearly infatuated, though they apparently hadn't admitted it yet? The sun was brilliant outside, almost harshly so when you were as fair-skinned as Chloe was, but inside the shop with the lake breeze coming in through the screened windows and the porch roof keeping the direct sunlight out, it was downright pleasant. She would miss these moments when she shifted to healing full time. At times she wondered if she was making the wrong decision, even though it had been a long-time dream to use her skills in that way.

Because she did have skills. She could use the stones, but she had other talents as well, like the one that told her that there was no question that her brother was smitten with one Kylee Jensen. From what she'd seen of him, he had been from the moment he saw her which was funny enough, but the fact that Kylee was so bound and determined *not* to be attracted to him made the whole situation just too delicious. She could get years of teasing her baby brother out of this. Not that he didn't deserve it, after the way he'd treated women all his life. The previous Brett Main was exactly the kind of man that Kylee should be running from. The new Brett Main?

Well that was the little cruelty of the whole situation, wasn't it? From the shell-shocked look of him, he was likely to do something stupid that spooked the poor girl right out of here.

Outside the little green car had scooted away and peace reigned in *This & That*. Chloe leaned over her tray of stones. The lapis was the wonderful deep blue of the Afghani highlands. Lapis had been a favorite in ancient Egypt and had been found in the tombs of ancient Ur. It was good for balancing the thyroid glands and promoting intuition, amongst other things. The trouble with most of the stones before her, and not just the lapis, was that most had gone years without cleansing or care that would recharge their healing properties. She really should suggest that a pamphlet go out with each piece that left the store. She had to remember to mention it to Lila. Or Kylee. The darn woman had a mind like a steel trap and if she agreed with it, whatever it was would get done.

The ding of the bell over the front door startled her because usually a footfall up the porch stairs announced anyone arriving.

She looked up and stopped, glimpsing a long, low-slung limousine with blacked-out windows double parked in the street out front.

The man standing in the store matched his infernal machine blocking traffic. He was tall, fair haired as a Teutonic God and built like you would imagine such a God to be. Broad shouldered, square jawed, jutting brow and eyes just as shuttered as the car outside. He wore an impeccable gray suit with a luster that suggested silk and screamed expensive, as well as an austere white shirt and pinstriped black and red tie. His shoes had the expensive luster of what could only be Italian leather.

Chloe did the once over and then returned to his face. The man's gaze was like a hot wind over parched earth and she had a momentary vision of night and eternal burning. Her heartbeat increased and for a moment she felt like a cornered bird. She swallowed.

"May I help you?" she asked.

"You are?" The man's imperious question came out with a slight German accent and he stepped farther into the shop.

Suddenly Chloe was sure that this guy's presence in her shop was about the last thing she wanted. She came around the counter to stop him.

"One of the proprietors of the *This & That*." She motioned at the store. "Is there something I can help you with?" For some reason she didn't want to give her name.

"Yes."

The word was so final that it made her think of the end of the world. Sweat started to bead between her breasts and along the edge of her braid.

"I am seeking something that was taken from my family years ago. You might say it was lost during the war. I have reason to believe that you may have acquired it in a recent business transaction."

Her heart pounding in her chest, she fought to be charming when everything about this man spoke of danger. It didn't take the way the jet stones on her necklace burned against her skin through her caftan to tell her that. She swallowed. "Well, that is interesting. I've helped inventory everything we've brought in. There's been nothing truly outstanding."

At least nothing matching this man's apparent wealth.

He waved a hand to silence her, before she was finished. "It is not composed of diamonds or rubies. In fact it is no more than a keepsake, a trinket, if you will. But it means a great deal to me and my family."

"Interesting. And you are? I don't believe you've introduced yourself."

"Johan. Johan Fehr."

He dipped his head in a slight formal bow and she wouldn't have been surprised if he flipping clicked his heels together or revealed a swastika sewn into the inside of his oh-so-pricey jacket.

"Well, Mr. Fehr. Perhaps you can give me a little better description of what it is you're looking for. Then I can check it against our inventory."

In two quick strides he stood in front of her. The store went dark. The stone necklace blazed against her chest, but all she could see was his eyes. Johan Fehr's fire-gilded eyes. She was swallowed by those eyes, consumed. Whatever Johan Fehr wanted, he was going to get because there was no way she could stop him.

"Show me," he said.

A part of her was screaming, no-no-no, but she obeyed, and pulled newly-bagged jewelry out from storage cupboards.

He swept his hand over them, then turned toward the house and she got the strange sensation that he was searching it, too. He turned to her in disgust. "It is not here. What have you done with it?"

"Tell me what it is and I will try to help you. Give me a hint, at least. A ring, a necklace? What?"

But Fehr just flashed her a look of such malevolent disgust she felt like a statue that could be turned to dust at a touch. She stood frozen as he swept out of the store, moving in long strides that barely seemed to touch the ground.

When he cleared the porch she collapsed back against the counter taking great heaves of air, and when that didn't work, ran out onto the front porch to gasp in the breeze as the long, low limousine oiled away down the street. When it was out of sight, the sun seemed to shine again and she sank down in one of the wicker chairs. Her nose held a charnel house scent that she couldn't place, but it had come in with the man. If she went inside the shop it would reek of him.

She smoothed her protective string of jet beads thankful that her morning meditations had chosen them for her today. Would she even have survived if she hadn't been wearing them? She pulled the neck of her caftan out and looked down her bodice. As she'd suspected, bright red spots marked where the series of jet beads had rested. She pooled the black beads in her hands but felt none of the tingle she usually felt from beads that had been activated. These she had cleansed and charged in sea salt two nights ago and in rock crystals last night. Now they lay in her palm as if they were dead.

Jet stones were great for arthritis and inflammation and for healing the grief pangs of death or separation. They also offered protection against evil spirits, magic spells and witchcraft.

She didn't know which one Johan Fehr was, and she didn't much care, but Johan Fehr was evil and he was looking for something.

It.

Give it back, Kylee's note had said. It could only be the bracelet.

The question was how she could tell Kylee that she was in serious danger.

CHAPTER 14

Feeling replete in almost every way, Kylee climbed out of the racing green Miata in front of the *This & That*. Brett, the ultimate throwback to a more gallant time, actually held the door for her and got a small kiss on the lips that threatened to become something more, until he held her away, touched her lips with his forefinger and said, "Later then."

He left her standing on the curb in the warm sun, the breeze playing in her hair. She felt slightly abandoned, but she refused to feel like she had to run after him. "Later then" promised there was more to come, didn't it?

She turned thoughtfully to the red and white house and spotted Chloe on the porch. Things must be slow then. Kylee waved and inhaled heliotrope-scented air, but Chloe barely raised a hand. Frowning, Kylee went up to the house.

"They'll be ready tomorrow."

Chloe looked at her blankly. She huddled into herself on the edge of her seat, her long string of usually shiny jet beads hanging dully from her hands. Even her thick lustrous braid seemed to have lost its shine.

"The posters and brochures, I mean. Chloe is everything all right?"

Chloe heaved a sigh and seemed to find renewed strength. She straightened, forced a smile and patted the seat beside her. "Come sit. That's good news about the posters etcetera. I need to talk to you about something."

Kylee lowered herself cautiously to her seat, because whatever Chloe wanted to talk to her about wasn't good. She braced herself. "Has something happened to Lila? Or Reggie?"

Chloe shook her head, her beads clacking together like brittle bits of glass, not the comforting soft sound of stone. Her jaw firmed and she shook her head before meeting Kylee's gaze. "While you were gone the store had a visitor."

Kylee went still. It couldn't be her mother. She was off somewhere on a cruise and had never been close to Kylee. She didn't even know where Kylee was at the moment, other than no longer traipsing the world. Kevin? Could it be Kevin? She waited for the little rush of anxious excitement that had always preceded their meetings, but it didn't come. Instead she just felt tired.

"My ex? Was it Kevin?" She held her breath waiting.

Shaking her head, Chloe gave a rueful smile. "Sorry. No. Worse, I'm afraid." Her expression turned grave, little worry lines furrowing between her brows. "I—I don't think this has to do with your private life, Kylee, but I do think it has to do with you. With that, to be specific." She nodded at Kylee's wrist and the bracelet she was absently rubbing.

"The bracelet?" She covered her wrist. "What are you talking about?"

Chloe sank back into her chair and grabbed onto the chair arms as if holding on for her life. "A man came into the store after you left and thank God you were gone. He said his name was Johan Fehr. He was big, athletic-looking and, frankly, scary. He came in like a customer but there was something phony about him like fool's gold amid a pan of the real thing. He was perfect and shiny, but his eyes gave him away—they were gray—like burning pits full of ash you could fall into and he aimed them at me." She shivered and once they'd started the little tremors just didn't seem to stop. Chloe seemed to collapse back into herself and huddle again.

"Oh my God, Chloe. Are you all right?" Kylee was on her knees beside her friend, pulling her into a hug. Chloe's skin was cold as ice in the shady porch.

Kylee leapt up, grabbed a chair and dragged it down the steps to the sunny lawn, then she ran upstairs and caught Chloe's arm. "Come on. You need the sunlight to warm you up."

Thankfully, Chloe came willingly enough, though her steps were halting. When she settled in the chair with the sun full on her, the shivers seemed to slow a little. Settled on the grass in front of her, Kylee caught her hands. "Now what did the guy want?"

"That's just it. He never said. He said we had something of his. A keepsake, an item of no great value except to his family, and he wanted to reclaim it. I asked what it was and he said I was to show him our stock." She shuddered so deeply it was like her heart could shake loose. "He looked at me and I *had* to do what he wanted. I showed him everything we had out here. He checked the rest of the house, too. At least I think he did. Then he said it wasn't here. He asked what had we done with it. Then his face cleared as if he knew. There was such pure hate in his gaze I felt like I could shrivel up and die right there." She shuddered again, but she held up her hand to stop Kylee from hugging her one more time. "The whole time he kept talking about *it*. Needing *it*. Wanting *it*. After he left I realized it was just like in your note. Give *it* back.

"Kylee, I think he wants the bracelet and he'll do anything to get it." She grabbed Kylee's hands, "He's evil. So evil that if I hadn't been wearing these protective beads, I don't know what would have happened. Maybe—I think—he'd own me if I hadn't been. I'd be his creature."

Her blue gaze had turned lavender with fear. Tears filled her eyes as she pulled Kylee into a hug. "You're in danger, Kylee. We have to guard you and keep you safe until we can get Reggie to cut that damned thing off your wrist. We have to get in touch with Lila—and Brett.”

The sunlight seemed to dim in the yard, though there wasn't a single cloud in the sky. Kylee sat back on her haunches and studied her friend. Chloe was clearly scared, something she hadn't expected to ever see, given the woman had always seemed a reserve of vast calm, esoteric wisdom, and humor. But that didn't necessarily mean she was right this time, did it?

The sun's heat seemed to catch in the bracelet and send warmth radiating up her arm. She considered the lovely piece of jewelry. It *was* lovely, but to consider it bait for something evil was a little farfetched. But then so were Chloe's stories about healing stones. Maybe this was just another of her more—shall we say—esoteric ideas.

She rubbed the bracelet and it soothed her. It was safe on her wrist where it was meant to be, and anyone wanting it would have to come through her. Heck if they could show her how to get the darn thing off, she'd gladly give it to him, but somehow the fact that it had attached itself to her suggested she shouldn't. She could take care of it. That was why the bracelet had come to her in the first place.

Now just where had that silly idea come from?

Catching Chloe's hands she faced her friend. “Chloe, I really appreciate you telling me this and I can see that this guy really scared you, but... but I think that I can handle this. I was scared when I got that note, but I've lived in your parents' house for a while now and I'm not scared anymore. I think—I think I can handle it. I'll be careful. I will. But I don't want you telling Lila or Reggie—or Brett.”

Chloe went to protest and Kylee held up her hand.

“No. I mean it. They'll just worry and stop living their lives because they're worried about mine. I've spent enough of my life imposing my needs on other people. I'm not about to do it this time. This is my issue, if it is an issue. Not theirs.”

Chloe's hand caught Kylee's and squeezed so tight it almost cut off the circulation to her fingers.

"Kylee, you have to believe me. This is too dangerous. These beads—you need to understand. When I put them on this morning they were full of protective power. Now they're empty. That thing—that thing in that man burned them out entirely. If he'd stayed much longer I don't know what would have happened." She clutched the beads close to her chest and swallowed. "Please listen to me."

Kylee stood and nodded, suddenly feeling stronger than she ever had. "I do believe you, and I will be careful. I promise. I will. But I want your promise that you won't tell the others. I want you to swear on—on the power of your stones that you won't tell them unless I agree."

Slowly, reluctantly, Chloe nodded. Then she took a deep breath, stood, and caught Kylee in a hug.

§

For Kylee, June 30th dawned with another cloudless, bright blue sky, though the radio said thunder showers might come their way. Chloe, however, said it wasn't going to rain because the stones weren't showing it. Kylee didn't know whether to believe Chloe because if she believed her about the weather, didn't it mean she might have to believe her about the man who visited the shop? There had been no further sign of him, but since their little talk Chloe's all-seeing gaze had always seemed to snag on Kylee. It was getting to be a drag.

Kylee ate a bowl of Cheerios standing up by the sink looking out the kitchen window—her usual morning routine. She would never get bored with the magnificent view, though her gaze kept straying to the place where she'd stood with Brett that night. She'd been standing almost right there when he'd kissed her that time. She could still smell a hint of his herbal aftershave with an undertone of rich wine. Just the thought of his touch on her arms brought a surge of heat through her and a flutter to her heart.

That wasn't a good thing. It was too soon for any involvement with anyone. What was it they said—that it took as long to recover from a relationship as you had been in the relationship? She'd been with Kevin for two years, but then had she really? In all that time had Kevin ever been truly committed to her or to them as a couple? She didn't think so and she wondered if she hadn't known it, too. Maybe that was why she ran after him so hard—she'd known it was going to end, too, and had been too weak to face it.

But it was too soon to be having feelings for Brett.

Of course, he had only dropped in to the house once since that night, though he had frequently turned up at the store at her break time and happened to have time for a coffee. And since what she had affectionately dubbed The Pastrami Lunch—capitalized because of that lovely kiss when he dropped her off—he'd called her at the store and picked her up for lunch a couple more times before he flew off to a wine festival in California. It was a good thing he didn't know about Chloe's visitor, because knowing Brett he would have felt guilty leaving—if he'd have gone at all. Since he'd been gone, he'd called her three times and was finally due back today.

A little shiver of anticipation ran through her.

She was trying not to get her hopes up that he'd call when he got back. He'd probably had a sober second thought about them during his time away. Time apart always gave clarity of sight.

Her silly, too easily broken heart did a ridiculous clench.

"Remember that feeling, Jensen. You don't need that," she muttered to her cereal.

Another bite of Cheerios and she focused on the view—the slumbering deep blue lake nestled against the far shore of hunched gray mountains with seams of new green growth. Someone had told her mountain goats lived there, but she'd never seen one. A lone powerboat furrowed its wave across the almost still water, but in her yard, the willow branches stirred like someone waking—

her garden hopefully. Or maybe herself. After the long, miserable slumber with Kevin she felt like she was finally waking up and living her life. She'd spent a whole week of evenings weeding and turning the soil. She'd planted lines of seeds of carrots, spinach and broccoli, her three favorite vegetables. She'd also planted a corner with zucchini and cantaloupe melon just to see what would happen, and from her window there were already faint lines of green in her garden. Things grew in the Okanagan. Maybe she could, too.

And she'd proved to Chloe and herself that her decision to keep Chloe's terrifying visitation from the rest had been the correct action. She was still here, wasn't she?

Thank goodness she'd managed to get through that first intimidating day at the house. After three weeks of sleeping—if not like a baby—then at least with interesting dreams of handsome men in roman togas who looked remarkably like Brett, the fear she'd felt that first day had faded. Even after Chloe's dire warning.

Wearing leggings and a flowing sleeveless tunic of bright yellow that she'd found on sale in a local beachwear shop—and of course, her friend the bracelet—she locked up behind her and headed down the steep hill to the store.

Parking in Lila's spot because she was away, Kylee tiptoed through the backyard lest she disturb Reggie's creative flow, because when Reggie was in that mode she apparently lived on caffeine and cola and forgot about normal things like sleep. She let herself in the back door to the kitchen, put on a pot of coffee to brew, and headed for the shop.

The place smelled of Chloe's sweet myrrh incense and leather from the small handmade purses Lila had taken on consignment after Kylee discovered them at the weekend craft market. They were just the perfect size for a woman to carry a few dollars, a brush, and a tube of lipstick while she was out walking. So far they'd been selling like hotcakes. Another small win for Kylee.

She had an hour before the store opened so she set about dusting and readjusting the displays to their best advantage. She'd tried out a new display system yesterday, leaving aside the artisan-specific jewelry in most cases, to focus instead on complimentary colors and designs. The result had been major changes to a number of display cases, but those changes had seemed to fuel the sales the store had experienced, too. This morning she planned to use some of the lovely sherbet-hued silk and pashmina shawls as background to a special display of Reggie's jewelry.

She unlocked the safe that held Reggie's designs, slipped two rose and gold-toned shawls off the wall display and opened the glass case. She carefully laid the rose pashmina so it flowed like waves, and then braided one of Reggie's chains with the gold scarf. The other pieces of jewelry she either pinned to the fabric or let fall so it looked like a cascade from a rich woman's boudoir. Lovely. Decadent. Desirable.

She stepped back to admire her arrangement. Just about perfect; she just hoped Chloe and Reggie and Lila liked it.

"You've been avoiding me."

Kylee almost fell as she spun to face Reggie in the beaded doorway. The curtain clacked softly as it fell behind her, or maybe it was urging Reggie not to fall down. The black-haired woman looked like she just about could: hollow-eyed, gaunt cheeked, and even her shoulders seemed sunken in.

"Reggie! You look like hell." Kylee ignored the jeweler's protests and caught her arm to lead her to an antique wooden chair Lila had found at another estate sale. Reggie sank down with a groan. She smelled of old sweat and sour coffee and looked like her tangled mop of black hair hadn't seen a brush in days. "You haven't eaten or anything have you?"

It came out almost as an accusation and Reggie jerked and looked up at her, eyes narrowed. "And you're just as good at changing the subject as you are at avoiding my inspection of that darn bracelet. It's been over three weeks, you know, since I asked you to let me take a sample." She looked down at her long narrow hands, the skin blackened by whatever she'd been doing. "And no, I haven't eaten. Frankly, I'm famished."

That was it. Kylee bundled her exhausted friend up and onto the porch. "You stay here," she said as if talking to an errant dog. "I'll be right back with something to eat."

It ended up taking more than a few minutes to toast bagels, dig out the cream cheese and fresh strawberries, and pour fresh coffee and steamed milk into two mugs. Then she lugged a tray with the food and two fresh washcloths—one soapy, one just wet—back out to the porch. Reggie was where Kylee had left her, her head back, eyes closed almost dozing, but she opened one eye when Kylee pushed out the door.

"Smells good." She managed to sit up and cast a look of absolute bliss at Kylee when she handed her the washcloths. She scrubbed her face, hands, and arms and then sighed. "You have no idea how much better that feels."

Kylee settled on the edge of another of the wicker chairs. "Maybe I do. I remember finally arriving in the town of Nouakchott after five days crossing the Sahara desert without much sleep and no showers. I expect it can't feel much different except I had sand embedded in my skin and you've had whatever that was." She motioned to the now-blackened washcloths.

Reggie sat back in her chair and wolfed down the bagel. There was nothing much delicate about Reggie at the moment. She looked ravenous. When she finally finished the last bagel half she licked her fingers, leaned back and sipped her coffee. "So why are you avoiding me?"

"I'm not." Kylee frowned and sipped her coffee. She wasn't, was she? But her hand covered the bracelet protectively. "I thought you were too busy to talk to me."

The soft slap, slap, slap of a jogger running past on the promenade was the only sound until Reggie sipped her coffee again and savored. Then she put the mug down. "You've really grown attached to that thing, haven't you? The bracelet, I mean."

The bracelet gleamed on her tanned wrist, the miniature doors like entrances to all the dream places you could hope for, each one more exotic than the next. "It's a lovely piece of jewelry. It doesn't belong to me so I'm trying to take good care of it."

"Well it's been on my mind. It keeps creeping into my head while I'm designing and it's just—it doesn't fit with what Lila usually brings home. It doesn't look like ordinary estate jewelry, though the Victorians did come up with some pretty ornate jewelry. Theirs was more about ornate enamels, drop earrings and broaches shaped like insects, flowers or leaves. Art deco had square motifs but none were doors like this is. Other than the idea of lockets, I can't think of any culture that glorified doors, at least not in their jewelry. Not like that. Not even today, really, though it's the sort of thing modern buyers would likely go for. Actually, looking at it on your wrist, I think other people would really like it."

She leaned forward, her bangs shadowing her eyes as she studied the bracelet on Kylee's wrist. "The thing is, I really don't think it's modern. Can I see?"

Hesitating, Kylee finally held out her arm. Everything and everyone kept coming back to the bracelet and it was getting frustrating. Reggie checked the edges. "There. See. That's where I ran my fingernail the night you moved in. In this light you can see it—the faint mark. That means that the silver is soft." She twisted Kylee's wrist this way and that in the sunlight. "And there, see?" She tapped her finger on one of the doors—a miniature that reminded Kylee of doors she'd seen in Morocco, complete with the tiny emblem of Fatima's hand in the center. "See those dark marks along what's been made to look like the iron casings on the door? I'd lay money on that being corrosion. There're spots of it in a lot of places." She dabbed her finger from place to place so Kylee just wanted to pull her arm back to protect the precious bracelet.

Yes, precious. It was cool and comforting and clearly the most beautiful piece of jewelry she'd ever worn. Definitely the most exotic. Reggie finally released her and she yanked her hand back, running her fingers over the lovely silver links on her wrist. "I'm really trying to take care of it, and I've tried to get it off a bunch of times, but the closure just doesn't work."

Not that she'd tried it recently. It was like the bracelet was becoming part of her. It felt at home where it was. As if it was meant to be hers—had been sent to her for a purpose.

Reggie was watching her. "Tell you what, now that I'm not up to my hip pockets in design and prototypes, when Chloe gets in, come on back to my shop. I'll take a small sample of the metal and send it in for analysis at the university. If they think it's old, we can take it in for them to see. Okay?"

"A scraping?" Kylee swallowed. "Won't that damage the bracelet?"

Reggie grinned. "Nah. We're talking microscopic amounts. You won't even be able to see it." She stretched and stood up, looking out at the lake. It was the color of steel, the surface smooth. There was no usual morning breeze and the air felt like it was holding its breath, just as Kylee had been while Reggie examined the bracelet. She walked out onto the steps so that she could see up to the mountains. "Wooee. There's a lot of dark clouds building up there. There's going to be one heck of a downpour later today."

Clumping back up the steps she paused. "Don't forget to come by. I'm going to head home now and take a shower and catch a few hours sleep, but I'll be back by noon, so stop avoiding me."

In other words she wasn't going to take 'no' for an answer.

With a thanks for breakfast, she left Kylee to clean up the dishes from the porch and return them to the kitchen. There, she watched Reggie leave and had the unkind thought that she hoped she wouldn't come back.

What the heck had gotten into her? She didn't think like that. Her hand closed around the bracelet. "If you're going to be a bad influence like that I'm not going to want to wear you? Hear?"

And so who was all woo-woo and ridiculous now?

The bell above the front door to *This & That* tinkled and Kylee whirled around. Damn. She'd left the front door unlocked when she brought the dishes in and the store wasn't supposed to open for another ten minutes.

She abandoned the dishes in the sink and hurried out to the store. A man stood there, tall, but not as tall as Brett and square shouldered in a wrinkled-looking gray suit. Someone she knew or at least recognized. Russet colored hair combed back unlike Brett's tousled look and, when he turned around, a gaze that swept over her and seemed to take in everything before coming to settle on her again. Okay, that might be a little like how Brett looked at her except without the heat.

Detective. That was it. The man who had been involved in the investigation into the death of the estate agent Lila had dealt with. Her skin prickled and her free hand came up to cover the bracelet.

"Can I help you?" she asked, keeping her hand down as she eased behind the counter that held the antique cash register.

"Corporal Danny Forester. I was wondering if a Lila Weber works here?"

"Yes," Kylee answered slowly. What was this? The guy knew she worked here. He'd interviewed her here already and been a bit of dick while doing it." She's the owner, but she'd not here right now."

The good Corporal ran long spatulate fingers back through his hair and shook his head. When he looked back at her there was a lot less confidence in his gaze. In fact, looking at him something was off. He had a couple of days growth of beard and eyes that were just a little scared and—wild.

"I should know that, shouldn't I?" he said. "I've been here before."

Okay, things were starting to get weirder. "Yes," she said keeping what she divulged to a minimum.

He rubbed her forehead and massaged his eyes. "Damn."

"Are you all right?" she asked, despite herself.

He didn't look at her, just shook his head and did a slow scan of the shop again almost as if it was brand new to him. "I—have some follow-up questions for her." He shook himself like a wet dog. Smiled. "Sorry. Do you know when she'll be back?"

"Uh, yeah. I guess. She's expected today. Maybe tomorrow, I think."

"You think. You can't be sure?"

"I—we—Lila keeps sort of an open schedule when she's out buying. She might get to a town only planning on attending one sale, but someone will tell her about something else and she'll follow the trail—sort of like a good detective would—should." Oh crap. She'd put her foot in it now.

The way his eyes narrowed at her she was sure he'd seen the bracelet and knew that he hadn't seen it the first time he was here. But it was an oversight. And why would the bracelet be important to him anyway?

"And can I get your name, please?"

He hauled out a notebook and Kylee almost froze. She so did not want to get involved with any police investigation, not that she had anything to hide, but something about this guy just made her cautious. He seemed confused—and a little desperate. But he stood there expectantly, pen and notepad in hand, and what excuse did she have for denying him?

"Kylee. Kylee Jensen."

"I think I've seen you around. You and a man in a little green car."

Kylee froze. How could he know about Brett? Brett hadn't been around when he was here the first time and they hadn't been out together since except that quick trip to West Kelowna. Unless the good detective had been watching them—her. Every hair on her body stood on end.

"I—I was here when you were here last time. That must be why I seem familiar."

He looked at her like he didn't believe her, but finally nodded, pulled out his wallet and handed her his card. "Could you pass that to Ms. Weber and ask her to call me, please?"

She watched him exit the store and down the front stairs. When he reached the street he stopped and looked back at the house as if he was going through some kind of struggle. Then he headed to a big brown sedan and climbed in. He looked like he was making notes in a notepad.

Kylee inhaled for what felt like the first time since the front bell dinged. What the heck was going on? Why wouldn't he remember having been here before and giving Lila such a hard time?

Outside, a cherry red BMW sedan pulled up across the street and three well-heeled ladies in brightly colored sundresses climbed out. They admired the lake for a moment and then turned to the store as Kylee hurriedly turned on the discrete "open" sign. It was going to be a long day until Chloe arrived.

§

Corporal Danny Forester sat in his old fast-food wrapper scented car and rubbed his aching head. What the hell was happening to him? The morning sunlight cut into his vision as if he'd been on a bender last night. He knew he hadn't been. The glare off the lake was enough to make him want to curl into a ball and his hands shook like an addict going through withdrawal. What the hell was wrong with him? His head had felt like it was full of nothing more than mothballs for the last three weeks—so much so that his Sergeant was starting to ride his ass. Wasn't he? He was doing better than he had been; at least he felt like somewhere inside this mothball-scented brain was the one that he'd been born with.

That was an improvement that had come over the last few weeks, because three weeks ago there was a period he could barely remember and even his notebook—the place he *always* recorded everything in an investigation—reflected that blankness. Sure there were a few notations, like the one with Lila Weber's name on it associated with the Burns investigation. Now it was more like someone had left a door open into his brain and mist kept rolling through and half-blinding him.

He shook his head and rolled his window down, hoping a breeze off the lake would help to clear his head. The trouble was, there was no breeze and the scent of dark coffee and fresh muffins just made his head ache. He needed help. He needed help bad. Not just to solve the Moira Burns murder case, but to figure out what had messed with his brain.

Hopefully the Weber woman could do that.

§

Kylee sold three silver and stone bracelets—one a Regulus—an amber pendant with entrapments, and six sets of earrings before lunch. She was busy with a customer looking at pashminas when Chloe swanned in at one p.m. She wore a caramel-colored caftan that set off the deep brown of her hair and had shed her layers of necklaces for a torque that was made of green discs of some kind of stone and a single large black disc of jet. Her hair was somehow twisted up and held with a single silver spike through her mane so she looked like a priestess of some ancient temple. A little twinge of envy ran through Kylee, but then she couldn't imagine ever dressing like that. She seriously doubted that Chloe would look like anything but a fish out of water if she dressed the same as Kylee.

A crowd seemed to flow in after Chloe, and Reggie's request to come back to the studio was soon forgotten. The detective's card still burned a hole in her pocket. She needed to talk to Chloe about it, because his visit had been so weird and she wasn't sure she should even pass his visit along to Lila. Her auburn-haired friend had too much on her mind these days, but Chloe would give good counsel. She always seemed to. Even if nothing had come of her dire warning.

The flow of customers continued, always more than one person could deal with, given the jewelry was all locked in glass cupboards. Kylee missed her lunch break and the afternoon coffee break looked like it was going to come and go, when the door jingled again and a familiar masculine presence filled the room. Kylee glanced up instantly aware.

Brett stood by the door, soaking up the admiring glances of the customers, then waited patiently until Kylee finished with her current customer before sauntering over to her. He leaned down. "You miss me?" whispered in her ear.

"Were you gone?" she asked, keeping her voice light, as she wiped fingerprints off the counter, because just his presence sent a tingle of warmth through her skin. Unfortunately, it probably showed.

"You know I was gone," he growled. "Napa. The wine festival."

She glanced up at him and didn't like the intense heat in his eyes. No one in the shop could miss it. She'd thought too much about him over the time he'd been gone. Entirely too much given she wasn't going to fall for him. She should just discourage him. She would. But she didn't want to hurt his feelings.

"Well I hope the festival went well for you." She went to turn away.

"I got you something." His husky voice changed, became eager, like a kid who couldn't wait to tell a secret.

She should just tell him she was busy right now. She should just walk away. But his barely concealed excitement was infectious. "You did?"

Crazy. Stoopid. She should be hightailing it for the hills instead of coming in for a crash landing with this guy.

He held up a white plastic bag she hadn't noticed he was carrying. "Could we go in the back?"

She glanced around the shop. Three other customers kept glancing her way and so did Chloe. Mind you, the women could just be admiring Brett—he *was* certainly worth admiring.

She shook her head, "Too busy." She checked her watch. "Maybe come back at three. I'm off then."

Then she left him for a customer and almost did a fist pump. Yes. She had shown where her priorities lay even though the wild, needy, childish part of her was jumping up and down wanting to see what he'd brought her. A man had brought her something!

She had to think hard to remember the last time that had ever happened.

CHAPTER 15

SHE WAS THE MOST UTTERLY CHARMING WOMAN he had ever met and certainly the most confusing. Feeling abandoned and just a tad nonplussed, Brett inhaled the shop's oversweet incensed air and followed Kylee with his eyes. He caught his sister's smug grin as she looked back to help a customer. Were they ganging up on him? Warning Kylee against him? Surely to God, Chloe wouldn't do that. He *had* changed his ways. He had, ever since he took the plunge and used his half of the inheritance to buy in as partner at Elkhart—not that he was telling anyone about that little venture. Not even Chloe knew he'd taken that step. It meant that he had to be responsible and that he no longer had a place in his life for his old wild ways. It also meant that he'd hadn't been sent to Napa Valley—he'd been chosen as co-owner to go on the week-long wine junket—and because he really needed to get some space.

In the few days he'd known Kylee she'd become all-consuming. She inhabited his dreams, both at night and waking. In fact he'd nearly ruined a vat of Shiraz when he almost let the temperature get too high during the cold maceration process. He could have totally ruined the color and boldness of the wine when he'd been daydreaming instead of paying attention. He'd finally announced to his partner that he was going to California just so that he could clear his head. Besides, he had figured it would focus him on business and he'd be surrounded by lovely California girls, too. It couldn't hurt.

But it hadn't helped. Not one bit. The week had stretched forever and the whole time he'd found himself thinking about Kylee, wishing she was with him or thinking about the things they could do when they were together again. Stupid. Idiot. Fool.

Just seeing her again, the way Kylee swayed away from him, his mouth went dry. Even trying to be stiff and unapproachable, she couldn't hide the fact that she was a woman who moved like a woman should, with the soft shift of hips, stretch and move of muscle under silk-soft skin. He'd felt those muscles when he held her in his arms. The soft lighting of the shop caught in the highlights of her blond hair and placed shadows in the arch of her neck. Those shadows would taste of lavender and strawberries. His body tightened and he grabbed hold of the glass case he stood next to.

"You okay, brother," Chloe said as she slid past him to help another customer. "Whatever you've got, I'd say you've got it bad." A wicked smile, but then her face went momentarily serious. "Stick around, okay?"

Then she was gone. What the hell did that mean?

Get a grip, Main. Kylee's putting you in your place because you ran off like a coward for a week, no matter what excuses you try and make about business. But she clearly liked his attention. The way the color had risen in her cheeks when he arrived. The way she avoided his gaze. She was every bit as aware of him as he was of her.

He looked down at the bag he was carrying and suddenly felt a little concerned. While he was at the resort hosting the wine festival he had noticed a blouse in the resort store window that had, for some reason, reminded him of Kylee. As blue as her eyes, and made of a gauzy fabric that would flow around her and was just as feminine as she was. On a whim he'd gone in and bought it. After all, he'd seen her closet. She had almost nothing.

But now he felt foolish. Giving a woman clothing seemed a little too intimate, though he'd done it enough times in the past. Most of the time, then, it had been lingerie—something entirely inappropriate for Kylee. Especially when he wasn't even sure he should be getting involved with her, given she was on the rebound.

Yeah. He told himself all these things.

It hadn't done a lick of good.

"Shit."

A couple of customers nearby looked up at him.

"Apologies. I'm just an idiot sometimes." He glanced in Chloe's direction because she could definitely provide advice—his sister was always free with it—but after her snide remark she was busy helping a customer so it looked like he was on his own.

He escaped the store and found himself on the sidewalk feeling a little panicked, standing across from the promenade and the lake. It lay placid this afternoon, disappointing the sailboat owners who were forced to run on their diesels, their sails flaccid in the still air. The sun beat down like a hammer onto an anvil, but the thunderclouds that had threatened this morning when he arrived home had all swept away eastward. He checked his watch.

Crap. Two hours. He had two flipping hours to find something a little more suitable to give to a woman he wanted to know better, but didn't want to scare.

He jogged down the sidewalk toward the bakery-café, sweat already starting to stand out on his body, to a trendy little home design store in the same complex and stepped inside into an explosion of fan-cooled air and... stuff. An eminently practical man, he really didn't "get" things like gnome lawn ornaments and things made of metal strips that looked like vases. How the hell did you keep a plant watered when the whole thing was holes? There were racks of scented candles worse than Chloe's incense that made him want to sneeze, and a display of jewelry made of ceramic flowers that were so far beneath the *This & That* that he just passed them by. Glass vases, wall clocks, she didn't need those because they came with the house. Small brightly colored garden flags with phrases like "Welcome" or "I [heart] Gardens". He couldn't see Kylee with those either.

The oscillating fan by the door sent a surge of cool air past him and a display of wind chimes shifted in the man-made breeze. A chord of musical gongs and tings reverberated through the shop and seemed to tremble deep in his bones. He stopped.

Turned. Amidst the deep gongs of the four-foot-long pipes and the high pitched ting-ting-ting of cheap Taiwan-made chimes, there was something—a series of notes that spoke of life and freedom and... happy. If there was anything he wanted for Kylee it was happy.

He tested each set of chimes until he found the one he wanted. Silver metal tubes hung from a black wooden circle. A long central string ended in a black wooden disc with an Oriental figure carved into it. He carefully took them down from the display and up to the counter, absolutely certain Kylee would love them, or he was no judge of people at all. They were wholly impractical, and yet they spoke to him and what the hell was that all about, anyway?

While he waited for the storekeeper to wrap them so that the first movement of the bag wouldn't give the contents away, he browsed through the store and found the one practical thing they offered. A set of high-end dead-bolt locks. Practical? He took two, one for each door to Kylie's house. That was the thing that had burned in his mind the most when he was at the wine festival. Concern.

Because he'd left without making sure her doors were even more secure, and even though she hadn't said anything. For some reason that bothered him.

§

Three o'clock came as the sun shifted over the westward mountains and shadows started to stretch out onto the lake, but there were still customers in the store. Chloe said she could handle it and, frankly, Kylee's feet were hurting. It had been a whirlwind of a day for a Monday. Surprising, but it showed that word of mouth was working to advertise the shop. A good thing. She'd sold so many beautiful things, Chloe had been a Godsend with her knowledge of healing stones that had seemed to really interest the customers. That alone had sealed the deal for a few sales, so it was something Kylee wanted to read up on.

She paused by the antique cash register just to breathe in the shop. It smelled of floor wax and silver cleaner and a customer's expensive perfume, along with Chloe's sweet incense that threaded into the air from the brazier on the shelf behind the cash register. The open windows stirred the pashminas along the wall so they seemed to almost breathe in the air. The pot lights glimmered on the glass jewelry cases and caught on her bracelet. She rubbed the little vine-wrapped door as had become her habit.

She needed to go see Reggie for that metal sample, but she really wanted to go see Brett. He'd brought her something! She was surprised at how that made her heart flutter a little. Silly heart. She was acting like a school girl the first time a boy asked her out. Again.

But then, that was her modus operandi, wasn't it? Hopeless infatuation and then let the guy hurt her. Nope, she had more control than that. She would not let her heart rule her anymore. As a matter of fact, maybe she'd let Mr. Brett Main just cool his heels and go let Reggie take that sample. Because she wasn't some kid crushing on the neighborhood lifeguard.

No, I'm crushing on the lifeguard all grown up.

She closed her eyes and shook her head. "Damn," she whispered.

"Problems?" Chloe asked coming up behind her to put a lovely iridescent labradorite silver pendant into the "hold" drawer while the customer left with her friends. She gave Kylee an appraising once over.

"No," Kylee shook her head feeling like she'd just stepped back into high school drama. "Just me. The too-stupid part of me." She slapped her chest over her heart.

"Aah," Chloe gave her an all-knowing look. "Let me guess. My errant brother."

Kylee sighed. "It's that obvious, is it?"

"That you like each other? Sure. I'm making the most of it, because you are sooo not Brett's 'type'." She hooked her fingers in air quotes. She gave Kylee an assessing once over. "Otherwise everything's still okay? No stalkers or anything?"

"Nada. So quit your worrying. You probably just read the guy all wrong. Maybe he was having a bad day."

"Bad eternity, more like. Don't believe me, but there was something very black in that man."

Kylee really didn't want to get into that discussion again, so she went with something more normal. "Here's the thing. How do you know if it's real when you've got a heart like mine that seems to go all soft and mushy every time a man looks at you in a certain way? How do I not get walked on?"

Chloe let her fingertips slide down the silver chain and pendant she'd given Kylee. The gold threads in the rutilated quartz caught the light. "This will help you to see the truth, but really, I think you need to look into your heart. Why does it need someone so badly? A lot of women I know actually need a man around to feel good about themselves because they've never learned who they really are. So they try to find their identity in how the man sees them."

Pondering this, Kylee ran her fingers over the brass keys of the old cash register. They were cool and lovely. Nobody ever made something like this big old thing today. It was all about minimizing and functionalism, while this old cash register was both functional and beautiful. It even had scroll work down its sides.

"I think what you're saying is that I need to give myself enough time to be sure of who I am before I add another person into the mix." The thought of saying bye-bye to Brett saddened her and it wasn't because he made her feel good about herself.

But Chloe was shaking her head. She laid her fingers lightly on the back of Kylee's wrist. "That's what a lot of people think I mean, but really, I'm just saying that you have to be sure of yourself and not just follow the other person's lead all the time. You have to be true to what you want, Kylee. That, most of all. Know what you want and go for it."

Chloe patted the back of her hand. "You should go. I think Brett's waiting for you, right?"

"Where did you get so wise?" It slipped out before Kylee could help herself.

"Wise?" Chloe's laughter filled the store in a rich, low timbered guffaw. "Woman, I've made all the mistakes myself. How else does one learn? I sure wasn't sprung from Zeus's brow. I've got a history just like everyone else and it isn't pretty."

"Even Lila?"

Chloe's chortles cut off. "Lila most of all, I suppose." She shook her head. "But that's her story and not mine to tell. So get going, would you? I've got reading to do and stones to assess and I'm getting less done with all the darn customers that keep coming in."

She made a show of shooing Kylee toward the curtained door to the back, and Kylee went—to get her purse and see Reggie. To do what she wanted, instead of what Brett expected.

Not that she really wanted Reggie to touch *her* bracelet, but the woman had been hounding her for three weeks now. The curtain clacked softly behind her as she went down the hall to the back of the house. The kitchen gleamed softly, the yellow cupboards, reflective counter, and brushed steel appliances all catching the sunlight through the bank of windows. Reggie's shop sat in the yard with the door and window open, an oscillating fan whirring in the window.

Taking a deep breath, Kylee stepped outside into the sunshine. It beat down like a hammer and the air barely stirred in the yard. She instantly started sweating and even the roses seemed wilted in the heat. A good day to jump in the lake. But first this and then see Brett. She shook her head. It was like the afternoon was one thing to dread after another. If she was going to cool things with Brett.

Her footsteps clumped on the rear stairs and she trudged across the yard to Reggie's open door. Classical music she would have never expected—Debussy, it sounded like—was background for a tapping sound that could have been light hammering. She paused, stroking the bracelet and taking comfort in the feel of the metal. She knocked on the door frame that gave onto a dark interior. Her nose curled at the scent of heat and hot metal.

"Reggie?" She poked her head into the shop, but was blind after the brilliant sunshine.

The tapping stopped. "Oh. Right. You're here. Finally."

Reggie sounded distracted from somewhere in the room. "Come on in," she said. "The heat's a beast today. The fans help a little."

Kylee stepped blindly inside into almost suffocating air until the fan at the window sent a cool jet past her, before disappearing to other parts of the room. Across the room something glowed red hot and radiated heat that only added to the baking from the outside.

"My God, Reggie. You're working in a furnace. How do you stand it?" Sweat was already running down her back and between her breasts. She thanked God for the next jet of fan air and followed it deeper into the dimly lit room.

Reggie shrugged from where she perched on a stool, a leather apron over her street clothes of a black sleeveless t-shirt and black shorts. A light over her worktable illuminated her black hair. It was plastered to her skull, her bangs held back by a hairband to expose her high forehead and huge brown eyes, with distinct bags of exhaustion underneath them. "It is what it is. I'm used to it."

She took a long pull from a plastic water bottle. "So you finally decided to come and see me. I was beginning to think I should start a betting pool on just how long you could avoid it." Another swig of water and Kylee could really understand the thirst, given she was parched just standing here.

"So what is all this stuff?" She motioned around the room. It was small, with a sizeable workbench in front of Reggie with a narrower bench down one wall where the glowing thing sat. Next to it was something that looked a lot like a desktop printer. The walls were lined with neat rows of tools, different sized hammers, pliers, punches, mallets, saws and others she didn't recognize. A set of tongs sat on the table beside her, along with what looked like a tiny anvil and a blow torch.

"Tools of the trade. Grinder." She motioned at something that looked like a stone wheel above a large sink of water. "Smelter." A motion at a stack of burned-looking bricks in the corner. "Kiln." The thing that looked like a boxy printer this time. "Grab a seat. I was just trying something out."

"I thought you went home for a rest," Kylee said as she perched herself on a battered stool. The workbench was a mass of scarred and stained wood, but on the top of the small anvil lay a tiny strip of metal about three inches long. She leaned forward to look at it.

"I did, but when I'm in creative mode I have a hard time settling down." She rubbed her nose and left a dark streak across it.

"Uuh," Kylee said and tapped her nose.

"Shoot. I always do that." Reggie grabbed a cloth and wiped her nose, but it just smeared the mark a little broader. "How's that?"

"Not great. You're sitting in a sweat box and you have dirt all over your face. You still look like you haven't slept in days. Have you?"

Reggie shrugged. "Don't remember. I've been playing with ideas inspired by your bracelet and art deco designs. This is going to be a board in a doorway with an art deco window made of Roman glass with filigreed silver."

Kylee could imagine the piece, but the bit of silver on the anvil sure didn't look like anything.

"Okaaaay." Against her better judgment she held out her arm. But she really wanted out of this darkness and heat. "You wanted to take a sample."

There was a moment while Reggie seemed to reconfigure her brain from her jewelry to the bracelet on Kylee's wrist.

"Right. I did, didn't I?" She got up and went to a cupboard, returning with a piece of what looked like parchment paper. Laying it on the table, she returned to her stool and picked up a knife. "Okay. Let's do this."

It took everything Kylee had not to pull her wrist back to her breast and leave. When she held out her arm the bracelet seemed hot and it got hotter when Reggie went to hold the lock. Reggie jerked and dropped it and frowned. "Well isn't that the damndest thing."

"What? What is it?"

"It's almost like an electric current runs through the bracelet. It shocked me." She caught Kylee's wrist and turned it this way and that under the light of a desk lamp that spot lit the glistening bracelet. "Well, no matter. We'll get this done and get the sample off to the university."

She caught the edge of the bracelet again and bit her lip, then swung Kylee's wrist over the parchment and ran the point of the knife over the edge of the lock. A few tiny curls of silver fell on the parchment.

Quick as a wink, Reggie folded the parchment to form a small packet with the sample inside. This she tucked it into an envelope that went into her shorts pocket.

Kylee sat there, feeling ready to weep. She shouldn't have done it. She felt sick to her stomach, almost like when she was a child and found a bird that had broken its neck against a window. She cradled her wrist against her chest and the heat was overpowering. She couldn't breathe and she needed to get out of here.

"I—I'm glad that's over with." She stood.

"Kylee? Everything okay."

"Yeah. Yeah, sure. Just great. But I've got somewhere I need to be. See you, okay?"

She beat a hasty retreat out the door and turned her face full-on to the sun because she wasn't okay. That little knife scrape had felt like a knife to her heart and that was weird, right? Was she flipping bonding to a flipping piece of jewelry, now? God, she was so stupid.

She shook herself, ran into the house to wash the sweat off her from Reggie's inferno—yup, that was what she was going to call that shop from now on—and stood there a minute, staring into her reflection in the mirror over the little guestroom sink. *So whatcha going to do there, Kylee? What is it you want?*

What she really wanted was someone to tell her what to do about Brett, but that wasn't exactly what Chloe had been talking about. If she knew what was good for her, she'd just grab her purse and climb in her car and head home. The trouble was, there *was* something about Brett and it *was* more than a physical attraction. At least she thought so. She liked the way he'd treated her—almost like a good friend, meeting her for coffee, checking her doors to make sure she was safe. Bringing her a gift back from California. Well maybe that wasn't what a friend did, especially not a friend of such short acquaintance.

So what's it going to be, Kylee?

The bracelet seemed to pulse on her wrist and reminded her of Brett's comforting hands on her arms. She was most likely a fool, but at this moment she wanted to know where this thing with Brett was leading. She did.

That decided, she headed out front, waved goodbye to Chloe and headed for the lakeshore and the café.

Yup. No one could ever say she wasn't a fool where the heart was concerned.

CHAPTER 16

Lila squeezed the SUV into the carport next to Kylee's faded Civic and turned off the engine. She sat there in the silence of the car glad to be home, but overwhelmed with what she had learned. She'd told Kylee it was a buying trip, but that wasn't wholly her purpose. Beyond the carport, the backyard baked in the hot sun and the patio furniture seemed hazed with heat. Fans churned the air into Reggie's workshop—she couldn't imagine working in there right now, but somehow Reggie managed. Hands still firmly gripping the leather-clad steering wheel, she glanced in the rearview mirror at the musty-smelling boxes in her back seat. Well, she actually had done some buying, but in some ways it felt like she'd gone through the motions. She pulled the baggie out of her pocket and once more read the note it contained.

GIVE IT BACK.

All the little hairs on the back of her neck prickled just like they had the first time she read it, except now, after her latest 260 mile round trip to Kamloops, she felt a little sick to her stomach along with the little chill of fear. She'd actually had her car heater running because she couldn't seem to get warm even though the sun was blazing.

At least Kylee was here. They could discuss what Lila had learned and decide how to deal with it. The big concern was making sure Kylee was safe.

She climbed out of the car and the afternoon heat slammed into her, almost making her dizzy. Yet it still didn't warm her. She leaned on the car for a minute—this whole thing had spooked her more than she liked to think. The boxes could just wait. First see Kylee.

Trudging across the yard, she headed for the kitchen.

"Lila? That you?" Reggie's voice along with the sound of stirring in the shop. Dark hair in matted strings, and wearing a black singlet t-shirt and black cutoffs, Reggie stood in the doorway. "I thought you were supposed to be back tomorrow?"

Sighing, Lila shook her head. "I came back early. I had to talk to Kylee."

"She left a while ago. She finally let me take a silver sample of that darn bracelet, but then she said she had somewhere she needed to be."

Lila glanced back at the carport. "But her car's still here."

"Then she must be headed some place local. Hey, if you've got a minute I've got something I want you to take a look at."

There was something excited and eager in Reggie's face that needed attending. Lila looked back at the house, because maybe Kylee was talking to Chloe or Chloe would know where she'd gone, then she nodded and followed the stone path across the lawn to the workshop. The wall of heat met her at the door scented of sweat and hot metal and stone.

"Holy moly, Reggie. How the heck can you work in this?"

Her friend grinned up at her and ran a work-blackened, long-fingered hand back through her matted hair. "Like always. I get going and I hardly even notice. That, and I drink a lot of water."

She went to a small fridge in the corner and pulled out two bottles. When Lila declined, Reggie downed one bottle's contents in one long smooth gulp and then opened the second. "Guess I was a little more parched than I thought. It's over here. I've been noodling with this for a bit and just finished. I'd like your honest reaction."

She stepped aside, drawing Lila over to her worktable and the mess of equipment there. A plain black cloth had been laid out with a silver pendant displayed on the center. It was about three inches long and made of tiny wood-grained sterling silver slats to look like boards in an arched doorway. The upper half, though, had been made like an art deco window, with fine silver strands arching up over the opening like the branches of a tree and holding in place a piece of smoky blue-gray Roman glass. A tiny lock had been placed on one side of the doorway and hanging from a tiny silver chain beside it, was a tiny ornate key. At the top, the pendant's bail—the loop that attaches to a chain—was subtly worked into the doorway so that it looked like a peak to the door.

"The designers sent me some of their sketches and the clothes were pretty tailored, but feminine. I thought this could go with their white blouses and flowing trousers." She held her hand to her chest just beneath her collarbone.

"May I?" At Reggie's nod, Lila picked the piece up. It was cool and heavy in her hand, but not so heavy it would be a burden to wear. "It is truly beautiful. Where did you come up with the design?"

Reggie shrugged. "Where do you think? Stupid bracelet's been on my mind, I guess. I just took the concept in a little different direction."

"Can you do earrings to match?"

"Can I do earrings?" Reggie rolled her eyes and pulled out a well-used sketch pad and pencil. "I'm thinking something like this." She swiftly penciled in arched drops of Roman glass with the same silver tree design encasing them. "Like windows framing the doors. So? Thoughts?"

Lila looked from the sketches to the mockup she held. "They're exquisite and the designers would be fools if they don't want them. I'd take it right now for the shop—or I'd steal it for my own wardrobe." She held the pendant to her chest, bare above a square-necked, fitted navy cotton dress, which at that moment felt like a sodden rag against her, given the sweat currently running down her back and front. "See? Looks pretty good, doesn't it."

Eyeing her, Reggie shook her head. "Everything looks good on you."

"Yeah, but this is spectacular." Lila replaced the piece on the soft black cloth. "Send them a photo and your sketches and I'll bet they'll be falling all over themselves. But now I have to find a certain little blond."

Reggie frowned. "She seemed kind of spooked. Scooted out of here looking a little sick."

"And that surprises you in this heat?"

But Reggie shook her head. "It's hot, but I don't think that was it. More like she was upset that I took that metal sample. She's real protective of that bracelet."

A little chill frisson ran up Lila's back. The bracelet again, but she only nodded. No need to bring everyone in on this—yet. She excused herself and headed for the house and blessed coolness. A quick change of clothes and then she had to find Kylee, because ever since she'd spoken to the Officer in Charge of the West Kelowna detachment of the Royal Canadian Mounted Police, she'd known that something in Peachland was terribly wrong.

And her friend was at its center.

§

Kylee found Brett seated outside the *Taste* bakery at the table she'd almost come to think of as theirs. The black wrought iron table was the same one she'd sat at that first day in Peachland and was the one where Brett had first found her. It was also the table he'd brought her to the first time he'd picked her up for coffee, and each time thereafter. It sat beside one of the concrete columns outside the bakery providing a little shade from the sun and shelter from the winds that could sometimes run up the lake.

Not that there was any wind today. The sun baked down on Brett where he leaned back in his bistro chair, his long legs stretched in front of him as he gazed out at the lake and the long-legged joggers in spandex running by. With his tan and his sun-streaked hair he was still that sun-bleached lifeguard that she'd crushed on so many years before.

And she was still acting like a school girl now.

Was she? She hadn't been following him around like a puppy, like she had when she was fifteen. She hadn't thrown herself at him. They'd had coffee and lunch a few times and there'd been those few luscious kisses, but she hadn't had that frantic feeling of *having* to be with him or she just might die. She'd felt that way with Kevin which, looking back, might be why he was able to take advantage of her.

For a moment she felt a little sad as she stood on the sidewalk just watching Brett sipping a plain coffee amongst the iced latte-toting *Taste* patrons, his aviator sunglasses hiding his eyes, but his tousled hair and strong jaw catching admiring glances from the women at the next table. He nodded and smiled at something the women said, but then he must have seen her. He raised his sunglasses, stood, and *smiled*.

Really smiled, with his eyes, with everything, actually. As if he really had missed her. Her knees went a little weak and her heart did a little jig so maybe that school-girl feeling was still there, but she inhaled and nodded and threaded her way through the tables to him. Strong arms surprised her with a hug she was totally unprepared for. Hug him back? Play it cool? Kiss him on the mouth? The cheek?

Darn it, she really was that stupid little school girl, except now Brett arms around her brought a sensation of—not wild madness, but completeness.

Thankfully, Brett ended the hug and held her away from him. "You really are a sight for sore eyes," he said. "It feels like forever since we had dinner together. I think we should do it again. In private." He held a chair for her. "What can I get you? Or would you rather get out of here?"

Dinner, not coffee. Dinner was the night he'd kissed her. Dinner was the day he'd held her close and rescued her from her fears after finding the note. For a moment she wondered what Lila had done with it.

"You're still drinking your coffee," she said in answer to his question and nodding at his half-filled cup.

"That's my fourth refill. Believe me, I could float away from here if you want to go, but I'm happy to stay if you want something."

The sun beat down on her head and shoulders, she really wished there was more of a breeze because she could feel the heat of Brett's gaze on her, even though his eyes were hidden behind his shades. "It's pretty hot here," she allowed.

"Leave it is." Brett stood and quickly went to bus his cup to a tray and came back to offer her his hand. "How about we take a drive?"

"But my car..."

"Is parked safely at *This & That*. You can pick it up later. I'll bring you back."

His hand still waited for hers and she hesitated, feeling like the world was watching and this was a fatal moment. Her decision now would set the future course of her life. Nervously she rubbed the silver bracelet and felt a comforting surge of warmth. It was the right thing to do. Brett had been nothing but a gentleman to her and he was the one who had come looking for her.

She accepted his hand and felt the gazes of the women at the next table flicker in disappointment, but the moment his fingers twined in hers she knew she'd made the right decision. If felt— right—good—solid.

"Lead on, McDuff." She smiled up at him.

They left the maze of tables and he led her down the street to the shade of a line of huge cottonwoods that ran their roots down into softly shifting lake water. Along the shore people sunbathed, or splashed in the water, their voices running out over the rippling lake. A lone swimmer paralleled the shore in slow steady strokes that spoke of distances covered and distances still to come. That was how she should approach this relationship, too. Not a run and a leap of faith like Kevin had been, but something intended for longer term. Something that brought them shoulder to shoulder instead of her always running after him.

His arm brushed hers and a tingle ran through her as she glanced up and found his gaze waiting. He'd felt it too; she could tell by the way he seemed to stop breathing for a moment. Then he squeezed her hand and helped her into his Miata, then climbed in himself.

"I missed you, you know. The whole time I was away." Lifting his sunglasses away, his green gaze met hers, the color of the leaves which stirred softly above them.

She smiled. "I missed you, too, though I was busy the whole time." Too busy to notice except at night when she finally had time to let her mind wander. It had invariably settled on him.

"I thought I'd show you around my Peachland," he said, gunning the engine. They cut out into the slowly moving traffic and cruised down the road along the waterfront, enjoying the little scenes: families picnicking; couples sunbathing together, holding hands. Then they swung over the little bridge that spanned Trepanier Creek and turned toward the highway.

"Where are we going?" she asked.

Brett just smiled mysteriously.

They turned north onto the highway and then immediately off onto a twisted switchback of a road that ran up the steep bluffs at the base of the mountains. The sky was deep blue above them and the view was spectacular, though not as good as from her little house. A developer had cleared all trees from the hillside to the north of them, and had planted a suburban housing development. It looked barren and unappealing without the pines and poplar she had come to associate with Peachland in her short time in the community. She couldn't see Brett ever living in one of those houses at all.

She was right. They passed the subdivision and the road swept up over the crest of the hill to a plateau of what looked like expensive homes on acreages. Sleek horses lounged in irrigated green fields. Gardens of rhododendron and roses and cedar spread around the houses, and vineyards laced across the flats and up hillsides. They turned off at a long driveway between two tall maples and a sign that said "Elkhart Winery" and *"Wine Tasting Tours"* in smaller print underneath. A silhouette of a large antlered buck was burned into the wood. Pale green vines ran back from the driveway on either side and seemed to take up almost all of the bench land. A light mist of irrigation reached her from a rainbow fall of water far out in the field.

"Some of the vines are still young, so we're watering," Brett explained.

The road curved around a stand of pine and came into a paved courtyard that would provide parking for tourists. Around it were three buildings. Three cars were parked in a line in front of a glass-fronted cedar-sided tasting room. Beside it lay a large barn-like building and on the third side was a sprawling house of cedar and stone with massive stone and floral gardens that had been shaped in the silhouette of the Elkhart. Tall weeping willows spread shade across the parking area and gave the air a luscious cool. Brett drove between the barn-like building and the house, and around to the back of the buildings to where a small, maple-shaded lawn held a picnic table. There he parked the car. Like the lawn at her home, the grass ended at the edge of a bluff allowing a wonderful view out over Peachland and southwards toward the blue-gray distance of Penticton at the southern tip of the lake.

Kylee took that in, but then slowly climbed out of the car as Brett came around to her. The lawn stood in front of one of the strangest houses she'd ever seen. Like the other buildings, it was cedar-sided in rich red-glowing oiled wood, but it was built like a low-slung bungalow, except that at one end the building suddenly sprouted a square-sided tower that rose three stories. The vineyard had clearly escaped its neatly-ordered fields, too, for grape vines grew up around the house, flowing over trellises and framing doors and windows.

"Oh my," she managed, for the house with all its oddity, intrigued her. "It looks like it's been scooped out of a European fairytale and plunked down here."

"Welcome to my home," Brett said, shattering all her preconceived notions of the man. He'd seemed so careful, logical, and practical that she'd expected him to live in a sleek steel and glass condo, and yet he spoke of Ogopogo and lived in a place like this.

"You live here?" She double checked.

"Well, yeah." His reply was almost bashful. He motioned to the picnic table in the shade of the tree. "Why don't you set yourself down and I'll get us something to drink."

He set two shopping bags on the table with a warning not to peek, and then loped toward the house's front door and disappeared inside. Kylee wandered over to the bluff edge for the view. Lovely, but not quite as expansive as the one she enjoyed from her house, because a curve of the long narrow lake blocked the view northward. The lake was the same iridescent blue she'd woken to every day since she'd arrived, the hills beyond gradually parching gray in the sun, and boats laying trails across the smooth lake water.

The silence was almost a visible presence except for the hiss of the irrigation and the high-up cry of an osprey that floated overhead on black wings. She turned back to the house and inhaled the scent of grapes and wandered toward the house. It looked quaint and almost magical the way the brilliant green vines encircled each window. She came to the door, open now. Unlike most doors today that were fabricated out of metal with a press-board core, this was clearly made of wood slabs tongue-and-grooved together and held in place by black iron strapping. It had what looked like a handmade black-iron door handle and the grapes were trellised to form an overgrown arbor that hung small clusters of still-green grapes around the door frame. With the darkness of the interior hiding its contents, it looked mysterious and yet familiar.

She frowned, but then Brett reappeared in the doorway, a grin on his face and two wine goblets and a bottle in one hand. He pulled the door shut behind him. "Come on."

He started back to the picnic table and caught her arm. Kylee didn't move.

The door... the way the grapes hung... but...

"Kylee? Is everything all right?"

His voice seemed to come from some other world that was at the other end of a long tunnel. She shook her head and stepped up the single step to the door and ran her fingers down the sun-warmed wood. The sweet scent of the grapes was here, too, like the scent Brett carried with him, and she knew that later in the summer if she stood here she would almost get drunk on the scent.

It just couldn't possibly be, but it was. What could it possibly mean?

"Kylee?" Warm hands caught her frozen arms and turned her to face him.

It was like being yanked out of a dream and she craned around to keep the door in view. He shook her slightly.

"Kylee, what is it. You look like you've seen—I don't know what."

She met his gaze then. "No. No ghost. It's just—this is going to sound really stupid—your door is on my bracelet." She held up her wrist and turned the delicate silver around until her favorite door was on the top of her wrist. Held it out for him and felt the warmth flow up her arm like a comfort as he caught her hand. "See? Right down to where the grapes are hanging."

She watched him match her theory check for check. Everything was there, including the little cluster of iron grapes that made the door knocker.

"How can that be, Brett? How can your house have a door that looks exactly the same as one in my bracelet?"

He was holding her wrist now and really studying the small door. Finally he shook his head. "No idea. A weird coincidence, most likely. The door is sort of similar to what you might find in Europe."

But the way the brown swirled in his gaze, he didn't think so anymore than she did. He caught her hand and led her back to the picnic table, reclaiming the bottle of wine and glasses he's set down on the grass.

In silence he poured the wine, a pale gold that smelled of peach, pears, and—violets. "Try it. It's a Viognier, a little old fashioned, a little more difficult to grow and ferment, but oh, so worth the risk."

He swirled the glass and then, uncharacteristically, knocked it back. She tasted cautiously.

"It tastes of peaches and—earth?" It did, as if sunshine filled her mouth, the essence of the Okanagan, with a little butter aftertaste. But they were changing the subject, even though she felt the door to Brett's place like a presence behind her. What did it mean? A warning? An invitation?

Her fingers ran over the comforting silver again. Not a warning. She was sure of it. No... she met Brett's warm green-brown gaze over the lip of her wine glass and they held. Held and she smiled and *knew*. The fact that the bracelet and the door were the same was more like a fate thing. A message. A warmth flowed through her and she felt Brett's presence like a magnetic pull. This thing with him was right and it made her suddenly self conscious. Would he read the decision she'd made? That she wasn't going to be afraid of a relationship with this man anymore?

§

The soft curve of Kylee's lips, their pale pink prints on the edge of the wine glass, the way she savored the wine thoughtfully, the way the soft breeze played in the pale strands of hair around her face, the way she met his gaze and this time held, all of them overwhelmed the unsettling coincidence of the doors. It simply had to be a coincidence, because Reggie had said she thought the bracelet was old. That meant they couldn't have used his door as a model and hell, even if they had, how could they have gotten the exact position of this year's clusters of grapes. It just wasn't logical. It *had* to be a coincidence.

He would hold to that because Kylee was here with him and there was something about her—as if the fear he'd always sensed in her had dissipated. He reached out and caught her hand.

"Did I tell you that I missed you?"

She nodded.

"The whole time I was in California all I could think about was getting home to this place—my vines—and you. Most of all you. I wanted to show you this place." It felt a little like he was baring his soul. What would he do if she didn't like it?

Behind her glass, she nodded. "It's beautiful here. It—it sort of looks like this tastes. Like sunshine and rich earth and all the fruit that both make possible." She gave him a shy smile that he'd grown ridiculously attached to in such a short time.

"I bought you something in California, but then I thought it was too—well—personal to give to you, so I bought you this." He pushed the bag from the Peachland Interiors shop toward her.

Sky blue eyes traveled from the bag to him and back again. "You really didn't need to get me anything."

But her trim fingers were eager as she opened the white bag and pulled out the long slim box with the photo of the wind chimes on the top. Her eyes grew round and she hurriedly opened the box and brushed past the tissue to lift out the chimes. A gorgeous ripple of sound filled the yard.

"Oh my goodness, Brett! They're beautiful." The softness of the barest breeze caught the long paddle and a different chord of music rang out across the vineyards in a tone so beautiful it could probably make the grapes grow. Her blue glaze flashed back to him as she set the chimes down. "Thank you! I'll hang them in the willow and they can sing me to sleep at night."

She leaned across the table to place a light kiss on his cheek, so close to his mouth that he almost turned into her. A surge of heat ran up through him and he wanted to take her in his arms, but instead he patted the white bag. "You aren't finished."

Kylee frowned and plumped back down on the picnic table bench. She pulled the deadbolt lock boxes out of the bag, looked at them, at him and then began to laugh. "Well better late than never, I suppose, but thank you. All of this will help me sleep better at night—not that I haven't been since I got into the house."

She seemed genuinely delighted in the chimes and locks. Her long fingers kept stroking the brushed steel of the chimes. Take a chance and give her what he'd really brought her back from California? She seemed more relaxed than she'd ever been around him.

Taking a deep breath, he pushed the gray plastic bag toward her. "Then there's this. Like I said, it might be too much. If it makes you uncomfortable, just give it back to me and it's done."

Jeezus, where had all his confidence gone? He felt like he was sinking into deep water and waiting for Kylee to throw him a lifeline, but somewhere over the last two weeks he'd made a decision to swim in deeper than he'd ever swam before and the shore was so far off he couldn't see it anymore. Only Kylee. His destination?

Hesitating, she accepted the bag, opened it, and drew out the beautifully wrapped present he'd carried onto the plane so it wouldn't get crushed in his luggage. Simple blue paper wrapped the box, and was held together with two-inch wide gold ribbon that had been hand tied into a huge golden, multi-looped bow.

Kylee's throat worked a little and her lips pressed into a line as she looked like she considered whether and where to begin.

"It's so pretty I don't want to open it." She looked up and smiled. She reached out and caressed the wind chimes again. "This is more than anyone has given me in years. And it's not even my birthday or Christmas. Are you sure you want to give me this?"

"Open it." Note to self, find out when her birthday is.

With a grin of delight she carefully untied the bow and removed the ribbon, then unfolded the paper so carefully he almost grabbed it from her and tore the box inside free. But that was rushing things and he couldn't rush Kylee anymore than he could rush the fermentation of an oak-casked burgundy. He forced his hands flat on the table.

When she opened the box and saw the tissue paper inside she looked up at him. "You bought me clothes?"

Should he apologize? Just take it away before she saw what it was?

Instead, he swallowed and nodded.

Cocking her head at him, Kylee paused. "You like to live dangerously, don't you? I've been told that buying clothes for a woman is one of the most difficult things a man can do because it's hard to understand a woman's style and taste." She grinned. "At least that was the world according to my ex. He would never even try to buy me clothes. A gift card, maybe." She was looking at him as if seeing him for the first time, or reappraising what she thought of him. In a good way, maybe.

"I guess I figured it can't be any worse than the chances you take when you blend a wine and go to taste it for the first time. A risk, just like life is a risk."

Smiling secretively she burrowed through the tissue and lifted out the blue top he'd bought her. Like he'd thought, the color was a perfect match for her eyes, the fabric fine enough it would flow over her trim body like a beautiful second skin.

"Oh my God, Brett, it's beautiful. I love it. I want to try it on." In a flash she was up and holding the fabric to her, her movements like dancing and his heart did an uncharacteristic flip flop. Crap. Maybe all Chloe's knowing glances were right.

"Well then, you must." He stood up and caught her hand, liking the familiar way her fingers curled into his. He led her to his house and inside, feeling her hesitate slightly, but as they stepped through the door together a flush ran through him from their joined hands as if they'd stepped through a magic portal. It sent his blood singing and his awareness of Kylee soaring. She was warm. She was alive and she was here, with him. In the dimness of his entryway, he turned her to him, set the blue top aside and pulled her into his arms.

CHAPTER 17

CLAD IN A SIMPLE LONG, SLEEVELESS CRIMSON TUNIC that skimmed lightly over her hips, black shorts, and athletic sandals, Lila left *This & That* out the front door and stepped back into the heat. The sun weighted her mane of hair around her shoulders so she wished she'd put it up. At least then the breeze would reach her neck—not that there was much breeze. The still air seemed to have sucked the life out of everything along the lake shore. Bathers baked in the sun. Even the ubiquitous splashing children seemed to paddle half-heartedly in the shallows. The sapphire-blue lake lay flat and barely rippled, like it was hiding something. Even the cars driving along Beach Avenue seemed ponderous and slow, pushing hot winds before them. She pulled on her Raybans and struck out for the bakery which was where Chloe had said she thought Brett and Kylee were meeting. Please let them be there. Please let them be there, and Kylee be willing to do what needed doing.

But Kylee wasn't at the bakery and neither was Brett. That they were probably together was a reasonable conclusion given Chloe's observations of the two of them. Their chemistry had been clear from the start and it was nice to see both of them taking the time to get to know each other. Brett, now that he was over himself, had turned into the kind of man every woman would like to meet. Thoughtful and kind, though still blessed with beach boy good looks and a hint of the devil.

She turned on her heel to head back to the store and her car.

"Lila Weber?" Male voice. Vaguely familiar.

She swung back around and found herself facing Detective Danny Forester looking significantly less certain of himself and significantly more rumpled than when she'd last seen the officious idiot. All the alarm bells went off in her head and she backed away a step.

"Of course I'm Lila Weber. But then you knew that."

Forester frowned as if he was trying to remember something. He still wore the suit he'd worn over a week ago, but by the look of his white shirt, he might have slept in it. His jacket he held in his hand, and his shirt sleeves were rolled up, but that hadn't helped against this heat. His shirt was massively sweat stained. He nodded. "I interviewed you, didn't I?"

What the heck? "Yes. And practically searched my shop and house. What can I do for you Corporal. I'm in the middle of things and I really need to be going."

Not the least because the RCMP had said that one Corporal Danny Forester was seriously AWOL from his post at West Kelowna Detachment. He hadn't been seen since the night of Moira Burns' death, when he'd been part of the team interviewing witnesses in the neighborhood where Moira had been hit. He'd apparently climbed in his unmarked vehicle and driven away. No one knew where. The police vehicle had been found at his house, but he hadn't been seen anywhere until Lila walked in with the report that he'd interviewed her in Peachland.

"I need to talk to you," he said, stepping towards her before she expected it.

"Well, I don't want to talk to you. I believe there are police looking for you and I intend to go call them, so I suggest you move on." She hauled her cell out of her purse and punched in 9 and 1.

He moved so quickly and smoothly she hadn't even seen it

coming. He had her arm by the wrist and the phone out of her hand. Then he punched the cancel button on the phone and pulled her into him so she inhaled his scent of hot iron and days-old spicy aftershave.

"Like I said, I need to talk to you, Lila. This is important. I don't mean any harm, but I need to figure out what the hell's happening to me."

"How the heck should I know? I hardly know you." She tried to pull away, but he wasn't releasing her. "I can scream and there'll be people all over you in no time."

He nodded and his brown eyes met hers. "I know. But I need your help, here."

His gaze was dark and desperate and but his grip on her arm eased.

"See? I'm letting you go. But if you could just sit with me a minute. Say, on that bench?" he motioned to a green-painted park bench set in tree-shade by the water.

She needed to find Kylee. She really did, but this man was one of the things Lila'd been wanting to warn her about. Maybe it would be a good idea to find out what he was all about.

"Five minutes. I can give you five minutes and then I'm out of here and I'm calling the police."

Not bothering to see if he followed, she strode to the bench and plunked herself down. Corporal Forester perched at the other end, his jacket across his lap. He looked out at the water, his skin pale under the tan.

"I don't know what's happening to me. I know I was in Kelowna. I know I was on an investigation, but the last thing I remember is interviewing a homeless guy and then everything goes cloudy, like I wasn't really involved. But I remember you because I was looking for you. I don't know why."

His hands were folded in his lap like a choir boy's and his throat worked like just saying the words caused him pain. Maybe the man had had a psychotic break. Maybe he was crazy as a loon and dangerous, but right now he just looked like a man who was thoroughly frightened. She frowned.

"Why tell me? Why not go back to your office and figure it out there? You've got an entire detachment of police to help you."

He shook his head. "Because if I go back there they're going to tell me I'm just as crazy as I'm afraid I am." He turned that sad brown gaze at her. "That's the thing. I don't think I am. I think— something happened during that investigation. I don't know what, but it was like I was suddenly along for the ride inside my own body and then suddenly I had it back again. Everything was so hazy I didn't know what to do. Then I remembered you. I was looking for you. What did I want?"

The man's story was so all-out weird she really should just stand and march right out of here. But he looked like an abused puppy right now, and by the look of him he was a proud man. He didn't like this anymore than she did. She sighed.

"All right. If you want to know, you came down to question me about the night of Moira's death. I saw her, you see." She told him about arriving late and the box of jewelry Moira had for her and how she'd left Moira alive. "That was the only business I had with her. I took the box and headed right out, because I was trying to get back to Vernon and it was already late. I got the sense she would be leaving almost immediately after me. She looked exhausted, but then those estate sales can be trying." She glanced sideways at him and saw him nod as he wrote in his black police notepad—habit probably, the way he managed his thoughts. When he was done, she continued.

"After you'd interviewed me you asked to see the box of jewelry I'd bought, so I took you into the kitchen where I was sorting things from the buying trip. You seemed really interested in the contents of that box—almost as if you were searching for something. When whatever it was, wasn't there, you seemed almost angry. You left. That's it. Until this morning."

He wrote his notes and then looked up at her, his gaze a trifle tired and a lot desperate. "That's all?"

"Everything." She nodded. "What were you hoping for?"

He sat back and scrubbed his fingers through his hair, then shook his head. "I don't know. For some reason I'm down here. Still down here. I should be back in West Kelowna begging the CO not to fire my ass, but I'm here hanging around like a bad smell. Beginning to smell like one too." He gave a rueful grin. "I need to know what happened and why. I seem to remember a small green sports car and a blond woman. Does that mean anything to you?"

Lila froze. That meant way too much, because there was only one person it could be. Tell him? Ask him about the note she still had in her pocket? The police hadn't seemed that interested, but Corporal Forester might be. Then again he might also be the person who put it in Kylee's house and terrified her. The heat seemed to have left the hot day and a too-cold breeze blew up the lake.

He seemed so earnest and so clear-headed at the moment. Take a chance and tell him what she knew and suspected? But who was to say he wouldn't come after Kylee then. No, that was one piece of information she wasn't sharing yet.

She checked her Longines watch. Five minutes were long past. Well, in for a penny...

"When I passing through West Kelowna today I went into the detachment. They were surprised I came in. You see they really have just focused on finding the hit and run driver. That's what they're calling it. I got to talking to the lead investigator and he said that aside from one half-crazed homeless guy who claims that the truck was guided by an alien that had been inside his head, there's nothing to indicate it was anything more than that. Except that one of their best detectives had suddenly disappeared taking some evidence with him."

Corporal Forester reached into a jacket pocket and pulled out a gleaming black leather daytimer that looked an awful lot like the one she carried. She had admired Moira Burns' diary and had bought the same kind last October from a little stationery store in Kamloops.

"This," he said looking at her with a pained expression. "I have this and I don't know why." He flipped it open to the date of Moira's death and ran a finger down the page. "It lists all of the purchases made at the estate sale. Everyone who was there. I figure this is how I tracked you here. The question is, why?"

"You wanted to question the last person to see her alive?" Lila asked. That was the logical thing, the thing you'd expect, except everything about Corporal Danny Forester and what he'd experienced suggested the situation was far from normal.

"Could be," he allowed with a nod. "But here's the thing— what I do remember—and you've got to know it's like I'm walking through a fog from the moment I questioned the sole witness—is that after I picked up the daytimer at the scene the only thing that mattered was finding you and the box you had. I climbed into my car and immediately left."

"May I see it, please?" she asked for the daytimer and after hesitating a moment he passed it to her.

Yup, there was her name, big as day in Moira's plump script. Among the list she recognized other names of the buyers she frequently saw at estate sales. Almost all those listed had small tick marks beside their names and a number—probably a receipt number given they were in numeric order down the list. All except one name. "Who's this I wonder? By the look of it, he didn't buy anything and yet she'd noted down his name."

She turned the diary toward him and tapped the page where it listed a James Murphy. "You know, when I showed up at the estate sale Moira actually acted relieved. I chalked it up to the fact she wanted to get the heck out of there and go home—she'd stuck around a couple of hours longer for me. But now that I think about it, she mentioned a guy—someone who'd never come to the sales before and he'd apparently hung around for a good long time. She said she had to roust him out of private areas of the house where it was like he was searching for something. She said that at one point he offered to buy all the jewelry in the house, if she'd just sign his papers and leave. Of course she'd already sold some things and accepted payment, and she'd promised my lot to me, so she turned him down. Apparently he wasn't happy when he left. Moira might have been nervous being alone."

Corporal Forester went thoughtful. "Something to look into. A man searching for something. The name's familiar, though I can't say I recognize it right now. Strange that he was looking for something and I apparently was, too."

A thought that was all too clear to Lila. She rubbed her arms against the chill. It made no logical sense that there could be a connection between the man who had freaked Moira out and Corporal Forester's searching through the jewelry she'd brought home. And yet where was the logic in Chloe's healing stones and yet she accepted that. There was a connection, because both of them had been searching for something. Something hidden in a box of jewelry the man in Kelowna never got a chance to see. Something that had been removed from the box of jewelry, as well as from the kitchen, when Corporal Forester inspected it. The only thing that fit that bill was the bracelet.

Tell Corporal Forester?

She glanced sideways at the man. He looked a little dissolute and a lot desperate in his rumpled clothing and his couple of week's growth of beard. Nope. Kylee was just too vulnerable with that darned bracelet on. A sitting duck, in fact, if that creepy compulsion seized the good officer again.

She checked her watch again—she'd been here half an hour—and stood. "I think you might be well-advised to return to your detachment. Perhaps you can follow up on this Jake Murphy. He might be your culprit. That is the word, isn't it?"

"Suspect. We call them a suspect. And yeah, I should." He scrubbed his face and stood beside her looking out at the lake. "You want to know the really scary thing? That witness I described—the homeless guy? His description of having an alien in his head? That's exactly how I'd describe what happened to me."

§

Brett's arms were solid and strong around her and she inhaled his scent of sunshine and vineyards, as heady as the wonderful wine they'd been sipping at the picnic table. Around them, the dim reaches of the house were punctuated by beams of light allowed in by windows, that left her with glimpses of the leather arm of a couch, the gleam of old wood, the vivid pattern of a pillow. She looked up at him, and took a chance, brushing his mop of sun-bleached hair back from his forehead and eyes.

"You know, I've decided I'm going to like you," she said. Saying the words felt like plunging into a dark pool trusting there weren't rocks underneath.

His hands came up to frame her face, his thumbs gently rubbing her lower lip. "That makes me happy. I've decided I like you, too."

His arms snugged her a little tighter to him and as easy as that, he leaned down, and she found herself waiting. The kiss, when it came, was just about everything she had imagined it would be—yes, she had imagined it. Had dreamt of that too-fleeting kiss at the house and the more lasting one on the wharf.

But this wasn't fleeting. His lips grazed hers and lingered, his tongue tasting as if she was one of his fine wines. His kisses trailed along her jaw, to her eyelids, and she felt her legs melting. This was how a man kissed a woman—with longing and promise and passion. Not like Kevin at all, with his tongue down your throat and grope methodology.

This man knew how to kiss, and she answered; wrapping her arms around his neck she kissed him back, trailing kisses down his throat, then smiling up at him.

"Oh. Damn. Kylee." He kissed her deeply then and heat surged through her body. His hands roamed down her sides and came to rest on her hips, pulling her into him so she could feel his reaction to her. Hard. A promise, and one she wanted him to keep, but he pulled away and smiled down at her. "Um. You wanted to try on that blue top."

His voice was a little hoarse and breathless and all her words had vanished from her head. She nodded. Because if the man could kiss like that, she was seriously looking forward to what came later. As a matter of fact she'd be kind of happy if it wasn't much later.

But she followed his lead as he indicated a washroom and she ducked into what must be a guest powder room with mottled marble tiled walls and a square white sink set into a black marble counter. Plush gray towels hung on the rack. She hurriedly pulled off her tunic and pulled on the blue top.

It hung to just below her hips, grazing her body in all the right places, with a slight peplum and longer hem at the back to give the garment a sense of movement. It was sleeveless and had a rounded neckline that mirrored the longer hemline in back. Across the front tiny blue beads set off a subtle design of a covey of delightful, stylized quail. It fit perfectly, the fine fabric like a second skin.

"You ready for this?" She called through the powder room door and ran her fingers through her hair to fluff it a little. A little lipstick and she was ready.

She opened the door and found Brett lounging on a low brown leather couch, his long legs outstretched. Across from him was a stone fireplace of natural river rock, with what looked like a carved-wood antique clock on the mantle. Dark hardwood floors were covered with a kaleidoscope of Navajo-patterned rugs and similar patterns graced cushions on the couch and a small ottoman. It was a masculine room, and yet it oozed comfort. She stepped out to him and pirouetted.

"It's beautiful, just like I thought and you got the size perfect." She pirouetted again and then did a little jig before settling herself on the couch beside him. "Where did you get so talented, picking out a woman's clothes and getting it so perfect?"

He looked mystified a moment and then grinned. "One does not grow up with a sister like Chloe and her friends, without some sense of fashion wearing off. And while we're asking questions, where'd you ever get so beautiful?" His hand skimmed her bangs back off her face. "Yup. Beautiful."

Beautiful? No one had ever called her beautiful in her life. She'd grown accustomed to cute, or gamine, or attractive. She swallowed.

"You really do know the right things to say, don't you? All those years of chasing women..."

He shook his head. "Nope. It has nothing to do with all those years. It has to do with you. You're beautiful and you need to know it." Pulling her into his arms, he kissed her again, until she felt breathless and flushed. He set her back down and nodded. "Yup. I stand by my assessment. So, you want to see the place?"

She did, so he gave her the grand tour of his house, the main floor with its heavy, masculine furniture in the spacious living room, but a thoroughly modern working kitchen in the back, complete with a magnificent wine cellar. A spare bedroom and then there was the set of stairs spiraling up into the tower end of the house. He led the way, taking her through a room that served as his office with all the modern computers, printers, desk and cabinets etc., and then up again. The top floor was a modern bedroom with a king-sized bed sporting more of the vivid Navajo print. A modern-styled dresser sat against one wall, while thick cream-colored Berber carpet covered the floor. A door led into a good sized ensuite with a jetted tub that could hold two and a glassed-in shower stall. Both the ensuite and the bedroom had massive windows that allowed spectacular views of the lake. The bedroom had a sliding glass door that gave onto a small verandah.

"Wow! No wonder you put your bedroom up here. You can see forever." She stood at the window peering out at the view she knew she would never get tired of. In the few short weeks she'd been here, she'd changed, she knew. And part of the change had been the way the Okanagan had gotten into her blood. "I love it here."

She realized what she'd said when she felt Brett's arms come around her and he cradled her against his chest. "We could love it here together," he said with a wicked gleam in his eye and nibble on her earlobe.

"Brett." She rolled her eyes and turned into him. "Not what I meant and you know it."

"Ah, but I've been known to change a young lady's mind. Care to wager whether I can change yours?"

He looked way too tempting, with the light catching the strong lines of his face and the way his polo shirt accentuated the breadth of his shoulders and his abs. He must have seen her weakening, because he leaned in to place the most sensual of kisses on her lips so her mouth opened in answer. She met need with need. Then he caught her shoulders and set her aside so she wanted to grab him by the collar and kiss him back. Now.

"Hold that thought. But we've got company."

Following his gaze out the window, she saw a bright red Ford Escape stirring up dust as it sped around the winery and into Brett's yard.

"Lila? What's she doing here?" Aside from interrupting something she really didn't want interrupted. Brett's kisses had ignited something that she thought she'd never feel again and this time she trusted those feelings.

"Looks like she's on a mission, the way she's driving," Brett said with a frown. He laced one last light kiss on her lips and headed for the stairs, concern written all over his handsome face. With a last lingering look at the bedroom, Kylee followed.

CHAPTER 18

To Kylee, Lila's sharp rap-rap-rap on the front door sounded like thunder in the dim silence of Brett's house. As she followed Brett down the stairs, the sunlight placed searchlights through the downstairs windows, slashing through the shadows until Brett opened the door. The heat rushed in at them as Lila stood silhouetted against the daylight, her auburn curls a medusa corona around her head and shoulders.

"Thank God. You're here." She plunged into the house without waiting for an invitation, her gaze catching on Kylee's attire. "Nice top. Very nice."

She strode into the living room and turned to face them, there was an unaccustomed edge to Lila's usually calm demeanor. Small beads of sweat stood out at the edge of her hair and her gold-tanned skin seemed suddenly pale. She caught Kylee's hand. "Are you okay?"

"Okay? Of course I'm okay." She glanced up at Brett. Better than okay, in fact. "I should be asking you the same thing. What's wrong Lila? You look like something bad has happened."

But Lila was already twisting Kylee's arm around, fumbling with the bracelet. What the hell? Kylee tugged her hand away and rubbed her wrist protectively.

"Lila? What is this? You never come up here." Brett stepped between them as if he sensed something was seriously off.

Lila looked from one to the other of them and closed her eyes. "Okay." She took a deep cleansing breath and exhaled, splaying her hands wide in release. Then she looked at them again and sank down on the edge of Brett's deep brown couch.

"Okay. Let me take this slow. Kylee, I've been worried about you ever since you got this." She fished in her pocket and brought out a piece of paper in a Ziploc baggie. "The note you found in your house the day you moved in. I took it, remember?"

A chill shivered down Kylee's spine at the way Lila's eyes seemed too wide and, frankly, a little scared. It was too similar to the look Chloe had had when the man had visited the store. Had Chloe told Lila? "I remember."

"Well I took it up to the RCMP on this last trip. I kept meaning to get in there sooner, but things just seemed to get in the way. So on my way back from Kamloops I stopped in to the RCMP detachment and asked for the officer who's investigating Moira's death." She shook her head and looked down at the note in her hands. "They said that they were investigating Moira's death as a simple hit and run. But the officer wasn't that Corporal Forester who came to Peachland to interview me. When I asked about him the guy I was talking to totally shut down. When I said that Forester had been to interview me in Peachland he finally said that they were looking for him. The guy had apparently interviewed one witness at the time that Moira was found, and then he'd taken a piece of evidence from the scene and left. They'd found his police car abandoned and that was it."

"What?" Confused, Kylee sank onto the arm of a chair, but the chill in the air seemed to be growing except where Brett stood close beside her. "But Corporal Forester..."

"So I showed them the note," Lila interrupted. "But they weren't interested and didn't see any connection to their case. Let's just say I freaked and left, because Forester *had* been asking questions in Peachland after he'd run amok in Kelowna and he'd been searching for something. The fact that he'd been searching for something and didn't find it made me think of the one thing that wasn't in the box when he went looking. That." She nodded at the bracelet. "I drove like a madwoman back to the store, but you weren't there. Corporal Danny Forester, however, was—not in the store, but he caught up to me when I was looking for you. We spoke."

She told them about the discussion and Moira's mention of a man who had apparently been searching the estate sale house and shook her head. As she spoke, the room got colder and colder and the air seemed to suck right out of Kylee's lungs. She shivered and wrapped her arms around herself for warmth. The new shirt was too thin for the chill of the house, but she suspected she wouldn't be any warmer outside, either. Kylee looked down at her arm at the soft gleam of the silver bracelet and somehow knew that everything Lila said was true.

And that meant Chloe's warning was, too.

The room went silent after Lila finished and her friend looked exhausted and drained where she sat. Sometime during her talk Brett's arms had come protectively around Kylee's shoulders and she leaned back against him. He was a source of warmth and strength when cold seemed to be everywhere. It helped thaw the fear that seemed to have immobilized her.

"This doesn't make any sense, Lila," Brett said, his arms tightening around Kylee. "Why would some cop come chasing down here after the bracelet? It means nothing to him. And why would he be spying on Kylee and me? So he mentions a green sports car and a blond woman. It could be someone else entirely."

Kylee shook her head. "No. I think she's right. There's—there's something unusual about this bracelet. We've all commented on how unusual it is. Its design. Its silver. The fact the stupid thing won't come off. Even the fact that one of the doors matches your front door, Brett. Just how does a door that was apparently made a long time ago come to have exactly your door in its design, right down to the grape clusters ripening this year? And there's something you don't know. Some guy in a limo came looking for the bracelet and scared the wits out of Chloe. He was searching for some keepsake that meant something to his family. He apparently wasn't happy when whatever it was, wasn't at the *This & That*."

"What!" Lila and Brett's voices exploded together.

"When did this happen?" Lila demanded.

"Why wasn't I told?" Brett said.

Kylee pulled out of Brett's arms and stood, frowning at the sudden interrogation. "It happened a few days ago and you were gone, Brett. I made Chloe swear not to tell anyone because I didn't want you all to react like this."

"But this is a real threat. A lead. We should let the police know," Lila insisted.

"And you need to get that bracelet off your wrist." Brett stood and caught her shoulders, peering down at her.

Okay, here was her test. What was it Chloe had said? What did she want? She raised her chin at Brett. "No. This bracelet is meant to be where it is. It came to me almost like it was fated and since then all manner of good things have happened. My job, my house, you..." She scanned his face for an indication that she wasn't signing their fledgling relationship's death warrant. "I'm sorry, but I'm not taking it off until it comes off like it's supposed to."

Lila threw up her hands in frustration. Brett's face worked as he struggled with too clear emotions—anger, fear, frustration.

"Kylee, you've been spending too much time with my sister. It's an old bracelet. That's all."

She stepped back, feeling the loss of Brett's arms, but she needed to understand what was going on when nothing made any sense. If Brett couldn't see what she saw, well then he was a little bit blind. "If you guys can't figure the clasp out, then something is seriously wrong. You're experts. At least Lila and Chloe and Reggie are, and they haven't been able to get it off any better than you could."

Rubbing her forehead with one hand, she caught his hand with the other. Her anxiety eased a little. It was like they were better together. "There's something weird about that Corporal's story. The way he describes himself as being in a fog."

"I'd say it's more the way he says he had an alien in his head like the homeless witness said. Guy's gone around the bend." Brett caught her shoulders again. "Don't worry, Kylee. I'm here and as long as I'm here I'll protect you."

She looked up into his green eyes and saw that he meant it. This guy was here for the duration—even if she didn't do things the way he thought she should. She could just let Brett protect her from whatever was out there. Wasn't that what she'd wanted with Kevin? Protection from the great unknowns in life?

She reached out a palm to stroke his face. "Thanks. That helps, but I think we need to do more than just worry about protecting me." She turned back to Lila. "I think we need to know more about this bracelet if we're going to understand why someone like Corporal Forester would want it."

"My thoughts exactly," Lila agreed. "That's why I did some digging to find out who the estate belonged to and where family might live. Apparently the home belonged to a Mrs. George Bristol. Her deceased husband had been a Colonel in the British Army before immigrating to Canada after the Second World War. They had three kids who now live in Vancouver, Toronto and Ottawa."

"So we're going to contact them and see if they know anything about the bracelet?" Kylee asked. It was almost like some of the class projects they'd undertaken together when they were kids in school.

"Hold on a minute." Brett pushed in between them rubbing his face. "Let me see if I've got this straight. You both think that there is something going on that places Kylee in danger, yet now you're going to go *research* it? Are you nuts? Wouldn't it make more sense to just cut the darned bracelet off her wrist and give it to the authorities?"

Just the thought of following Brett's suggestion made Kylee's stomach clench. She covered her wrist protectively. The warm colors of the Navajo carpets and the dim lighting suddenly went dark and cold. Brett looked too big, too threatening where he stood. She fell back a step.

"Not this bracelet. No." she said. She cradled her arm against herself and both Lila and Brett looked at her strangely.

"Now that is strange," Lila whispered. She stood up and approached and Kylee backed up a step, shaking her head.

"Kylee? What is it, sweetie?"

Her old friend was too tall, her hazel eyes had gone dark and threatening. Why hadn't she seen it—Lila was a threat not a friend. Kylee backed up another step, and her hand clutching her wrist where the bracelet pulsed, yes actually pulsed. She would not let anything happen to her bracelet.

From somewhere in the darkness beyond Lila, she heard a voice: "What the hell's going on, Lila?"

Someone who she'd always thought would protect her, but no longer. Lila who she'd thought was her friend—a lie. The betrayal brought tears to her eyes. She really was what Kevin had said—a needy nothing who could never be worth the time it took for a friendship—or a relationship. She couldn't breathe with all the old pain that filled her chest.

"Kylee? What are you seeing? We're your friends, remember? We want to help. We won't try to cut the bracelet. We promise."

It was like a cloud over the moon suddenly passed away and Lila's beautiful face was before her. The darkness left and it was just a dimly lit room with beams of sunlight lacing dust motes through the shadows. The scent of clean leather and wood oil hung faintly in the room along with the scent of vineyards and sunshine. Brett's scent.

She swallowed. What was she doing? Her legs started to give and strong arms caught her.

"Let's get you outside into the sunshine," Lila said and Brett half-carried her out the vine-laden door to the picnic table where the wind chimes still lay.

She sagged onto the bench and rubbed her clammy brow. "Wow. What was that?"

Lila knelt in front of her while Brett kept a warm hand on her shoulder. A good thing because she felt like a cold wind had blown right through her and almost blown *her* away.

"I've never seen anything like it." Lila shook her head, her soft curls swaying. "You went white as a sheet and it was like you weren't there at all—not in your eyes anyway. Something feral and trapped looked out at me."

Lila caught her hand and started to rub her fingers. "You're freezing."

"You've got no idea how it feels from inside." Kylee kept her voice light, fighting for normalcy. It didn't quite work. "It—it was like I wasn't quite there, but something else was and it was afraid and you were the enemy." And that was the truth, now that she thought of it. At least as far as she was going to reveal. She wasn't going to tell them about all her insecurities.

Lila frowned and stood. "I don't believe this psychic stuff, but this is the third person who described feeling like there's someone else inside them. That can't just be a coincidence. There's something going on here."

But Brett was shaking his head. "What? You're suggesting Kylee's possessed, now? Isn't that just a bit of a stretch?" His fingers tightened on her shoulder.

The weird thing was it could be true, even though she didn't want it to be. She looked up at the two of them: her best friend, the man she was falling for. Their gazes flashed as they faced each other, both clearly not happy with each other.

"You know damn well that I don't believe in that stuff anymore than you do, but look at what we've got, Brett. I wish you'd seen Corporal Forester and how shaken he was. He didn't strike me as anyone who would leap to the conclusion of possession, and yet he said that he felt like something else had been in his head. Sound familiar to you?" She looked meaningfully down at Kylee and a wave of fatigue swept through her.

"Guys," Kylee said, holding up her hands. She just couldn't deal with this right now, with Brett's vehement denial most of all. When she looked up at him all she saw was his concern, as if he saw her suddenly as an invalid. She wasn't. She needed to make that clear. "Can we just not talk about this anymore? Lila, I'm tired. I want to go home. Will you take me? Tomorrow's Canada Day and it's going to be busy."

Lila nodded and Kylee gathered up her new wind chimes and her purse from the table.

"I'll drop by later to put those up for you and put in the locks." Brett said, coming close beside her and stroking her face.

"Don't," she said. "I want to take a long hot bath and then I'm going to go to bed."

Why she was turning him away, she wasn't sure, but it was her own decision—not whatever had just happened in the house. She just didn't appreciate being looked at as something broken. She might have been once, but she wasn't anymore and didn't want to be around someone who made her feel that way now.

She left with Lila, riding silently down the switchback road down to lake level and then back to *This & That* after Kylee mentioned that she wanted to reclaim her car. The long day still lingered on, but the sun was starting to fall toward the top of the hill. People still frolicked in the lake, though, and decorations had gone up for the events Lila had said occurred on Canada Day. Red and white bunting now festooned the front of the *Taste* bakery café. The red and white flag with its ubiquitous maple leaf had appeared everywhere in the space of a few hours. Even Chloe had managed to put small bouquets of tiny flags in each of the copper flower pots festooning the front porch. The flags looked like strange blooms amidst the white and red geraniums. Then Lila drove them around back and pulled into the carport.

"Can I borrow a laptop?" Kylee asked.

Lila's finely plucked brows rose. "You figuring to do some research this evening?"

Kylee nodded. "Something like that. What was that guy's name again? The British Colonel?"

"George Bristol?"

That was him. "I think I'm maybe going to do a bit of an Internet search on him. See if I find anything."

"And I'm going to contact his family, if I can find them," Lila said and slung an arm around Kylee's shoulder. "You know, you were pretty hard on ol' Brett back there. You basically cut him off at the knees. He was just trying to help."

A little pang of guilt ran through her but she shook her head. "I'm not a baby bird, Lila. I'm a big girl—now. I realize that. I don't have to have some big strapping man around to make me feel safe."

Lila looked at her out of the tops of her eyes, but it wasn't in doubt. She grinned. "Maybe not, but there's plenty of pleasure to be had in sharing a life with someone. Don't forget about that."

Like Lila was anyone to talk. She'd filled her life up with work and, it seemed, nothing else. But Brett was a good guy. Someone she really liked. Kylee sighed and nodded. "I'll think about it."

§

The next day, Canada Day, bloomed bright and promised to be as hot as the day before had been. Canada Day, the Canadian version of the American's Fourth of July, was the celebration of the birth of the nation. Kylee woke early, and sipped a cup of rich coffee in the kitchen with the door open to let in the cool morning air and the scent of sage and the baby's breath that grew wild on the hillsides. From outside came the sounds of song sparrows, the croak of a raven and the taunt of a magpie along with the soft gong. Underlying it all, the wind chimes sang in the somnolent breeze. She'd hung the chimes on a hook on the eaves of the house, just outside the door, until she could decide where she really wanted them. The soft music only leant itself to the silence of the morning.

Another sip of the dark brew and she flipped open the laptop. She didn't need to be at the shop until noon. Last evening after her bath, she'd sat here at the table in her shorty pajamas sipping tea and researching Colonel George Bristol, late of the British Army.

Surprisingly, there had actually been a Wikipedia entry, not that it told her much. But then, she really didn't know what she was looking for, did she? She rubbed her—no—*the* bracelet. What she really wanted was a clue as to where he might have got the bracelet and why it felt so important. Not that she knew it was, but it just *felt* like it was.

After listening to Lila talk last night she could no longer deny the fears Chloe had, but she was going to figure out what was happening.

Colonel George Bristol had been born in 1920, the second youngest son of a family of minor British nobility with a long history of service to their country. His father had lost his leg in the First World War. So George apparently signed up as was expected of a son who wouldn't inherit much of anything. Apparently there was nothing distinguishing about his early career, but then the Second World War began.

Bristol had been in Africa in the British 8th Army serving under General Ritchie in the disastrous tank fight against Rommel. He'd been with the defeated British Army as they retreated from Tobruk and made their way across North Africa toward Alexandria and Cairo, Rommel in pursuit. Along the way, Bristol had apparently led a small force charged with slowing Rommel down. The article didn't say what had happened, only that Bristol arrived in Alexandria with very few men and after that point his fortunes changed. He was part of the successful force that repelled and defeated Rommel's Panzer division. From

North Africa he went on to a number of other successful ventures, including the British force that successfully defeated the German force on Lake Tanganyika. After the war had ended he had retired and emigrated to Canada.

"Okay, George Bristol. So just where did you happen to pick up this little trinket?" She sat back in her chair and absently rubbed the bracelet, because for some reason she was sure that it had been Bristol who had found or purchased the bracelet, not the woman he had married after he came to Canada. An odd conclusion based on nothing but a hunch, really.

She scrubbed her fingers through her hair and closed the computer. She'd tried online searches for jewelry with door motifs and hadn't learned anything more than what Reggie had told her. There just wasn't anything that came close to the style and delicacy of what she wore on her wrist. Hopefully Lila was having more luck contacting the family.

She stood up and moved around the room, washing her teacup, cleaning the counter of crumbs from last night's dinner. She should wash the floor; she swept it at least. The wind chime softly gonged outside the door and she slid her feet into flip-flops and went out the door and down the stairs to stare back up at the place where she'd hung the chimes. It wasn't the right spot for them.

Back up the stairs, unhooked the chimes and she marched out to the willow tree. She found a hook already in a major limb that must have been placed there for holding a lantern or something. Hung the chimes there and stood back, still unsatisfied. What the heck was the matter with her? She wasn't one of those women who couldn't make up their minds. But this morning even this decision eluded her, just like the answer to the bracelet eluded her.

She was pretty sure she knew why, too. Brett. She had unfinished business with him, even if his doubts about the urgency to understand the bracelet infuriated her. In the cooler light of morning she could forgive his doubts. Heck, she had them herself. Just how was she supposed to find out anything about some old bracelet found in an estate sale? And why would anyone want it? Sure, it was unique, but it was just a bracelet. It wouldn't be impossible for someone to make a pretty good replica. From what she'd seen, Reggie could do it. Regulus jewelry was nothing if not intricate and meticulous. But from what Lila had said, the Corporal *had* been looking for it, just like the guy at Moira's sale had been looking for it and just like Chloe's creepy visitor had been. Or something had compelled them to.

That was the thing, wasn't it? The story of being compelled sort of resonated with her because she'd felt like that herself when she put the bracelet on. She'd felt like that a little as well, when she'd first kissed Brett. Well, not exactly compelled that time, but as if it was meant to be and she had known it. Even though she hadn't. She shivered at those thoughts because being possessed didn't sound at all attractive.

But being with Brett had felt right and it wasn't some stupid bracelet telling her that. It felt really right, and she'd left him last night like there was a problem between them.

Shoot.

She checked her watch. Just coming on nine thirty. She had time to run up to Brett's now that she knew where he lived. She could apologize and make things right between them.

She grabbed her trusty daypack and locked up the house, then started her Civic and rumbled down the hill and along the highway before turning back up into the hills. The traffic on the highway was a madhouse of Canada Day travelers and she caught glimpses of the Peachland shoreline and the hordes of revelers. They'd basically shut the road down for the afternoon parade and evening party. The event would end with a massive fireworks show that she'd been looking forward to watching from a lawn chair planted in her front yard, glass of wine in hand. In her imagination, Brett had been there beside her.

The Civic chugged up the steep Trepanier hill to the plateau with its horse farms and wineries and the scent of ripening grapes in the air. If she hadn't smelled it, she never would have realized there was such a scent as sunshine. She turned at the carved Elkhart sign and followed the long driveway in and around the winery buildings to Brett's house. The place baked in the sunshine, its front door closed, its windows reflecting back at her.

She climbed out of the car and thumped the door shut behind her hoping that would give him warning. But there was no Miata at the front of the turreted house, and no sign of movement. She went up to the front door and knocked. Waited. No answer. Sighed.

"He's not here."

She turned around, seeking the source of the voice. A man came limping toward her across Brett's lawn leaning heavily on a cane. He was a tall lanky guy, about sixty years old, with the sun-creased brow and crow's feet of someone who had stared out at far too many sunrises. He wore a faded-to-white denim shirt and worn jeans, and had salt-and-pepper gray hair just down over his ears. Most memorable, though, was an easy wide smile which, as he stuck out his hand, exposed a row of perfect white teeth.

"You must be Kylee. I'm Frank—Frank Roberts, and I can see by your expression you haven't a clue who I am, but I've heard plenty about you." His hand was big, warm and enveloping, but twisted in the joints. He gave a single shake and smiled down at her. "Brett's talked non-stop about you. I haven't seen that in him in maybe—forever. I think the boy's a tad smitten and now I see why."

"Nice to meet you." She tried to be business-like, but a warm flush rose up her shoulders. No one had ever been 'smitten' by her. Smitten. Such a quaint, old fashioned word, but it suited Frank Roberts because he came across as just a little square and a lot old fashioned. He probably wouldn't approve of the fact that she'd been seriously thinking of taking Brett to bed as part of her apology. It had been a stupid idea anyway. Well—maybe not that stupid.

"Is he going to be back soon?" She tried to hide her disappointment.

Frank's gaze twinkled as he rubbed his chin and leaned on his cane. "I suspect he's standing in your driveway right now and wondering where you are."

"You're kidding." Could she have passed him on the drive over?

"Nope. He has a particular way of flying out of here in that sports car of his whenever he's headed in your direction. A little more desperate to get there, I'd say."

That darn flush again. She couldn't meet his gaze. "Well, then, I guess I'd better be on my way, and not take up your time."

"Kylee, sweetheart, you are welcome here anytime. Maybe come up for dinner sometime. You and Brett can walk the vineyards and he can show you some of our newer vintages. The boy's a good vintner. Better than I ever was, that's for certain. Best thing I ever did, hiring him and letting him buy in. Takes a load off an old man."

Her turn to grin. "You aren't old. Whoever told you that lied."

Chuckling, he shook his head. "'Fraid not. It's my bones as told me. Rheumatoid arthritis."

"I'm sorry." And she was. His twisted hands and his limp looked painful.

"Don't be. We all got our crosses, now don't we?" He shook his head and looked her up and down. "But you are a pretty sight for an old man's eyes. Unusual bracelet."

Kylee froze and her hand went protectively over her wrist. "Thanks. It's not mine. It belongs to the store." Swallowing back sudden nervousness, she glanced back at her car. "Well, thanks for all the compliments, but I guess I should get going and go find Brett. If he comes back please tell him I was here." Then she abandoned him for her car and almost sent gravel spraying as she accelerated out of the Elkhart Winery yard.

She was shaking on the trip home and she didn't know why. Frank Roberts had been nice. Kind even, and totally nonthreatening. It was herself that was the problem. She was getting totally paranoid and really, she should be begging Reggie to cut the darn thing off her wrist—but she couldn't. It was like she'd do anything to protect the bracelet and that just wasn't sane. She rubbed the bridge of her nose feeling a headache coming on. The bracelet was a warm weight on her arm. Soothing—like a shackle, maybe?

She shivered again.

Instead of going home, she decided to brave the crowds in Peachland and took the back streets to reach the carport of *This & That*. She parked behind Lila's Explorer partially blocking the lane and hurried into the backyard. Reggie's shop was closed up tight, thank goodness, so the jewelry maker was finally getting some much-needed rest. Kylee knocked on the kitchen door and stepped inside. The kitchen smelled of sugar and spices and a perfectly formed Bundt cake sat cooling on a rack on the counter.

"Lila?"

"Out here," Lila's voice drifted back from the shop.

Kylee headed down the hallway and pushed through the beaded curtain to find Lila with a cup of tea studying the view out the window. The sunlight through the windows caught in her hair that was pulled back in a tangled pony tail. She still wore her yoga leggings and tunic. "Sorry if I smell, I was just cooling down before my shower." She looked back out the window. "Lots of people out there."

"Sure are." Kylee stepped up beside her. Not only was the promenade along Beach Avenue full, but so was the street. The town had arranged a vintage car rally and so there were antique cars parked along the side of the road. At noon they'd all start their engines and join the Canada Day parade, but right now car aficionados from around the Okanagan Valley had joined the tourists to eddy around the cars draped in red and white flags. "Looks like there's lots of people."

"Uh-huh. Enough that I was thinking I might have made a mistake not opening earlier. There're a lot of wives and girlfriends with those men out there."

Kylee looked down at herself, still in her shorts and t-shirt. "I'd offer to open, but I'm not exactly dressed for it."

Lila shook her head and glanced down at her. "I wasn't asking, just thinking out loud." Her gaze caught on the bracelet and held a moment. "I made some calls last night and found Colonel Bristol's family. I talked to the youngest daughter. She remembered the bracelet but didn't know a lot about it except her dad used to joke about it. Call it his luck. It was one of a number of things he had brought home from his time in the service. Apparently he served all over the world—Hong Kong and Singapore after the war. North and East Africa during it. She hadn't thought of the bracelet in years and hadn't even realized her mom still had it.

"I don't know what that tells us," she finished and sipped her tea.

"Bristol apparently served in North Africa in the British 8th Battalion. He was part of the fight against Rommel. I found him on Wikipedia." She told about how he had had an undistinguished career until as part of the retreat, he took a small force out to slow Rommel's pursuit through the desert. Things had seemed to turn around for the British at Alexandria and she ended her story with her fingers once more rubbing the bracelet.

"So what are you saying?" Lila asked around another sip of tea and a smile at a young couple swinging a little girl between them. The child's blond hair flashed in the sunshine and they looked the epitome of happiness.

Looking away from the family and down at the bracelet she decided to try out a new idea. "What if he got the bracelet during that mission to stop Rommel? You said he called it his "luck", so he had to associate it with something momentous in his life.

And Reggie said the metal looked like it had the kind of patina like it had been eroded. Sand, maybe? That would fit with North Africa. Believe me. They have sand there. I couldn't get it out of my clothes or off my skin. There was sand in the food and sand in the tea I drank and sand in my hair." She gave a little shiver. "I don't miss that."

"Gee. I can tell." Lila gave her a friendly nudge with her elbow, but then looked thoughtful. "So you're suggesting the bracelet is actually lucky? That's a little farfetched, isn't it?"

For a moment Kylee hesitated, but then she took a deep breath. "It's like I said yesterday. It's been lucky for me. Everything good has happened since I put the bracelet on. Even those great sales that first day in the shop, remember?" And definitely there was Brett, given that Frank Roberts had described him as "smitten".

But Lila still looked doubtful. "Well, when I asked about the provenance of the bracelet, Bristol's daughter suggested I talk to her eldest brother. Apparently he spent a bunch of time interviewing his father at one point because he had the delusion of writing a biography of the Colonel. She said he never wrote the book and she wasn't sure if he still had the notes, but at one time he'd collected all his father's old diaries and letters from their mother. He might remember something. I would have called him last night, but he lives in Chicago. He's some kind of international patent lawyer."

She took another sip of tea and glanced over her shoulder at the antique brass clock that sat inside a glass bell jar. "Guess I should get on that. And you should get home and enjoy your last few minutes of leisure before another deluge of sales. I have a good feeling about today."

She headed for the back of the house and her shower, leaving Kylee to finger the bracelet again and stare out the window. Lila could make the call, but she already knew she was right about how George Bristol had come by the bracelet. The bracelet itself had told her, not that Lila would believe that. She, like Brett, was too determined to believe only what they could experience with their own senses. In some ways she was, too, with one exception. She felt with her heart. And when she'd expressed her theory to Lila it had been like a bolt ran from the bracelet right through her. Right to her heart.

Certainty dwelt there, just like Brett did.

She headed out to find him.

CHAPTER 19

He stood in the yard of Kylee's place, the breeze barely carrying the morning cool under the sun's assault. Of course Kylee wasn't home.

The lake was a mirror of steel blue and the worn mountains across the water a wilted gray-green that made him think of water-starved grapes clinging to life. It was going to be a scorcher and he just had to hope that he hadn't ruined things between him and Kylee. Even though the automatic sprinklers had clearly kept the lawn and Kylee's small garden green and growing, the air smelled more of heat and pine. Days like this, you understood that the Okanagan was basically a desert. Without the lake it was nothing, but add water and anything grew.

Like vineyards and orchards and market gardens.

At the moment he felt a little like the land without water—parched—and a little frantic that he might not see water again. Because Kylee was his balm. How the heck it had happened, it was hard to understand. He'd sworn off women for the time being. He wanted to focus on the winery. And then a small blond woman had danced by his car.

He stood where he'd stood with Kylee looking out over the lake, feeling her beside him, listening to the faint sound of the chimes as they gonged softly in the breeze. Everything, even the fresh-scented air, reminded him of her. She was a troubling woman; passionate, but delicate. He needed to go slowly with her, if he could get back into her good books. This morning, as soon as he thought it was a decent hour—he didn't know whether Kylee was a morning person like him, or not—like his sister—he had climbed in the Miata and headed for Kylee's house. He'd needed to apologize. It was her bracelet, or at least it was on her arm. Though he'd just been trying to protect her, he had no right to run down her idea to at least understand where the bracelet came from.

But she wasn't here and the urge to apologize was like a piece of food lodged in his throat. He had to get it out. Out on the lake, the statutory holiday meant flocks of boats sailed the blue waters of the lake. He looked down at his watch. It was getting close to parade time and the time *This & That* would be opening. Kylee must have gone down early. Go meet her at the shop? Take her for coffee? The bakery café would likely be a madhouse.

Well, at least head down and catch her at the store and tell her he needed to talk to her. Yes, that was the ticket. Maybe make a brief apology and tell her he'd make it up more fully later. After the shop closed.

That made sense. Then he'd head back to the peace of the winery and get busy with the accounts and orders Frank had set aside for him to go over. With Elkhart still just establishing their vines, they were somewhat dependent upon grapes bought from neighboring vineyards. Brett had spent part of the winter identifying the grapes that they needed and then Frank had developed contracts with the growers. Brett needed to check them over to make sure the yield and varietal's ratios were correct. And then he needed to get back to thinning and positioning the vines with their new grape clusters. It was intensive, sometimes emotional work when he had to actually remove fledgling grape clusters, but he knew that done properly, decreased yield could lead to improved wine quality.

Sort of like giving up all the other women had let him meet Kylee. He ran his fingers back through his hair and shook his head. "And she'll be so flattered that I think of her like a piece of fruit."

He really could be an idiot where women were concerned.

He climbed back in his car, resolved to make it to *This & That* regardless of the madness it was going to be driving into the town, and turned the car around in the gravel driveway. A young couple pushing a stroller rattled down the side of the road and he stopped to let them pass before turning onto the pavement. The man was a bespectacled, slope-shouldered fella, the kind who immediately screamed milquetoast accountant, with fine blond hair that already seemed plastered to his overlarge head with sweat. He walked beside a brown-haired woman pushing a stroller who looked like she was still getting rid of her baby weight. A newer family then, and he considered them with a new appreciation. Was that what he wanted with Kylee?

His heart did a solid thud-thud that told him yes. Damn. He had it worse than he thought.

He smiled at the family and nodded at the man. Halfway down the hill he recognized Kylee's beat up Civic chugging up toward him. He slowed, flashed his lights, but she apparently didn't see them. He pulled a u-turn and followed her right up and into her yard again, pausing long enough to admire her long tanned legs and perfect form as she climbed out of her car and placed her hands on her hips to look at him. She shook her head.

"Let me guess," she said as she ambled toward him and he climbed out. She looked flushed and pretty as hell even in the worn shorts and t-shirt. "You waited for me here while I was up at your place and down at the store." She grinned up at him. "I met your partner. He tells me you like me." She arched one brow.

"He did? I thought it was obvious."

"Good." She stood on her tiptoes, caught hold of his shirt front and pulled him down to her to kiss him.

Now that was a surprise.

§

The surprise on Brett's face was actually humorous when she pulled back from her kiss. His green eyes had gone dark and lustful. It made her glad she'd let the kiss linger until his arms had come around her and he'd pulled her close. His lips had answered her and then slipped up to taste her cheeks and neck and earlobes. Then he'd pulled back from her.

"Not that I'm not totally appreciative, but what's this all about?" he asked.

"Would you believe an apology?" And so much more. When she'd climbed in her car to head from the store to her place she'd known that the next time she saw Brett something wonderful was going to happen. At least she wanted it to. "I realized I was a total dork last night. You were just urging caution and care. Like maybe you didn't want anything to happen to me." She cocked her head at the house. "So you care to come in?"

She ran her fingers up his forearm and somehow even that was sensual. Heck, just touching this man sent little shivers of electricity shocking through her. Their one major clench at his house had left her breathless and barely able to think. She wanted more than that. It had been a long time since she'd been with a man and she'd never been with anyone who interested her as much as Brett.

She laced her fingers though his and he nodded, so she tugged him after her toward the house and up into the kitchen. "Did you see the chimes? I hung them in the willow."

"I heard." He came up behind her and nuzzled her neck as she unlocked the door and she nearly dropped the keys. His arms came around her and he pulled her in tight so she felt how he wanted her.

Okay hands, stop shaking and make these keys work faster.

She finally got her hands to work and the door swung open. Brett shoved her inside and she turned to him, met his need with her own. It was as if flood gates had opened inside her, her need for this man. She ran her hands up over his hard chest and swallowed back her fear. "I want you."

Oh God, she was forward and she felt the heat run up her shoulders and into her cheeks so she was mortified, but Brett only smiled. "You don't have to be embarrassed, Kylee. I want you, too. I have since I first met you."

"Really?" And she hated the doubts about herself that seemed to show. She shook herself. "I think I knew that and just didn't want to deal with it."

His hand gently, so gently cupped her cheek. "You'd been hurt. Badly. You needed time."

"Nope. Wrong. I needed to meet someone like you." She began to tug his shirt-bottom out of his jeans. "And now I have."

She found the bottom of his shirt and let her fingers slide over masculine skin. He jerked slightly at her touch and then his hands found her waist, picked her up as if she weighed nothing and had her butt on the table, his body between her bare legs so fast she knew he'd done this before. Probably many times.

It didn't matter. It didn't. It was what men like Brett expected of their women. *But what did she expect? Who was she kidding?* She wanted this just as much as he apparently did. She held her arms up to help him strip her t-shirt off. Tugged his shirt up and off his shoulders so he pulled it off and tossed it on the table behind her. Then he stopped, his gaze, his hands skimming her flesh leaving her heated and aroused at the way he looked at her. The green of his eyes blazed.

The pads of his fingers burned up her arms, across her collarbone before trailing over her breastbone to the pale downy line down her abdomen. Then his palms came up to cup her breasts, his thumbs lightly, so lightly she gasped, caressed her nipples through the lace of her bra. She couldn't help it; her eyes half-closed and she arched into his grasp as she ran her own palms up over the rock hard of his abs and pecs and then down again toward his belt. Her fingers caressed the softer flesh there and ran along the denim edge of his jeans.

"Kylee," he breathed and slipped her bra off her shoulders, his fingers miraculously having dealt with the closure. His lips trailed from her mouth, to her neck, his hands lightly teasing on the flesh of her breasts. Hot breath nuzzled her shoulder and she sagged against him, as his mouth trailed lower and finally, finally found her breast. She gasped at the pleasure of his moist mouth suckling. Of his tongue on her nipple, his other hand so busy on her other breast, playing her. The blended feelings bringing a gushing feeling of warmth to her core.

"Oh God, Brett. I want you." She pressed herself against him and clutched his head as his hands ran up her sides sending quivers through her again and again. Her skin was on fire and he was the flame. There was only one way to quench it. "Should we go upstairs?" she whispered as she kissed his hair, his brow, his lips as he stopped pleasuring her breasts and brought his head up to hers.

He leaned his forehead against hers, his green gaze locked on her own, the heaviness of his need between them. A palm cradled her cheek, thumb trailed over her lower lip. Then he tilted his head sideways toward the old kitchen wall clock.

"When do you need to be at work?" His voice was rough, soft. His throat worked.

"The store opens in an hour. I—we—we could—I'd still have time to shower and get down there."

His swung back to her. "Is that how you want our first time to be?"

"I know I want to make love to you." She wasn't sure what he meant.

His face softened in a smile. "And you have no idea how much I am glad to hear that, but I think our first time together deserves not to be rushed. I want to enjoy it and not be bound by a clock. Besides..." His hands skimmed from her face, down over her sides, then returned to cup her breasts, sending a zing through her core. He grinned wickedly and leaned down to whisper in her ear. "If you want me now, just think how badly you'll want me in a few hours."

His hands slipped down to her bare legs and ran fingers light as feathers up the insides of her thighs. Where they met, he pressed his palm into her and she rose up to his hand. His brow rose and he stepped into her again, pressed his confined hard length against her and ground it in. His hands pulled her hips into him, then slid up over her breasts as he whispered into her hair.

"Yes I want you right back, Kylee. Badly. But I'm prepared to wait to do it the right way." And with that he released her and stepped away. She felt shell-shocked and ravenous and naked and embarrassed that he'd turned her down. No. That was her old needy self talking. He'd only delayed it to let the anticipation build.

She trailed her fingertips down his muscled torso to the bulge in his jeans and more heat flooded through her. She licked her lips. So maybe there was something to this anticipation thing. She met his gaze. "So tonight?"

He stepped into her then and caught her chin to tilt her lips to his own, but he didn't touch her. "Wild horses couldn't keep me away."

The heat in his words sent her own flaring and she could almost come just with the thoughts of what was to be. But she nodded when he stepped away and slid off the table, legs a little wobbly so Brett caught her arm.

She looked up at him. "I, uh, think I'm going to go take a shower and get ready."

"How 'bout I wait for you and drive you down—saves you from having to find parking?"

"Sounds good. It won't take me long to get ready."

He nodded and released her. As she went to leave the room she promptly bumped into the door frame. God, she was so hot for that man.

Behind, she heard him softly laughing.

She was going to have to make the shower a cold one.

§

One tepid shower, forty-five minutes and a couple of *verrry* steamy kisses later she was standing in the back yard of *This & That*. She was still trying to get her legs under her, not to mention get her hair in order, because Brett's last act had been to grin and muss it for her. Damned man.

Damned man because she couldn't get his scent of vineyards and warm earth out her nose, or the feel of his hands off her skin. Her mind kept wandering to that bulge in his jeans and how it would feel. Another warm flush ran up through her and oh God, she had it bad. Just standing here her core ached, and when she moved, the feel of her leggings and the whisper on her skin of the blue top Brett had given her just about sent her over the top.

Get a grip, Jensen. She inhaled the heated air of the patio. Reggie's workshop was still closed up—she was taking the day off, though she'd said she might be in to help at the shop. The brightly colored lawn furniture had been moved and a tropical bird-patterned napkin was snagged against one chair leg so someone had enjoyed lunch out here. Probably Lila. She retrieved the abandoned napkin and went into the kitchen. It gleamed like she'd first seen it, all of Lila's most recent treasures all sorted and stored two days before. The Bundt cake sat in a place of honor on the table, its top drizzled with icing, rich with fresh vanilla. The scent of a spiced iced tea filled the room along with the sunlight and she grinned. She felt like this room, all full of sunshine and anticipation.

Yeah, anticipation, damn him. Brett would come back for her at six and then they could do as they wanted. Only six hours. She could last that long, though the way her body ached for his hands and other things, she might just explode.

Getting rid of the silly grin she was sure she wore, and putting on as close to a businesslike expression as she could manage, she pushed through the beaded curtain into the shop. Empty, but outside on the front porch she saw Chloe and Lila seated together. Something had them laughing. Beyond them lay the crowds of Beach Avenue with its display of antique cars and beyond it, the cool blue foil of the lake. She pushed out the door to join them. Chloe checked her watch, pulled out a dollar and handed it to Lila.

"You win. She's more dedicated than I thought. Or my brother's really turned over a new leaf."

Kylee frowned and looked from one woman to the other. "Pardon me?"

Waving a gracious hand, Lila stood up wearing a summer white boat-neck dress that clung to her figure and reached demurely to her knees. She wore white sandals with snake-shaped straps that ran up over her calves. "It was nothing, Kylee. Just a little wager. I said you'd be here on time, but Chloe here was sure that you and Brett would hook up and you'd be late." Her lush lips quirked in a grin as she met Kylee's gaze. "Looks like it might have been a near thing, though."

"You—you were making wagers about me?" Kylee didn't know whether to feel offended or pleased.

Chloe stood, today wearing a tunic of black and white harlequin diamonds over calf-length leggings and a set of silver chains set with more jet beads and a pendant. A single carnelian burned red in each ear. She patted Kylee's cheek. "Not you, dear. Your sex life."

She breezed past before her words fully sank in and Kylee stood there, trying to deal with the crimson that flushed through her skin as the two women entered the shop laughing. Lights flicked on in displays.

"Would you go put the sign out?" Lila's voice wafted out to Kylee. For the Canada Day celebration Lila and Reggie had painted a sandwich board of red, white and silver. It advertised the fact that the shop was open in a design similar to the posters and flyers Lila had put out this morning.

The sign leaned against the porch wall so Kylee grabbed it and carried it down to the gate, appreciating the opportunity to recover from her blush. Darn women, anyway. She settled the sign right next to the gate through the hedge that guarded their front garden from the crowds of people. A group of young women saw the sign and followed Kylee inside.

"You're both just jealous," she hissed at Lila and Chloe and they burst into laughter before heading off to help the shop's first customers.

The shop gleamed. They'd cleaned all the displays, including shining the brass antiques and oiling the old wood. They'd brought in new stock to make sure they had a larger than usual number of moderately-priced earrings so the earring display was packed. The pashmina still had pride of place, but so did a rack of silken scarves so sheer Scheherazade would drool. Kylee turned to help one of the young women who was admiring a Regulus necklace made to look like overlapping fish scales, each scale on the front sporting a small unique design and a small semiprecious stone.

Surprisingly, the young woman bought the necklace, even though it was one of the more expensive pieces in the store. It just proved how much money was in the area, and how you could never assume anything about the customers. With that in mind, Kylee stayed busy as women escaped the crowds cramming the street for the parade and took refuge in the relative cool of the store. When the parade started, with the customers' agreement, they closed the store for thirty minutes and gathered on the front porch to watch the parade and drink lemonade that Lila provided.

Antique cars drove by gleaming in the sunlight. Marching bands from the local high school high-stepped past as did the pickup truck with a country band in the back, complete with a caller and a troupe of square dancers following behind. Small locally-made floats celebrating Peachland's peaches and other produce came past followed by cowgirls dressed in their finery, the silver on their horses' saddles and bridles flashing in the sunshine. The air smelled of suntan lotion, cotton candy and popcorn. Then the parade ended and from down the lake toward the center of town came the sound of more music.

"That'll be the hoedown starting. The Chamber of Commerce went all out this year what with it being Peachland's centennial. They've got a dance and a corn roast with a beer garden that'll go until the fireworks start," Lila said as she ushered her customers back into the store.

The break didn't seem to dampen the shoppers' spirit. If anything the break seemed to settle their decisions and Kylee enjoyed a number of sales in quick succession. The steady flow of customers continued the rest of the afternoon until the time neared the dinner hour. At quarter to six Brett pushed through the beaded curtain just as Lila brought the sandwich board sign back up onto the porch. She stepped inside as Brett came up beside Kylee. She swallowed and felt guilty though they hadn't even touched. She was so aware of him even the pale blond hairs on her arms seemed to stand up and bend toward him.

Lila closed the front door behind her and leaned against it, a satisfied gloat on her face. Chloe paused behind the cash register for all the world looking like her mouth was full of yellow feathers. They knew what was going on. They could probably see the steam coming off her and Brett's bodies.

"So. Brett," Lila said casually. "I've been thinking about rearranging the store and now that we've cleared out so much inventory I thought this would be the perfect night. I've asked Kylee to stick around 'til seven. We could use your strong back, too." Somehow she managed to keep a straight face even through the snort coming from the direction of the cash register.

Kylee shot a sidelong look up at Brett and registered the barely concealed dismay. Well she didn't mind getting in on a little of the kidding. She turned around. "I'm so sorry, Brett. I should have called you, but we were so busy I totally forgot."

Okay, well she wasn't quite as good at keeping a straight face as Lila. Her lips curled and her chest threatened and finally she succumbed to an out and out guffaw. "If you could see your face..." she chortled and turned to Lila and Chloe. "And you are both very bad women and very wonderful friends. Now that you've put this poor man through hell surely you're going to let me play hooky these last five minutes." She tapped her watch and Lila relented.

Kylee pirouetted around, and wrapped her arms around Brett, and stood on tiptoe to kiss him. "There. I'm off the clock and they can tease all they want. I don't care."

Brett's arm came around her and he led her to the door and out onto the porch. The sky was still brilliant blue, but the sun had fallen over the tops of the western hillside toward evening. He took her in his arms then, and gave her a kiss filled with some very big promises for the evening. From inside the store came a Chloe-hoot as she fanned herself behind the cash register.

Heat rushed into Kylee's cheeks, but Brett just caught her hand and tugged her after him down the stairs. "Come on. I think there's a party here somewhere."

CHAPTER 20

WHAT BRETT WANTED TO DO WAS USHER KYLEE to his car parked down the street and then drive like a madman up to his place to get Kylee where he wanted her; which was in his bed. But he'd be damned if he was going to live up to all the expectations of a bad boy that his damned sister and her friends obviously had. Nope, he was going to show Kylee a good time, sort of woo her a little. He'd waited this long since meeting her—a first for him. He could wait longer. Hell, for Kylee he could wait forever, because hadn't he been waiting for her all his life?

Around them the evening crowd pressed down the street, laughter and friendly screams filling the air as the youngsters played at throwing each other into the cool blueness of the water off the wharfs that punctuated the lakeshore. Out on the water, the boats were already setting up in a huge offshore semicircle, jostling each other for the best fireworks viewing spot. Here and there the wonderful scent of barbecued hot dogs and hamburgers came from food trucks and family picnic tables. His stomach growled, but even the aroma of wonderful food couldn't compare to the scent of Kylee.

He pulled her into his side and her arm came comfortably around his waist. "You know, this morning took about every ounce of my self-control, so just so you know, there is only one way this day is going to end."

Her big blue eyes went a little wider and she wet her lips and somehow managed to brush his arm a little firmly with her breast. "Well that is—quite the promise, sir. My aim is to make sure you keep it, you hear."

Her taut nipple seemed to burn into his skin and he leaned down to place a too-brief kiss on her lips. Dammit, just being around her got him aroused, and with the hard-on he was sporting it was going to be damned uncomfortable walking around. He pulled her out of the crowd, down to the beach, and raised an eyebrow at her in mock sternness.

"Unless you want me to have you on the ground right here, you better behave. You hear?"

All mock innocence, she studied her hands. "Aah, shucks. I wasn't doing nothing."

"Like hell," he said, his voice just a little too raw with desire.

She looked at him out of the tops of her eyes. "But you liked it, didn't you?"

He looked down at himself. "You know I did and so will everyone else at this rate. So we go down to the beer garden, maybe have a glass and dance one dance so that sister of mine doesn't think that all I want to do is ravish you, and then we can leave. Deal?"

"Deal," she grinned sweetly. "And just so you know, I might not be wearing any panties under these leggings. Race you to the beer garden."

Before he could swat her delectable behind, she scooted up the beach and into the crowd. So that was how she wanted to play this, was it? A game of cat and mouse. A titillating evening of across the room glimpses, and searching, always leading to the inevitable pleasure of finding each other. If anything it made him hotter. And the thought of no underwear....

Damn.

He bounded up the beach after her, but she'd already pushed farther into the crowd and he only caught glimpses of her bright blond head. He shoved through the crowd after her.

She was quick, this woman. Like a sprite in a forest, the way she would disappear from view and then suddenly reappear on a street curb waving, or angling one leg for him to admire as she stood on the first rail of a fenceline that bordered the lake. He spotted her talking to a couple with a stroller. He vaguely recognized them as her neighbors, but then the crowd closed around them. When he reached the spot near a German restaurant, they were gone and the crowd pressed in around him so he could barely move.

People jostled against him as he craned to see her. No dice, and not much chance of spotting her in this restaurant crowd. He needed to get going. She'd said she'd meet him at the beer garden. Actually she'd said she'd beat him to the beer garden, dammit. He wasn't going to let that happen. He elbowed free of the people waiting for seating in the courtyard restaurant, passed lineups waiting at a Mexican foodtruck and reached the center of the street. The crowd had thinned here and he broke into a jog. The beer garden wasn't that much farther.

The tents and tables that the Chamber of Commerce had set up covered the green town common. It lay across the street from the main line of stores and Peachland's famous octagonal church-come-museum. A band had set up in a gazebo at one end of the green, with an area clear for dancing, but the rest of the green was cheek-by-jowl tables inside bright blue wire fencing. A corner had been cordoned off which held roaring half-barrel barbecues roasting hot dogs, hamburgers, and onions. His mouth watered at the scent.

He hurried up to the crowd around the beer garden gate, but there was no sign of Kylee in the press of people. Odd, because she'd managed to stay in front of him the whole way down the street. He searched around the lineup, but there was still no bright blue blouse and no slip of a woman with sunlight in her hair. He megaphoned his hands.

"Kylee! Kylee Jensen, I concede the race!"

Still no sign of her. Well, perhaps she got waylaid. She *had* been talking to her neighbors. Leaning against one of the antique-looking streetlights, he settled in to wait, but something didn't feel right. She'd been just as eager as he'd been. It had been a race and Kylee struck him as someone who wouldn't back down. Not the way she'd teased him before she took off.

Nope. Something definitely wasn't right. He started back the way he'd come, scanning the crowd, shoving through knots of people in case she was hidden behind them. By the time he reached the German restaurant lineup again he was starting to get concerned. There was the whole bracelet thing. The woman in Kelowna had been killed.

Don't be stupid. That was a hit and run accident, no way anything like that's going to happen here.

But a tight knot had formed in his belly and, damn it, he had to find her.

"Well look who's here. So where's your girlfriend, Romeo?" Chloe's voice seemed to cut though the crowd as she and Lila stood in line for the restaurant.

The gloating grin faded from his sister's face as he turned to her. "Geeze, Brett. Is everything okay?"

Shaking his head, he joined them in line. "I can't find her. We were having a race to the beer garden and she just never showed up." He checked his watch. "It's been half an hour now. I waited fifteen minutes and she shouldn't have needed that much time. She was ahead of me the whole way down the street."

Chloe and Lila exchanged glances.

"That's not like her," Lila said, concern placing two small lines between her brows. "She wouldn't want to worry people, not even in fun. Chloe, I'm going to help him look. You hold our place in line."

"Like heck. Three sets of eyes are better than two." She followed them out of line and into the crowded street.

"Brett, how about you stay down around the beer garden and wait. You can search that area again." Lila patted his shoulder.

"Don't worry. She'll show up. Chloe and I will work our way back toward the store. If we haven't found her by then we'll come back and decide what to do next, okay?"

It wasn't what he wanted to do at all. He wanted to sweep all these silly revelers away so that only Kylee and he remained on the street. It had been a stupid idea to stay in town when all he wanted to do was be with Kylee. He'd been an even bigger idiot to let her get away. Some protector he was. Maybe it was just a sign that all those years as a love 'em and leave 'em kind of guy was all he was good for. He wasn't meant to have a long term relationship. But either way, he had to make sure Kylee was safe. That blond sprite was everything at this moment.

"All right. We meet at the beer garden in twenty minutes. After that I'm calling the cops."

Twenty minutes. That would make it almost an hour since he'd lost her. It was beginning to feel like a lifetime.

§

The day seemed to wilt around Lila even as Brett disappeared back into the noisy crowd. Down at the beer garden, a new band had started their first set with a rousing rendition of Smoke on the Water. The Chamber of Commerce was going to be real impressed with that one. Still, close around Lila and Chloe, people were punching their arms in the air in time to the music. But the press of people was too much and it felt like it would have been a better day to just be inside cocooned with everyone you cared about. The blue of the lake had turned dark and murky, even though the sun laced the far mountains with gold. The warm air had suddenly been replaced by a colder breeze off the lake. Lila shivered and pulled her fine red pashmina closer around her shoulders.

"He's scared," Chloe said as she watched her brother become just another bobbing head in the crowd. "I haven't seen him look that pale since we got the news about our parents' accident."

When her friend shivered, Lila slipped her arm around Chloe's shoulder. "It was hard on you both."

Chloe turned back to her. "Yeah. It was. But Brett seemed to feel that he had to be strong for the both of us. I think it almost killed him doing it. He was like a crazy man at the hospital with them day and night, and then we lost them anyway. He kept sending me home to get some rest, but he never left. Not once. It'll kill him if something's happened to Kylee. I've never seen him like he is around her. Gentle and caring and hell, he's actually courting her—not some slam-bam, thank you ma'am. It's been almost too easy teasing him!" But there were tears in her eyes.

"It'll be okay," Lila said, trying to keep a confident face. Because this wasn't like Kylee at all. She might do silly stupid things with her heart, but otherwise Kylee was solid, a realist. It was why Lila had always loved her—someone who could love so deeply, but see the truth and the humor of her failings, too. "How about you take the lakeshore and I'll do the sidewalk side. Between the two of us, we should be able to see everyone. You'll see. We'll probably find her talking to someone. She probably just lost track of time."

Chloe's expression said she didn't believe that any more than Lila did, but she had the good grace to nod. They separated and started back down Beach Avenue, keeping each other in sight.

All the terrible things that could have happened kept playing through Lila's mind and she had to fight the bubbling worry down otherwise she might come apart. It was she that had encouraged Kylee to stay—sure, the woman had obviously wanted to—but it was Lila's fault that she had. And if she hadn't asked Kylee to give them a hand at the *This & That* she wouldn't have found that darned bracelet. It was her along with Brett who had acquiesced when Kylee demanded to keep the bracelet. She could have dealt with the whole situation so easily; it was her store, her bracelet, she wanted it off Kylee's arm. But she'd let it remain there and put her friend in serious danger.

She scanned the crowd of mixed generations all enjoying the evening together, and momentarily lost sight of Chloe in her harlequin tunic, then spotted her slightly farther down the promenade. Lila waved and caught up. She was going to have to pay attention to spotting Kylee, not spend her time making up horrible versions of what could have happened to her. Nothing had happened. She was just off somewhere with someone she'd met. That was all.

Kylee wouldn't abandon Brett. Especially not the way the two of them had looked at each other tonight. Tonight had been something special to the both of them and it didn't take a rocket scientist to figure out what was up.

Her heart beat a little faster as she kept searching the crowd. They were getting close to the shop and unless Kylee showed up soon she was going to have to conclude something had happened. Unless Kylee had shown up to meet Brett. There was always that hope.

They reached *This & That* with neither of them spotting the bright blond head of their friend. Chloe left the promenade to join Lila on the sidewalk. "So what now, boss? Keep going?"

Lila checked her watch, scanned the crowd again, and then glanced at the shop. Could Kylee have come back here for some reason? "Maybe we should check inside and if she's not there, we head back to Brett. The police will be the next step."

Together they pushed through the gate and headed for the front door. The place looked dark and forlorn in the fading sunlight, but above the sky was still a glorious blue with golden spotlights catching on the humps of the mountains across the lake.

"Lila?" The masculine voice spun her around to find Corporal Danny Forester at the gated entrance to the yard, another man at his side. Forester looked better than he had last time she'd seen him. Rested, though there was still something haunting in his gaze. He wore a clean white shirt rolled up to the elbows and trim fitting jeans. He'd also shaved, which undid the dissolute, slightly manic look he'd had previously. The man with him was obviously another cop. Tall, like Forester, with short black hair and an athletic build, but the "tell" of the cop was in the eyes. They looked deep, those eyes, and assessed everything they saw. Right now he was assessing her and the shop. He wore a polo shirt and jeans too, with a windbreaker over that, which in the warmth at this time of day made her think he had something under it he was trying to hide.

"Corporal Forester. What brings you to Peachland on so rowdy a night?"

The crowd was flooding around the two men, jostling their shoulders as the revelers made their way toward the music.

Forester nodded. "What we were talking about last time we spoke. The case." He had to raise his voice to be heard over the noise.

Glancing at the crowd, she walked back and opened the gate. "If you want to talk, perhaps you should come in." She looked back at Chloe, waiting in the shadows by the porch. "We've a matter maybe you could help us with, but we don't have a lot of time."

They clumped up the porch and Chloe let them in and flicked on lights in the store. Corporal Forester sighed and then motioned to the other man. "This is my partner, Corporal Jasper Stone. I asked him to come down here with me after I turned myself in to the detachment. I'm not supposed to be doing this, but something's come up with the case." He glanced at his partner. "We've had a little disagreement about coming down here, but I figured there was more you weren't telling me last time we met. I brought Corporal Stone because it might give you more confidence that I'm on the up and up."

"I'd check their identification," Chloe said, her gaze never leaving Forester's partner's face.

It was a good idea. "May I?"

The two officers pulled out their wallets and displayed official looking badges and ID. Chloe peered over Lila's shoulder.

"Satisfied?" Lila asked.

Chloe held one of the stones in her necklace and reached out to lay her fingers on each of the badges. Finally she nodded. "Jet helps dispel evil spells. These are okay." She looked up at the men and her gaze seemed to linger on Corporal Stone's face. She frowned watching as the two men put their documents away.

"So what's happened with the case? Have you found the truck that hit Moira?" Lila asked.

Forester glanced at his silent partner. "Actually we've done one better. We've found both the driver and the truck. Fellow was a local contractor named Jake Murphy—the same name as was written in Moira Burns' diary. Apparently he'd been at a potential job to do an estimate just down the street from the estate home, but for some reason turned up at the estate sale. His truck had damage consistent with the accident and we're pretty certain the DNA from the evidence we've lifted off the front end will match Moira Burns."

But Forester was now looking away, and his partner's jaw had clenched so tight it pulsed.

"There's something else, isn't there? What's happened?" Because she needed to be out there looking for Kylee. Just the fact Corporal Forester had shown up somehow made her friend's disappearance all the more serious.

Forester shoved his ragged brown hair off his forehead. Finally he nodded. "Thing is, when we arrived at his house, he didn't answer the door. We checked with the neighbors and no one had seen him since the night of the incident, so we broke in. We found him hanging in his kitchen. He'd used an extension cord to do the deed."

Unbidden, Lila's hand rose to her mouth. Chloe exhaled in a rush, "Oh my God."

Forester nodded. "That's not the most interesting part. You see, he left a note. It was barely coherent. It started off with one line written over and over and then finished with the words: *So much strangeness in the world. Aliens.*"

"But... but isn't that the same thing your homeless witness said?" Lila asked. "It doesn't make sense. Why would a business contractor and a homeless man use the same phrase?"

Sighing, Forester shook his head. "You're forgetting, it was my descriptor as well. But maybe the repeated line in the note will make it a little clearer." He glanced at Stone who looked like he'd rather be anywhere else in the world than here. "It said over and over: *Get out of my head.*"

CHAPTER 21

THE SWIRL OF PEOPLE AROUND BRETT, THE LAUGHTER and the jostle of friendly shoulders had first become an annoyance, but now they just left him laced with fear for Kylee. Dusk was settling over the Okanagan and a light wind had picked up and cooled the air. Along the road and in the common area of the beer garden small twinkling lights flashed on in all the trees. It made him think of a small towns in Italy and southern France where plazas lit like this had cafés which spilled out onto paving stones and the tinkle of wine glasses. He'd spent some of his most pleasurable moments there and had daydreamed of taking Kylee sometime.

This though, this was just macabre. Too many people. No sign of Kylee and the smell of spilled beer was enough to turn his stomach. In the falling light, the laughing faces around him just looked tortured, and more people were pressing into the area all the time. Where the hell were Lila and Chloe? They should be back by now. Unless something had happened to them, too.

If anything, the wind ran colder, even in the heated press of the crowd.

Thirty minutes after Lila and Chloe should have found him, he finally spotted them, the crowd parting around Lila who stalked like a runway model through the hordes with Chloe on her heels and two men following.

Brett stood on tiptoe and waved, and Lila adjusted her direction toward him. Please let them have found Kylee. Please.

But there was no sign of her when Lila arrived. She might still be one of the most elegant women he had ever met, but at the moment she looked shaken and diminished. Chloe crowded in beside her and placed a reassuring arm around Brett's waist.

"How're you holding up, bro?"

"Not good. You didn't find her then?" He wanted to throw up. He wanted to punch whoever had stolen Kylee. Actually, he wanted to stomp all over them until they were ground into dust or grape juice.

Lila shook her head. "There was no sign of her, but we did run into help. "Brett, this is Corporal Forester and Corporal Stone of Kelowna RCMP. They've been conducting the investigation into Moira Burns' death. They found the driver of the truck that killed her, but he'd killed himself."

"What does this have to do with Kylee?" He eyed the two cops. One looked like he had a whole lot of better days behind him and one looked resigned—like he didn't want to be here.

Chloe squeezed him. "It's weird stuff, Brett. You sure you want to hear?"

He ripped loose from his sister. "Just tell me what the fuck is going on!"

Lila turned to the plain-clothed police officers—detectives, then. "Would you tell him what you've told me?"

The worn-down cop's shoulders seemed to slump a little as he told about the hit and run, and the finding of the homeless eyewitness who'd ranted about an alien in his head, and aliens driving the truck that hit Moira Burns. Then the tale took a really wild-assed turn as he talked about showing up in Peachland and how his head was a fog and he didn't really remember anything except glimpses of a green car and a blond.

In an instant Brett had him by his collar. "What the fuck have you done with Kylee?"

He slammed the detective against the light standard next to them, and wanted to bash his head in. "If you've hurt her, I'll kill you," he growled into the cop's ear, but strong hands hauled him away by the shoulders. Lila and Chloe inserted themselves between himself and the cop.

"Brett, stop. Just listen," Chloe said, waving her hands in front of him as if he was an enraged bull. Maybe he was. Maybe he didn't fucking care.

He stopped himself and hauled in a deep breath. No, Kylee wasn't going to be found if he just went nuts. He shrugged off the other cop's hold and folded his arms across his chest. Frankly, he was surprised he wasn't under arrest for assaulting an officer. "All right. I'm listening."

Settling his shirt on his shoulders again, Forester continued. How good old-fashioned police work had found the truck, and then the driver—dead with a suicide note and the weird-ass use of the word "alien" again."

He scanned each face looking at him. "Aliens? Are you fucking kidding me? Chloe I can understand because she'd always talking about some woo-woo shit—sorry, sis. But you, Lila? And you? You're cops." He turned to the two men, "You can't be buying this."

Stone looked like he'd rather be any other place in the world, but Forester was shaking his head. "You think I want to believe? I don't know if it's aliens or something else, but I do know something was in control of my body."

"Brett, there are many cultures that believe in possession. The Buddhists with their hungry ghosts. Christians with their exorcisms. Lots of others."

"That doesn't make them real." No way. No how.

"Brett, do we really have to debate its reality right now? What matters is that Kylee is missing and that when Corporal Forester first came into the store a month ago, he was asking about the box I got from Moira. He actually searched it and seemed upset that whatever he was looking for wasn't there. What if it had been, but I didn't show it to him? There's only one thing that fits that description, Brett. Kylee's bracelet. She'd put it on while we were emptying the box and she hadn't been able to get it off, so she wore it to help the customers. She was wearing it when Corporal Forester was there."

Fists clenched, he swung back to Forester. The man shook his head. "That's the thing. I don't remember it at all. I knew there was someone named Lila Weber I'd come to see because her name was in my notes, but I don't remember any of what she's telling you now at all."

"So you say." He so wanted to bop the guy. Demand he tell where Kylee was.

"Listen," Stone intervened. "Getting angry isn't going to find Kylee Jensen. There're five of us here. I suggest we get a bit more methodical. I suggest we mount a grid search. I've already called the West Kelowna detachment and asked them to start checking vehicles leaving town. They're radioing the cops already here to keep an eye out. I suggest we break into a couple of teams and search more methodically, including the side streets. I'll take Chloe, here. Forester and Mr. Main will be another team. Ms. Weber I'd like you to stay here in case your friend returns of her own accord. Everyone agree?"

Brett glared at Forester as everyone exchanged telephone numbers. At least he could keep an eye on the guy.

§

Darkness and fear. Kylee hunkered down in the musty scent of old wood, dry rot, and mouse droppings. The old wood wall pressed into her back, the sound of the crowd and the music outside the door almost as overpowering as the fear that kept her immobilized. Her hands weren't tied. Neither were her feet, but due to the pacing figure in front of her she tried to be as small and unnoticeable as possible. If she was really small and really unnoticeable, maybe she could turn it to her advantage.

The hollow sound of his footfall seemed to echo inside her. The sound of revelry as people partied along the lakeshore came from a dream, another world where Brett existed with his protective gaze and Lila and Chloe acted like two plotting matchmakers. But Brett wasn't here. Kylee cowered in the corner of the second floor of the old octagonal church with only the faintest of light sneaking through the louvered windows on the church's eight sides. There was no one here except her captor and with the boisterous noise and blaring music, no one would hear her even if she yelled. Besides, the church stood off by itself, backed on one side by the highway, on another by a public washroom and on the other by a commercial building that was certainly locked up tight this evening. It left her trapped.

She wished she was truly alone when the pacing figure stopped in front of her. She pressed back farther into the wood behind her wondering how she could feel so cold when the room itself smelled of heated air and dust from the day's sunshine. How could her lovely flirtatious race with Brett have gone so wrong?

She'd wanted him so badly her whole body had ached with her need for him, but she'd played along with his delayed gratification strategy knowing that their coming together would be even sweeter for it. So she'd teased him running off into the crowd toward the main part of town; the spire of the octagonal church, her target. Let Brett catch *her* this time.

She'd made it a game—stay out of his sight, but keep sight of him. She'd found spots to stop and pose provocatively for him and then skittered away laughing before he could catch up as the crowd flowed between them. It had left her breathless. She'd been flushed and warm and she'd beaten him by a mile and had come up to the beer garden to lean against a streetlight chuckling to herself. Just how hot and bothered would Brett be when he caught up to her? The thought of his hands on her, pulling her into him brought a flare of heat and a throb to her core. Oh, what they would do this evening. She closed her eyes and inhaled his scent because it was branded on her.

Then she had heard her name.

"Kylee?"

Her eyes flashed open. Who? Because she didn't know many people in Peachland, though she was starting to. Then she recognized him, though it had taken her a moment, out of context and alone as he was.

Glasses that caught and reflected the light of the million little lights in the trees. Narrow shoulders and thinning blond hair. Her neighbor. What was his name? After that first day of introduction, they had waved to each other whenever he and his wife had pushed their stroller past, or when she'd driven past their little house in the hollow.

"Tom. Hi. Are you out for the evening? It's fun, isn't it?" She laughed and waved at the crowd and the gazebo where the band played a rousing country tune. A few brave couples had started to dance. She'd passed him and his wife and baby earlier on the race down Beach Avenue, but they'd said that the crowd was getting too big and they were heading home.

"Are you here alone?" he asked.

She glanced at him. His gaze was intense as he waited for her answer. "Oh, no. I'm waiting for someone."

Her boyfriend? Could she call Brett that? After tonight? The word felt silly and juvenile. Her lover. She was waiting for her lover. She stood on her tiptoes craning. Just where was he.

"Where are Mary and Marica?" she asked turning back to Tom. "I thought you were heading home?"

He brushed his hair back and grinned, but there was something different about him. "It was Mary who spotted you here by yourself. She sent me over to get you. She wanted to invite you for dinner; we haven't really had a chance to see each other since we popped in that first day." He cocked his head at the old church/museum. "The crowd's a little thinner over there. Easier with the stroller and all."

Brett should be here any moment, but it would just titillate him more if she wasn't here. Let the poor man think he'd won, but she knew better. Besides, she wouldn't be long.

She nodded, "Just for a moment. In this crowd I don't want to miss my friend."

They threaded through the crowd, the trees placing silhouettes against the darkening blue sky. Tom was right that the press of people lessened significantly once they got closer to the church. The commercial area ended and the church sat dark and empty up a slight incline from the road. There was no one around, not even using the washrooms.

"Where are they?" She stopped.

"Just up here." Tom grinned back at her and caught her hand. "Marica was getting overwhelmed by the noise so Mary brought her up here for a little peace. I'm one of the volunteer curators so I've got a key." He dangled it from a finger.

But something didn't feel right. Not right at all.

"Um. I think I better get back to my friend. Why don't you tell Mary I'll drop by your place on the weekend."

"Come on, Kylee. This won't take a minute." She went to pull away, but his grip was iron. Make a fuss? A scene? He was only asking for a minute and they *were* neighbors. She didn't want to insult them. She allowed herself to be led up the last step to the church entrance and waited while he opened the door.

The inside had been dark. She should have known. She should have turned on her heel and run because Mary and Marica wouldn't be waiting in the dark. She shouldn't have been so trusting that she followed him inside, so he could slam the door behind her. No Mary or Marica. He'd grabbed her by the shoulders then and forced her up the rickety stairs in case someone came in. And now here she was. Trapped.

She glared up at the narrow shouldered man. She could almost believe it wasn't Tom Beaton before her. His eyes seemed to pick up the meager light and glow like ash-covered embers in the darkness. A bitter almond and iron scent came off of him.

"Why are you doing this, Tom? What do you want with me?" Keep him talking. Make him see her as a person. Wasn't that what all the television shows said you were supposed to do if you were abducted?

"I want nothing of you, Kylee Jensen. I just want what you bear."

"What I bear?" She looked down at herself. Blue top. Black leggings. A pair of flats and the crystal necklace Chloe had given her that was supposed to symbolize truth. Well the truth was she was in a heap of trouble. Her fingers found her favorite grape arbor door on the bracelet. The bracelet.

She slid her wrist behind her and glared up at him. "You're going to have to do better than that, Mister. As a matter of fact this whole scene is a bore. I'm out of here."

She shoved to her feet, but before she could move he backhanded her.

Her head swung so sharply right she heard her neck crack. Pain blinded her for a moment and she staggered back against the wall, slid down onto her heels, a power bar on the wall outlet digging into her back. She tasted blood and brought her hand to her cheek. Hot. Hurt. Tears filled her eyes. Fear filled her chest, because this guy actually hit her. He really would hurt her...

"What is this? I don't understand why you're doing this to me?" A little sob caught at her words.

"I want the bracelet."

Her fingers went to her wrist to cover the piece of jewelry. "It doesn't want to come off."

She wouldn't let him take it. The fact that he'd apparently abducted her to get the bracelet said that he shouldn't get it. Something bad would happen if he did.

As if in answer the bracelet pulsed warm against her skin. Holy shit! She lifted her fingers almost expecting the thing to be glowing. Almost as if it was using energy, like Chloe's stones. Protecting her, like Chloe's jet stones had protected her from the man in the shop?

She clenched her eyes shut for a moment because this whole situation was so unreal. Tom Beaton, the man so proud of his little girl, who with his wife, brought a newcomer a pan of brownies, just wasn't the kind to abduct anyone. Not if she was any judge of people.

Of course she hadn't spotted Kevin for the heel he was, either.

No. That had been a matter of the heart and she wasn't doing that again. Things with Brett were different. Just like this Tom Beaton was different as night and day from the man she'd met previously.

"If—if you want the bracelet so badly why not just take it off me?" She forced a shaky laugh. "We've been trying to get off me for days."

He suddenly loomed over her, his eyes two glowing coals. "It will not come off, that I know. Not until you have done your part in this. At least not while you live."

Holy crap. Kylee cringed back. She had to get out of here. She had to find Brett. They had to stop this man or whatever was in him, because she did NOT want to die and she seriously doubted that anything good would happen if he got what he wanted.

She and the bracelet had to get away. Okay. She'd have to play along for time.

"What's so important about the bracelet?" She held her breath, not sure she wanted an answer.

His head snaked around toward her and she felt like a cornered mouse. "What is it to you, little one? Nothing that will help you, certainly. Let us just say that the bracelet possesses certain—qualities—that I find attractive." He hooked his fingers around his final word and continued his pacing.

What was he talking about? Was there something more to the bracelet? Had she really felt something while she wore it? The protectiveness of it. The heat. The surge of pleasure through it when she was with Brett. Did she really believe this was more than a crazy man talking? If it was, she was in serious trouble.

She looked around searching for a corner, a bolt hole, anything, but there was nowhere to hide. *Get a grip, Jensen. You dealt with being dumped and having your nose rubbed in it every day for three months.*

Yeah. Sure. You turned into a zombie.

No. She came home and did what she needed to. She came to the one place she knew she'd recover—to Lila's. And she had. In the space of a month look how well she'd done. She was over Kevin. Yes, she'd entered another relationship, but both of them were taking it slow. Coffee and dinner and hanging out together, but nothing more except what had been planned for tonight. Well, she was darn well going to live through this because she wanted the chance to be with Brett—even if things didn't work out with him long term. Life wasn't about permanence—it was about making connections with people and if sometimes those connections ended, well so be it. Life went on. But she didn't believe her connection to Brett would end anymore than her friendship with Lila had.

She felt stronger just thinking about it. She would not die here. She wouldn't.

"My boyfriend's out there looking for me right now. He'll find me."

Tom Beaton or whatever he was, stopped his pacing in front of her again. "Why? Why would he look in this church? Have you a connection to it?"

That was true. She didn't have any connection to the church at all, except for her first morning here. Brett wouldn't know about it.

"I thought not. My car should be here soon and we'll be able to leave."

That brought her upright. She couldn't let that happen. If he got her away from here, she was doomed, of that she was certain.

Outside the light was fading, leaving the church interior in almost solid darkness, but her eyes had adjusted now. Tom Beaton paced an aisle in front of her as she huddled between what looked like two large work tables. The center of the room was filled with a single massive table that, from where she was sitting, looked like it had piles of rocks piled on it. That and a fringe of tiny trees.

That made no sense at all.

Then she remembered Nora Kallaher and her chatter when she'd first met Kylee and showed her inside the church. She'd mentioned that the second floor was used by the local model railroad aficionados. They were building a perfect likeness of Peachland at the turn of the century, she'd said. That had to be what she was looking at. Was there some way she could use that knowledge to help herself? If she could just distract Tom for a moment, she might stand a chance. The stairway leading down to the main floor and the entrance lay just across from her. She could see the top of the stairs across the room under the railroader's table.

She scanned the tables to either side of her. Nothing. She had no idea what was on them. So what was around her? Her fingers splayed across the floorboards and her elbow hit the surge protecting power bar on the wall. She stopped.

A lot of power bars had a bank of on-off switches. Instead of having to turn off a lot of individual machines, it was easier just to turn off the power bar. Wouldn't model railroaders have a bunch of machines to turn off, too?

Tom was still pacing, stopping every few minutes to scan his phone. Probably awaiting a text that the car that was supposed to take her away had arrived. Thank goodness the town event would make getting close to the town center difficult, but she couldn't expect that to last forever.

She shifted position, watching Tom all the while. She got her feet under her and pretended to ease her back muscles. Her fingers slipped over the square shape of the power bar. There. Right on the top, a single button.

Tensing, she waited for Tom to reach the farthest arc of his pacing. He started to swing around, so he'd be a little off balance.

She stabbed her finger and bright overhead lights suddenly flashed on over the central table. Train wheels started whirring.

She threw herself forward, sliding under the railway table as Tom stumbled. His feet and legs seemed to get tangled as she belly-scrambled across the dusty floor.

The stairs were there. Almost there. Tom roared behind her as he raced around the corner of the table.

§

It was all useless. Brett scrubbed his face and pinched the bridge of his nose to try to smooth out his emotions. There was no way he was going to show any sign of weakness to Forester who stalked silently beside him as they walked the streets that paralleled Beach Avenue. They'd already covered the streets up beyond the bakery/café, while Chloe and Corporal Stone worked their way north from the beer garden. Now Brett and Forester were checking the streets back from the café, heading south to meet up with the other search team. If they didn't find Kylee, Brett wasn't sure what he would do. Go a little crazy, possibly. Funny how when you lost something you realized just how much you cared about it. Chloe could tease him all she wanted; he just wanted Kylee back in his life.

Only one block back from the revelers along the lake and it was like you were in a different world. No one walked these streets. The scattered streetlights spread pools of light through the lingering dusk, but otherwise everything was in shadow. Most of the houses were dark, their residents presumably enjoying the street party. Cars lined the street edge. Even dogs seemed to be indoors rather than risk them getting out of fenced yards while the crowd was in town.

They reached another sidewalk leading up to a house and Forester turned in. In the house, a drawn curtain couldn't hide the TV glow in the living room. Sighing, Brett followed up to the front door. Forester knocked and soon the sound of footsteps came to the door. It opened slightly and an elderly woman peered out past a security chain.

"Yes?" Querulous. Her gaze caught on the two men and she pushed the door a little farther closed.

"Corporal Danny Forester, West Kelowna RCMP. We're looking for a missing woman. She's about five foot four, blond, wearing a blue top and black leggings. Have you seen anyone like that, or anything suspicious?"

Old blue eyes peered out at them with suspicion, but then she shook her head. "No woman, no."

For the umpteenth time, Brett's heart sank. There were so many people at the celebration and so few people around to ask. So far no one had seen anything, while out on Beach Avenue the crowds were oblivious to what was going on around them.

The old woman unlocked her chain and swung the door open. She wore polyester pants and a floral blouse with a matching sweater. When you have nowhere special to go, you have to make every place special, Brett supposed. She frowned. "There was one of those stretched cars—a limousine—that got stuck across the street trying to turn around about ten minutes ago." She hefted her chin at the street. "I went out to make sure he didn't damage my lawn. Driver was nice enough, but he asked what would be the best way to get to the old church in town. Said he had to pick someone up there." She shrugged. "I told him he was out of luck here, because the street doesn't run all the way through. He'd be better off going to the other end of town and trying to get through the roadblock."

Something about her story caught Brett's attention. "The old church? Why'd he want to get there? Museum's closed this time of night."

The old woman shrugged again. "I didn't think to ask him. I just wanted to protect my lawn. My late husband made it his life's work to get a perfect lawn and I don't take too kindly to tire tracks on top of it. These youngsters these days. They don't think anything of driving over the edge of the pavement." She tsked softly.

"The church. That could be it." Brett nodded at Forester. "Apparently there was some guy in a limo asking after the bracelet at the store. He scared Chloe, but left in a limousine with darkened windows."

Forester thanked the woman and the two of them retreated back to her precious curb.

"Tell me," Forester demanded.

Brett was already loping down the street toward the next block that would take him back to Beach Avenue. "The museum's down by the beer garden. It used to be a church. It doesn't get used much, and it's set back by the highway so it's a little private, too. Lots of shadows. If Kylee beat me to the beer garden like it looked like she was going to do, it would be the perfect place to hold her until someone could come and pick her up. Someone with a limousine." He shook his head. "A stretch limousine just isn't something we see here except during grad season."

He was running now, Forester beside him, because the more he thought of it, the more it made sense.

They hit Beach Avenue and stopped dead in the press of people.

About a mile along the curve of the lake stood the commercial part of Peachland, tonight decked out in lights and the wafting sound of party music. The church stood in shadows at the other end of all that mayhem.

"Damn. That car could be there now. It's going to take us at least twenty minutes for us to get there," he said.

Forester looked him in the eye. "I know you don't trust me, but trust me now." He led off in a ground-eating stride, elbows out, shoving through the crowd like a knife as he fished a phone out of his pocket. Where people pushed back, he announced "police". People backed off and let him through like the prow of a boat, Brett closely bringing up the rear.

But there was no running the mile. That was impossible with the clots of people, not to mention the folks staking their claim with lawn chairs on the road, set up to watch the fireworks that would come with full dark. On the murky-scented lake, the circle of boats had grown, gleaming like rings of fireflies on the water. The first stars were visible overhead and he had so planned on being with Kylee to watch all of this—preferably from the safety of his bed, the hiss of the vineyard irrigation, and the booms of the fireworks their only music.

Still, Forester made better progress than Brett expected. They reached the supervised swimming area. Ahead the press of people increased. Past the swimming hole with its rope swings and diving board, there was no more beach, just a three-foot drop down to the water. Metal fences kept people from falling down, but it also constricted the crowd's ability to ease the press of people. Forester paused.

"Here." Brett grabbed his arm and turned them away from the lake into a side street of small, old-fashioned two-story houses much like his parents' house. "We bypass the crowd," he yelled and started running, even though other people had shared his idea. He bumped against people, tossed an apology over his shoulder and was gone. He didn't care if Forester was with him, he just knew he had to get there because it *had* to be where Kylee was. She sure as heck wasn't on the street. He'd have found her if she was.

He cut back down to Beach Avenue past the firehall and the old garage that had become another trendy sidewalk café, tonight filled with people enjoying a late dinner. The air carried the scent of hamburgers, grilled salmon, and pizza. Wine and beer glasses tinkled.

The street was a solid mass of people pressed into a too small an area. The lights of the beer garden blazed, as did the spotlights on the band playing on the gazebo stage. People moved to the music, their faces a sea of expressions he couldn't fathom. Happy, he supposed, while all he could manage was frantic. Southward, the café was connected to a string of closed shops, guarded from the street by a sidewalk and a little grilled fence. People perched on the fence and park benches, beer glasses in hand, so clearly the beer garden had escaped its boundaries.

"This isn't good," Forester said, coming up beside him. "Too much booze and not enough police presence. I've counted three officers all with auxiliary partners. Not enough if things get unruly. I've alerted Stone to our twenty—our location. He'll call it in to the detachment." He patted his cell phone pocket.

"The church is just down here." Brett led them behind the worst of the crowd along the front of a real estate office and a beachwear store. Beyond was the concrete block bunker of the public washroom and sunk farther into shadow closer to the highway, was the white and red painted church.

Was that a thump at the doorway? Over the music and the crowd noise it was hard to tell.

He leapt up the narrow set of stairs that led to the front door. "Kylee!"

A muffled cry came from inside.

CHAPTER 22

The air in the church reeked of old wood oil and the iron scent of her fear. The dust under the model train display made Kylee sneeze as she frantically belly-crawled toward the escape. Heck, fox-hole soldiers would be impressed with her speed. But was she fast enough? Had to be. The tangled legs of Tom Beaton weren't tangled anymore. He was coming for her. She had to move and move now.

She slid out from under the table at the top of the stairs, scrambled up and half fell, half threw herself down them just as Tom's hand grabbed the back of her new blue blouse.

No. She wasn't going to let him stop her.

The delicate fabric ripped as she yanked loose and leapt down the stairs two-three-four at a time, hands sliding on wood railing. A crash said he was right on her heels.

The door. Where was the door?

There. Arched, stained glass windows on either side marked it.

She crashed into a display case and reached the door, yanked on the handle but the darn thing wouldn't open. It *had to* open.

Something grabbed her hair and yanked her back. She turned, kicking and screaming and pounding with her fists. Please let someone hear her. She tried to get her knee up between his legs, but he was too wise for that. Even his spindly arms were stronger than hers.

"Help! Help me!"

His hand came up and tried to muzzle her. She bit down hard.

Behind her something crashed against the door. Someone was there! She screamed and then bit down hard again on the hand muzzling her. Tom groaned and then hit her, his fist catching her on the temple.

The room spun around her, her knees folded in pain. She sagged against her captor and his breath was in her face like copper and iron, his gray eyes glowing like smoke in a fire and she was lost and burning, too. Her wrist was on fire, but she truly believed that as long as she felt that pain this thing in Tom Beaton couldn't hurt her.

And then suddenly the gray eyes were gone and strong familiar arms came around her. "Kylee? Kylee, are you all right? Are you with me?" Kisses on her cheeks, on her fluttering eyelids, and finally on her mouth.

Warm and tasting of rich wine and warm earth.

"Brett?" She fended him off to look at him. "Is it really you?"

"It's really me, babe." He picked her up and swung towards the door. "I'm taking her to the hospital," he said over his shoulder.

Then Corporal Forester was there and so was another man. They had Tom Beaton handcuffed between them, but Beaton didn't look the same—he was smaller, shaken-looking and mumbling to himself. And right by the door waited Chloe and Lila, concern on their faces. Forester had Beaton by the chin and was peering into his eyes as if looking for something.

"It's not here," Forester said and looked back at his partner, his eyes narrowed. "It's not in me." He went to his partner and peered into his eyes, then turned to Kylee and caught her chin. When he was done with her he grabbed Brett's jaw and forced him to meet Forester's gaze.

Brett yanked away, still holding Kylee. "What the hell are you doing? Leave her—me—us alone."

"I'm checking you're you, okay? I know this thing, whatever it is. It could be in any of us." Forester shook his head. "You're okay."

Forester went over and checked out Lila and Chloe. "Dammit, it was here, but now it isn't. Where the hell is it?" He turned back to Tom Beaton and Kylee shivered.

"Brett I'm fine. I am. A little bit knocked around, but he didn't do anything but slap me a couple of times."

He just growled that he was getting her out of here.

"Brett, please. I can walk myself." To prove it, she made him release her and limped to the door. She must have turned an ankle on her race down the stairs, but it wasn't bad, and with every step it felt better. All she really needed was to get out of here. She made it to the door and Lila swallowed her in a hug. Chloe crowded in to make a threesome.

"Thank God you're safe. I just about freaked when Brett told me you were missing," Lila said.

Nodding, Kylee held up her arm. "It's about this. There's something the matter with Tom." She motioned to the man virtually hanging in the police officer's hands. "Or there was. Something inside him." She looked back at her friends and wondered if it was really them looking back at her. She shivered. At least Forester seemed to think they were all okay. Poor Tom Beaton was muttering to himself and whining to the two policemen. She yanked her gaze away. "I just need to get away from here."

"Of course you do." Lila started to usher her down the stairs, but Kylee resisted.

"With Brett. I want to get out of here with Brett."

Lila frowned and so did Chloe. "You sure?" Lila asked.

"Never more sure of anything in my life." She glanced up at Brett and caught his hand.

With admonishments from Forester and Stone to come in to the detachment to give a statement tomorrow, Kylee left with

Brett. The police were going to be a while dealing with Tom Beaton and trying to find the limousine that had apparently left Peachland just as they were breaking into the church. Luckily, Brett had thought to park his car at this end of the town when he'd planned on bringing her to the beer garden.

He led her through the crowds and the roadblock to the car and helped her in. When they'd made it onto the highway, the little green sports car accelerated until they turned up Trepanier hill. She felt the moist air of the vineyard before they turned down the driveway and came to a halt at the door to his house. There, he held the car door for her and then pulled her into his embrace.

"I really thought I might have lost you," he said into the rhythmic hiss-hiss-hiss of the spraying irrigation and the faint strains of music from down by the lake.

She looked up at his handsome face, his eyes hidden in the darkness, and out at the night-laden view. The last of the light was leaching from the sky, but across the lake a half moon rose above the gray hills. "I think you might have, if you hadn't come when you did. He said he'd kill me to get what he wanted. This." She held up her wrist and shivered.

His warm hands ran up her arms and pulled her more tightly against him. "Then tomorrow we're cutting the damned thing off. You hear?"

He tilted her chin up. "Understand?"

She nodded, though there was no way in hell that was going to happen. But the argument could wait for another day and he placed the most gentle of kisses on her lips that erased all her chill. He slid his arm around her shoulders and tugged her into his side.

"How's your ankle? Do you feel like a little walk?"

She inhaled the night bloom of damp irrigated air over sun-warmed earth, the medley of ripening grapes and dry grass that was a wonderful counterpoint to his body's scent of warm earth and wine. A little nod up at him and, "Sure."

After the cooling breeze off the lake, the air on the bench of land was still warm on her skin. She felt encased in a moment in time with Brett. The lawn was dark around them, and the long rows of the vineyard were sketched on the shadows of the hillside. Out on the lake, the water was a reflective night sky sparked with the fireflies of the boats at anchor waiting for the fireworks. The half moon placed long finger of light across the water's surface as if pointing at her—them—as Brett led her from his yard, through a small grape arbor-covered gate and into the long lines of the vineyard.

The soft sound of crickets stilled as they entered; overhead came the sound of bat wings. She looked up to see them and Brett smiled down at her. "The best darn pest control going, the bats and the swallows. There's a mess of bat colonies living in the old school house down along the water. They're so endangered these days, that they refurbished the schoolhouse around the bat colony, if you can believe it. But they keep the insects down."

The soil was soft underfoot as he led her out into the vineyard under the gaze of the moon. It caught on his hair and in his eyes when he looked at her, and he looked at her often. As they went, he'd stop every so often to gently twine a vine back in place in the arbor, or he'd smile at the swell of a cluster of grapes and would regale her with the tale of agonizing over the decision to keep of this particular cluster of grapes.

"You talk about them as if they're your children," she said, liking the way the moonlight caught the angles of his face.

He shrugged and grinned down at her. "In a way, I guess they are. As a vintner, you shape every part of the grape's existence from growth on the vine, to the pressing, to the fermentation, casking, and aging. It's my decisions that can turn a mediocre wine into a great one."

"And you love that."

His eyes were dark, all the green lost as he gazed down at her. "I think—I love the connection. It *means* something. At least to me. My legacy, maybe. Who knows, maybe a hundred years from now people will be talking about the Elkhart the way they talk about the vineyards of Champagne or Burgundy."

He looked so part of the place, with the echo of grapes in his scent and the moonlight flickering on his skin. Could she ever look so... like she belonged? "You've got deep roots here."

"Yeah," he nodded. "I do. I can't imagine living anywhere else."

"Funny." She looked past him then, afraid of baring herself too much to him, and yet wanting him to understand. "I totally get it, but if you'd asked me two months ago I wouldn't have understood. This place. These people. They really are home."

"No," he said, his voice a quiet rumble as he put his arms around her. "You are. Home, I mean. Like I can't imagine Peachland without you in it. But you try to leave, and no matter how much I love this place, I think I'd follow. That's what I've figured out, what you mean to me."

His face was shadowed as he leaned down to her, his lips gentle as the moon as they brushed against hers. "You see, bracelet or not, I think we're meant to be together." He pulled back so he could look into her eyes. "Believe me, I never thought I'd hear myself saying that."

There was disbelief in his voice and such boyish wonder in his eyes, that she couldn't help herself. She caught his collar and leaned up to kiss him firmly. His hands found her back, then slid down to her waist, then hitched her into him firmly as if they might never be sated. If it was possible, she could get drunk on this man. He made her wonder at the beauty of the world and forget the ugliness and pain that was behind her. His answering kiss deepened and he groaned into her.

"I think..." His mouth slid to her neck. "I think, maybe..." He nibbled her ear. "I think maybe I've had enough of walking tonight. What do you say?"

When he pulled back to look at her she was breathless enough that all she could do was nod. A toe-curling fire spread through her core and she leaned into him and breathed in his scent of sun-drenched grape vines. Swallowed, pulled away and raised her brow. Smiled.

"You know, I still don't have any underwear on..."

Mock horror filled his face. "Then we'd best do something about that." Arm around her waist, they wandered back through the long lines of vines, and through the grape arbor gate and then to his house. There, he unlocked the door and welcomed her inside with another long kiss. This one straying from her mouth back to her neck and under her hair, his hands cupping her head, fingers in her hair as she pressed herself against him.

He pulled back and cupped her face. He must have seen her wince the barest amount when he ran his palms down the side of her face. He dropped his hands to her shoulders. "After what you've been through tonight, we don't have to do this you know." He kissed her brow, her lips almost chastely.

And there was no way in heck she was letting him get away this time. "No way, buster. I didn't wait this long and escape a bad guy for nothing." She caught his head and pulled him down to her and kissed him long and hard. When she released him she met his gaze with challenge. "See. I'm fine. Better than fine."

Apparently he didn't need any further urging. He grabbed a bottle of wine and two glasses and, holding her hand, led her up the stairs. For a moment she almost cringed at the déjà vu of Tom Beaton dragging her into the church. But this was Brett and this was his cozy house.

His bedroom was filled with the white light of the moon, marking it with light and shadow. He set the wine and glasses down and came to her, where she stood by the door. This was his landscape. Let him ask her in. He shook his head and caught her hands.

"You're beautiful, you know."

She shook her head. "No. Lila's beautiful. I'm just..."

He leaned in and covered her mouth with a kiss. "Beautiful and she doesn't even know it. A shame, that," he whispered into her ear.

His mouth trailed across her throat, the lightest of kisses setting her skin alight, teasing her as his lips found the edge of the neckline of her poor torn beautiful blue blouse. His mouth paused there and her mind filled in the sensations that would come when his mouth travelled a little lower. Her nipples hardened and she wanted him to touch her, hold her, but strangely he hadn't touched her with his hands. Only his mouth, gently urging her neckline a little lower, then darting back to her mouth to ravage.

She sagged against the wall behind her and his arms came up to either side of her head. He braced himself on the wall and peered down at her so intently she swallowed. A slow smile curved his lips, as she reached for him and pulled his shirt up out of his jeans and up over his back. Bare chested he faced her again, strong arms she imagined he had developed both swimming and wrestling wine barrels, once more braced to either side. He said nothing.

Tentatively at first, she stroked his strong chest. Let her be the aggressor. After tonight she was strong enough. She ran her palms down over his pecs feeling the strength of muscle, the hard nubbin of his nipple, the smoothness of flesh. Down to his narrow waist and hips and the plain brown belt closure there. The hard lines of his muscles created shadows that arrowed down over his belly button to disappear suggestively below his waist. She swallowed and met his gaze again. She wanted to press her skin against his, wanted to feel that hardness and strength against her. Feeling shy but determined, she grabbed the bottom of her blouse and pulled it up over her head, then dropped it on the floor. A shame, but even if the fabric hadn't been torn, the lovely blouse would be ruined to her forever.

She looked up at him waiting, his dark gaze smoldered and heated her skin.

"Why stop there?" he growled, and an embarrassed flush flooded up through her. She'd never been forward like this. Ever. But she took his dare and slid her leggings down. Stepped out of them, still caught in the circle of his arms.

One dark brown brow arched at her. "Those are panties. I thought you said you weren't wearing any."

"I lied." She grinned and looked down at the lacy things she wore, a purchase specially made for this eventuality. Taking a deep breath as she caught his belt buckle, "How about you? Are you a tighty whitey kinda guy or into boxers?"

The buckle fell loose and she glanced up at his face as she quickly undid the jeans button. His expression had gone tight with expectation as she unzipped him and let her fingers barely touch him before she pushed the denim down over his hips to the floor. He stepped out of them. Tighty whiteys that gripped his ass very nicely. She cupped him in her hand and he throbbed against her palm. She squeezed and a little gasp of air escaped him.

She liked that she could have that effect and leaned in then, and placed a string of kisses over his chest and followed the shadow line down to his waist and the waiting bulge of him. No man had ever let her undress him before. Not if she wasn't naked first. Through her bangs she peered up at Brett, his eyes were heavy lidded as if he was holding his breath waiting.

She tugged his underwear down and cupped him in her hand, stepped into him and ran his hard length against her belly, then stood on tiptoe so he hung between her legs and ran him over the silk of her panties. His heat sent her own soaring and she rocked against him.

Brett groaned and his arms finally came around her, pulled her into him, his face buried in her hair, mouth on her neck, her shoulder, her breast as he picked her up and pressed her against the wall. Then he suddenly turned and carried her to the bed. Tossed her down on its softness and laid himself beside her.

"This has got to go," he said, and with a quick flick of his hand, her bra was undone and he slid it off her shoulders. "And these."

Two fingers hooked in the silken sides of her panties and pulled them down, leaving her to wiggle her fanny out of them.

"Good girl."

He ran a finger lightly over her skin, sending shooting sparks of sensation through her flesh. Just how he held such magic in his hand she wasn't sure, but she felt like one of his wines must feel, plucked and fermenting to create sweet magic inside her. She ran her fingers over his chest and smiled when he shivered.

"I was right, you know," he said as he stretched himself beside her. "You are beautiful. You just don't know it yet. I'm here to show you."

She figured she was going to enjoy it.

§

Moonlit flesh trembled under his hands as he eased Kylee onto her back beside him. His hands smoothed her skin as he raised himself and tasted her lips, then went walking southward to her breasts, his hands smoothing, soothing, her flesh. The night was cool on heated skin, Kylee's scent of heated lavender and strawberries counterpoint to the scent of sun-warmed earth and moisture through the open bedroom window. Her gasp as he took her nipple into his mouth almost broke his resolve to go slowly.

Damn, this woman was desirable and precious and made more so by his determination to go slow, to make it last. To make whatever was between them last. He lingered over her breasts, playing there, then slipped down her body to the small mound and tasted, stayed, and enjoying the small tremors that ran through her body. Enjoyed it more when her back arched and a small cry escaped her. He lifted his head and found such wanton desire in her eyes it almost stopped him.

They were wide dark pools, her lips parted and her face flushed dark in the moonlight. Her pale hair was tangled around her face and the curves and valleys of her flesh only promised bliss. Her breast moved up and down rapid as a bird's.

"I think I will always love you like this. You look like a dove finally set free, but almost afraid to fly." He smiled and smoothed her damp hair back from her face. "Come fly."

She came up off the bed and into his arms, so fast he nearly toppled them both off the bed. Her long legs twined around his waist, her slim arms around his neck.

Pressing her back onto the bed, her hold on him only loosened when he hung above her, his hard length pressed between them. She licked her lips almost nervously and it charmed him completely. Then her slim fingers caressed him and his whole body tightened.

Beautiful, chaste, and a little harlot. What man could want more?

"Hold on," he said and fished a small wrapper out of a bedside table. She helped him slide it on, her touch an erotic slide that made his breath hitch. He caught her and pressed her back, pressed between her legs and she opened for him, her gaze, huge and liquid and locked on his. And then he entered and his groan of pleasure was matched by Kylee's soft cry. Had he hurt her? He didn't want to hurt her.

He stroked her face. "Okay?"

She nodded and he began to move, slowly, so slowly, reveling in her warmth. Rocking them together in the velvet softness of her so she was like a flower unfolding around his length, accepting him in and he wanted more. Wanted to lose himself in this woman, know her from the inside out. He lifted himself up still joined with her and pulled her onto his lap. Caught her hips and continued the slow process of pleasuring her as his mouth sought and found the tight peaks of her breasts. The double sensations of soft and hard made him want to thrust deep, but instead he held back, aroused by the length of her neck as her head fell back in pleasure, as her small gasps escaped her, as her hands gripped his shoulders and she actively thrust herself to meet him. Deeper, if it was possible, she found a way. Her gaze under lust-heavy lids made his blood surge. She met him as an equal, taut thighs around his middle.

She leaned in and lightly bit his nipple, her hands sliding down to his ass as she drew him in. Wanted more and demanded. He caught her soft buttocks and swung them both off the bed, her legs locked around him as he backed her to the wall. He thrust as one hand sought her softness where they were joined and she jerked once more, cried out and shuddered around him. Molded into him wanting more.

One hand braced against the wall, he sped up his thrusts and Kylee met him for each one. Her small heels beat at his ass as she arched her back toward him, as her hands gripped his shoulders, raked his back and he was in her and he was in this thing whatever it was for the long haul, because he thought he might love this woman. Heat exploded up through him and the top of his head blew away, as from outside came the distant boom-boom and the night lit up with the brilliant sunbursts of fireworks. He thrust once, twice, three times into her and felt her shudder soul-deep around him.

Cradling her to him, he carried her to the bed and collapsed beside her, as the walls of the room were painted red and gold and blue from the Peachland fireworks. He stroked her, loving her, cherishing, because looking into her night-darkened blue eyes he was going to do this again and again and again. As long as they both shall live.

§

Heaven. She was in heaven and the pleasure set her body ringing like a bell. On the rumpled sheets of Brett's bed, the night air cooled their sweat-slicked bodies, but not completely. No, never completely because just inhaling Brett's musky scent of sun-heated grape vines and just one look at the lust still in his eyes let her know this wasn't over. Not tonight. Not for a very long time. Forever?

His touch, as he ran his calloused fingers down her side, could almost make her come again. She snuggled in closer to him, and he tugged her into his chest.

"So just where were you hiding away all these years," he said, his voice a comforting rumble in his chest, his heart a steady counterpoint.

"Not hiding. I just didn't know what I was looking for. So I guess I was looking in the wrong places. Corporate boardrooms and the like." She looked up at him and found him studying her. He looked so serious she had to grin. "Who knew I should have been wandering through wineries?"

He hugged her and, giving into a wanton urge, she looped a leg over his hip, felt him harden against her. Helped him along with a little wiggle of her hips and giggled when he swatted her rump.

"You plan on exhausting this old man?" he asked.

"This old man feels more than a little up to the task." She'd never been an active pursuer in her lovemaking, but this time she pushed him onto his back and swung a leg over to ride him.

Ride him, she did.

§

The fireworks were long over and the sky was turning light when Kylee woke from a doze. She was warm and alive and safely in Brett's arms, her backside snugged against his groin from the last time they'd made love. She felt herself color a little at the thought. Just what hadn't they done last night? Brett was obviously a very skilled lover and she—was not. Still, he'd put up with a willing student and she'd learned a lot. Learned she liked this man a lot more than she ought to, given the short time they'd known each other. Was she just doing it again? Throwing herself at a guy because she was too desperate not to be alone?

A niggle of doubt made her squirm with discomfort and so did a lump in the bed. She shifted, trying to get rid of it, but Brett shifted behind her and pulled her back against him. Warm breath on her neck as lips found her ear. "You planning on sneaking out of here? Because it's not going to happen. You are here to stay, madam."

Just what was he saying? That he wanted to waste the coming day in bed together, or something more? The way his lips trailed down her shoulder and his hand snaked around her to caress her breasts and then slip lower, she forgot what the question was. She enjoyed the eroticism as he pressed into her once more from behind and rocked them together as the sunrise flooded the sky with peach and apricot fingers. When they were sated, he pulled her up with him and led her to the open window and out onto the small iron-railed balcony where he wrapped his arms around her from behind.

The lake was awash with the warm colors of the sky, the cool night breeze gradually warming in the angled sunlight. Behind them the last of the irrigation stopped leaving them in a silence broken only by the distant cry of a bird. Brett started behind her.

"What is it?" she asked, loving the way his arms came around her and the way their bodies seemed to fit together.

"A pheasant. There used to be a lot of wild ones around here, but I haven't seen one in years—not since all the development. They're a rare bird now. They don't do well with all the housing, and all the dogs. Too much civilization." He turned her around in his arms and lifted her two hands to kiss them and then leaned down to caress her mouth with his. "Did you ever think maybe you're like the pheasant and you weren't meant to live in all that civilization down on the coast?" The lightest of kisses. "Maybe you were supposed to be here?" Another kiss. "So we could meet?" Still another kiss. "And do this?"

He pulled her hips into his and she felt his desire, felt her own answer.

"Just what have you done to me, Kylee Jensen? I've never wanted anyone like I want you."

"I know. It's impossible, isn't it? Like a magic spell."

"Maybe." He swept her into his arms as if she was no more than a child and strode back into the room to toss her onto the bed. "Doesn't matter, though. I know what to do about it."

She pulled him down to her and they welcomed the day in with another tangle of limbs and joyful lovemaking.

It was when they lay winded on the rumpled sheets together, her head on his chest, his hand gently fondling her breast, that she realized something was missing.

"The bracelet," she said, sitting bolt upright, Brett's caress momentarily forgotten, as her fingers closed around her empty wrist. "Oh God, Brett. It's gone? It's gone."

A darkness seemed to cross before her eyes and she elbowed him aside as she fumbled in the bedding. Pulled duvet aside, finally forced Brett off the bed. Nothing. Yanked sheets back, pulled pillows aside, and finally spotted the dull gleam of silver. She pounced on it and pulled the bracelet out, then took it to the balcony doorway to examine. A relieved sigh escaped her.

"Thank goodness. It's not broken."

Brett took it from her to examine. "You're right. All our nighttime gymnastics, must have somehow done the trick to open it." He ran the small key through the lock and the bracelet became a loop, then swiftly slid the key through the lock again and the bracelet hung loose across his palm. He shook his head. "Opens like a charm, now. I don't understand what all the fuss was about."

She held out her wrist to have the bracelet put on, but Brett held it away. "No way in hell am I letting my girl have that thing on her arm again. There're too many unanswered questions about it."

My girl? He said my girl? A warm sunny feeling flooded her chest that was just as wonderful as all of their lovemaking. She stood on tiptoe and kissed him. "Then maybe we better get ready to face the day and get it back down to Lila. Besides, if we show up much later, it's only going to give them more fuel to tease us."

His arm snaked around her waist and he pulled her into him. "Let 'em tease." Tossing the bracelet onto his dresser, he hauled her back toward the bed once more. Kylee slipped loose and beat him to it.

As the sun was nearing noon, they finally showered, dressed, and made it out to Brett's sports car. He drove them down the sage and baby's breath-scented hillside. Kylee was certain anyone who saw them would know exactly what they'd been doing because she couldn't seem to get the stupid cat-that-ate-the-cream smile off her face and Brett seemed to have a matching one. And then there was the touching. His hand kept slipping off the gear shift to her knee or to run one electric fingertip up her thigh until she was really considering just asking him to turn the car around again, but the bracelet sat in her lap, its lovely silver confined in a plastic Ziploc baggie. And then there was the police. Corporals Forester and Stone were expecting her at one o'clock.

Beach Avenue looked amazingly clean and civilized after the past night's festivities. The joggers were back along the lake though their strides might be a little shorter. The folks at the bakery/café shuffled and wore dark sunglasses as if they were nursing hangovers, and the lake spilled placid waves against the shore. Only a few families were at the beach even though it was a hot day, and even those families seemed a little more subdued than on other days. But the garbage had been picked up and aside from the brightly-colored Peachland banners hanging from the light posts, no one would have known that there had been a blow-out party in the town the night before.

They pulled up in front of *This & That* and found Chloe, Reggie and Lila all seated, talking on the front porch. The talking turned to whispers when Brett and Kylee climbed out of the car. The whispers went silent when Brett twined his fingers in hers to walk beside her up to the stairs. He ushered her up them in front of him and then stepped up beside her.

"Morning," he said.

Chloe snorted. She wore a sunny yellow, sleeveless, hip-skimming caftan and white shorts. "Afternoon more like. Where you been, or should I ask?"

Even Reggie, in her usual black cargo pants and singlet, and Lila in a lovely lavender smock could barely hide their smirks behind their coffee cups. Kylee felt the blush flood up over her shoulders to her cheeks. She was suddenly too aware of how she wore one of Brett's white t-shirts tied at the waist over her leggings.

"Gee, she sure do blush awful purty," Reggie deadpanned.

Kylee looked skyward. "Okay, so we spent the night together, all right? Enough said?"

"Oh no! You're not getting off that easily." Chloe shook her head, her thatch of necklaces—blue lapis with jet today—rattling. "You're the first 'friend' my brother has been with. I want the low-down. Is he really as good as all those other women said?"

Oh my. The way her cheeks were burning, much more and she'd bleed.

"Hey!" Brett interrupted. "I'm right here. Kylee's not going to kiss and tell any more than I am, so get your dirty little mind out of the gutter, or better still go have your own affair, Sis. Then you can tell us everything."

He sniffed the air. "That coffee?"

"On the stove," Lila said.

Brett shot a look of question at Kylee.

"Please."

"Then wait here and don't let these three witches pick your brains for details." Then he disappeared into the house leaving Kylee to settle uncomfortably onto one of the other chairs. Silence descended.

"So?" Lila asked. "You're all right after last night?"

It took Kylee a moment to realize that her friend was referring to her abduction and not to the replete ache of a body well and truly used. "I felt safe with Brett. To be honest, the whole incident seems like it happened years ago." She shook her head.

"Amazing how the mind will protect itself," Reggie said.

"That and a good roll in the hay," Chloe chortled. "Sorry. It's sort of written all over your face, woman. My bro must be better than I thought."

"Damn. That's what I was afraid of. Is it really that obvious?" She looked from friend to friend to friend and got her answer.

"Well not to change the subject or anything but something aside from your teasing came out of my wild night." She dropped the baggie she'd had in her hands onto the wicker coffee table. "Let's just say it came off in the midst of everything."

Lila's brow arched.

"You can say that," Chloe mumbled and Reggie snatched the bracelet up and dumped it out of the baggie into her palm to examine.

Brett returned with their coffee and a plate with four pieces of toast, and settled on the arm of her chair. "So Forester and company want to interview Kylee at one, right?"

"Just before they left they said they'd conduct the interview here, rather than you going into the detachment. I said I'd pass the message along," Lila said, her gaze seriously scanning the two of them before a smile lit up her eyes. "I can't tell you how worried you had us last night, Kylee. Just how did he trap you?"

The memory of that evening with the heat, the smiling happy people all around her, and her anticipation of Brett finding her and what would come after, all came flooding back to her. And then Tom Beaton appeared out of nowhere and she'd let him lead her off somewhere, just like she'd let Kevin lead her off on a wild goose chase for his own benefit, not for hers. The difference this time, was that she'd taken action and freed herself.

Brett's warm hand found her shoulder and the memory faded. She was here on the porch with her friends. The sunlight off the lake caught in the streaks in his hair. Brett who was settled. Brett who had pursued her and who had been there to find her last night. Brett who had invited her into his life—a life that was connected to place. Here. Now. Her place, too. Her hand slipped up over his as Lila smiled and Chloe, having taken the bracelet from Reggie, played with the clasp. She slipped the bracelet around her wrist and the key through the clasp.

She held out her wrist for them all to admire as a brown unmarked police car pulled up front and two tall figures climbed out.

Chloe turned her wrist from side to side to study the bracelet. "It was simple, just as we thought. The key just goes through the key hole."

"Hey," Danny Forester said as he clumped up the stairs, Corporal Stone on his heels. "I see everyone survived the night. That's good."

"Better, even," Brett said. "We got the damned bracelet off."

Chloe glanced up as if she felt everyone's gaze turn her way. She held up her wrist and then went to unclasp it. Frowned. Tried again.

And again.

"Oh crap."

ABOUT THE AUTHOR

Karen L. Abrahamson s a well-traveled writer who has explored cultures and countries around the world. Home, however, brings her back to central British Columbia, Canada that has inspired a number of romances, including the well-regarded *Unlocking Series*. She is the author of literary, romantic and fantasy fiction. She lives on the west coast of Canada with two Bengal cats that aren't quite as well traveled as she is. When she isn't writing she can be found with a camera and backpack in fabulous locations around the world.

If you would like to get an automatic e-mail when Karen's next book is released, sign up at her website, *www.karenlabrahamson.com*. Your email address will never be shared and you can unsubscribe at any time.

A Special Request from the Author: Word-of-mouth is crucial for any author to succeed. If you enjoyed this book, please consider leaving a review at Amazon, Barnes and Noble, or any other e-tailer, or on Goodreads; even if it's only a line or two, it would make all the difference and would be very much appreciated.

To find more of her writing, visit

www.twistedrootpublishing.com.

SNEAK PREVIEW
UNLOCKING HER HISTORY

PROLOGUE

THE NIGHT AIR OFF OF OKANAGAN LAKE CARRIED the warm, wet heat of the daytime like the luscious heat off a living body. It smelled of deep water, the pine of the dry hills and the faint scent of boat diesel from Peachland marina that was just down the road. The beach lay silent as it was supposed to at this deepest hour of night. Just gentle waves lapping over fine gravel and the occasional splash of the ducks that slumbered with their wings over their heads near the shore. They were as blind to his presence, as were Peachland's puny sleeping residents.

Uphill from the water came the low rumble of the long-haul trucks on their midnight rides down the highway and from farther uphill came the yip of some kind of animal. Dog? No, something wild. He had no time for that sort of thing. He brought his attention down to the stately old white house stained gray by the night, its red trim turned the color of midnight shadows. That was his destination.

Like a shadow himself he crossed the street, keeping to the shade of a huge old cottonwood, then slunk around the corner away from the water and down the back alley until he reached the two-car carport that he had marked when he first assumed this body. It was a good body, ready for action and unassuming. He had located it through his usual agency and then moved into it to regain what had been kept from him.

Darkness filled the carport as he slid past the mini SUV and into the yard at the rear of the house. It was a small yard made smaller by the workshop that filled the left side of the space. He inhaled the forge and solder stink of an artisan. To the right was a high cedar fence and a small vegetable garden, while at the back of the house stood a flagstone patio with cushioned wicker furniture, the cushions tipped up against the night dew. Someone in the house paid attention to details. That was not a good thing.

The rear of the house held the kitchen area, he'd ascertained that during a prior visit. The body smoothly knelt beside the door and used fine fingers to extract tools from a small vinyl case. He relinquished control of the hands and let the body do its work. Lean in and listen for the soft clicks, feel them through the thin metal picks. There, one pin shifted. There, another. A third. A fourth and he stopped, inhaled and drew power out of the darkness, then blasted it into the alarm system that ran through the doors and windows. The bitter scent of burned wiring curled into his nostrils as he shifted the door handle.

The rear door swung open onto darkness and he inhaled the breath of the two women sleeping in the bedrooms above.

He slid inside and pulled the door softly closed behind. The kitchen was rich with the scents of basil and thyme, the dark smoke of red wine, and an undertone of silver. That was what he sought. Like smoke, he followed the scent down the hall, but stopped before the door into the jewelry shop. The scent of was stronger here. Silver and gold and the arcane vibrations of stones and crystals, but a silly curtain of plastic beads blocked him from it. Well, he had come this far.

Gently he eased the strings of beads aside. He slid through the curtain, then let the curtain fall back into position, the beads clacking softly.

He sniffed the air again. Silver, but he was not sure. This body was not as attuned to the nuances of scent as the policeman had been, and even that that was a far cry from the body he normally rode. But the bracelet had come off the woman. He'd felt it as surely as if he had stripped it from her arm himself. It had been like a gong had gone off in him; one level of the ancient curse removed and one less level of power for him to recover.

Fists tight he strode around the room. The faint taste of the ancient silver still lingered on the air. After almost losing the woman to him, they now must be aware of their danger. If it had come off her wrist had they locked it up, then? Could that be it?

He shoved behind the small cash register counter and found the safe in a cubbyhole in the house's inner wall. It was a safe intended to protect the shop's goods from the usual depredations of the common criminals who might live in this backwater of central British Columbia. A backwater town in a backwater country.

He set the thief body free to ply the combination lock and dreamed of the power that would come with success. An old foe vanquished. Power returned. The long handle of the safe turned with a low thunk and he pulled the foot-high door open releasing a gust of silver-and-stone-scented air.

His eyes burned. His nose watered as he hauled a stack of black velvet trays out to inspect. Some cursed person had placed jet stones in the top tray. He set it aside to examine ornate silver necklaces. Earrings with cabochon emeralds. A silver pendant fashioned like doors, with silver filigreed trees over an ancient glass window. He stroked the exquisite piece. Someone had labored hard over this.

Quickly he rifled through the trays. It had to be here. It had to, yet all of these pieces were marvelous—but new. Not what he wanted at all!

Stymied, he stood. He strode around the room fighting the desire to smash the glass counters, sweep down the displays, ram a fist through the large windows to make the women pay. By all the hounds of hell and the infernal flame that burned within him, the bracelet was his! He *would* make them pay.

On impulse he pulled a bag from under the counter and poured the safe contents into it.

A movement of air, a whiff of roses. He spun around as a woman with moon-pale skin and wild curls pushed through the beaded curtain.

"I've called the police," she yelled as he mowed her down, smashed into a glass display case and leapt for the front door. The sound of glass shattering followed him as he yanked at the door. The lock tore through the sash sending a bell wildly ringing and he was out and across the porch, down the stairs and gone, loping up the street.

A fool. He'd been a fool to do that, but for the bracelet he would do anything.

The breeze off the lake shifted direction. From the north it came, carrying the scent of peach and cherry orchards and a hint of ancient silver. He kept going, following the trace northward on the long runner's legs and stopped once he had crossed the small creek called Trepanier. The town spread behind him, suburban houses strung along the lakeshore that curved gently southward toward the heart of the old town of Peachland. Ahead stood a large, three-story, L-shaped building of apartments surrounded by gardens.

Redolent of myrrh and frankincense, the scent of power billowed out at him. He stood there, the water running beneath the bridge, the man's blood running in his veins and satisfaction running in his ancient brain.

Here. The bracelet was here, pouring its magic out a condominium window. That meant one of the women had done the foolhardy thing and placed the bracelet on her wrist. His bracelet. He would deal with her.

In the distance came the scream of police sirens echoing over the lake. Time to get off the street and make his plans.

CHAPTER 1

T HE CLOCK ON CHLOE MAIN'S BEDSIDE TABLE said two in the
morning when her phone burred in her ear and dragged her out of
a luscious dream of... The dream vanished as she bolted upright
in bed, her long braid catching on the darn bracelet on her arm.
She almost tore the hair out of her head, so that by the time she
fumbled the phone up she was solidly awake.

"Hello?" she asked, scrubbing at her eyes to avoid the sleep
that wanted to descend again. The white cotton sheets and duvet
were warm and inviting.

"Chloe, it's Lila. There's been a break-in at the store. The
police are here. Can you come?"

At the shakiness in Lila's voice, Chloe's skin went cold. All
possibility of returning to sleep disappeared as she swung out
of bed onto the cool hardwood of the shadowed room. "Are you
okay?" She didn't bother waiting for a reply. "I'll be there in ten.
Five even. Just let me get clothes on."

She hung up and swung around the room with its wide
queen-sized bed and its old fashioned dresser beside the sliding
glass door opening out to the condo patio. The floor-length sheer
curtains billowed from the breeze through the narrow opening
she'd left open for fresh air. Underwear first. The good thing was
that her trusty caftan tunics and her braided hair meant she was

pretty low maintenance. A midnight blue tunic and leggings and cool water palmed over her face. She grabbed an amethyst crystal off her livingroom shelves, a cream colored shawl, then took the stairs down to the basement. There she aimed her silver Camry out onto the road and followed the headlights the half mile down the beach to *This and That: Jewelry and Unsung Treasures.* Nothing moved on the street as she pulled into the curb at the front of the store behind a marked Royal Canadian Mounted Police patrol car and a large SUV.

Compared to the other sleep-darkened houses the red and white house was an opal ablaze with light. She pushed through the gate and ran up the steps and inside, the bell above the door tinkling. She stopped. Leastwise she was stopped by a constable blocking her way and someone examining the broken front door latch.

"Excuse me, Ma'am, you can't come through here." The cop was tall, young, still baby-faced and wasn't that a comment on her ripe old age of thirty four. He had eyes the color of azurite, and onyx-colored hair, but she'd be darned if she was going to let him get in her way.

"Like heck I can't. Lila Weber called me. Is she all right?"

She went to march across the shop to the beaded doorway into the back of the house, but he caught her arm. "If you're a friend of Ms. Weber's why don't you go around the side of the house? She's being interviewed in the kitchen."

She read the guy's face, then scanned the room. An officer was busy photographing the area behind the counter and the guy she'd almost run over when she burst inside was back examining the door. Crime scene. This was a crime scene she was standing in. Her chill went deeper. She tugged the shawl tighter around her shoulders and stepped outside, to take a deep breath, then ran around the side of the house to the backyard. Light blazed from the kitchen, exposing another officer busily doing something to the house's back door. She eased past and into the sunny kitchen that didn't quite feel so sunny at this time of the night.

The room was a lovely one, built almost like a summer kitchen with bright windows in a long row over counters that ran most of the length of the room. The walls were white, but the cupboards were yellow. Bright spots of turquoise ceramics on the counter and on the wall made the place feel like a summer day in the tropics—except for the woman huddled at the table.

The nook sat at one end of the room, with bench seating around three sides and a lone chair on the fourth. At the moment Lila was seated forlornly on the nook bench across from a uniformed police officer. Lila was the owner of the house and one of Chloe's partners in *This and That,* but at this moment she looked nothing like the together business woman she usually was. Her head of long auburn curls had gone wild around her head and her hazel eyes had gone palest green. In the absence of her silver rings she twisted her fingers and her flawless skin was almost as pale as the room's walls.

"Lila! My God. Are you all right?" She pushed past the uniformed police officer who sat in the chair and slid into the nook bench beside Lila to give her a hug. Under normal circumstances Lila might be the most composed person in the world, but at the moment everything about her shouted scared. Even her aura was off kilter and tarnished.

Small shudders ran through Lila's body and Chloe quickly stripped the shawl off and draped it around Lila's satin-pajama covered shoulders, then slung her arm around her friend and pulled her into a hug. "It's okay. We'll get through this. We will."

"She was just telling me what happened," said the officer— another youngster, with the same cookie-cutter sternness.

Lila nodded and wiped at her eyes. "I'm sorry. I feel like such a ninny. I was asleep but something woke me. I came down stairs for a drink of juice, but then I heard something from the shop. I don't know what I thought it was, but for some reason I grabbed the phone and went into the store. He scared the heck out of me when he shoved past for the door."

Shivering, she pulled the shawl tighter around her pearl-pink pajamas.

"How about I make us a cup of tea?" Without waiting for an answer, Chloe pushed free of the table and put the kettle on to boil on the gas range. She found a good Indian loose leaf tea that she added to the water and some chai spices that smelled pleasantly of cardamom and pepper. When everything was boiling, she added sugar and milk and then strained the result into a teapot. Carrying the pot and three mugs, she went back to the table to play mother and pour the tea.

The heat of the spicy tea helped cut her own chill and Lila's trembling seemed to lessen. Chloe faced the officer. "You have questions for me?"

"Just a few. I've already taken Ms. Weber's preliminary statement. There'll be some detectives who will probably want to ask more tomorrow."

Chloe met Lila's eyes and they both sighed. They'd both had enough to do with police for a lifetime over the past few days when their friend and *This and That's* star employee, Kylee Jensen, had been abducted and held prisoner. It seemed to have something to do with the bracelet Chloe now wore. She covered the incriminating bracelet with her hand and nodded. "What do you need to know now?"

Lila shook her head. "I'm so sorry I wasn't more help. It was dark and I really didn't get a good look at him. There was just a flash of lighter-colored hair and then he was gone. The way he ran away I'd say he was younger, though."

The officer made a note of it and then looked up. "I was asking Ms. Weber for an estimate of the value of the stolen goods."

"Stolen?" Chloe turned to Lila. "You said a break-in..." The image of the officer photographing the space behind the store's counter suddenly filtered in. "Oh my God. The safe! But things were in there to be protected!"

Lila shook her head, her eyes welling with tears. "I knew we were getting more high-priced inventory and with Reggie's design's too, I knew we needed to improve our security. I just hadn't gotten around to it what with everything happening with Kylee and the bracelet."

Chloe's gut felt like she had just swallowed a granite boulder. "There was a lot in there," she said, considering. "Reggie had finished her samples for the Milan show and so they were all in there, too. They were one-of-a-kind pieces. I had a stones in there that I thought were going to work for my crystal therapy." She looked at the officer and swallowed. "I'm going to need to think about it, but off the top of my head I'd say the value of the goods was probably at least twenty to twenty-five thousand dollars. I can pull together a complete list for you." And kick herself as she itemized each piece.

"With descriptions, please. We'll be wanting to check the local pawn shops of course. And any photographs would be helpful as well."

"Of course." She caught Lila's ice cold hand and squeezed it knowing that her hand was probably just as cold. She felt frozen, numb except where she held onto her mug.

By the time the police left it was going on five in the morning and the summer sun was rising over the mountains on the other side of the lake. Nerves still frothing so there was no way she could sleep, Chloe sent Lila upstairs for a shower and set to making breakfast. Apparently the detectives would come to ask their questions later this morning.

In the quiet of the kitchen she sliced fresh apricots and peaches and washed fresh cherries, all from local orchards. Then she toasted English muffins, pulled out the almond butter and homemade Saskatoon jelly and carried a tray with the food and a fresh carafe of coffee out through the debris of the store, trying not to look at it. On the front patio she sank down on the wicker couch with its tangerine and turquoise pillows and looked out at the lake.

Okanagan Lake ran eighty-plus miles north-south in south central British Columbia and was the kingpin of a string of long narrow lakes that drained into Washington State. Okanagan Lake was deep and the home of the mythical Ogopogo lake monster, but mostly it was a summer playground for boaters and kayakers and people who came to visit in their recreational vehicles. But this sunny July morning it was just a quiet silver lake, the breeze barely placing a ripple on the fine surface.

The still water rustled along the fine gravel beach across Beach Avenue belying the disturbance she felt at the store. She'd felt a premonition of bad things to come when she'd put the bracelet on, but who knew it would be this?

She held it up to admire in the morning light. The bracelet was a mysterious piece. It had come to *This and That* in a box of odds and ends from an estate sale and Kylee, after digging it out of the mass of jewelry, had put it on. From there things had gotten weird with the estate sale agent murdered; Kylee's abduction at the hands of her neighbor Tom Beaton; and a string of men who had claimed that they had been possessed by aliens. One of them had committed suicide from guilt at what he'd done. The others were dealing with the aftermath and suffering mental breakdowns.

She poured herself a cup of coffee and sipped it while waiting for Lila. Of course whether all these happenings had to do with the bracelet was a matter of some debate.

The bracelet itself was intriguing. Apparently an antique, for its silver showed signs of wear, it was comprised of a series of seven small doors, each linked to the other by delicate silver chains so they formed a cuff that that was cleverly closed by a small ornate key that fit through a lovely scrolled keyhole. The trouble was, apparently once you had the bracelet on, it didn't want to come off again. That had happened to Kylee, until the piece had fallen off in bed almost as if the bracelet itself decided when it should come off. Now it was here to stay on Chloe's wrist.

Each of the seven doors was unique. One was an arched silver door with grapevines twined around it. Another had a tiny gargoyle face for a knocker. Still others had hinges that looked like something out of an elfish kingdom, while another had leaf-shaped hinges. One of them looked like a classic Dutch door with separate upper and lower doors sections. Another was solidly square with raised lintels and a fatima hand knocker. The last, her favorite, was what looked like a wooden door bound with iron strapping and large iron knobs—at least it felt that way when she ran her fingers over it. It reminded her of something you might see in North Africa. Some of the doors even had tiny ornate locks and chains hanging from them so they were as secure as the bracelet apparently was on her wrist. Apparently that was more secure than the shop safe.

Sighing, she looked out at the lake.

Along the paved walkway that ran along the beach, the few early morning joggers slapped their feet on the pavement as they loped past wearing spandex. Their pooches did a doggie jog beside them. From uphill came the low drone of early morning traffic. She breathed in air heavy with warm lake water and the promising scent of fresh baking from the bakery café down the street.

Peachland was a good town. It was a small town that still had its 'old timers,' but it was being dragged kicking and screaming into becoming a destination for vacationers. With that came subdivisions to support all the people who were moving into the area for the country lifestyle. Up the hillsides from the lake many of the old orchards had already been torn down and replaced by houses.

"And isn't that just a depressing thought to start the day with." She reached into her pocket and pulled out the amethyst crystal. She'd forgotten to give it to Lila. The stone was known to protect against burglars and ward off violence and danger. Too little, too late, it seemed. She stuck the stone back in her pocket and sipped her cup of coffee. The caffeine wasn't going to help her nerves any.

The bell over the shop's front door dinged quietly and Lila stepped out onto the porch, her curls a damp mass around her shoulders. She'd dressed in a pair of navy Capri pants that showed off her long legs, and a sleeveless lavender top that skimmed her body, but the lack of sleep showed even through her carefully applied makeup. There were bags under her eyes and she wore a haunted look along with her usual many artful silver rings. Sinking into her throne-backed wicker chair, she closed her eyes.

"I swear every muscle in my body aches and he didn't do anything to me other than knock me over."

"Fear can do that. It tightens all the muscles. So does shock, and you've had one."

The early sun illuminated Lila's once well-known beautiful face and brought the copper out in her hair. "Maybe they should market it as an alternative to isometric exercise. I might do yoga, but I feel like I've been through a war. I'm going to feel this for a while." Her lips curved, but then she sighed. "I called Reggie. She's coming right over. Thank goodness one of us has had a full night's sleep."

Any appetite Chloe might have had evaporated. "I was the one who convinced her to put her designs in the safe. They'd have likely been left alone if they'd been in her shop."

"That, my friend, is a silly thing to say. How were you to know someone would break in?"

What could she say? Out on the water a V of Canada geese were playing chicken with a lone yellow kayak. The wind was picking up some and a small shiver ran up her back. The familiar sense of foreboding settled on her shoulders. No good was going to come of this. Over the years she'd learned to listen to her feelings.

Her hand closed over the stupid bracelet that had caused for so much trouble for Kylee.

"You think it might have something to do with the bracelet?" Lila asked.

Chloe turned to her and realized that Lila had been watching her and the way her fingers seemed drawn to the slim band of silver. Chloe shrugged. "Who knows? Probably not. I mean the bracelet wasn't in the store so there'd be no reason to break in here, would there?"

Lila looked thoughtful, but nodded.

A clatter came from inside the house. Through the windows Lila had opened after the police were finished, the beaded curtain clacked and then, "Holy shit!" Footsteps hurried across the hardwood and the bell dinged above the door as Reggie pushed out onto the porch. She sagged onto the wicker loveseat, shoving her black Cleopatra hair out of her face. "What the hell happened?"

"We had a two a.m. shopper. I surprised him in the store," Lila said, her skin paling even in the warmth of the sunshine.

"The place looks like a disaster," Reggie said, looking back at the door. She wore her usual camo fatigue pants and a black tank top, a look that belied her actual kindness. "The lock's torn right out of the door frame."

Chloe nodded. "Another thing to take care of. How about I get a pen and paper so we can make a list?" She heaved herself up out of the chair knowing she was really just being a coward delaying telling Reggie about the safe and the fate of all of her custom pieces. She went through the shop and retrieved paper and pen from the kitchen and returned in time to hear Lila telling the bad news.

"The safe was open. The thief took everything."

Chloe stood just inside the door as the muscles tensed across Reggie's shoulders. Then they sagged. "You're kidding, right?"

Lila shook her head as Chloe stepped onto the white-painted porch. The scent of the red and white petunias and baby's breath in the hanging copper pots along the porch rail was almost enough to make her nauseous. She collapsed in her chair again and sighed. "I'm so sorry. I was only trying to help."

Reggie frowned. "What are you talking about?"

"The fact that it was me who convinced you to put your pieces in the safe. It's my fault they were stolen."

"Well that's just plain stupid, isn't it? The crook could have broken into my shop as well. In fact, I need to check that. I guess I also need to let the designer know about our little setback and get busy trying to reproduce what we've lost." Reggie nodded. "Write it down. Contact Milan designers. And make a note of seed pearls. If I'm going to re-do some of those pieces. I have an idea to take them over the top to downright gorgeous."

Feeling a tad overwhelmed at her old friend's graciousness. Chloe dutifully acted as scribe as they brainstormed temporary closure signage, getting the front door repaired and the security system updated along with a myriad of other tasks. They decided to use the opportunity to repaint and restain the store. Then Reggie excused herself to check on her workshop in the back and Lila stretched and stood up.

"I think I have an appointment with a broom to get rid of the glass, and you my dear need to be as good to yourself as you were to me. Go home. Take a shower and get a bit of rest. I'll call when the police arrive."

Chloe stood, prepared to argue that Lila had been through enough, but Lila stopped her with a hug. "Who else would be here within five minutes in the middle of the night? You are one heck of a good business partner and one wonderful friend. Thank you. I don't know what I would have done without you."

In truth both Kylee, who lived up the hill, and Reggie who lived in West Kelowna would probably both have responded almost as quickly, but Lila's first thought had been to call *her*. She hugged Lila back and read the fortitude on Lila's face. She needed time alone to get herself put back together. Maybe they both did after the long night.

Chloe left Lila to clean up and headed out to her car.

CHAPTER 2

"Seems like we've been here before," Jas Stone said as he pulled the unmarked police sedan into the curb in front of the big, old, red and white heritage house. The traffic on Peachland's Beach Avenue was fairly mild for only a few days after the Canada Day celebration that had brought hordes of people to the parade and party. A lot of those people would be vacationing in the area, but this morning the usually popular beach was surprisingly empty. Maybe it was a result of the big "Closed for Restoration" sign on a sandwich board in front of the store. Knowing a small town like Peachland, there probably wasn't an inhabitant of the town who didn't know the place had been robbed the night before. The sign probably contributed to the fact there was a parking spot open right in front of *This and That*.

"Like returning to the scene of a crime," Danny said.

Jas turned the ignition off and glanced at his partner. Corporal Danny Forester was looking up at the house with an uncertain expression. He wore his usual khakis and a blue polo shirt. He ran his hands through his thatch of red hair. If anything the motion managed to make his hair look worse.

The guy was still coming down from a bad bout of something that had him AWOL from work and spouting weird stuff about having been possessed by an alien. Thankfully he'd had the smarts not to mention the latter point to the brass at the West Kelowna RCMP detachment, so he had been allowed back on active duty with only a reprimand on file. That and the Commanding Officer had asked Jas to keep an eye on him.

"Figure they'll be happy to see us?" Jas asked, thinking of the long-haired beauty he'd partnered with on the search for Kylee Jensen. Chloe had been her name. Chloe Main, but that was about all he knew. They'd both been focused on finding her friend. The last time he'd been here had been here was only a few days ago to take Kylee's official statement.

"If I was them, I think I'd rather not have us dropping in. I mean the abduction and now this? In Peachland? A domestic violence case, maybe. Public mischief or kids drinking. We hardly ever get a break-in, and now this."

"Welcome to the big city," Jas said to the community-at-large as he climbed out of the car and followed Danny to the house. It was odd, but the place looked, well, bruised today. Like a domestic violence victim who was trying to hide her scars. Maybe it was the fact the front door was off and there were two workmen removing the front door jam, but the place had the sense of being pushed off its foundations.

Danny stepped past the workmen, into the shop with Jas on his heels—broken display case, glass swept into a corner. Fingerprint powder on the cash register counter and around the door. "The owners around?" Danny asked. "Lila Weber?"

"In back," said one of the workmen and nodded toward the hall beyond a beaded curtain.

"Kitchen, most likely," Danny said and led Jas down the dimly lit hallway.

"Hey," Danny said as he entered the kitchen. "Guess who."

There were three women there. Tall, auburn-haired Lila Weber was on the phone at the counter. As usual she looked cool, collected, and as lovely as the minor celebrity she once was. According to Danny, a Google search for Lila Weber turned up that she had been the lead in a favorite cult film about a mythical hero who fell in love with goddess. She'd never done any acting after playing the goddess and either by choice or circumstance had fallen back into obscurity. But boy did she still have cheekbones.

She nodded the two of them to the table where Chloe sat along with another woman who looked like a cross between an action hero and Cleopatra. But it was Chloe who held his attention. She was dressed simply enough in a loose-fitting yellow tunic that set off the tan of her skin and the hip-length column of her braided dark brown hair. But it was her eyes that held him. When she looked up at him, their deep blue seemed to turn intense lavender. An optical illusion, of course, but it was seductive as hell, especially with her lush mouth.

Totally unprofessional, dude. He stopped himself and let Danny take the lead. Keep an eye on the guy and all that. That was where his attention was needed.

Chloe slid out from behind the table and extended a hand. "Detective Forester, isn't it?. And Stone." She seemed to frown as she briefly glanced in his direction, then turned her attention to Danny again. "We've just been working on the list of what was stolen and trying to come up with a more accurate estimate. Unfortunately I might have underestimated things a bit when I gave a figure to the officer last night."

She looked back at the table. "This is Reggie Lewis, our jewelry designer—Regulus Designs. I think you met the other day. Remember that name because she is going to be famous. Reggie, these are Detectives Forester and Stone. They arrested Tom Beaton." Beaton was the man who had abducted Kylee Jensen. Oddly, he also claimed he'd been possessed by aliens—when he was lucid at all. He was currently being held in the Kelowna Regional Hospital psychiatric ward for observation.

The black-haired woman colored briefly as Jas shook her hand. "It's Corporal actually. For both of us. Detective is used on Municipal police forces, or on television. Not for the Mounties."

He caught an unhappy flicker across the Chloe woman's face, so she obviously resented being corrected. Reggie motioned to the seating. "Did you want to interview us here?"

Lila, having just hung up the phone, joined them.

Danny glanced at Jas. "How about if we start with Ms. Weber?"

"Together. Sure." There was no way in hell he was letting Danny Forester conduct an interview alone given the short time since his AWOL period. They guy still couldn't fully explain where he'd been or what he'd done, just that he remembered being at the scene of the hit and run of an estate agent, and then he'd come to Peachland and started watching the women at *This and That*. It was creepy as hell that they were back here, and Jas wasn't taking any chances.

"How about on the back patio," Lila said and Danny nodded.

"You might want to take some water," Chloe offered.

Danny accepted, but Jas made it a rule not to take anything from either victims or suspects. As he stepped outside, he glanced back at the two women at the table. Chloe was watching. There was almost laughter in her eyes.

Fifteen minutes later he was beginning to figure out why she'd been laughing.

At the rear of the house the smallish backyard was half taken up with a raised flagstone area that served as a patio. Like the front porch of the house, there was an expensive looking set of wicker patio furniture complete with brightly colored cushions.

The whole effect was one of pool-side lounging, the only trouble being that there was no pool and no breeze either. With no shade over the patio he was frying his ass off here in his standard-operating procedure summer weight sports jacket. He *could* take it off, of course, but he was already sweating like the proverbial pig. Danny, meanwhile, looked like he was just getting comfortable, seated on one of the wicker chairs as he eased Lila Weber into her recollection of the night before.

Jas, had preferred to remain standing. Let the interviewee and interviewer develop rapport. He could always jump in if Danny went off the deep end or missed something. He found his mind wandering, wondered whether Chloe Main used this patio to get that tan of hers. She really did have great almost violet eyes in creamy, sun-kissed skin and what looked like a mane of hair judging by the thickness of her braid. A man could lose himself in those eyes and get tangled in that hair. Too bad she hid her shape in those hippy–style caftans. She'd been wearing something similar when they'd searched for Kylee Jensen together.

And that was not what he was supposed to be focused on. He yanked himself back to the interview.

Thirty minutes into the interview that felt closer to an hour, the dark-haired Lewis woman stepped out of the house, nodded and let herself into the small workshop—jeweler's workshop, probably. Made sense. Then workshop fans started pouring more hot air out onto the patio and he seriously thought about shooting them out. If not for the paperwork involved in the firing of a service revolver, he might have.

Instead he shifted position and lasted another fifteen minutes by which time he was pretty sure his underwear was sodden.

For the third time Danny was taking Lila Weber through her description of the suspect. He'd tried a straightforward cognitive interview, and had gone on to more probing questions, all to no avail. Now he seemed bent and determined to use the questionable practice of having her imagine she was standing outside the store and seeing the suspect running toward her.

Lila shook her head. "That's the weird thing. I don't see anything. It's like one of those blurs on TV when someone moves really fast. Like the Flash or something. I don't get *anything* clearly and I'm usually really good a noticing details."

Danny sighed and looked up at Jas. How the hell did the guy stay as cool as he looked in this heat? Jas felt like his skin was frying and yet ol' Danny–boy's redhead skin seemed just fine.

"I 'm going to ask a few questions about whether there might be any connection to the Kylee Jensen case," Forester said.

Jas opened his mouth to stop the interview right there, but what the hell. If Danny wanted to waste his time on that kind of question, it gave him a chance to get out of this heat.

"Tell you what. Why don't you finish off here and I'll head inside and get Ms. Main's statement," he offered. Better to be accused of leaving his partner than of condoning this line of questioning.

He didn't wait for a reply, because he really was dying here. He let himself inside and the back door clicked shut behind him. He sighed at the coolness, just as the amethyst-eyed beauty stepped into the kitchen from the hall.

For a moment he didn't know what to say. She stood there in the sunny white and yellow kitchen with its brushed stainless fixtures, looking almost as shocked at his presence.

"Uh. Sorry. Water. Uh... I needed water. It's damn hot out there."

And by the glint in her eyes she knew perfectly well it was— in fact she'd likely been laughing at him the whole time he'd been out there! Just what did she have against the police. No, make that what did she have against him? She *had* been less than talkative the night of the search. His momentary pique faded at the light in those eyes and the faint scent of something dark and floral she wore. From somewhere in the recesses of his memory, the word freesia came to mind, like an incense stick trailing smoke into the room. Interesting, just as his reaction was. It had been a while since someone got him interested.

"The water's in the fridge," Chloe said, and moved into the room, her numerous necklaces clicking together as she shifted to the counter and opened a drawer. She pulled out a long narrow box with a colorful picture of what looked like a many-armed man with an elephant's head. Hindu god, though the name escaped him. A whiff of sweetness and spice made him almost take a step back. God preserve him, it *was* incense.

With long, deft fingers she pulled out a stick and replaced the box in the drawer, before lighting the incense stick with a barbeque lighter. A long thread of sickly sweet smoke poured from the tip of the stick and the bracelet around her wrist caught in the sunlight through the windows. Then she looked at him again, her brows arched above those eyes. "The water's there—or would you prefer tap water? There're glasses in that cupboard." She nodded to the cupboard beside the fridge.

"Uh. Yeah. Thanks." He pushed off from the door, feeling like he was shoving though deep water. He should know, he'd spent an earlier part of his career on an RCMP deep-water rescue team. But this wasn't like him—at all.

The woman—Chloe—the name suited her somehow—turned to leave.

"Your friend out there mentioned a few things that I'd like to ask you about."

Chloe paused, questions filling her gaze. "Ask away, I suppose. What would you like to know?"

He fished in his jacket pocket for his notebook. "Ms. Weber indicated that you were responsible for locking up the previous day. Is that correct?"

"Of course. I was minding the store because Kylee was away for the day." Her hand strayed to the silver bracelet she wore—the same one there'd been all sorts of talk about as being the reason for Kylee Jensen's abduction. A lot of claptrap if you asked him.

"Tell me about it."

She sighed and turned back to him, the incense stick purling a trail of smoke into the air. "I went through my usual procedures of course. I cashed out and then I pulled the most valuable displays and a few other things for the safe. I locked them up and that was that. I thought you wanted the list of what was taken. It's on the counter right beside you. I've made two copies so that there's one for the insurance as well."

He noted her comments in his notebook and looked back at her. "You mentioned other things for the safe. Like what?"

Shaking her head, she looked down at her hands. A momentary expression of guilt crossed her face. "There were Reggie's sample pieces and some of my crystals—the ones that looked most suitable for my healing practice."

Jas frowned and raised his brows in question. "Healing practice?"

She met his regard. "Yes. Healing. With crystals. They have certain resonances within them that act on the human aura to calm and purify. I'm in the final stages of opening my own healing clinic."

"Uh—huh ." With a straight face he made a show of writing 'crystals??????' in his notebook and glanced back at Chloe. Apparently his face hadn't been as straight as he figured, because her lips were pressed into a less than happy line. Not exactly what he'd been going for when he'd decided to interview her. He needed to diffuse the situation, but *come on*, healing crystals?

He flipped his notebook closed and considered a moment. Well in for a penny... his mom always said. When she wasn't busy spending their last penny on some-or-other fortune teller.

"I see you're still wearing the bracelet. Don't tell me *you* can't get it off now?" he tried a smile. A laugh together would ease the tension in the room.

But the woman's face went still and guarded. Her one hand closed over the bracelet in question."Now why would you mention that? It's a whole lot of hokum, isn't it?" she asked softly.

The incense in her hand trailed smoke signal challenges across the gap between them. What could he say? His first inclination was to say yes, but his single mother raised him not to go out of his way to offend people.

"Well. Hokum might be a pretty strong word. I think I'll go with strange. Or odd." Or unfounded or, like healing crystals, stretching the bounds of credibility.

Her gaze narrowed as if she read his real feelings. "I can see that you don't believe in much, Detective Stone."

"Corporal. Corporal Stone."

"Of course. Because detective is on TV or municipal police." She quoted his words back at him and there was a miniscule shake of her head as if she thought use of his correct title was minutia. "Now unless you have some additional questions for me, I really should get back to cleaning up the store. We've a lot to do before we can open for business again."

She ducked out the door, her soft footfall rapidly fading. Damnation, he *did* have a question or two more for her. The guilty expression was hiding something. He grabbed a bottle of water from the fridge and followed her, pushing through the clacking curtain of beads.

She'd stuck the incense stick in a small brass holder and set it before a small bronze Buddha figure on a shelf behind the ancient-looking cash register. She glanced at him briefly, but carried on with her work, sweeping the glass up into a bin, taking down the jewel-toned scarves and folding them into a box. She righted a mannequin that had been knocked over, removed the array of necklaces from its headless neck and brushed off its black velvet covering. She left the tall shallow earring display alone— those glass cupboards hadn't apparently been touched by the perp, but the glass display counters she emptied out and placed each item in a small silk bag, then shifted around the room, sweeping everything out. She had a graceful way of moving, as if she listened to music and he wondered what kind of music it would be. Something with sitars and chanting, probably.

Totally not his thing, even though her cream top shifted over her and gave tantalizing glimpses of the curves of her body. This was no girl-woman. Chloe Main was most definitely a woman.

While she worked he tried to stay out of her way, but then she slid behind the cash register counter and pulled out two trays of stones, one purple and one black, and began sorting through them. She looked up as if she'd first noticed him. "Is there something else?" All business.

He really should just go. Forester would be a much better interviewer for this woman, given that so much about her just set him off. Let Forester interview her and then the two of them could get out of this madhouse of women who claimed that a bracelet was grounds for kidnapping and that crystals were the perfect thing for healing. The whole story about the bracelet was just so farfetched. And all the talk about possession was another ridiculous leap farther, even if Forester seemed to believe it, too. The Beaton character—well he'd clearly been off his rocker when he took Kylee. Psychotic breakdown or something, that was all. The shrinks would figure out what was going on.

"Uh, yeah." He followed her to the counter while she picked out four small stones of each color. Shaking the stones like dice, she went to each corner of the room and placed one stone of each color carefully together on the floor or window sill

When she returned, she turned a look on him like it was a dare. "Crystals. Jet and amethyst for protection," she said and waited. "I don't want there to be any more break-ins."

As if a few stones around the room would do any good.

He pulled out his notebook again and met her dare.

Look for *Unlocking Her History* at your favorite bookstores or e-tailer.

Romance and Adventure
from Twisted Root Publishing

If you enjoyed this book, you might
enjoy other titles available from Karen L.
Abrahamson in your local bookstore or
wherever e-books are sold.

www.karenlabrahamson.com